the PEARL

OTHER BOOKS BY ANGELA HUNT

The Justice
The Note
The Immortal
The Shadow Women
The Truth Teller
The Silver Sword
The Golden Cross
The Velvet Shadow
The Emerald Isle
Dreamers
Brothers
Journey

With Lori Copeland:
The Island of Heavenly Daze
Grace in Autumn
A Warmth in Winter
A Perfect Love
Hearts at Home

Web page: www.angelahuntbooks.com

The Women of Faith Fiction Club presents

the PEARL

BY ANGELA HUNT

W PUBLISHING GROUP™

www.wpublishinggroup.com

A Division of Thomas Nelson, Inc.
www.ThomasNelson.com

So he took me in spirit to a great, high mountain, and he showed me the holy city, Jerusalem, descending out of heaven from God . . . The twelve gates were made of pearls—each gate from a single pearl! And the main street was pure gold, as clear as glass.

—JOHN THE APOSTLE, FROM REVELATION 21

One

As my prerecorded voice began extolling the virtues of a Posture Perfect Mattress, Gary Ripley, my producer, came through the doorway and shoved a stack of freshly printed hate mail beneath my nose.

"New batch." He dropped the pages onto the desk. "Thought you might want to stir something up in the next hour. The what-to-do-with-Grandma topic is getting old."

I cocked an eyebrow at him, but he only grinned and leaned against the wall, lifting his hands in a *don't-shoot-the-messenger* pose.

I picked up the first letter, which opened with a string of expletives, then pronounced me the worst excuse for a counselor the world had ever seen. *"The advice you gave that woman in Atlanta came straight from the pits of hell,"* someone, probably a man, had written. *"Leave her husband? Marriage is for better or worse, but you want to overturn God's laws and institute your own."*

I felt my cheeks burn as I leaned back in my chair. Though I had grown accustomed to vitriolic mail of all types, criticism never failed to sting. Beneath the bluster and bravado I'd adopted as part of my radio persona, I constantly worried that I would hurt someone in a reckless moment of glib patter.

"Gary"—I glanced over my shoulder—"do you remember a woman calling from Atlanta?"

"Yeah." He snapped his gum. "Yesterday. You told her to pack up and run like mad."

"That was the abuse case, right? The woman with the broken jaw?"

Gary nodded. "The husband had put her in ICU the month before. How could you forget that one?"

"I didn't forget." I fingered the edge of the paper as I studied the e-mail. "I just wanted to be sure I remembered it correctly."

No, no cause for guilt on this one. God did want us to weather good and bad in our marriages, but I have never believed he intended women to be used as punching bags. The nameless coward who had sent this note could bluster all he wanted; my counsel in that situation had been sound.

I slid the paper to the desk and glanced at the clock. Nine fifty-eight, so I still had two minutes until the top of the hour, followed by eight minutes of news and commercials. Plenty of time for a break.

I flipped through the remaining e-mails. "Anything interesting in here?"

Gary shrugged. "The usual. People calling you intolerant and a hardhearted witch. Oh, and one calling you a child-abuser."

I snorted a laugh. "Because I told that one woman to swat her kid on the rear?"

"That's the one. The lady says she's going to report you to Social Services."

"She'll have to catch me swatting my kids first." I stood and stretched, then pressed my hands to the small of my back and grinned at my producer. "My kids never need swatting. They're angels."

Gary made a face at that, but he didn't argue. Truth was, my kids *were* good kids, and he knew it. At eighteen, Brittany Jane's only major flaw was her stubborn refusal to keep food out of the cluttered cave she called a bedroom, and Scott Daniel, age five, was a bundle of pure delight.

Taking advantage of the break, I left the studio as Gary followed. We visited the coffeemaker in the snack area, filled our mugs with liquid caffeine, then stood and drank, enjoying the quiet break while keeping a careful eye on the clock.

Our building, owned by Open Air Communications, housed several radio stations—among them WUBN, the Gulf Coast's hard-rock headquarters; WSHE, soft rock from the sixties and seventies; WNAR, home of the county's best jazz; and WCTY, the voice of new country. At any given hour you could walk down the halls and peer into studio windows of a half-dozen broadcasters, all saying something different on the invisible airways that carried our words, healthy and perverse, across the nation.

Sometimes the thought left me feeling a little dizzy.

Gary took a final sip from his mug, then pointed to the clock. "Time."

I nodded, then followed him down the hall. A door swung open as we passed WCTY, allowing a stream of country music to flow through the hall. I shook my head as the lyrics followed us: *I'm so miserable without you, it's like having you here.*

As Chad Potter, our sound engineer, punched up the theme music for my show, I slipped back into the air studio and took my place behind the desk.

On the phone, a half-dozen blinking buttons flashed at me; each of them representing someone who had called and remained on hold through the commercials, the news, and the theme music. I would never cease to marvel at the patience of some callers. Most of them would hang on even through the monologue I delivered at the beginning of every segment.

As the theme music faded, I settled the headphones on my head— the better to hear my producer and sound engineer from the control room—and leaned forward on the desk.

"Welcome back, friends and neighbors, to another hour of the *Dr. Sheldon Show.* You know, some people look for flowers and robins as a herald of spring; I look for the Nordstrom catalog. I know I'll be on the cutting edge of fashion just by perusing its contents, and this year I was not disappointed. Now I know some of you may think it's not possible to be fashionable by osmosis, but I beg to differ. I mean, what is fashion, but clothing that's *in* one year and *out* the next? Right now my closet is stuffed with things from when I first got married, so something tells me I'm about to ride the crest of high fashion once again."

I paused to pick up my notepad, then ruffled the pages in front of the mike. "As I flipped through the catalog this year, though, one group of products confused me. I don't know if you've seen these things in the stores yet, but what is the deal with toe toppers and foot tubes? I mean, have you *seen* those things? I suppose they're for wearing with slides and sandals, but they kind of defeat the purpose. The toe toppers—I know, it's hard to imagine anything with that silly a name being practical—are half a sock. They start at the toe like an ordinary sock, and end at the arch of your foot. Now I ask you, what is that about? Do you wear them with high-heeled, elegant sandals? And have this terrycloth *thing* hanging out?"

Silently I counted out a beat, then laughed. "And foot tubes—have you seen *those*? They're like the calf warmers we all bought when that Jennifer Beals movie came out . . . you know, the woman welder who wanted to—*Flashdance*, that was it. Anyway, these foot tubes are like calf warmers, but they cover only the middle part of your foot. Your tootsies and your heels are still left out in the cold to freeze or sweat, depending on whether you're wearing them in Montana or Florida."

Looking through the rectangular window that opened into the control room, I saw Gary holding a hand over his face. Because he knew women comprised the majority of my audience, he tolerated my female-oriented monologues, but just barely.

"Toe toppers and foot tubes." I breathed a heavy sigh into the mike. "Somebody please tell me this fad will pass."

I glanced up at the list of names on the computer monitor, then pressed the first button on the beige plastic phone. "Carla! Welcome to the show."

"Dr. Diana! Goodness, I can't believe I'm really talking to you."

I cast Gary a *didn't-you-tell-her-to-get-to-the-point?* look, then shoe-horned a smile into my voice. "Have you seen those toe toppers in the stores yet?"

"No—and I agree, they sound silly."

"I think so. But how can I help you today?"

"It's my mother—I mean mother-in-law. She's mousy—I mean *mouthy*—good grief, I'm nervous!"

"Calm down, Carla. We haven't lost a caller yet." I glanced up at the computer screen, where next to Carla's name Gary had typed *MIL insults her constantly. Advice?*

Though the woman might be nervous simply because she was on the radio, I knew her anxiety might also have arisen from the fact that her mother-in-law could be listening . . . so I'd have bet my bottom dollar that *Carla* wasn't her real name.

My caller exhaled into the phone, eliciting an agonized expression from Chad at the soundboard.

"Okay. It's like this—I love my husband, I really do, but his mother is driving me crazy. Everything I do, she has to criticize—my clothes, my cooking, the way I keep house. I have a job, you see, so what does it matter if the shelves get a little dusty? Her son doesn't read books anyway, so what does she care? And lately Joe and I have been talking about having a baby—"

"Joe is your husband?"

"Yes. Sorry, I should have said that."

"And how long have you been married?"

"Six months." She exhaled another deep breath, obviously grateful that I had taken control of the conversation.

Flashing a grin at Chad, I silently tapped the windscreen on my microphone with two fingers, reminding him that I knew better than to huff and puff into his expensive equipment.

"I'm glad you called, Carla, and I'm glad you didn't wait to address this issue. Because if you allow this situation to continue, you will be dealing with the problem for as long as your marriage lasts—which, in my opinion, won't be long past your fifth anniversary. Men who allow their mothers to criticize their wives tend to lose their wives' respect, and respect is one of the most important ingredients in marriage."

I paused a moment to let my words take hold. "Let me ask you this, Carla—do you know much about your mother-in-law's history?"

"Um . . . not really. Should I?"

"It might be helpful. We'll talk about your husband in a moment, but first let me remind you of one of my favorite profound sayings. Are you ready?"

"Yeah, sure."

"Here it is: Hurt people . . . hurt people."

In the control room, Chad played the blast of a trumpet, the usual sound effect for one of what he called *Dr. Diana's pronouncements.*

Grinning at him, I pulled the mike closer. "If your mother-in-law is honestly vindictive toward you, she may be acting out of pain. Somewhere, someone has hurt her badly, and she has not yet learned how to deal with that hurt. You may be the source of her pain, through some direct or indirect action, or her issues may spring from something completely unrelated to you."

"So what do I *do* about it?"

"You do this—first, you ask your mother-in-law if you've done something to offend her. Say you've noticed that she seems out of sorts around you, and ask if you can do something to make things right. If she names something—say, for example, you inadvertently ran over her petunias—then apologize and offer to replant her flowers. If, on the other hand, she denies her attitude or says you've done nothing to hurt her feelings, then your conscience should be clear.

"Second, you talk to your husband and tell him you love him dearly, you admire him to death, but you married him, not his mother. So the next time his mother criticizes you, if he doesn't politely excuse himself and lead you out of Mama's presence, he'll be disappointing you tremendously. Leave and cleave, Carla—that's what marriage is about. Leaving the parental nest and cleaving to your spouse. If your husband doesn't want to be firm in the face of his mother's wailing—and believe me, she will wail the first few times he stands up to her—then you'll just have to resign yourself to the fact that you married a spineless mama's boy."

In the control room, Chad clicked a key and sent the wail of a frustrated baby over the airwaves.

I grinned at him while Carla sputtered protestations. "But I thought men who took care of their mothers were, like, *programmed* to take care of their wives! My mother always said I should notice how a boy treats his mom, and he was always so deferential to her—"

"There's a vast difference between treating a woman with respect and kowtowing to her every demand." I lowered my voice and leaned closer to the microphone. "I know it's not easy, Carla, but your husband might need a *lot* of encouragement before he'll be able to stand up to his mom. I wish you'd noticed his disposition toward docility while you were dating."

"I did notice his—whatever you said. But I was sure he'd change once we were married."

"Men don't change, sweetie, apart from acts of God. They fossilize."

I cocked my index finger toward Chad, who clicked the next button and took us into commercial. After pulling the headphones from my ears, I picked up the telephone. The promo for Nutriment Weight Loss Solutions dropped to a muted mumble when Chad saw I held the receiver.

"Carla," I spoke into the phone, "we're off the air now. Listen, dear, I'm not saying you should give up on your husband. I'm saying you and Joe need to open the lines of communication. Tell him you love him, make him feel like your protector. That's probably all he needs to rise to the task. If you make him feel like he can take on the world, taking on his mama will be a lot easier."

"I'll try." Carla sniffled into the phone, a sound I'd heard a thousand times, but still it got to me. "Thanks, Dr. Diana."

"You're welcome, sweetie. God bless."

I disconnected the call, then glanced at the computer monitor where a queue of bright green rectangles listed all holding callers. Gary moved interesting people straight to the top of the list; he relegated weirdos or off-topic calls to the bottom.

Rarely did we resort to bottom-feeding.

Four callers were now waiting—according to Gary's notes, the woman at the top of the queue was dealing with a blended family, the man after her was calling about a troubled sixteen-year-old, and the name beneath his belonged to ten-year-old Tiffany, who wanted to ask a question for her school report. The last caller, Lela, was wondering about the wisdom of leaving her money to a spoiled grandchild.

Lifting a brow, I peered through the rectangular window before Gary's desk. Lela was bound to strike a nerve with my local audience, so she must have sounded like a real dud to earn last place in the lineup. Though my show was syndicated and broadcast on sixty-two stations nationwide—with new stations signing on every week—the folks in Tampa cared deeply about elder issues. Probably 75 percent of the people in my local listening audience were retired snowbirds, particularly in this month of March.

Through the wide windows separating me from the technical brains of my program I could see Chad, my engineer, hunched over his board, his magic fingers adjusting knobs and sliders whose functions remained a mystery to me even after five years in radio. Gary, my producer and call screener, hunched over the phone, his brow crinkled in concentration as he greeted another caller. His hands moved to the keyboard, and in a moment he'd click *enter* and send the information to me.

As the commercial played out, I settled the headset back on my head and glanced at the computer screen. I didn't often buck Gary's suggested order, but I wasn't in the mood to discuss blended families. The ten-year-old might be more fun.

I clicked the button for line three as the intro music faded away. "Tiffany, honey, are you there? This is Dr. Diana."

A heavy breath whooshed into the phone, then, "Hello?"

"Hello, Tiffany. Did you have a question to ask me?"

More heavy breathing, followed by a decidedly childish giggle. "Is it really you?"

"It really is. And I hear you have some kind of school report to write?"

Another loud exhalation. "Yes."

"What's your topic?"

Yet another heavy sigh. "Dr. Diana."

I laughed. "You're doing a report on me? Well, sweetie, I hope you're kinder than my critics. Is there something special you wanted to know about me?"

"Yes."

I smiled. "And that is?"

"Ask the question, dummy. She's waiting."

Despite Tiffany's obvious proximity to the phone, I had no trouble hearing a woman's sharp voice. A second later, Tiffany exhaled again, then asked, "Do you have any pets?"

I clenched my fist, wishing for a moment that I could climb through the phone line and speak a few strong words to whoever would burden this tender ten-year-old with a label like *dummy*.

"Yes, sweetheart, I have a pet." I spoke in the warmest tone I could manage. "I have a Chinese pug, a little guy we call Terwilliger. He spends most of his time in my son's room, 'cause they're the same age. They're best friends."

Tiffany laughed, a lovely two-noted giggle. "He sounds cute."

"He is, honey, and he's smart, too. Sometimes people look at him and think he's not so smart, 'cause he has this little mashed-in face, but they're wrong about him. Terwilliger—we call him Twiggy for short— is a great little dog. And he doesn't care what people think, 'cause he knows he's okay in my book." I hesitated. "You understand, sweetie?"

"Uh-huh."

"Is that all you need from me?"

"Uh-huh."

The woman's voice shrilled again in the background: "Say thank you, idiot, and get off the phone."

Rage burned my cheeks. "Who is that, Tiffany? Your mom?"

"Uh-huh."

"May I speak to her, please?"

No answer but the clunking sounds of a telephone in transit. A second later the woman's voice came over the phone, the sharp edges smoothed away. "Hello?"

"Are you Tiffany's mother?"

"Why, yes, I am."

"She's a charming little girl."

"Why, thank you."

"What's your first name, dear?"

"Anna."

"Well, Anna, I don't know your situation, and I suppose I could be way off base, but I do know this—your daughter deserves better than you're giving her now. Maybe you're having a bad day or something, but no child responds well to words like *dummy* and *idiot*. What I've heard from you in the space of two minutes amounts to verbal abuse—"

A definite click snapped in my ear. I glanced up at Gary, who shrugged as if to say *she's gone*.

"Well, folks," I said, aware that Tiffany and her mom might still be listening. "Let's remember one thing, shall we? Sticks and stones may not break bones, but they certainly can wound a spirit. If you have to give your child a nickname, let it be something endearing. My husband has always called our daughter *sweetness*, and"—I forced a laugh—"he calls me *gorgeous*, whether I measure up to the name or not. But he makes me *feel* gorgeous, and that's what we need to do for our loved ones . . . give them room to soar."

Pressing the next button, which took us into a twenty-second pre-recorded bit of patter, I glanced at the call screen, where a new name had appeared at the top of the queue. Gary's thin voice filled my right ear: "A live one coming through. Be careful—he may be a crank."

"Got it."

I read the detail line, where Gary had typed: *Tom—thinks his wife is planning to leave him. Sounds desperate.*

Nodding, I picked up a pencil and tapped it to the syncopated rhythm of my ten-second lead-in, a hyped-up, whispered version of my name recorded over a funky Latin beat.

I felt good. The morning had offered a string of interesting calls, all practical problems without a single tedious question about capital punishment, politics, or abortion. I had strong opinions on those issues, but so did my callers, so the resulting merry-go-round resulted in frustrating radio for host and audience alike. On the few occasions callers did manage to bring up one of the irresolvable topics, I usually ended up having to cut them off, particularly if they became abusive. I didn't mind disconnecting rude callers, but afterward I always had to spend another hour defending my actions to well-meaning folks who thought "free speech" meant "free access to the airwaves."

As the intro died down, I punched the button for line one. "Hi, Tom! Thanks for calling the show."

"Dr. Diana?" The voice came out garbled, as if the man were strangling on repressed emotions. His tone, coupled with Gary's warning, raised my adrenaline level a couple of percentage points.

I straightened in my chair. "I'm here, Tom. Did you want to tell me about your wife?"

"She's leaving me."

I waited only a second for him to continue, then hurried to fill the dead air. "How do you know she's leaving?"

"She's outside putting suitcases in the car. And she's taking my little girl with her."

I looked up at Gary, who crossed his arms and nodded.

"Tom"—I rested my elbows on the desk—"I'm not sure there's anything I can do for you at this moment. Have you talked to your wife about why she wants to leave?"

"Yeah. She's found another man—she's moving in with him. I told her it would just about kill me if she left, but she doesn't care."

"I'm sure she cares, Tom, but perhaps she's confused at the moment."

"She doesn't give a flip."

I stiffened at something I heard in his voice, something jagged and sharp.

"She doesn't even care that I got the gun out of the dresser drawer. She saw me pull it out, but she just kept moving toward the car, dragging my daughter with her."

I pressed my hands to the headphones as the muscles in my chest constricted. "You have a gun?"

"Right here in my hand. It's loaded, too."

I looked at Gary, whose concerned expression had intensified to panic. Chad, on the other hand, looked almost gleeful at the prospect of unexpected drama.

"Tom, you need to put the gun away. You must have frightened your wife; perhaps that's why she's leaving with your daughter."

"I'd never hurt them." He paused, his words hanging in the silence as if he'd paused to question his own statement, then he pressed on. "But I'm going to kill myself. And when she comes back into the room to see if she's forgotten anything, she'll find me lying here. And maybe she'll pick up the phone, and you can tell her why I did it."

I braced my hands against the edge of the desk. "Whoa, Tom. I don't think I can cooperate with your plan. And we shouldn't rush into anything."

Oh sweet Jesus, I need you now.

My mind raced backward at warp speed, summoning up the standard protocols in crisis counseling. When a patient threatens suicide, the counselor has to stay calm. Remove the weapon if possible. Take charge. Insist you're not going to leave, you will get help, and anything is better than suicide. Be loving, but above all, be firm.

Silently praying for wisdom, I leaned into the microphone. "I'm glad you called, Tom, because I want to help you through this. You've gone through a lot today, but this is not going to be the end of your world, you understand? Your wife is leaving. But even if she drives away with your daughter, she can never take away the special relationship between you and your child. You'll always be her father, right?"

As Tom mumbled incoherently, I picked up my notepad. Grabbing a Sharpie someone had left on the desk, I wrote *CALLER ID?* in block letters, then ripped out the page and flashed it toward the window. Gary read the note, then nodded.

"Yeah, I'll always be her father." Tom was weeping now, his ragged voice scraping like sandpaper against my ears. "But I don't want her to remember me like this."

The adage I had so glibly recited only a few moments before flittered through my brain: *Hurt people . . . hurt people.* Would Tom hurt someone before the day ended?

I scrawled *CALL 911* on another page, then yanked it from the notebook and held it up. Gary made the OK sign, then hunched over the phone.

I had to keep Tom talking. "You don't want her to remember you like *what*?" I gentled my voice. "Tom, I know you're confused, but you have to see the illogic in your statement. You don't want your daughter to remember you as sad and upset, but would you rather she remember you as a bloody corpse on the living room floor?"

"I'm in the kitchen." I could barely understand the words through his sobbing.

"Think, friend. Let your daughter remember you as a man who recovered from a temporary loss and grew strong enough to be the father she needed as she grew up. How old is your daughter, Tom?"

More weeping, then, "Four."

"Four? Oh, Tom!" I released a dramatic sigh, a breathy stream of air that defeated the purpose of Chad's prized windscreen. "You haven't had time to see her lose her first tooth, walk to her first day of kindergarten, or smile at her first boyfriend. Don't you want to be around when she goes on her first date? Even if you're not with your wife, don't you want to be nearby when your daughter wants to talk to someone about her relationship with her boyfriend? Don't you want to be the man who walks her down the aisle on her wedding day?"

He did not answer, but I wouldn't give up—not as long as I could hear him sniffling.

I had to distract him. "I have two children, Tom. A son and a daughter. I don't talk about them much on the program because my daughter's at the age where she doesn't want to admit she even has parents."

Dead silence on the other end of the line. A flicker of apprehension coursed through my bloodstream, then I heard another sniff.

He was still with me. Frantic, I pointed at Gary, giving him the sign to open his mike. I needed feedback from someone, and I didn't want to pull words from Tom if he didn't feel like making small talk.

"My kids," I said, giving Gary purposeful direction. "They're something, aren't they?"

Gary shot me a deer-in-the-headlights look through the window, then leaned into his mike. "Your daughter's a wonderful girl."

I sent him a grateful smile. "Yes, she is. And that, ladies and gentlemen, is the seldom-heard voice of Gary Ripley, my producer. Gary's listening, too, Tom, and we're going to get you some help."

"I don't want help." Tom's whisper was faint and flat, the voice of defeat. "Thanks for trying, Dr. Diana, but if you'll just tell my wife why I did it—"

"My son, however, loves having his mother around—then again, he's only five." I pressed on, not wanting to give Tom an opportunity to sign off. If I could keep him listening, even arouse a little indignation, the emergency rescue personnel Gary had called—*please, God, let no snafus arise on that end*—would have time to reach my distraught caller.

I rattled on as if I hadn't heard Tom's last words. "Most five-year-olds are wise enough to realize they didn't spring from the primordial ooze and parents had something to do with their appearance on earth. My daughter, on the other hand, has decided that eighteen equals complete maturity and she should be allowed to do as she pleases."

Gary's wide eyes warned me away from the topic—talk of the tumultuous teen years would not comfort a suicidal caller.

I backed away and tried another approach. "What's your daughter's name, Tom?"

He hesitated, cleared his throat, then said, "Casey."

"That's a lovely name. Is she your only child?"

"Yeah."

"Children are wonderful, aren't they? I didn't think I would ever be a mother. My husband and I were married five years before we became parents, and our first child arrived through adoption. For three years we tried to create a biological child, then the doctors told us the odds of pregnancy were pretty much one in a million. So because we wanted a baby more than a pregnancy, we adopted our beautiful daughter. I thought our family was complete, but apparently God had other ideas. Twelve years later, surprise! The rabbit died—or, in this technologically advanced age, I suppose I should say the home pregnancy test proved positive. My husband and I found ourselves on the receiving end of an unexpected pregnancy, and now when I look at my son I see undeniable proof that God still works miracles. My boy is a little angel, as delightful as any kid you'd ever want to meet . . . and I'll bet he's a lot like your Casey."

I glanced toward the control room, hoping Gary would have some sort of update for me, but he had turned away, concentrating on whatever he was telling someone on the phone. His voice was a dull murmur in my headphones, not clear enough for me to catch his words.

Without missing a beat, I returned to the tale of my family's creation, a story I'd told a number of times at pro-life rallies and mother-daughter banquets. For security reasons I rarely talked about my family on the air, but this was an exceptional occasion.

"I love my children, Tom, and I'm sure you love your Casey, too. I'd lay down my life for my kids, no doubt about it, but I know it's also important that I be there for them. Because I want to be around for my daughter's wedding, I try to eat right and exercise a couple of times a week. Because I want to be able to play ball with my son, I don't smoke. In a way, I guess you could say I'm living for them—and I know you are, too. When parents love their children, living for them just comes naturally. Wouldn't you agree?"

More sniffling sounds, followed by a muffled, "Yeah."

"That's great, Tom. I'm glad you feel that way, too." I forced what I hoped was a relaxed laugh. "Just this morning my little boy bounced into my room and woke me by covering my face with kisses. At first I thought I was dreaming, but when I opened my eyes, he was standing beside me in his little pajamas, dragging his monkey by one arm. I asked what he was doing, and he said, 'I'm kissing you good morning, Mommy. You kiss me good night, don't you?'"

My next laugh wasn't at all forced. "Isn't that sweet, Tom? I'll bet your Casey sometimes does things like that." I narrowed my eyes, listening intently, then smiled when I heard his reply.

"Yeah, sometimes she does. She likes to stand on my feet when we dance. 'Course it's not really dancing—it's me rocking back and forth while she stands on my boots and hangs on to keep from falling off."

Frantic hand-waving from Gary's window caught my eye. He pointed toward Chad, who was holding up a sign: *SWAT TEAM OUTSIDE THE HOUSE.*

I closed my eyes as my uneasiness shifted into a deeper and more immediate fear.

"Tom, I need you to do something for me. You called today to talk, and I've enjoyed our conversation very much. But I'm in the business of providing help, so we have done our best to help you. I've just learned some people have arrived outside your house."

"What kind of people?" An edge in his voice verged on the threatening. Apparently Tom couldn't see out a window from where he stood.

"Well, your wife and daughter are out there, right? You said they were outside. Have they come back into the house?"

"Nobody's come in."

"Did you hear the car leave?"

"I didn't hear anything. The windows are closed, 'cause it's cold outside."

He definitely wasn't calling from Florida.

"I'm glad it's quiet. Listen, Tom, I want you to put the phone down and go outside to see if your daughter and wife are still in the driveway. But before you go, promise me you'll leave your gun on the kitchen table—we wouldn't want to frighten Casey with it, would we?"

The edge melted away, leaving only soft concern. "I wouldn't want to do that."

"Fine. Leave the gun on the table, Tom, and step out the front door. Make sure Casey is okay and give her a hug for me."

I winced as the phone rattled against something hard—probably the kitchen counter—and the studio went silent as we held our breaths and listened. Perhaps this was the one occasion where dead air would not be a curse.

I slid my hand toward the next button, wondering if we should go to commercial in case something went drastically wrong. I glanced at Gary, who was staring up at the clock, counting the seconds. Ten . . . fifteen . . . twenty.

Hurt people . . . hurt people.

How long would it take to subdue a man? Surely longer than it would take to *shoot* one . . .

I glanced at the computer screen. Chad had cued a station promo to run next. In five more seconds I would hit the next button and go with the promo, but—

Gary's voice buzzed in my ear. "Diana? Why are you waiting?"

"I don't know why I'm waiting." I spoke into the mike, filling some of the dead air. "I just think I should."

We heard sounds—muffled voices, a shout, and odd clunking noises. I flinched as a new male voice rumbled over the phone line. "Is this Dr. Diana?"

"It is. Who are you?"

"Sergeant Michelson, of the Memphis police. We're in the house."

"And Tom? The man I was speaking to?"

"One of our officers subdued him, and he's safe. We're taking him to a hospital for a psych exam."

From the control booth, Chad triumphantly punched the next button, and a glance at the clock told me why he'd been quick to cut off the conversation. Local news aired at the top and bottom of every hour, and a suicidal man in Memphis, Tennessee, didn't qualify as local news.

I picked up the receiver to continue my conversation with the police officer. "We're off the air now, Sergeant. Were the wife and daughter outside?"

"They were gone by the time we arrived. But after the 911 call came in, we kept listening to your show so we'd know what was happening inside the house. When he went out the front door, two of our people went in the back to secure the weapon."

"Thank goodness." I leaned back in my chair as relief flooded my bones. "And you'll make sure he gets help? Unless he does, he may try something again, Sergeant. And suicidal people don't always use a gun."

The cop's short bark of laughter had a bitter edge. "Tell me something I don't know, Doc. But thanks for your help."

I hung up the phone, then paused to bow my head. As the newscaster in the next studio read the news, I exhaled a deep breath and let the Spirit pray for me. The best I could manage was a heartfelt, "Thank you, Lord, for averting a tragedy."

When I finally looked up, I leaned into the mike to ask Chad to run the long promo and a two-minute sound bite after the news. I needed a quick trip to the ladies' room and a splash of cold water on my wrists.

I slipped off the tall, padded chair and moved toward the doorway, waving to Gary as I left. If the SWAT team had fired upon Tom or he'd gone outside with his gun, that call would have resulted in an unmitigated disaster . . .

Heaven had smiled on me this morning.

Two

DR. STEVE SHELDON EXITED THE SMALL STOREROOM his staff jokingly referred to as his *prayer closet*. The appellation was not off the mark, because he often retreated to the confined room when he needed a quiet place to pray. His tiny office held too many files and charts to be closed off when he needed real sanctuary, yet sanctuary—and silence—was what he'd wanted when he realized his wife had a seriously disturbed caller on the line.

He'd been listening, as he always did, on a pocket-sized transistor radio left over from his college days. The small and unobtrusive ear-piece allowed him to work while he listened to Diana's show, a far better option than flooding his office with topics that were often not suitable for the ears of young children. Most of the time he was able to concentrate on his patients and listen to Diana in the background; this morning, however, he'd been in the middle of filling a cavity when he realized his wife was facing serious trouble.

He had immediately finished with his patient, handed the chart to Melanie Brown, his dental hygienist, and retreated to the storeroom. Melanie must have realized the source of his distraction, for she didn't once rap on the door to disturb his concentration. His patients could wait, and they did—children rarely clamored to greet their dentist.

Now he sidled past Melanie and grinned at six-year-old Joseph Walker, who sat in the reclining chair like a stiff-armed plastic doll. "Hey, Joseph." Steve perched on a padded rolling stool. "Miss Melanie tells me you have a beautiful smile. Mind if I take a look?"

The clearly petrified kid nodded, then slowly lowered his jaw until a quarter-inch gap appeared between his lips.

"Sorry, partner." Steve grinned at the boy, then pulled the surgical mask over his face. "But you're going to have to give me a crocodile-sized smile so I can see all your choppers."

With an agonized expression, Joseph Walker complied, his gaze rolling up to the ceiling.

"My son's only a little younger than you." Steve pressed a gloved fingertip to the edge of the boy's upper teeth. "And he's already lost a tooth, can you believe it? I thought he'd wait until six to lose his first tooth, but he's growing up real fast. He already likes the Tampa Bay Bucs and can name every player in the starting lineup—with a little prompting."

Steve's gaze drifted toward the boy's eyes in case a spark of interest flickered there. But as the metal tip of his probe encountered the enamel of a bicuspid, Joseph's eyelids lowered and clamped tight. But the brave lad spoke.

"I loss a toof when I was five." The blue eyes opened and sought Steve's.

"Then you're a big boy just like my Scotty." Steve smiled, hoping to offer reassurance, but he knew the sight of smiling eyes above a surgical mask would likely do little to ease Joseph's tension.

Better to hurry and put the kid out of his misery. Keeping up a steady stream of comforting chitchat, Steve checked the molars, asked Joseph to bite down, and noticed that the boy already had a sizable overbite. With his small jaw, he would definitely need braces in a few years.

No need to mention orthodontia to Joseph. Mrs. Walker would need to know, though.

Steve dropped his probe onto the tray, then clapped his hands.

"You're all done, kiddo." Snapping off his rubber gloves, he rolled them into a ball and tossed them toward the trash can, which Melanie opened at the appropriate instant.

"What teamwork—you, me, and Miss Melanie." Steve unhooked the paper shield from the boy's neck. "Together we'll keep those cavities away, okay? So when you're as old as I am, you'll have all your own teeth."

Joseph nodded wordlessly.

"Good boy. Now, Miss Melanie's going to give you a toothbrush, a tube of toothpaste, and let you pick a toy from the treasure chest. I'm going to go to the desk and talk to your mom. You're doing a good job on the brushing, Joseph, so keep up the fine work."

Joseph slid out of the chair and followed Melanie to the playroom while Steve met Mrs. Walker at the reception desk. As she frowned and wrote out the check, he explained the boy's future need for orthodontia. "He has a small jaw and a sizable overbite. He's still growing, but I think within the next couple of years you should take him to an orthodontist for an evaluation."

Mrs. Walker's brow lowered like a thundercloud. "How can you know that when he doesn't even have his permanent teeth?"

Steve forced a polite smile. "Baby teeth are smaller than permanent teeth, and his teeth are already crowded. He'll be fine for a while, but since orthodontia is expensive, I want you to be prepared."

Mrs. Walker sighed loudly, then handed her check to the receptionist. "If it's not one thing, it's another. I don't know why I ever wanted to have kids. They're costing me a fortune."

"They *are* expensive," Steve agreed, backing away. "But they're worth it, don't you think?"

Mrs. Walker heaved a weary sigh as she turned on her heel. "Ask me later, Doc, after I've had my dinner and a cup of coffee."

He watched in bemused dismay as Mrs. Walker called her son from the playroom, then pulled him toward the front door. Melanie witnessed the scene, then approached the reception desk.

"Makes you wonder about American motherhood, doesn't it?"

Steve shook his head. "Don't judge Mrs. Walker too harshly. She has six others like Joseph at home, and each one of them either has or will need orthodontia."

He grinned at his hygienist, knowing she had a twelve-year-old son. Over the six months she'd worked for him, he had learned that her husband had walked out on them years ago, but she seemed to manage single motherhood as well as any woman he'd ever met. "Tell me, Melanie, do you ever wonder why you had kids?"

Her blue eyes sparkled. "Oh, I know why. 'Cause I got swept off my feet by a fast-talking, two-timing, no-good glob of bucket slime."

Steve tilted his head, not quite sure how to respond, but she patted his arm. "Don't you worry about me, Dr. Steve. My boy B.J. and I are doin' just fine. As long as he doesn't drive me crazy wanting the latest Nintendo game, we'll make it."

She crinkled her nose and looked toward the receptionist. "You got more kids for us to torture, Gerta?"

Gerta Poppovitch, the woman who'd been administrating the office for the last fifteen years, ignored the hygienist and fixed Steve in a steely glare. "For you, Dr. Steve, Tommy Oliphant has been waiting ten minutes in room two." She slid a bright yellow chart across the blue Formica counter. "And for you, Melanie, here's the chart on Audrey Williams, a real charmer. On her last visit she bit our hygienist."

Melanie pretended to shudder. "I suppose it's a good thing my tetanus shots are up to date."

As she stepped forward to get the chart, Steve checked his watch. Diana was beginning the third hour of her show. At noon he'd have to call and congratulate her on a problem handled well.

Whistling, he moved down the hall to where Tommy Oliphant waited.

Three

GARY RIPLEY LEANED BACK IN HIS CHAIR AND GRINNED at the string of lights. All ten phone lines were blinking; they hadn't stopped since the SWAT team intercepted Tennessee Tom in the last hour. Diana had come back on the air and continued, cool as a cucumber, but Gary had been sweating bullets the entire time she talked to the suicidal man. It was a good thing she pulled it off, a *great* thing, or the press would be calling her "Dr. Death" or "Dr. Die" from this day forward.

A phone line at the far right of the bank of buttons began to blink. For an instant he stared at it, wondering how a caller had managed to access one of their private lines, then he hurried to press the key.

"Morning Show."

"Is this Ripley? Diana Sheldon's producer?"

"Yeah—can I help you?"

"Conrad Wexler, vice president in charge of network talk shows. Just wanted you to tell Diana we've heard about what happened on your show this morning—"

Gary's stomach clenched.

"—and we're amazingly proud of her. My assistant is trying to get the story to the TV networks for some prime-time airplay. Shoot, if

Barbara Walters can do a special on that ten-year-old kid who foiled a bank robbery in Houston, she can certainly do one on the talk-radio shrink who stopped a family massacre in Tennessee."

Gary looked at Chad, who was oblivious to everything but Diana's chatter.

"It, um, wasn't exactly a massacre, sir. The guy was threatening to kill himself."

"But his wife and family were outside, right? And he had a loaded gun?"

"Um, yeah. Apparently."

"And in the good doctor's professional opinion, could the situation have escalated?"

Gary glanced through the window at Diana, who was trying to convince a woman that wearing a formal white gown to her fifth wedding wasn't such a good idea.

"I'll have to ask her. I do know she was nervous."

"Then it was certainly a *potential* massacre, and our Dr. Diana averted it. That guy could have gone outside and killed the wife and kid, then turned the gun on himself. He could have taken out one of the SWAT guys. It happens all the time—I read about something similar in the paper just last week."

Gary bit his lip, not wanting to argue with a head honcho. Wexler had to be calling from L.A., headquarters of the Prime Radio Network and home to all the big-name national radio talk shows. Diana was only a small star in the Prime Radio crown, but today might bring her an opportunity to shine a little brighter . . . which would reflect nicely on her producer.

"Prime-time TV would be great, sir." Gary swiveled his chair to keep his star in view. "Diana would be a natural."

"I know she would. You tell her I called, and keep us in the loop if you hear anything else from Tennessee. Maybe we should think about changing the focus of her show—what would happen if we made it more suicide-centered?"

Gary made a face. "I, um, don't think she'd buy that, sir. She wants to keep the show focused on family problems."

"So where do you think suicides come from? Messed-up families."

Gary studied the dusty ceiling tiles before answering. "I think Diana would say she wants to help families *before* they get majorly messed up. Besides, if we did nothing but suicides, we'd be bound to lose a few. And people get sued for things like that."

Wexler fell silent for an instant. "You're right, the liability would kill us. But the drama, man, the drama!" He blew into the phone. "Well, you tell her I called and to keep up the good work. You, too, kid. You'll hear from us."

Gary opened his mouth to say good-bye, but the phone had already gone dead. He dropped the receiver to the desk and glanced up at the caller screen—Diana was now talking to a fifteen-year-old girl whose mother wouldn't let her get a tattoo.

"It's *my* body," the girl was saying. "And if I want a tattoo, I don't see why I can't get one."

"At fifteen," Diana said, "you're only a shadow of the person you will one day be. Your tastes will change as you grow older, and the tattoo you love today may be the mistake you hate in twenty years. Listen to your mother, sweetheart, and keep the peace at home. When you're older and on your own, if you still feel you *must* have a tattoo, then you'll be able to get one. But until that time comes, remember one thing—Mama knows best."

Gary grinned. Part Erma Bombeck, part Dr. Laura, and part Emily Post, Diana had an answer for everything and everybody. Despite her show's growing popularity, until this morning she had been one of the best-kept secrets in America.

Now he had a feeling everything was about to change.

Four

BRITTANY SHELDON PULLED HER BOOKS TO HER CHEST and leaned forward, one sneakered foot flat on the floor, the other flexed to propel her out the door.

As the bell chimed, she rose with thirty classmates. "Hold it," Mrs. Parker called. "Read the last three pages of *Hamlet* for homework. Find out what happens to the prince—and count on a quiz tomorrow."

Brittany moved toward the door, then rolled her eyes as her best friend, Charisse Logan, fell into step beside her. "Gonna read that play?"

"No."

Charisse grinned. "Gonna fail the quiz?"

"Probably."

"And you don't care?"

"Got that right."

They followed the crowd into the hallway, where sunlight streamed over the sidewalk and spilled onto the dented lockers clinging like barnacles to the walls of Seminole High School. After finding her own locker, Brittany twirled the dial as Charisse leaned against a concrete pillar and snapped her gum.

"I hate Mrs. Parker. Did you see that skirt she had on? I'll bet she's had it since the eighties. I swear, I think the fabric was plastic."

"Mrs. Parker is retarded." Brittany slammed her heavy English book into the locker and wondered why she'd even bothered to carry it to class. She was practically cross-eyed from reading Shakespeare and all those stuffy British writers Mrs. Parker adored. Why couldn't they read something *interesting* for a change?

A squeal cut through the roar and crash of students and slamming lockers. "Brittany Sheldon!"

"Oh, brother."

She turned in time to see Sierra Smith threading her way through a group of sophomore geeks. Sierra, an eleventh-grade varsity cheerleader who seemed to bounce through the halls even when she wasn't wearing sneakers, was so perpetually bubbly she wouldn't recognize a snub if you got in her face and told her to take a flying leap.

Charisse lifted a brow. "What do you think *she* wants?"

Brittany snorted. "Probably wants us to sell flowers or something for the prom."

Apparently oblivious even to the goofy looks from the geeks, Sierra kept coming. Finally she stood beside them, a positively putrid package of perkiness. "I'm so glad I caught you girls! Did you hear the news?"

Brittany modeled a look of exaggerated curiosity. "Golly gee, what news?"

The cheerleader beamed. "Your mother! She saved some guy's life on the radio this morning. He had a gun and everything, but she managed to talk him out of killing himself while somebody called the police."

Brittany glanced at Charisse. "And how would you know about it?"

"Mrs. Hamilton plays the radio in the library every morning, and she let us listen when things got interesting. It was so awesome! Now they're giving updates on the news every hour—"

Cutting Sierra off with an uplifted hand, Brittany gave her a plastic smile. "Thanks, Sierra. You're so right. I have the coolest mom!"

She waited until the bubbly girl bounced away, then suddenly unsmiled. "Let's get out of here."

Charisse slowed her gum-chewing. "You wanna ditch?"

"You bet." Brittany glanced over her shoulder, then set out toward the parking lot with long strides. Her pickup truck waited there, her chariot of escape.

Charisse double-timed to keep up. "But—"

"There'll never be a better day," Brittany said, thinking aloud. "I heard about my mom's little adventure, you see? And I was so upset I forgot to check out or call to get permission to go home. All I have to do is tell Mom I was worried about her, and she'll write me an excuse." She shook her head. "I feel like such a stupid baby. I can't go to the bathroom without a note from my mother."

"Join the crowd," Charisse said, then added: "So it'll be okay if your friend goes with you?"

Brittany shrugged. "You're upset, too, and you want to keep me company. If your mom doesn't buy that, I'll have my mom call her. No problem."

"But where do we go? Your mom'll be home in a couple of hours, and my mom is probably still in bed—"

"We go to the beach." Brittany tilted her face toward the sun, already hot and bright. "And we start working on our summer tans."

Charisse's narrow face beamed. "I like the way you think, girl."

"Thinking's easy"—Brittany narrowed her eyes as they moved from the mob on the sidewalk into the unpopulated parking lot— "when your mother is a flippin' genius."

Five

"YOU WERE JUST TOO COOL, DR. SHELDON."

"Thank you, Charity, but I was only doing my job." Charity from Buffalo was a regular caller with a penchant for sharing quotable quips, and I knew she had called with more on her mind than praise for my performance earlier that morning. Gary was doing his best to screen all the gushing calls.

I glanced at the clock. We were winding down, and I hoped Charity had something worthwhile to share as we moved into the close. "What's on your mind today?"

"As I listened to your program, I couldn't help but think about oysters. Do you know much about oysters, Dr. Sheldon?"

Oysters? The woman was determined to send us out on an irrelevant note. "Can't say I do, Charity. I don't even like to eat them."

The woman's gentle laugh rippled over the airwaves. I didn't know much about this woman, but I pictured her as about sixty with clipped gray hair, glasses, rouged cheeks, and a librarian's love of reference books.

"Oysters are one of nature's most wonderful creations. When a grain of sand enters their shell, they don't even try to eject the irritation. Instead they embrace it, pull it close, and surround it with their very essence. In time, their ability to wrap beauty around trouble results in a pearl. That's what you did today—you wrapped beauty around the trouble in that man's life and saved a lost soul."

With a lot of help from above.

I tilted my head toward the mike as the clock advanced to 11:58. "Thanks for sharing that, Charity. I must admit, I never cared much for slimy oysters, but I *do* like pearls. Thank you for your kind comments, and thanks for calling."

I cocked a finger toward the control room and Chad hit the next button. I signed off over "the bed," two minutes of funky rhythms designed to send listeners on their way with an upbeat attitude, careful to keep a light note in my voice as I wished my audience a good day and a good attitude.

No sense in letting the world know I felt as wrung-out as my grandmother's dishrag.

"Talk to you tomorrow," I finished, keeping an eye on the clock counting down the seconds. "And remember—the next time you have a problem, don't do anything you'll regret. Call me, and let's talk it out."

The music faded, Gary slumped in relief, and I slipped the headphones from my ears. Inside the control room, the noon news would have begun to blare from the speakers, but in my soundproof chamber the only noise was the quiet thump of my own heart.

I took a deep breath and lowered my head, not wanting Gary or Chad to see the play of emotions on my face.

Man, oh man.

I propped my elbows on the desk, then dropped my head into my hands. I'd had a live one today, and by the grace of God alone we had managed to pull success out of what could have been sheer disaster. If Tom from Tennessee had blown himself away on the air, or hurt his wife and kid—

Chad would have used the ten-second delay to keep the sound of a gunshot from reaching the airwaves, but the delay button wouldn't have been able to disguise the fact that something had gone terribly, drastically wrong. No matter how we tried to spin it, the world would have been witness to Dr. Diana Sheldon, pop psychologist and queen of morning radio, spectacularly failing a desperate caller. Within minutes the national media would have smelled blood in the water, and the tabloids would have engaged in a feeding frenzy. People who never listened to talk radio would have heard every gritty detail . . .

"Diana?" Gary's voice came through the intercom speaker at my left hand. "Can you come in here? I have news."

"In a minute."

I swiveled my chair to face the thick gray wall behind me. My coworkers had decorated every spare inch of space in the control room next door with girlie pictures, but nothing hung here except a promotional banner for the station.

WFLZ, the Voice of the Gulf Coast.

My voice could have blown it big time today.

I reached back and picked up my coffee cup, then brought the brew to my lips. Cold coffee wasn't the most appetizing thing in the world, but it was wet and my throat was dry. I needed to be on my way after gathering a quick report from Gary, because Scott Daniel would be standing in a line of kindergartners at the Gulf Coast Christian School, waiting for chauffeur moms to arrive.

I needed a minute, though, to gather my thoughts. The media might still pick up the story of my suicidal caller, but now it would play as a feel-good feature, not a news brief. We might even get some good publicity—and good publicity was priceless. My program was doing well, airing in several major markets, but something like this could propel us to the level of Paul Harvey or Rush Limbaugh . . .

I slipped from my chair and grabbed my purse from under the desk, then passed through the doorway and into the hall. A half-dozen interns stood outside, their eyes wide.

I hesitated. Young guys were always hanging around the Open Air Building; radio attracted them like a fistfight draws a crowd. But never before had they congregated outside my studio.

I passed through them, then turned. "Hey, guys, what's up?"

They nodded in wordless greeting, then a multiple-earringed kid who didn't look a day over sixteen hurried to open the door for me.

"Thanks." I gave him a puzzled smile, then stepped into the control room, pulling the door closed behind me. No sense in letting the interns eavesdrop if Gary had bad news to report. Anything could have happened in the last hour, including Tennessee Tom's suicide while in police custody.

I dropped my purse on the worn couch behind Gary's chair. "Well?"

Gary spun around to face me, a grin overtaking his usual preoccupied look. "Dr. D, what can I say? You were unbelievable this morning. The phones haven't stopped ringing."

Long ago I learned not to pay much attention to gushing praise, but kind comments from a coworker always filled me with a rush of warmth. Still, I couldn't have handled that call alone.

I shrugged. "I wasn't that unbelievable, and I nearly blew it at least once. I did what any crisis counselor would do."

A glint of wonder filled Gary's eyes. "Still, it was pretty impressive."

"Your husband called a minute ago," Chad added, glancing up as his big hands roved over the soundboard. He was monitoring the news being read two studios away.

"Steve called? Was something wrong?"

"He heard the show," Chad answered, using the computer mouse to drag and drop a commercial into the lineup on the monitor. "He told me to tell you he had been praying for you."

For Chad, a rough-edged agnostic, to even pronounce the word *praying* was something of a miracle.

"Really?"

"And what Charity said there at the end was good." Chad shrugged as he stared at the flickering meters on his board. "She seemed to tie it all together."

"That oyster analogy is as old as the hills, but yeah, it did fit well." I sank onto the couch against the wall and shifted my attention to Gary. "Anything else important?"

Leaning against the console, my producer delivered the next bit of news with an air of solemnity. "Conrad Wexler called."

"Wexler?" I tapped my fingers on my knee, trying to place the name.

"He's the vice president of talk shows for the network. Our boss."

"Oh." Wide-eyed, I met Gary's gaze. "So—are we fired?"

His grin widened. "Apparently we nearly gave him a coronary, but he loved what he heard. Told me to congratulate you on a job well done and mentioned that he was planning to alert the media. I wouldn't be surprised if the people from ABC News or *People* magazine show up on your doorstep this week."

"As long as they don't come today." I glanced at the clock mounted above Chad's board—twelve minutes after noon already, which meant I'd be so late that Scott Daniel might get anxious.

I pulled the straps of my purse to my shoulder. "I've got to run, guys. I'll come in early tomorrow, though, to tape those promos we discussed earlier—"

"Let me sleep on this latest development," Gary interrupted, "and maybe I can think of something to highlight what happened here today. Nothing that will come across as exploitative, but maybe something punchy like 'Dr. Diana can handle your 911 call'—"

I couldn't stop a shudder. "I don't think we want to encourage suicidal callers. If we give desperate people an audience, they're likely to call and kill themselves on the air just because they know they can."

Gary sank back, his body language suggesting he'd been hurt. "It was just a thought."

"I'm glad you're thinking. But let's think some more."

I gave him a grin, then stood and reached out to touch Chad's shoulder. The burly sound engineer could be as explosive as a chunk of C-4, but he knew how to solve all kinds of technical problems. I didn't know what we'd do without him. "Good work today, Chad. Thanks for your help."

He tossed a quick smile in my direction. "No problem, Dr. D."

Six

AFTER GIVING HER RESTLESS YOUNG CHARGES A STERN glance, Kathy Marshall bent to peer out from beneath the portico where a line of cars was creeping along at slug speed. The sun had disappeared, and the now-gray sky, heavy with drizzly rain, sagged toward the parking lot where moms and minivans waited with headlights on and windshield wipers beating in rhythm.

Rain always seemed to activate the wiggle gene in her kindergartners, and the visiting balloon artist hadn't done anything to calm them down. Taking advantage of the extra time afforded by their rain-canceled recess, he had taken pains to fashion a different balloon animal for each child—long, thin creations that were now clasped tightly in twenty-two pairs of small hands.

Mrs. Hawthorne, a vegan earth mother who drove an old VW bus that probably burned more fossil fuels than any vehicle in the line, leaned sideways to open the door for her squirmy daughter.

"Here you go, Placentia." Kathy caught the door and opened it wide, then helped the little girl into the front seat. Mrs. Hawthorne, apparently assuming that Kathy had things under control, leaned back against her seat and tapped the steering wheel in time to the Beach Boys tune playing on the radio.

Kathy forced a smile as she dragged her hand through the pile of McDonald's wrappers wedged into the space between the seat and the door. "Placentia, where's the seat belt?"

"It's there." Placentia pointed toward her mother's belt, hanging loose from the opposite door.

"Not your mother's belt, honey. *Your* belt. I can't let you ride away until you are safely tucked into your seat belt."

Mrs. Hawthorne, obviously oblivious to Kathy's rapidly ebbing patience, begin to sing: "And we'll have fun, fun, fun, now that Daddy took her T-Bird away."

"Mrs. Hawthorne." Leaning over the child, who began to bat Kathy's cheek with the tail of a balloon brontosaurus, she assumed her best let's-be-serious expression. "Can you help me belt your daughter into this seat?"

"Of course." Mrs. Hawthorne gave Kathy a wide-eyed smile, then jerked her thumb over her shoulder. "Get in the back, Placentia, where the belts work."

"I doan wanna!"

"You need to."

"But I wanna ride in front!"

Lifting both hands, Mrs. Hawthorne gave Kathy a helpless shrug.

Dimly aware that she was exhibiting a less-than-flattering pose to the other children in line, Kathy dived into the backseat of the car, then pinned Placentia to the seat with her forearm. The girl sang along with the Beach Boys, keeping time by bopping Kathy's cheek with the balloon—

If she ever invited another balloon artist, she ought to have her head examined.

Finally she felt the seat belt click. With difficulty she extracted herself from between the VW's bucket seats, then slammed the door with a bit more force than necessary.

Closing her eyes, she slowly inhaled as the next car approached.

"Miss Marshall?"

She looked down to see Scott Sheldon holding his balloon centipede with both hands.

"Yes, Scott?"

"My balloon doesn't have any legs."

Careful to keep an eye on the approaching car, she smiled at the boy. "Yes he does, Scott, we drew them on with black marker."

"But those aren't legs, they're just marks. Everybody else's animals have legs that bend."

She opened her mouth to answer, but at that moment Mrs. Lipps opened the door for her daughter. Reaching for Jacqueline Lipps with one hand, Kathy nodded to Scott. "We couldn't very well put a hundred bent legs on that balloon, could we?"

She bent to help Jacqueline into the car, belted the child in, then gave Mrs. Lipps a weary smile.

When she returned to the line, Scott Sheldon was waiting with another question. "Miss Marshall?"

Kathy lifted her hand, waving the next car forward. She ought to send Scott to the end of the line because his mother was nearly always one of the last to arrive. But he'd think she meant to punish him if she did, and somehow she couldn't stand the sight of pain in those big blue eyes.

As the next driver inched forward, Kathy turned her attention to Scott. "Yes, honey?"

"If I bring him back tomorrow"—his gaze shifted to the long, unbent balloon in his hands—"can we maybe give him a couple of legs?"

Kathy laughed softly as she motioned for Kimmie Jones. The quiet little girl was carrying one of the cuter balloon creations, a poodle that almost looked like a poodle.

"I tell you what, Scott." She winked at the boy as she placed her hand on Kimmie's shoulder. "Bring him in tomorrow and we'll see what we can do."

Turning to smile at Mrs. Cragle, Kimmie's mother, Kathy bent to buckle the girl's seat belt.

She was digging for yet another belt clasp when she sensed commotion behind her. The rising wind was spitting rain onto the children and making the girls squeal. She turned in time to see Natalie Wright throw up a hand to keep rain out of her eyes, then a gust of wind snatched the balloon kitten from her grasp.

Leaning on the open car door, Kathy called out a warning as Scott Sheldon ran after the balloon. The kitten flitted across the sidewalk, then landed in a puddle in front of Mrs. Cragle's front fender. Kathy took a step to haul Scott back into line, but the car door blocked her way. She sidestepped, intending to move around it, but the car lurched and she heard sounds that froze her scalp to her skull—the clasp of a safety belt, a soft thump, and a faint splash.

"Stop!" Terror lodged in her throat, making it impossible to say anything else. Something in her voice must have struck fear into Mrs. Cragle, for the woman's wandering foot slammed on the brake. Kathy pushed her way past the car door and covered the distance to Scott Sheldon in three frantic strides.

He lay chest down on the wet pavement with his head turned so she could see that his mouth was slightly open below eyes as wide and blank as windowpanes.

Seven

"DON'T YOU HAVE TO GO?"

Gary's comment broke my concentration. I had moved toward the door several minutes ago, but I paused to check the plastic correspondence tray mounted to the wall. Gary usually printed out new e-mails after the show, but some of our eager-beaver interns often pulled mail from the Web site while the show aired and dropped copies into the tray. Technology never ceased to amaze me, but I was usually grateful that I could hear so much from so many people in so short a time.

Though I was running late, I hadn't been able to resist skimming through the stack, hoping for a virulent piece of hate mail that might serve as a springboard for tomorrow's program. After today's drama, anything less than dazzlingly controversial would seem like a snooze. I might even tackle an abortion letter tomorrow, if I could find someone who'd debate intelligently instead of screaming at me.

Deep within the recesses of my purse, my cell phone played its melodic ring.

"Rats." I tucked the stack of printed pages under my arm, then began the laborious process of digging past wallet, checkbook, and sunglasses case in search of my Nokia. I had to be quick if I wanted to catch it before the automatic voice mail picked up.

I found the phone after the second ring, glanced at the digital readout, and saw "Steve's Car" in the caller ID box. Why would my husband be calling from his car? He usually ate lunch in his office, but maybe he'd known I'd be swamped after such a stressful show and was offering to pick Scott up himself, sparing me from a mad rush to the school. Or maybe he'd decided to take me and Scott Daniel to lunch. An impromptu celebration certainly fit the occasion.

The phone had sent him to voice mail, so I dialed his cell number and waited for him to pick up. "Steve?"

"Honey, it's me."

I frowned as I caught Gary's eye. My husband wasn't the type to state the obvious. I turned slightly and lowered my head. "Everything okay? You don't sound like yourself."

"There's been an accident at the school."

Something cold slid down my spine, leaving a trail of dread in its wake. "What kind of accident?"

"They say Scott's dead." My husband's voice, usually so calm and soothing even in the most trying circumstances, broke into shards. "They've got to be wrong, but I'm on my way to the school to see what the trouble is."

As my knees turned to water, I sank onto the couch. "Scott Daniel? *Our* Scott?"

"They said he was hit by a car." His words grated and cracked as they tumbled over one another. "It's raining, you see, and apparently the driver didn't see him step into the road . . ."

His strangled voice died away, and some part of my brain wondered how he could simultaneously drive and relay this terrible message. But a cloud, formless and heavy, swallowed up that insignificant thought as it began to fill my brain.

Jesus, Lord, this news couldn't be true. Don't let it be true. Take my life, my body, my *world*, but don't take my son. You couldn't do that, you wouldn't do that. Let him be hurt, let it be a mistake, let this be a dream . . .

"Of course it's not true." I said the words automatically, gripping the phone so tightly my fingers hurt. "You go there, and you'll see. I'm leaving the station now. You call me when you know what hospital they've taken him to, and I'll meet you there."

"Okay."

The line clicked and Steve was gone. Somehow I stood and turned toward the door.

"Everything okay?" The look on Gary's face told me he knew nothing was as it should be.

"Scott's hurt." I stared at him as a series of words and stuttering images filled my brain. "I'm to meet Steve . . . someplace. He'll let me know."

Gary slipped from his tall chair. "Your hands are shaking, Diana. Let me drive you."

I would have protested, but a quick glance at my hands confirmed his observation. Besides, having Gary to negotiate Tampa traffic would leave my mind free for more important things . . . like taking Steve's next call and straightening out this horrible mistake.

Nodding, I turned toward the door. "Okay."

I paused, frustrated by the moment Gary took to murmur something to Chad, then together we pressed through the crowd of starry-eyed interns still loitering in the hall.

"You might want to take an umbrella, Dr. Sheldon," one of them called. "It's raining outside."

Ignoring him, I concentrated on placing one foot in front of the other. After the news I'd just received, how could a little rain possibly hurt?

Eight

DRIVING MORE CAREFULLY THAN USUAL BECAUSE OF the rain, Gary turned the car onto the six-lane Gandy Boulevard and drove west toward the bridge and Pinellas County. Diana and Steve lived in Hunter's Green, an exclusive gated community between Largo and Seminole, but on the west side of Tampa Bay. Brittany, their daughter, attended Seminole High School, while Scott went to a private kindergarten at a church near the family home. Diana was usually careful to leave the station as soon as the show had finished, but even on the best of days she was one of the last mothers to arrive at the kindergarten pickup, depending upon the pace of traffic from Tampa.

He risked a glance at his stunned passenger. Though almost twenty years his senior, he'd always thought his boss an attractive woman. At this moment, however, the color had fled from her cheeks, the liveliness from her eyes. She sat very still, her eyes narrow, one hand clutching the seat belt across her chest.

He summoned the courage to speak. "Did, um, Steve give you any details?"

Keeping her eyes on the road ahead, she shook her head. "Not really." She spoke slowly, as if carefully considering each word before pronouncing it. "He said something about the rain . . . and about a car. I suppose somebody bumped Scott Daniel as he waited in the pickup line. But it can't be serious. Those people are very careful, and cars *crawl* through that portico where the children wait on rain days."

Gary sighed. Thank goodness. The show was going well, and today had been a red-letter day. He couldn't afford to have his star sidetracked by a family emergency.

"I'm sure Scott is fine," he said, handling the car with more confidence than he'd felt when they left the station. "Now, where are we going?"

Diana didn't answer, but the hand on the seat belt tightened until he could see the white bone of her knuckles.

"How am I going to get my car?" Abruptly, she gave him a pointed look. "How am I supposed to get to work tomorrow?"

"Don't worry, just give me your keys." He forced a smile. "I'll go back and get Chad, and when he gets off we'll take your car to your house. That way you can hook up with Steve and you won't have to worry about the car."

He pulled left to pass a slow-moving truck. "Diana, we're near the bridge. Where are we going? Did I hear you mention a hospital?"

"I don't know." Her face had drawn inward, a pale knot of apprehension. "Steve's supposed to call when he learns where they took Scott." She tossed her head slightly, as if shaking off the shock that had attacked her in the studio. "I think"—she gestured left—"you should head south toward St. Pete. They'll probably take him to All Children's."

Nodding, Gary increased the pressure on the accelerator. The Gandy Bridge would deposit them in St. Petersburg, and with a little luck they'd reach the leading children's hospital before Steve, who'd be coming from his office in Clearwater.

They were fortunate to have a specialized children's hospital in the area. Gary didn't know much about kids, but they were resilient, weren't they? His mother had always said kids practically had rubber bones. And doctors worked miracles these days.

Threading his way through the traffic, he gave his passenger a confident smile. "Everything's going to be fine."

Nine

GARY HAD NEARLY CONVINCED ME THAT STEVE'S CALL was nothing but a terrible mistake when my cell phone chimed again. I dived for it, catching it before the second ring.

"Steve? Gary's driving me, but which hospital?"

My husband spoke in an odd, flat voice. "No hospital, Di. They've taken him to the medical examiner's office. I'm here now, waiting for you."

I stared at the windshield, where the wipers thumped out an encouraging beat. *Not . . . dead . . . not . . . dead.*

"But—why? Surely they need to get him to the hospital."

The cellular silence between us filled with dread, then Steve's voice broke. "He's gone, sweetheart. His neck was broken. He wasn't breathing when the teacher reached his side, and the EMS personnel never found a pulse."

I looked at Gary, who was doing his best to act as though he wasn't listening. Seeing him—my employee—reminded me that I was a person with some authority.

"Listen, Steve, he can't be dead. Remember when that little girl down the street fell in her pool? She had no pulse. She didn't breathe for nearly ten minutes, but they revived her in the ambulance."

"But her mother had been doing CPR . . . and her neck wasn't broken."

I closed my eyes as horrific images pushed and jostled and competed with each other for space in my brain. My boy could not be dead. This was a mistake; it had happened to some other child or it hadn't happened at all.

"How can they be sure that's what happened to Scott? I want him taken to the hospital; I want the doctors to do CPR or whatever they have to do. Little boys don't go from being perfectly healthy one minute to dead in the next—"

"Diana." He whispered my name in a tattered voice. "We're waiting for you here at the ME's office. Come as soon as you can . . . because I don't think I can do this without you."

Do what? Give up on my son? I wouldn't do that, I *couldn't* do that, but if I had to go there to demand that they act in a reasonable manner, I certainly would. And if Scott Daniel was dead, if there was nothing else they could do—

A wave of pain threatened to engulf me, but I pushed it back and backpedaled away from that thought.

"Where *is* the ME's office? I haven't a clue."

"Ulmerton Road, about a mile west of the sheriff's department. I'll meet you outside."

He disconnected the call, but I sat for another three seconds with the phone pressed to my ear before I realized he had gone. Without warning, without so much as a good-bye.

My beloved Scott Daniel would never leave like that.

I turned to Gary, dropping my phone into my purse. "We have to go to the medical examiner's office. It's on Ulmerton Road—I think I know the building."

Gary nodded wordlessly, and I felt an instant's relief in knowing I wouldn't have to repeat anything Steve had said. After all, Gary had heard half the conversation, and surely he knew they didn't take still-living little boys to places that had more in common with a morgue than a hospital.

A morgue. Upon waking this morning, I could not have named a place less likely to house a meeting between myself, my husband, and my son.

I lowered the phone and dropped it back into my bag, then stared at the tops of my knees, bony lumps beneath the hem of my plaid skirt—a skirt I had liked until ten minutes ago. Now I knew I'd never wear it again.

I shifted my gaze to the window, then propped my elbow on the car door and stared at the traffic trailing by. Something had gone terribly wrong at that school. Some teacher had messed up, some driver had been reckless, and some principal had been out of his mind to even *think* of letting the children line up on a rainy afternoon like this one. Some EMS worker had been careless or lazy—why else hadn't they done something to stop the spark of life from leaving a perfectly healthy little boy?

Someone—perhaps many someones—had committed a grievous wrong today, and I would not rest until they had been confronted and made to realize the vastness of their mistake.

Scott Daniel Sheldon was not supposed to die today.

My baby lay on a steel table, his narrow chest covered by a sheet. His eyes were closed, his lashes pale fringes upon cheeks that had been rosy and warm when I kissed them this morning.

I cupped the smooth cap of shining blond hair against my palm. His name leaped to my tongue and stuttered against the back of my teeth, but I could not speak the name of a living boy in the presence of this empty shell.

So I stared at the child on the table, cold and pearl blue in the fluorescent lights. The hollow mockery before me did not seem capable of containing a life as robust as Scott Daniel's, but on the cheek I saw the scrape from his fall last week as we skated on the driveway. I had warned Scott that he wasn't ready to go down the steep slope, but in the minute I turned to pull mail from the mailbox, he tromped up the grass. I looked up in time to see him launch himself and sail down, his eyes wide with terror and his mouth open in a gleeful squeal. And, as I had feared, his skates hit the crack at the intersection of driveway and sidewalk and he went flying; fortunately, a patch of Floratam sod cushioned his face-first fall. His cheek, however, had encountered a stray rock.

Now I brushed my fingertip across the shallow scar. Scott Daniel, bone of my bones, blood of my blood, had inherited more than my blonde hair and blue eyes. My stubborn will had also passed through the placenta that fed him, yet it was somehow tolerable in this package . . . perhaps because he had also inherited his father's easygoing smile. The first time I held him in the delivery room, I knew he was a special gift, a boy God would use for some glorious purpose—

But not this. This—this death, this day, was not God's plan. This was completely wrong.

To my left, Steve was sobbing softly, one hand pressed to his face, the other across his chest in a primitive defense posture. *It won't help,* I wanted to say. *Something evil attacked us today, God stood back and allowed it, and for a moment, at least, the world turned upside down.*

I would not have been surprised to learn that in the last hour terrorists had destroyed the United Nations or an earthquake had ejected California into the sea. Surely God had been sleeping . . . and surely he would make things right.

But how?

I turned to my husband, the hideous and alluring question on my lips, but he had closed his eyes to the sight of our dead boy. The medical examiner, a quiet man in a white lab coat, stood near the door, respecting our time with our son. He had met us in the lobby and explained the accident, but the words had fallen upon my ears like an overturned can of Tinkertoys, jumbled and disorganized.

He gave me details, not answers.

None of this made any sense.

I don't know how long we stood there, but after a while I found myself in a small lobby decorated like the lounge at the car dealership where I routinely waste three hours every six months: leatherette couch against the wall, oak-laminate coffee table with chrome legs, dozens of tattered year-old magazines stacked on a matching table at the side of the couch.

I heard the crackle of cheap vinyl as I sank onto the sofa. Why did a morgue need a lounge? This wasn't a place where one came to wait for an outcome.

A moment later, I understood. As if he'd been summoned by some wireless pastoral-emergency network, our pastor, John Thompson, arrived. Breathless and red-faced, he pulled me to my feet, gave me a quick embrace, then greeted Steve in the same way.

"I'm sorry it took me so long to get here." Pastor John pulled a handkerchief from his pocket and offered it to Steve, who was still weeping freely. "Please, Diana, Steve, let's sit down. I'm sure you want to talk about this, and I'd like to pray with you."

Dry-eyed and shivering, I sat, but all I could see when I looked up at the man in charge of shepherding my eternal soul was an employee on autopilot, a man who routinely offered prayers for the sick and consolation for the grieving. I was a professional counselor; I knew how easily words of comfort became rote.

I stared at him, indignation mingling with rising disbelief. How could he comfort us? Though we had often talked to him at church, he had not known Scott Daniel. To my knowledge, he had never taught my son a Bible verse or prayed with him—Sunday school teachers and the kindergarten staff had done those things. Scott Daniel had not yet made a profession of faith, so Pastor John had not even baptized him.

I doubted he had ever heard my beautiful son laugh.

The pastor tugged at his pocket, probably looking for another hand-kerchief, then halted when he looked into my dry eyes. I would not weep before the man responsible for the kindergarten where my son died.

A flush colored his face as awareness thickened between us.

"I'm sure you want to know details of the accident." Looking away, he clasped his soft hands and lowered himself into a charmless chrome-and-vinyl chair. "I've talked to the teacher, the parent driving the car, and the police officer who wrote out the report."

"Tell us." My voice sounded chilly in my own ears. Beside me, Steve was noisily blowing his nose, but I had never felt less inclined to weep. "Tell me why my son is dead."

The pastor blanched, then spread his hands and looked to Steve. "The kindergarten teachers had all the children in line for rainy-day pickup. Only one car can fit beneath the portico at a time, you know, so the children were growing restless. By 12:15, however, most of the students had been picked up."

I took the blow without flinching. If he intended those words to carry a payload of guilt, he succeeded. By 12:15 I was usually crossing the Gandy Bridge, nearly at the school, but today . . .

Today I had been celebrating in the control room.

Still avoiding my gaze, Pastor John brought a hand to the back of his neck. "The kindergartners had animal balloons, you see—a balloon artist had visited the classroom and entertained them by making those twisty animals. When the little girl beside Scott lost her balloon in a gust of wind, he ran after it. Unfortunately, he darted in front of a driver who was distracted with buckling her child into the front seat. The car struck Scott from behind."

I brought my hand to my temple as a sudden dart of pain scorched the back of my brow. My angel was lying in the next room for the sake of a five-cent balloon?

"Given his height and the point of contact," Pastor John continued, "the police officer figured the impact broke Scott's neck instantly. The teacher could not get a pulse. When the EMS technicians reached us at 12:23"—finally, his gaze crossed mine—"Scott was gone."

Twelve twenty-three . . .

I had been sitting in the studio, grinning while Chad and Gary praised my silver tongue and quick-thinking wisdom. They had been crowing because I saved a life . . . but what if my delay had caused my son's death? If I'd been on time, would things have been different?

No, a rational voice assured me. Even in the best of circumstances, I hardly ever made it to the church before 12:25. If this had been an ordinary day, I still wouldn't have arrived in time to keep Scott from being hit.

So why didn't someone else prevent this accident?

"Where was the teacher"—my fist bunched at my side—"while my son was running into the road?"

"Kathy Marshall was standing right beside the children." A faint thread of rebuke lined the pastor's voice. "She was close enough to reach out and tap Scott on the shoulder, but he surprised her, darting out like that."

He lowered his gaze to the mottled commercial carpeting. "Kathy feels terrible about this, as do we all. But the police officer and the other teachers have assured her she did nothing wrong. No one can predict the impulsive actions of a child."

My temper flared. "Perhaps you should."

A strangled sound came from my husband's throat, but I pressed on. "Aren't you supposed to make allowances for the impulsive actions of children? No one can predict car accidents, either, so we make people wear seat belts even to drive around the block."

Pastor John gave me a look of patient exasperation. "We've painted a yellow line on the sidewalk. The children know they are not supposed to step over it unless they are escorted by a teacher. We drum that rule into their heads from the first day of class. Unfortunately, in his hurry to save his classmate's balloon, Scott forgot."

So now it was Scott's fault. The man was blaming my five-year-old child for his own death.

I rubbed my temple as the pastor kept apologizing. His words said "I'm sorry," but all I could hear was "Please don't sue us."

As if my husband would ever sue the church where he was an elder and a Sunday school teacher.

The door opened again. The white-coated medical examiner stepped in and handed Steve a clipboard. "I'm sorry to intrude, but this is necessary," the doctor said, his eyes filled with sadness and his voice rough. "The state of Florida requires an autopsy for all traumatic deaths. After the autopsy, we will release the body to whatever funeral home you select."

Steve looked at the clipboard as if he had forgotten how to read. "And this is?"

"We need permission to autopsy the body, so you'll need to sign at the bottom. The second sheet is a list of local funeral homes. You may select one now or make inquiries and call to tell us which one you'd like to use."

Did he really expect us to shop for a funeral home as if we were buying a new car? As the keeper-of-the-family-checkbook, I was usually the one who researched things like appliances and furniture, but I could not imagine how one went about choosing a mortician to care for one's child after an autopsy.

I watched in abject horror as Steve signed the first form, then flipped to the second page and put an *X* next to the box for Whitlow's funeral home.

I gave him a quizzical look. "Why them?"

His hands trembling, he offered the clipboard to the doctor. "I don't know. The name sounded familiar, I guess."

The doctor took the clipboard, then nodded. "They're good people. I'll have the director at Whitlow's give you a call."

I lowered my head into my hands as the words echoed in the silence.

Our pastor cleared his throat. "Will you want to have a service at the church?"

Steve didn't hesitate. "Of course, Pastor—and we'd like you to do it."

A surge of bile rose in my throat. I wasn't sure I wanted this man anywhere near my baby, but what other options did I have?

"I'd be honored." Pastor John nodded, then stood, undoubtedly anxious to get back to doing whatever he did all day. Tonight when his work was finished, he'd go home to his wife and three sons, none of whom had ever been struck by a car on church property. None of whom had ever even been in the hospital, much less the morgue.

Steve lifted his head. "We need to call Brittany—get her out of school, I guess."

I winced. How did one go about asking the school to release a child in this situation? "Excuse me, Mr. Principal, but Brittany Sheldon's brother has died. Yes, died. D-I-E-D. If you'll send her home, we'll be sure she has a proper note tomorrow."

"Why?" My voice broke. "It's not like she has to rush to the hospital to tell her brother good-bye." I glanced at my watch. "She'll be home in a couple of hours. Let's tell her then."

The words rolled off my tongue even as my brain resisted the idea of sitting down and sharing this disastrous news with our daughter. If I could put off telling Brittany, I could give her a few more hours of life in a world where horrible, unthinkable things did not happen on rainy Monday afternoons.

Pastor John lifted his hands, reminding me of how he stood to address the congregation after the call to worship on Sunday mornings. "Shall we pray together before I go?"

Steve bowed his head; I blinked in incredulity.

"Father God," the pastor prayed, stepping forward to drop a hand on each of our shoulders, "we know you are the healer of broken hearts. You know the pain of losing a son, and you have walked through the valley of the shadow of death. Be with Steve and Diana now, be the rod and staff that comfort as they walk through this time of grief and sorrow. We ask these things in the name of Jesus, our Lord."

Steve was weeping again, and something in the prayer brought tears to my own eyes. But they were not tears of grief—they were flecks of irritation.

I didn't want a rod and staff—I wanted my son. And God couldn't understand my pain; how could he? He was God, he knew how the play would end. Yes, he lost his beloved son, but only in a finite dimension, and he knew he'd have his son restored after three days.

I stared at the floor, my watery eyes blurring the floor covering into a homogeneous smear. I'd always heard that God understood our pain, but at that moment I couldn't believe it. Comparing his loss to mine was like a millionaire losing a hundred bucks on a bad day in the stock market.

"We'll be praying for you, Steve and Diana." The pastor's deep voice rumbled into my thoughts. "I'll be praying that God would show himself near and dear in this time of trouble."

How could God be *near* when he had obviously been napping this afternoon? And *dear*? Somehow the word didn't fit this situation.

I had been a Christian since childhood, and I'd never felt inclined to hide my faith. At the station, I'd borne more than my fair share of cutting remarks because I professed Christ. I'd learned that you could be a Buddhist, a Muslim, a Wiccan, or a multi-pierced moon-worshiping pagan without eliciting too much comment, but you couldn't be a born-again Christian without attracting various versions of the uplifted brow and snide smile. Yet I had always remained faithful to my testimony, speaking clearly and often even a little eloquently about the reality of faith and God's enduring love.

So was *this* how God repaid me for years of faithful service? Where had his love been today? And why would God, who had so miraculously given Scott Daniel to us only five years ago, abruptly call him home on a rainy day in March?

Another thought—one I'd ignored earlier—jabbed like a splinter in my heart, radiating waves of agony every time my mind brushed against it. At 12:23, I had been thinking about work and radio—*why hadn't I known?* I should have felt something; my mother's heart should have intuited that my son was in trouble. The Spirit of God should have alerted me to the danger, but I heard no inner voice, felt no warning premonition . . .

Something had gone horribly, drastically awry.

Pastor John opened the door and left, leaving Steve and me alone in the silence. For a long moment we sat like statues under the hum of the fluorescent lights.

Finally Steve reached out and took my hand. "Let's go, darling." I stood with him, but as we passed through the doorway he turned right toward the parking lot while I turned left toward the room where my baby lay.

"Diana . . . where are you going?"

"To see Scott Daniel."

"But you've seen him."

I pulled my hand from his grasp and took another step toward the large, cold room. Odd, how that lifeless room called to me. "I need to see him again."

Something in Steve seemed to soften. He took my arm and led me back into the place where our baby lay on a steel table. Someone had wheeled in another sheet-draped body during our absence, and the form beneath it was definitely adult. No mourners stood near to remark upon it.

How could I leave my son with a stranger?

After pulling back the sheet, I ran my fingertips through Scott's hair, noticing how, even in death, gold sparked among the fair threads. He had been born with a wealth of white-blond hair, and when the other boys cut theirs short and wore moussed spikes, Scott had allowed me to keep his in a longer style. His hair was as soft as a kitten's ear, as sweet as baby's breath . . . and after today it would be out of my reach.

My mind flashed back to the crazy days of my teenage years, when after football games we drove along River Road in Rockledge, carefully managing the curves of that oak-shrouded road while searching for the fabled mausoleum. According to local legend, a man had buried his wife on his property in a glass-covered casket, and if you peered into the coffin you could see her hair and nails still growing.

It wasn't true, of course. Nails and hair were dead once they left living follicles and nail beds, but you couldn't have convinced me of that at sixteen. We never did gather the courage to visit the mausoleum . . . never did actually find the place. Now, standing with my son, I would have wagered there was no glass-covered coffin on River Road. Who would want to witness a loved one's decay?

I wanted to remember Scott Daniel as he was this morning—a joyful, curious little scamp. The boy who held my face to give me smacky kisses that never failed to smear my lipstick. The boy who rode on his dad's back while they stomped around the house waiting for dinner to materialize from my disorganized kitchen.

I'm not sure how long we stood there, but after a while I felt the gentle pressure of Steve's hands on my shoulders. "Honey, we have to go."

I bit my lip and nodded, then allowed Steve to lead me toward the door. Like a bandage long stuck to a wound, I felt myself being pulled from the son I had succored and birthed and nurtured. And as Steve guided me through the parking lot, his arm around my shoulders, I hunched forward as the agonizing pain of separation tore me in two.

How long would it hurt? The counselor part of my brain knew the pain would ease in time, but my heart didn't buy it.

My heart felt they should bury us together.

Ten

I THINK EVERY WOMAN, IF SHE IS HONEST, WILL ADMIT to having a contingency plan in case disaster befalls her family. In more thoughtful moments over the years, I had mentally mapped out the funerals of both my husband and my parents.

My parents proved unexpectedly helpful in this regard, having prepaid and preplanned their funerals years before they passed away within months of each other. They had both sensibly opted for cremation instead of burial, thus avoiding all the hassle with a casket, viewing, and graveside service, yet I always thought I would bury Steve if he were to die unexpectedly. My reasons had nothing to do with superstitions about the body, nor did I think myself morbid enough to spend long hours sitting in a cemetery revisiting his memory. I wouldn't need any kind of special setting for that—the Lord had used him to mold and shape my life over the past twenty-two years, so I would take him with me no matter where I went.

No, I had thought to have Steve buried for my children's sakes. At some point Brittany and Scott Daniel might appreciate a permanent memorial to their father. As a popular and beloved dentist, Steve's practice was practically a community institution, and I thought it might be nice for my children to visit a quiet place and commemorate the life they had known all too briefly.

I had made tentative plans for my parents, my husband, and myself (no frills, no media, no open casket, thanks). What I had never considered was planning a funeral for one of my children.

The day after Scott Daniel's accident, I lay in bed with a migraine, nauseous and disinclined to speak to anyone. In the preceding hours I had retold the story of Scott's accident several times, enduring fresh agony with each retelling. I couldn't speak anymore, couldn't tell another visitor or caller how my son had died.

Fortunately, Steve rose to the occasion, handling the details of death as deftly as he'd handled things in the ME's office. He arranged everything with the funeral home, choosing a small white casket lined with silver-gray satin, and a burial plot beneath a live oak at Serenity Memorial Gardens. We would have a funeral service at the church without the casket, in deference to any of Scott Daniel's classmates who might attend, then we'd have a simple service at the graveside for family members.

Tuesday afternoon, Steve came into the bedroom and described all this for me, inviting my comments of approval or disapproval, but I could only stare at him. Only once did I gather enough strength to break through my paralysis—Steve had gone into Scott Daniel's closet and brought out a white shirt and the navy blue blazer I'd bought for Scott to wear last Easter. My boy had looked like a blond cherub in that coat, but he'd worn it only about ten minutes before shucking it onto the Sunday school table and joining his little friends on the playground.

I rose out of bed when I spied the blazer in Steve's hand. "Not that. That's not Scott Daniel."

Steve gave me a look of sheer exasperation. "What, then?"

"Wait." Steeling myself to the necessity of action, I went into Scott's bedroom and rummaged through the closet until I found his favorite shirt—a child-sized Tampa Bay Buccaneers football jersey. I stood there, the jersey in one hand, and wondered what else he should wear. Steve had been carrying only the shirt and jacket—weren't the dead allowed to wear pants?

I shook my head. I didn't care how the funeral home people usually did it; my son would be fully dressed when we said good-bye for the last time. I pulled a clean pair of underwear from his drawer, found two sports socks with no holes in the heels and a pair of black knit basketball shorts. The funeral director might think the shorts undignified, but I didn't care. Scotty had loved them.

Taking the clothes to our bedroom, I dropped them into a shopping bag and handed it to Steve. "Tell them to dress him in these."

Steve peeked into the bag. "They told me he'd only be visible from the waist up."

"Take all of it." I bit my lip. "What about shoes?"

Steve closed the bag. "He didn't wear shoes to bed, did he?"

"Get his tennis shoes. I don't want him going—I don't want him to have bare feet."

I watched Steve walk away, noticing for the first time how weariness showed in the drooping slope of his shoulders. He needed rest. I needed rest. Both of us needed to close our eyes in healing sleep, but neither of us could. Not yet.

Strange, isn't it, how we assign metaphors of sleep to death. We speak of putting the body to *rest,* of people falling *asleep,* and meeting again when they *wake.* We even dress a casket to look like a bed, with pillows and ruffles and satin linings. But I knew Scott Daniel wasn't asleep—according to all I believed in the Bible, to be absent from the body meant to be present with the Lord, so my son wasn't sleeping in any sense of the word. He had vacated his fragile body, and we would treat it tenderly, but he would have no more use for that bit of mortal flesh until the day Jesus returned and refashioned it for use in his kingdom.

I knew all the relevant theology. Before getting my masters in psychology and my doctorate in counseling, I'd graduated from a Christian college with a degree in biblical studies. As a counselor and a radio talk-show host, I'd been dispensing the proper answers for years—God doesn't send trouble, but he allows it. Death is not a final good-bye, but a temporary parting. Tears endure for a night, but joy comes in the morning.

Funny how the answers didn't feel at all proper when the time came to deliver them to myself.

As the hours until the funeral ticked by, the pat responses felt less and less comforting. We had entered a surreal world where time and ordinary life seemed somehow suspended. Brittany, who had received the news in shock followed by noisy tears, floated through the kitchen only when we left it, then retreated to her bedroom. The counselor in me knew she needed someone to talk to; the mother in me was too paralyzed to volunteer for the role.

Our house filled with food as strangers rang the doorbell and handed over warm casseroles, speaking in hushed voices as if we, not Scott, were asleep. Kathy Marshall, Scott's teacher, and Winnie Cragle, the woman who had hit him, dropped by to blubber apologies that buzzed against my eardrums like static from a foreign radio station. People I didn't even know sent letters, notes, and e-mails. Cards sprinkled the foyer tiles, dropped through the mail slot in the front door. The phone rang so insistently that we turned the ringer off and let the answering machine relate the pertinent details: Funeral Wednesday morning, 10:00 A.M., Gulf Coast Community Church. In lieu of flowers, please send contributions to the Scott Sheldon Memorial Fund in care of the church, and together we can help children in need . . .

The memorial fund had been Steve's idea, of course—on Tuesday I had not been able to string two coherent thoughts together, let alone come up with a plan as meaningful as this one. Yet Steve knew our situation would attract media attention, so why not arrange to have good come out of tragedy? With the money from the memorial fund, we could do something practical the next time we heard about a family left homeless by fire or a child who lacked decent clothes for school.

At the time, I thought the memorial fund was Steve's way of making sure "all things work together for good" proved true. As for me, I didn't feel at all inclined to help God out.

On Wednesday morning I dressed with numb fingers, fumbling with the buttons on my white blouse. Was a navy-and-white suit proper attire for a child's memorial service? As a rule, the people of our church didn't wear black to funerals, for how could we mourn when our loved ones were in heaven? I understood the sentiment, but wearing red or green or pink to my son's service seemed about as appropriate as wearing a negligee to church.

Moving in a fog, I went downstairs and joined my family in the black limo provided by the funeral home. When the car pulled through the neighborhood security gate, the unexpected click and whir of cameras snapped me out of my stupor. A phalanx of press people stood beside the landscaped entrance while a local news van, satellite extended, idled at the side of the road.

"That's got to be her car!" I heard someone call. "Dr. Diana!"

Some still-functioning part of my brain realized that the national media had picked up the story. I hadn't read a newspaper in two days, nor had I spoken to anyone from the network. Gary had called Monday night to say they could run prerecorded "best of" programs for at least a week, and his reassurance had been enough to mute the tiny lobe of my brain eternally preoccupied with career.

Ignoring the reporters' shouted questions, the driver sped away, taking us to the church where we alighted in a private area, then walked to the front pew of a crowded sanctuary.

I didn't turn around. In the place ordinarily filled by a casket stood an easel bearing a twenty-by-twenty-four-inch photograph of my heaven-sent miracle, my smiling boy. Two extravagant bouquets stood beside the picture, spangling the front of the church with red roses, baby's breath, and silver streamers.

Some idiot had tied a balloon to one of the flower stands.

I lowered my head as tears stung my eyes. I might never be able to look at a balloon again without thinking of the senselessness of Scott Daniel's death . . . which meant that for the rest of my life I'd be sending regrets to birthday party invitations.

Drawing a deep breath, I opened the printed program. The brief publication listed Scott's full name, his birth date, and the date of his homegoing. It listed his survivors—*a child has survivors?*—as his mother, his father, his sister. All four of his grandparents were in heaven . . . and that thought, at least, brought a twisted smile to my face. He'd be well looked after until we joined him there.

My smile vanished a moment later. Beneath the order of service, some well-meaning imbecile from the funeral home had written, "Heaven needed another angel, so they sent for the brightest and best."

My empty stomach churned as I glanced at Steve. Aside from bad theology, the sentiment was cloyingly maudlin. Had he approved it? Probably. In his current state of mind, he would not have wanted to raise a fuss about anything.

The minister spoke, a woman sang, the children from Scott's kindergarten class walked up in wide-eyed silence and dropped crayoned pictures onto a table near his photograph. Later—in ten years, maybe—Steve and I would look through these tributes.

On Steve's left side, Brittany sat as quiet as a stone, her arms crossed at her waist. I looked at her during the kindergartners' promenade, expecting to see tears in her eyes, but she was staring at the carpet, one sandaled foot swinging in a restless rhythm.

Were we keeping her from the *mall*?

I averted my eyes as shame scorched my cheeks. The counselor in me rose up to waggle a finger and point out that as a teenager, Brittany was not well-acquainted with death. Her grandparents had lived miles away; they had not been part of the daily fabric of our lives. I could not expect her to mourn as we did; I really shouldn't expect anything from her at all. Right now she was mourning Scott Daniel with shock and silence. In time she would miss her brother, then she would learn how to deal with the loss. Children were amazingly resilient, weren't they?

At the conclusion of the service, everyone stood while Steve, Brittany, and I walked alone out of the church. After sliding into the waiting limo, I saw a crowd emerge from the church, their curious eyes following us as we pulled away for the drive to Scott Daniel's final resting place.

The fog-filled dream through which I had been sleepwalking ended at my baby's graveside. Seeing him in the open box, seeing the box next to fresh-turned earth, my anguish burst the last shreds of my control. I wept like a woman who has never known the release of tears. Alone with the pastor and my family, I bent and ran my fingers through Scotty's silky hair one final time.

I wailed when Steve pulled me away so they could close the casket. He tried to lead me toward the car as they removed the spray of flowers, but I resisted until Pastor John took my other elbow and gently helped Steve escort me forward.

As we stepped out from beneath the funeral canopy, again I heard the clicks of camera shutters. Security had kept the press at bay during the graveside service, but now that we were in public, the press considered us fair game. Steve slipped his arm around me, sheltering me from the intrusive cameras.

We drove home, where a posse of church friends was guarding the house. I gave them a glassy-eyed nod of thanks, then slipped out of my jacket, dropped it on the antique pew in the foyer, and climbed the carpeted stairs.

My baby, my miracle child, had moved to heaven, and I wanted to join him. I walked toward my bedroom, then whirled in an abrupt about-face and entered the little room I had wallpapered with red-uniformed tin soldiers on one wall and the Tampa Bay Bucs logo on the other.

With the quiet of the house wrapping around me, I kicked off my pumps and curled up in the middle of Scott Daniel's twin bed. His favorite toy—a rubber-faced black-and-yellow monkey beloved since infancy—sat propped against the pillow.

I pulled the monkey close to my heart and breathed in the scents of my son, then whispered the prayer I had recited at his bedside since his infancy: "Now I lay me down to sleep . . ." If God was merciful, perhaps he would fulfill that prayer and take my soul to join Scott Daniel's.

After a while my eyelids drifted shut, and I surrendered my senses to blessed numbness.

Eleven

SITTING IN THE FOYER OF HIS SILENT HOME, STEVE stared at Scotty's just-delivered portrait and felt a lone tear trickle down his cheek. His only begotten son, the child of his heart—

Now, God, I can empathize with you.

He missed Scotty dreadfully, and knew he would continue to miss him as the years lumbered forward. During every ball game, soccer tournament, and fishing trip, he would yearn for his son's companionship. Time might lessen this gnawing grief, but nothing would prevent Steve from missing the lighthearted boy who had suddenly disappeared not only from their lives, but from their futures.

Steve would attend no high school basketball games to watch Scotty play. There'd be no first car, no driving lessons. No teaching him how to shave and reminding him to use deodorant. No heart-to-heart conversations about girls, sex, and how to know when love is real.

He'd have no grandchildren through Scotty's branch of the family tree—and since Brittany was a grafted branch, no biological grandchildren at all. Not that it mattered . . . but he'd be lying if he said he hadn't thought about it. Most men want to father a son to carry on the family name, and he'd been no exception.

Leaning against the staircase banister, he closed his eyes and opened the door on a host of memories too precious to revisit amid the bustle of a houseful of guests. Scotty as an infant, mewling and helpless in Steve's hands. Scotty as a toddler, teetering forward in that ridiculous padded snowsuit Diana had made him wear to guard against bruises. Three-year-old Scotty excitedly blowing out the candles on Brittany's sixteenth birthday cake, then clapping in delight while she fumed.

Steve released a choked, desperate laugh, then opened his eyes. Such memories could be dangerous . . . if he wanted to make it through this time with his faith intact.

He picked up the picture, considered hanging it at the foot of the stairs, then decided to wait. Yesterday he had given their minister a copy of Scotty's most recent studio portrait, and Pastor John had been kind enough to have it enlarged. One day Diana would appreciate that kindness, but Steve didn't think she was ready to have a twenty-by-twenty-four-inch photo of their lost son staring her in the face first thing every morning.

In a few months she was certain to remember the portrait and ask about it. Then he'd bring it out so they could hang it in the den, a bright spot where they could enjoy it every day. And in years to come, as Brittany and her husband and kids came over to gather around the television to eat popcorn and watch animated videos, they could look up and see Scotty's picture, and think of him waiting for them.

In heaven. Steve had always thought of the place as being similar to life insurance—it was something you desperately needed, yet didn't need to contemplate—but now he found himself hungering for eternity. With Scotty there, heaven would feel more like home than this house did without him.

Twelve

BRITTANY SHUT AND LOCKED THE DOOR TO HER room, then kicked her shoes in the general direction of the closet. Terwilliger the pug lay curled in a pile of clean clothes she'd pulled from the laundry basket. Looking up as she approached, he opened his mouth in a panting smile and waggled his stump of a tail.

"Dumb dog." She stared at her clothes, now covered in white pug hairs. She'd have to throw the whole pile back down the laundry chute.

The dog would probably pester her to no end, now that the Scottster was gone. Ignoring him, Brittany perched on the edge of the bed and picked up the phone, then punched in Charisse's number.

"Hey."

"You back?"

"Yeah."

"How was it?"

"How do ya think? It was a funeral."

"Man." The phone line hummed for a second, then Charisse added, "You okay?"

Brittany leaned against the headboard. "I guess."

"What's it like at your house?"

"Quiet. There's a bunch of people in the kitchen putting food away. Mom's in Scotty's room, and Dad's in his bedroom. Nobody's talking much."

"Bummer."

Brittany shrugged. "Nobody but the Scottster ever talked much anyway. He ran his mouth all the time—so much I always wanted to slug him."

Charisse laughed, then clamped off the sound, apparently remembering that funerals and laughter didn't exactly go together.

"So—you wanna do something later?"

"Maybe. This place is creepy."

"Wanna go to a movie?"

Looking up, Brittany studied the dust tails hanging from her ceiling and stirring slightly in the breath of the slow-moving fan. "I guess."

"I can pick you up. About ten?"

Brittany considered. Ordinarily she had to tell her parents where she was going—a rule she found restrictive and stupid, considering that she'd be a high school graduate in two months—but neither Mom nor Dad seemed in any mood to care right now. And with all the coming and going at the house, she could probably slip out and not even be missed.

"Yeah, pick me up at ten. Let's hit the late showing."

"Anything special you want to see?"

"Something to make me laugh."

After hanging up, Brittany leaned back on her pillows and crossed her arms. The house was an absolute disaster, with assorted church people stumbling all over themselves downstairs. People she didn't even know were answering the door and tending some strange mourners' buffet in the kitchen while her parents had gone into seclusion. Mom had managed to hold herself together until the cemetery, then she absolutely lost it. And Dad, who'd been openly weeping since Monday, had pretended to be strong when Mom crumbled like a sandcastle hit by the incoming tide.

She tugged on the sleeve of her sweater. What if *she* had been the one hit by a car? Would her parents be carrying on over her like this? No sense in asking, really, because hypothetical questions were generally stupid. Still, the thought rankled—would they weep for her in the same way?

She knew her parents loved her. Mom had a baby book stuffed with photographs, and she had loaded her vanity in the master bath with fancy-framed pictures of Brittany in Christmas dresses, dress-up costumes, and tutus from ballet lessons. When she was little, her parents entertained her for hours with the story of how they had prayed for a baby to love, so God sent them a chosen child through the miracle of adoption. They talked about how they went to the hospital to pick her up, how they thanked her "tummy mommy," how they kissed Brittany and hugged her and dressed her in special clothes they'd picked out just for her—

But she'd been a kid then, and easily entertained.

When she was small, Mom and Dad had done everything parents could do for a daughter . . . until the Scottster arrived from out of the blue. Then everything changed.

At first she, too, had been caught up in the miracle of Scotty's conception. The idea of having a little brother was cool, especially after having been an only child for so long. But by the time Scott was born, she was thirteen, and ready to make her own life with her friends.

She had loved the Scottster—after she recovered from the initial embarrassment of walking around with a big-bellied, forty-three-year-old mother. But if movie stars like Jane Seymour could have babies in their forties, why not her mom? Mom had always kept herself in good health, and she didn't let herself get *too* repulsive while she was pregnant. Brittany even used to exercise with her after the baby came; the two of them would lie on the carpet in the den and do sit-ups while Scotty rocked in the baby swing, fascinated by the flailings of the women in his little life.

Yeah, the Scottster had been cute as a baby, and in the early days she had begged to baby-sit. "Maybe when you're older," Mom had answered, and Brittany sulked because her mother didn't trust her enough to handle an infant. Her first baby-sitting opportunity came when Scotty was two, and by the time he had passed his third birthday, Brittany was sick and tired of being asked to "stick around" to watch the kid while her parents ran to the store or went out on the weekends. Didn't they know teenagers had a constitutional right to a social life? Couldn't they understand that no high school student wanted to be caught dead with a toddler in tow?

"You're killing my reputation, Mom!" Brittany yelled one night. "People think he's *my* kid!"

That was an obvious lie, since Scott was as blond as moonlight and Brittany's hair more the color of a bonfire. Truth was, she didn't look like either of her parents, though well-meaning friends were quick to assure her she acted just like them.

Sheesh. As if that were a compliment.

Last year she and her parents had agreed on a compromise. Brittany would be asked to baby-sit no more than two nights a month, and in return she'd be allowed to stay out until midnight two weekend nights a month. Her parents still clung to the antiquated notion of an 11:00 P.M. curfew, but she and Charisse had found a way around it. After all, when two adults tumbled into bed at eleven after a long day of work coupled with dealing with a little kid, they weren't exactly vigilant about guarding the driveway. And a nice climbing oak grew right outside Britt's window . . .

The dog, tired of being ignored, jumped onto the bed and sat next to her, then dropped his chin to her knee. He blinked his round eyes, then looked at her with a woebegone expression.

As Britt dropped her hand onto Terwilliger's round head, her gaze fell upon an odd shape jutting from the dust ruffle at the bottom of her bed. Reaching down, she felt the hard bumper of the Ford F150, the red truck Scotty loved to "drive" all over the house. He must have had it in here Sunday night when she'd gone out with Charisse. He was probably chasing the dog with it.

Unexpected tears clouded her vision, and she blinked as she brushed them away. Death really rotted. The abruptness was the worst thing about it. The Scottster had been here one morning and gone the next. She'd had no warning, no chance to tell him good-bye or say she was sorry for all the times she acted like a snot when he didn't deserve it.

Wonder Boy could be a pain sometimes, like when he wanted to come into her room while she was trying to talk on the phone. A couple of times he'd managed to overhear choice information and blab it at the dinner table, and more than once she'd wanted to wring his scrawny little neck.

But she had never wanted him dead. God above knew that. And she had loved her brother—it was hard not to love his cute little face and those chubby cheeks. But though she would miss him, she'd leave the weeping and wailing to her parents.

If God counted the number of tears people shed for others (and why wouldn't he, if he counted hairs on heads?), then her parents had wept enough today to fill her quota, too.

In the last three days, they'd probably done enough for a lifetime.

Thirteen

MARCH TIPTOED UP TO APRIL WHILE I WASN'T LOOK-ing. The seasonal change is subtle in Florida. Our March winds are alley cats, and our April showers light. No tulips raise their heads to herald a new season here, no daffodils or hyacinths sprinkle our flowerbeds. If I had been more observant, I would have noticed the flocks of thong-clad spring breakers descending to cover the beaches, and the migrating, hoary-headed snowbirds who fly northward right around Easter . . .

I realized April had nearly arrived when I returned to work the Monday following Scott Daniel's accident. The eager girl at the reception desk had turned the page on her huge calendar a day early, and the vast amount of white space caught my eye before I noticed the watchful look she gave me—a sympathetic smile anchoring wary eyes, as if I were a bomb that might explode with the slightest shift in emotional pressure.

I saw the same look mirrored on dozens of other faces as I negotiated the maze leading to our studio. I walked down the hallways with measured steps, returning the fragile greetings with a nod and a stiff smile, determined not to let anyone crack the thin veneer of composure holding me together.

Gary had said I could take another week off if I wanted to, but I knew returning to work would bring normalcy back to my life. I'd been a working woman for so long I didn't know how to relax at home. Because I began my radio show while I was pregnant with Scott Daniel, I used to joke that you could measure the length of my career by the number of my son's birthdays.

I wouldn't make that comment anymore.

The friends and church members had all gone back to their own lives; Steve and I had washed the casserole dishes and Tupperware containers and returned them to their owners. Now the house felt empty, though it was still fragrant with flowers sent in a vain attempt to brighten our gloom.

As though that could possibly help.

Nothing could dispel the gloom haunting our home. You could shine a searchlight into the vaulted halls of my heart and the resident shadows would viciously snuff that beam like a puny candle flame.

Yes, we knew our son was in heaven. Yes, we knew Jesus had promised to bear our burdens. But those promises were like engravings on a tall marble wall, far beyond my reach and cold as death itself.

With relief I entered our control room and closed the door behind me. Chad and Gary sat in their places, while a pot of fresh brew bubbled beneath the coffeemaker on the counter.

"Morning, guys." Though I'd had two cups of coffee before leaving the house, I crossed the room in search of my mug.

Gary responded first. "Good morning, Diana."

I caught the guarded look Chad sent him, but charitably pretended not to notice.

"Um, Dr. D?"

"Yes, Chad?"

"I was real sorry to hear about your little boy."

This from a man who had attended the memorial service and would probably have run the other way if I had tried to thank him for coming. But I understood. People like Chad weren't comfortable with overt emotion of any kind . . . and this situation was loaded.

"Thanks." I found my mug, held it on my palm for a moment, then turned to face my coworkers.

"Guys, it's been a tough week at my house, but I'm a professional in the studio. I'm not sure what's going to happen today—actually, I'm not sure of anything anymore—but I'm going to do my best to carry on as usual. I just wanted to say that up front."

Turning back to the coffee machine, I picked up the pot. "Anything good in the mail this week, Gary? I feel like starting off with something divisive—maybe a juicy piece of hate mail."

When I glanced back, Gary had squinched his face into a *how-do-I-tell-her* look.

"Spit it out, guy."

"Um—90 percent of the mail last week was condolence letters. The other 10 percent was just stupid stuff."

I winced. "Nothing really interesting?"

He fidgeted on his stool, his knees shifting back and forth like the legs of an overanxious adolescent. "Gee, Diana, you're like a national hero. I haven't seen anything like this since the nation rallied around that pregnant woman whose husband died when the plane went down on 9/11."

My mind whirled. "But I didn't do anything."

"Doesn't matter. You were a hero to lots of people before this happened, and then Tennessee Tom called on the same day you lost your son—" His features tensed, as though he was suddenly aware he'd broached a difficult subject. He swallowed hard. "Now nearly everyone admires you."

I exhaled softly. I had not read the stories, but well-meaning friends had dropped off multiple copies at the house. Nearly every newspaper in America had picked up the story about how my son died minutes after I talked Tom Winchell of Memphis, Tennessee, into going out to meet a SWAT team. I couldn't blame them. No news editor worth his salt would pass up a story that rich in irony.

"What on earth do they admire me for?" I asked. "Not cracking under the pressure?"

Gary flushed as he looked away. "For getting through, I guess. For bearing up under the cameras and all."

I poured a packet of sugar in my coffee and stirred. I didn't want to be any sort of hero; I didn't want my private grief to overlap my work at all. On the other hand, I'd been in the radio business long enough to know the price of celebrity—if you create an appetite for your material in an audience, you shouldn't be surprised when the audience hungers for more. The key to survival is in knowing how much you can give without being eaten alive.

I took the spoon from my coffee mug and dropped it on a tray stained with the leavings of a week's worth of sloppy coffee drinkers, then turned to face my staff. "This is what we'll do. We'll take the first five minutes of the monologue to talk about the accident, and I'll thank our listeners for their support. I'll tell them we are working through our loss, but I'm still committed to the show and helping them with their problems. Then we'll cut to the most ridiculous caller you can find."

The dimple appeared in Gary's cheek. "You want Matilda?"

A caller springing completely from Gary's imagination and penchant for mimicry, Matilda was our ace in the hole whenever things got slow or we needed to voice an outrageous opinion that proper Dr. Diana simply couldn't verbalize. Most of our listeners were perceptive enough to realize Matilda was a fictional figment, but occasionally we did get letters from listeners who were convinced sixty-nine-year-old Matilda McGuillicutty really did live in a freezer box outside the Lake Bongo Vista Horseshoe Stadium.

"You bet. Have Matilda call and ask about sending her goldfish to therapy or something, and before you know it we'll be back on track."

"Perfect!" Gary spun around to scribble on his legal pad, and I knew he'd be thinking hard about what Matilda could say.

"Anything on the newswire?" I glanced out the window, where one of the ubiquitous interns was gazing wistfully at the soundboard, no doubt dreaming of the day he'd be allowed to push buttons and slide thingamajigs.

"One of our state senators is proposing a bill that would allow transsexuals to adopt children," Gary muttered in a distracted voice. "But you don't want to tackle that today, do you?"

"Why not? I'm an adoptive parent."

Before last week, I had been an adoptive *and* a biological parent . . . but I wouldn't think about that now.

I sipped from my coffee, pulled a thicker-than-usual stack of correspondence from the tray on the wall, then headed toward the door. "I'm going to the air studio to read through these. Yell if you need me."

Gary didn't even look up from his notes. "Sure thing."

In truth, I wanted some time alone, and the padded and sound-proof walls of the air studio seemed infinitely more soothing than the girls-in-bikinis-wallpapered control room. Gary and Chad were sharp young men, but neither of them could truly appreciate what had happened in my life. Last week, in an instant, I had lost a child. The most precious thing those two had ever lost was probably their virginity.

Nodding at another starry-eyed intern, this one a young woman, I slipped into the air studio and perched on my chair. The head-phones dangled from the boom, but I left them hanging, knowing Gary would understand I wanted quiet. When I wore those, I could hear every murmur and roar made in the often-busy control room. Gary would hail me on the intercom if he needed me.

Steeling myself for horrific spelling and a fresh assault of emotion, I pulled on my reading glasses and began to skim the letters and printed e-mails. From all over America my listeners had written, some bemoaning my loss, others urging me not to give up.

Did they think I was suicidal? I had been wounded, but I still had a husband, a daughter, and a career. In the last week I'd been too numb to act like much of a wife, mother, or career woman, but I would find my footing soon.

Maybe.

One woman from Idaho reminded me that the pain would lessen in time, for she had loved and lost, too, and loving and losing was better than not loving at all.

"Original," I murmured, turning another page on my desk.

The next two letters assured me that my son was now an angel in heaven. Wrong.

I flipped the page. The next note came from a medium who offered me a chance to speak to Scott one final time—for a reasonable fee. "If you like, we can barter a deal," the so-called psychic wrote. "Free radio advertising for one year will get you three thirty-minute sessions with your son's spirit. Call me today, Dr. Diana—I know that little guy wants to talk to his mommy!"

I wadded that page with one hand, then flung it toward the trash can where it—and its author—belonged.

The next letter came from a lawyer offering her services in case I wanted to sue the school, the driver, or the state of Florida for any reason whatsoever. Another handwritten note came from a barely literate woman who had no legal experience whatsoever, but was convinced I could persuade a jury to give me five million dollars, a million for each year of my son's life.

"*Think of all the things you could do with the money,*" she had scrawled across the bottom of a sheet of notebook paper. "*You could end hungry around the world, starting right here in air town. Sence I know your to busy to feed all those kids, I'd be happy to take care of the money for you.*"

"Sure you would," I muttered. "But it'd take a lot more than five million to satisfy your greedy soul, wouldn't it?"

I glanced toward Gary in the window, but he was busy with something at the computer and not looking my way. I satisfied my urge to vent by tossing the last letter into the garbage, too, and found myself wishing that I could meet some of these idiots face-to-face. As a radio personality, I'd grown used to receiving letters from all sorts of zanies, but never had they struck so close to my heart.

They weren't all bad. Sprinkled among the outrageous letters were cards and notes from kind people who knew how to string words together in a reasonably coherent pattern. Most were from women, though several came from men. I blinked back tears as I read these, and wondered if I should take some of them to Steve. He had been handling his grief reasonably well. He had gone back to work the day after the funeral and seemed to find comfort in staying busy.

Nighttime was the most difficult part of the day, and the family dinners we had enjoyed were rapidly becoming family history. Scott Daniel had been the glue holding us together, for Brittany certainly had no desire to eat dinner with her parents. Every night this past week, after coming home from school, she had gone straight upstairs to take a nap, sleeping through supper. With no desire to disturb what was certainly an adolescent coping mechanism, Steve and I ate take-out on TV trays in the den, pretending to watch the evening news so we wouldn't have to speak. Later, as I slipped into bed, I would hear the beep of the microwave downstairs as Brittany warmed up whatever leftovers she could find in the fridge.

My daughter had proved remarkably unflappable, and once again I marveled at the emotional elasticity of children. She had wept when we told her about the accident; she had stood with crossed arms at the graveside, an obvious defensive posture revealing volumes about her frame of mind. But logic assured me she could not blame herself—a common danger with children—nor could she blame us, for Scott's death could not have been more accidental.

She would miss him, we all would, but she would go on. She had her circle of friends, and she had a new life for which to prepare. In less than six months she would be leaving the nest and heading off to college. I would not want her wings to be laden with grief or guilt.

Without warning, tears stung my eyes. I dropped the letter in my hand and pulled off my glasses, swiveling my chair to block anyone watching from the windows as I swiped wetness from my lower lashes.

I had wanted to come back to work and return to the routine of ordinary life. I had even hoped that listening to the problems of others would take my mind off my own situation, but if my emotions kept ricocheting like this, how would I ever get through the day?

I reached into my pocket and pulled out a tissue, then furiously dabbed at my eyes. I had to get a grip. This control room, with its microphone and buttons and flashing phone lines, was blessedly removed from my home. At home, time had stopped, appetites had ceased, and the flesh-and-blood people had become ghosts while Scott Daniel laughed and giggled behind every corner . . .

I still listened for his tread on the stairs, paused at the threshold of his room at night, waited for his kiss to rouse me in the morning. His shoes, which still fit in the palm of my hand, littered the floor beneath his bed, and his favorite juice boxes lined the bottom shelf in the refrigerator.

My home had become an alien place, but here at the station . . .

Here I was safe. Scott Daniel had never even visited the Open Air complex. This place held no memories of him, so here I could find relief.

Glancing at the clock, I saw we had five minutes to air. Framed by the window linking me to the control room, Gary perched on his stool, his eyes intent upon me.

Giving him a thumbs-up, I reached for my headphones, then settled the band over my head.

"You okay?" His voice sounded thin in my ear.

I set my hands to the task of positioning a pad of paper and a pencil within easy reach. "I'm fine. You might want to pull up a couple of extra comedy bits, though. If you see me start to lose it, just let them roll, okay? I think I'll be fine, but sometimes I surprise myself."

"Don't worry, Dr. D," Chad breathed into the mike. "We've got your back."

Nodding, I took another sip of the fragrant coffee, then rubbed my hands together and took a deep breath.

Another week, another Monday morning, another show. But the first without Scott Daniel.

Fourteen

I WAITED UNTIL STEVE'S OLD BMW SHUDDERED TO a halt, then wrapped my hand around the seat belt across my chest. "I really don't want to do this. It's not too late for us to go home."

Steve halted, his hand on the door. "This will be good for us, Diana. Give it a try, just this once. If you absolutely hate it, I'll go alone from now on."

I blew out my cheeks, ruffling the bangs over my eyes. "I don't know why you need this. You're a mature man, you can find peace in your faith. And you're married to a counselor, for Pete's sake—"

"I need to do this for *me*. And I think you need it, too, though that stubborn will of yours has blinded you to your own need at the moment."

Unable to face him, I turned my eyes toward the window. If I looked over and saw a smile on his face, so help me, my palm would itch to slap it off.

"Have it your way, then."

As I unfastened the seat belt, I marveled again that Steve had even been interested in attending a support group for bereaved parents. The week after the accident he'd dropped a few hints about visiting the grief recovery group at our church, but I vetoed that idea before the words could finish leaving his mouth. Open our hearts before people who *knew* us? Having a pap smear in the middle of I-275 at rush hour would be far more appealing.

When he came home with a brochure about this parents' support group, I'd been adamantly against it, too. We didn't need help, we didn't need the exposure, and we sure didn't need to share one blessed word about our private grief with the world. Ever since taking my first radio job, I'd been careful to guard my family's privacy. Life was hard enough for my children because their dad had cleaned the teeth of practically every other kid in the county. My radio exposure had increased the pressure, especially on Brittany, who'd been a tender thirteen when I took to the airwaves.

"It's hard enough having two doctors for parents," she once whined to me. "But having Dr. Diana for a *mom*? People think I should never have any problems!"

With her plea in mind, I tried to distance my private self from the job. I refrained from using my radio voice in neighborhood conversations, I described my occupation on parent questionnaires as "communications," and I never offered to bring my kids along when the station booked me for promo appearances. My radio listeners knew I had a son and a daughter; thanks to the national media, they now knew my son was dead. That was all I wanted the world to know. My memories of Scott Daniel were too precious; I would not dilute them by sharing them with the world.

Not being a celebrity, however, Steve had never had to divide his life between public and private worlds so his sense of potential publicity land mines was undeveloped, at best. A good man with nothing to hide, he had no fear of the media and believed most reporters were friendly and sympathetic.

Ha!

I shuddered to think of a reporter lying in wait, then plying Steve with a smile and an innocent question about our family. Steve would erupt like Mount Vesuvius, spewing stories, snapshots, and quotes that would not always be understood by people outside our family circle.

Even before the accident, Steve *loved* to talk about our kids to anyone who would listen. Now the sympathy of strangers seemed to assure him of Scott's uniqueness, but I didn't need assurance. Scott Daniel was a special blessing from God, and I didn't need anyone to remind me of that.

The single reason I agreed to come tonight, the *only* way Steve could ever get me to appear at such a public venue, was my belief that Christian wives should submit when their husbands won't back down.

Of course, that belief hadn't stopped me from resisting during the drive from our home to this little frame building in Largo. On most occasions when we disagreed, I convinced Steve to swing around to my point of view. But he hadn't been in a swinging mood tonight, so here I was . . . because I respected my husband and wanted to please God.

And because Steve had promised I would have to come only once.

I glanced up toward the small building that had obviously been a home in a former lifetime, probably sold to the city as the population moved out of the urban center. A sign hanging from the porch eaves announced that we had come to the "Pinellas County Community Services Center."

Sighing, I picked up my purse and opened the door. Steve had no idea what I was risking in this act of submission—exposure, for instance. What would the press say if word got out that Dr. Diana Sheldon, professional radio psychologist, was attending a support group for desperate, pathetic parents? The idea was ludicrous.

Besides, I could already predict exactly what variety of psychobabble we'd be served tonight. I knew about letting go and moving on; I knew about venting and releasing and identifying the stages of grieving. My rational brain understood why I could burst into tears at any moment for no reason at all, and my scientific brain had begun to count squares on the calendar, for such outbursts usually tapered off after a period of forty days. The ancients had been wise when they allotted that length of time for mourning—physiologically, we humans seemed to require forty days to regain our equilibrium after a significant personal loss.

Steve and I were on day sixteen, still in the heart of the unsteady stage . . . yet another reason why we shouldn't be appearing in public.

Yet Steve apparently needed outside help, and it was only after he threatened to attend this meeting alone that I decided to rethink my position. Yes, I wanted to honor my husband's wishes, but I was also terrified of what he might say if I weren't along to stem the tide of words. Unaccompanied, he might freely talk about me, my job, or the pressure of raising a child in the spotlight of celebrity. My dear, naive husband might air our personal problems and feelings to anyone who would listen, even if one of them happened to be a reporter, a freelance writer, or a neighbor with a glib tongue.

I agreed to join him with two stipulations. I would speak as little as possible, lest anyone recognize my voice, and while we were in the meeting Steve would refer to me by my middle name, Juliet. According to the brochure, the group maintained a no-last-names policy, but I knew how friendships could spring up outside the confessional circle. No way was I going to let someone drag our family onto the pages of the *National Gossip*. That rag had already printed a grainy photograph of us at the cemetery.

The sound of Steve's footsteps on the gravel grated against my nerves. "Coming, *Juliet*?"

I gritted my teeth at the sound of sarcasm in his voice. He thought I was overreacting. He thought my security concerns resulted from paranoia, and he probably believed my desire to disguise my identity sprang from pure egotism. But in this age of reality television and overnight celebrity, I would take no chances.

I slid out of the seat, brushed the wrinkles from my skirt, and joined Steve on a narrow sidewalk that led into the community center. The place looked like most city-owned buildings—a little dingy and too garishly painted—but it was brightly lit and uncluttered. Through the screen door I could see wooden floors glowing with a patina of long use, and folding chairs stacked against the wall. A dozen chairs had been arranged in a circle in the center of the room, and most of these were filled by men and women of all ages. None of them were smiling.

Steve dropped his hand onto my shoulder as we paused to open the door, and I felt a sense of relief when I walked through and stepped out of his reach. Our disagreement vibrated like a force field between us, and I knew it wouldn't dissipate until we had successfully navigated the evening.

I spied two empty seats and strode toward them, leaving Steve to follow, his heavy shoes clunking against the wooden floor.

He flashed a smile around the circle of faces. "I'm sorry we're late."

"It's all right. You must be Steve and Juliet. I'm Mary Fisher." This reply came from a heavyset woman with a throaty voice. I sank into a chair, dropped my purse onto my lap, and rested my forearms on it, well aware that I was transmitting a forceful message in body language: *Don't come too close.*

Steve, on the other hand, sat down and leaned forward, then opened his hands in an apologetic shrug. "We didn't mean to interrupt. Thank you for allowing us to come."

As if they would turn us away! The sight before my eyes proved one of my mother's old adages—misery *did* love company, because these had to be the most miserable-looking people ever assembled in one room.

"You are welcome." Mary's voice was an echoing purr in the room. "You are among friends."

I resisted the urge to jam my finger down my throat. As a counselor, I had sat in the lead chair and murmured those same words many times, so I knew how automatic they were. Any vague hope I'd harbored of finding *real* help was shattered by Mary Fisher's appearance—she had adopted the uniform of a garden-variety social worker, a type I knew well from graduate school. Though she was probably on the far side of forty, she wore her gray-streaked hair long and straight. Her eyes, round with concern, peered out at us through untrimmed bangs, and her full patterned skirt flowed over her thighs and puddled on the floor like curtains in a formal dining room. Her skin was pale, for she was surely an indoor girl who only went outside to hug trees in the moonlight, and her lips were lined from the habit of pressing them together in thought. She wore no wedding ring, so odds were good she was liberated, divorced, or lesbian, and I knew without looking that if I were to peer into her purse I'd find a cell phone, a voter registration card establishing her affiliation with the Democratic Party, and a bottle of echinacea. Once she hit fifty, she'd be carrying ginkgo biloba, too.

"We are gathered here tonight," Mary said, her wide eyes sweeping the group as a heavy charm bracelet jangled at her wrist, "to support one another through one of the worst tragedies that can befall a loving parent. We are here because we have been united by loss. We are here because we care, and we long to care for others. We may have lost our children, but we have not lost the ability to care."

I closed my eyes. The sentiment in here was so thick you could haul it up by the bucket and sell it by the pound.

"Steve and Juliet—"

The sound of our names snapped me back to attention.

"—I'm sure you'd like to get a feel for things before you speak, so why don't we let the others start us off with introductions?"

She looked around the circle, her eyes wide with appeal, and finally one gray-haired man shuffled his feet and met my gaze. "My name's Ted." He shifted his blue eyes to Steve, then reached out and clasped the hand of the frail woman beside him. "We lost our son ten years ago. He was murdered on his way home from his after-school job, and his killer has never been found."

As a murmur of sympathy ran through the circle, I wondered how many times they had heard his introduction. Had Ted been coming to this group for ten years? The psychologist in me protested, but the parent in me understood. If someone took Brittany from me, I wouldn't be able to let the matter rest until the police found the killer and helped me answer a single question: *Why?*

A red-haired woman next to Ted lifted her hand like a child in school seeking permission to speak.

Mary nodded. "Go ahead, dear."

The redhead looked straight at me. "I'm Tilly. My daughter died from a drug overdose six months ago. She was only fourteen. I know who killed her—those nasty punks who make pills available to innocent kids. What I can't understand is why nobody's doing anything about it."

I looked away, lest Tilly read the thoughts in my eyes: lose the anger, lady, or it'll eat you alive. And don't forget who swallowed those pills—your daughter made the choice, right?

"I'm Meg—and I lost a baby at birth." The sweet girl who uttered this clutched at her young husband's hand and sent an apologetic smile winging toward Mary. "I feel a little like I don't belong here, because I didn't have much of a life with my baby. You all had a chance to really *know* your children—"

"The loss is the same," Mary interrupted. "You belong here, never doubt it. Loss comes to us through different situations, but we feel the same emotions. Sometimes we feel anger, sometimes despair, and sometimes we try to bargain with ourselves or with our conception of a higher power—"

"I don't blame God."

I stiffened as my husband spoke.

"God gave us our son five years ago—I'm sorry, I should introduce myself. I'm Steve, this is my wife, and we lost our five-year-old son in an accident only two weeks ago."

Another murmur of sympathy rippled through the circle, but this time it felt about as genuine as canned laughter. What did these people know about us?

"And I don't blame God—we weren't supposed to be able to have kids, you see, so when Di—when my wife got pregnant, we were thrilled. We saw Scotty as a gift from God, a miracle, and we just *knew* God was going to do something special with his life. That's why we're having a hard time with his death. Why would God take something he'd given us so miraculously?"

"That's an interesting thought, Steve." Mary's smooth voice flowed over us like honey on a raw burn. "But not everyone here believes in God, you know. If you do, that's fine, and I'm sure it helps if you can visualize life in a larger picture. Life brought you an unexpected gift, and now circumstances have taken it away. So what was the reason for that life? Was it not to love and be loved? Isn't that why we are all here? If you look at it that way, even a simple flower has a purpose—to bloom, even for a day, and bring pleasure to others."

I resisted a sudden urge to laugh, for my dear husband was staring at Mary as if she'd suddenly sprouted dandelions on her scalp. "I don't understand what flowers have to do with my son, and of course we loved Scotty. But there's more to life than love."

"Really?" Mary tilted her head, then spread her hands. "Group?"

"Love is all there is." This from a big-haired woman in tight jeans. "My son had Down syndrome and he was the embodiment of love. Some people are amazed I could miss him like I do, but I can't help it. I feel like I've lost an angel who flew into my life for a few years, then flew away."

"Love doesn't go very far when you're dealing with teenagers— you've got to have a lot of steel in your spine, too." Tilly's eyes flashed. "I loved my daughter and I miss her, but there are times I'm actually glad I don't have the hassle anymore. Then I feel guilty, but the truth is, raising a teenager is hard. All those nights I waited up because I didn't know where she was, or what she was doing, or who she was with—well, it was hard on a single mom. Now all I have to cope with is her absence—and, well, sometimes that's easier than coping with her presence, if you know what I mean."

As Tilly's voice faded away, Ted reached over and patted her hand. I felt a rueful smile cross my face. These people weren't likely to find answers here, but at least they had found companionship.

"I know how frustrating the teen years can be," Steve said, his voice softening. "But we hadn't reached that point with Scotty. Even so, somehow I doubt life with him would ever be hard. You may think I'm biased, but he really was a great kid. Everybody loved him and he loved everybody. That's why we were so sure God had a glorious future mapped out for him . . ."

As his voice trailed away, Steve looked at me. I knew he was hoping I'd pick up the conversational ball and run, but I couldn't. Even if I had wanted to participate, at that moment a lump the size of a football was lodged in my throat. I knew I'd be bawling like a newborn if anyone so much as looked my way.

I shook my head in a barely discernible gesture, then looked down to study the dusty toes of my shoes. Steve had brought us into this emotional huddle, he could get us out.

Fifteen

REACHING ACROSS THE CONSOLE, STEVE POWERED OFF the car's AC. Though the night was heavy and warm for April, the chilly breeze emanating from his wife threatened to frost the windshield.

He turned the BMW through the twisting side streets of downtown Largo, then headed south on Starkey Road. A light rain had begun to fall during the meeting and the highway shimmered beneath the streetlights. April showers were supposed to bring May flowers, but this rain held only the promise of more tears.

He had been the only one to cry during the meeting. All of the people in the circle had lost children, and, after hearing the others' stories, he knew none of them had yet arrived at a place of acceptance, whatever that meant. Yet he was the only one who wept.

Had the others learned to master their emotions? Or had their grief evolved to some feeling too deep for tears?

He glanced toward his wife, who sat with one arm propped on the door, her face turned toward the window. Diana had been too angry to cry. She had not spoken during the meeting, and her chilly attitude had silently warned everyone away. Even Mary, who could probably warm the cockles of Scrooge's heart, had deferred to Diana's frostiness and left her alone.

A few months ago Diana's aloof behavior would have embarrassed him, but embarrassment now seemed like such a trivial emotion. Once you have broken down in hiccuping sobs before police officers, church friends, your hygienist, and a medical examiner, what else on earth could possibly prove embarrassing?

At work, he'd been careful to maintain his composure before his young patients—children didn't understand loss, and in a perfect world, they shouldn't have to encounter death and disaster. But today's kids lived in a fallen world where Bad Things happened all too often.

He brought his hand to his jaw as a sudden dart of guilt pricked him. Diana was angry, but she was also in pain. He recognized it in the set of her jaw, the watery glint of her eyes. Stoicism was part of her nature, so she wasn't easily given to tears. He had always admired her strength, but now it seemed unnatural that the man of the house should weep and wail while the woman watched with glassy eyes.

He supposed part of his wife's self-control resulted from her work. The act of absorbing other people's heartbreaking situations had to toughen the heart somehow . . . or had her heart been tough all along? The most common comment he heard when people realized he was married to the famous Dr. Diana was "I don't know how she can sit around and listen to people's problems all day."

Maybe Diana was good at what she did because she had a heart strong enough to weather the emotional storms that knocked most people off their feet.

She wasn't unbreakable, though. Two nights ago he had come home to find her standing in the den, the contents of a half-dozen photograph albums scattered over the couch and coffee table. The desperate look in her eyes had alarmed him, and the fury with which she wailed, "I can't find one!" made him wonder if something inside her had snapped.

"You can't find what?"

"A picture of Scott Daniel snaggle-toothed. You know, a picture with his front tooth missing." She raked her hand through her hair, then stood there, one hand clawing her scalp as if she could dredge information from her brain. "How could we forget to take a picture of him like that? We knew he wouldn't stay that way forever!"

He had joined her in the middle of the mess, trying his best to remember the last time he'd taken the camera from the desk drawer. "Didn't we take pictures at his birthday party?"

"He had both his teeth then. He didn't lose his front tooth until January."

Steve pressed his hand to his chin. He had hauled out the video camera at Christmas, so they'd have those memories, but he couldn't remember shooting any pictures of Scotty's gap-toothed smile.

"We didn't do it, did we?" Tears were streaming down her face, but she wasn't really crying, it was more like an overflow of emotion. "How could *you*, a dentist, not think to take a picture of him like that?"

He opened his mouth, not sure if he should defend himself or soothe her, and suddenly she was in his arms, beating his chest with slow, heavy thumps while she wept in earnest.

No, Diana wasn't unbreakable.

Reaching through the empty space between them now, he squeezed her arm. "Is Britty home tonight, or did she go out?"

Diana lifted one shoulder in a shrug. "I'm not sure. She may have left a note on the kitchen table, but you didn't give me time to check."

He removed his hand, hearing the accusation in her words. After rushing home from the office, he had time to do little more than wash his hands and grab a slice of pizza from the box on the counter. She, on the other hand, had been home for at least three hours, but she'd say she had been busy reading letters or preparing for her show.

Still . . . he would keep trying to offer an olive branch.

Determined not to be drawn into a fight, he drew a deep breath. "Britty spends an awful lot of time at Charisse's house. Have you met the girl's parents?"

"Brittany is eighteen, Steve, she's not a toddler anymore. We don't have to request detailed biographical sketches of her friends' parents."

"But shouldn't we at least know what they're like? She's over there four nights a week."

"I've spoken to the woman."

"When? When you called their house looking for Britty?"

She turned, a swift shadow of anger sweeping across her face. "Why the sudden interrogation? Brittany and Charisse have been friends for three years. I hardly think they're about to run off and become drug dealers."

He took pains to keep his voice level. "I'm just saying we need to keep tabs on our daughter."

"Why? So God won't snatch her, too?"

Steve blinked, stunned by the force of his wife's reaction. He did not answer, but drove through the security gate, greeted the guard in the gatehouse, then turned down the street that would lead him home.

Silence reigned until they pulled into the driveway. As the automatic opener lifted the creaking paneled garage door, he gripped his wife's hand. "Diana, I know you're hurting. I know you didn't want to come tonight, and I appreciate the fact that you did. But just now I wasn't talking about Scotty. I only wanted to know about our daughter."

"Brittany's fine."

"Is she? I haven't seen much of her in the last two weeks."

Diana reached for the door handle. "She's doing better than either of us. Think about it, Steve—she lost less than we did, so she'll recover quicker. She lost a brother, but her world never revolved around Scott Daniel the way ours did. Plus, she has her friends to take her mind off things."

"Maybe she needs more than friends. Maybe she needs someone to talk to."

Diana arched a brow. "Like who?"

"Well . . . like a counselor."

Her nostrils flared. "Are you *nuts*? *I'm* a counselor, and she doesn't need anyone else. If I were to send her to someone, she'd think she was damaged goods or something. I'm sure she's only experiencing ordinary emotions in an ordinary way. We're a normal family, Steve, probably a lot better than normal."

Steve slammed the steering wheel with the meaty part of his palm. "What's *normal*? I must be nuts, Diana, because I can't find normal anymore. I get up, I get dressed, I go to work, but nothing feels right. You might be Superwoman, but I felt the need for this support group tonight, and somehow it helped to know other people have felt what I'm feeling. I can't help thinking that Britty might benefit from someone who can listen to what she's thinking and help her sort through all this."

"Brittany has us to talk to. Have we ever turned her away? If she needs to talk, she'll come to us."

"Will she?"

The question hung between them, unanswered, and for an instant Steve saw uncertainty flicker in his wife's eyes. Then her face froze in a mask of resoluteness.

"She would come to us." Her voice rang with finality. "I believe that with all my heart."

Sixteen

THAT NIGHT I TOSSED AND TURNED FOR THE BETTER part of an hour. When Steve's deep breathing assured me that he had nodded off, I slipped out of bed and padded down the hall. A thin strip of light and a faint stream of music had poured from beneath Brittany's door at eleven when I went upstairs to bed. Now her room lay as silent and dark as my own.

I walked past her closed door and hesitated at the threshold to Scott Daniel's room, breathing deep.

Everything I'd heard at the support group tonight told me I should go back to bed, close my eyes, and concentrate on tomorrow's tasks. If I couldn't move past this loss, I'd become as pitiful as Ted, who still sought comfort and counsel after ten years of bereavement.

But the heart and the mind speak with two separate voices, and the cry of my heart could not be ignored. Trailing one hand along the papered wall, I stepped into Scott Daniel's room and felt my flesh pebble in a shiver of delight.

Amazing, that after sixteen days a room could still retain the essence of a living, breathing boy. In the dim glow of the automatic nightlight I crossed to his dresser, then fondled the ears of a stuffed bunny, a beribboned gift I had meant to slip into his Easter basket.

Quietly opening the top drawer, I trailed my fingertips over the neat piles of underwear and socks. A shuffle of baseball cards had been shoved into the corner—I pulled them out, tapped them into a neat stack, and placed them in between the pairs of rolled tube socks.

Opening the second drawer, I instinctively recognized the things I sought—a swirl of unlaundered T-shirts and sweaters, still smelling of Scott Daniel Sheldon.

I pulled his Buccaneers sweatshirt from the melee and pressed it to my face, breathing in the scents of cookies and grass, boy and school paste. Then, still clutching the shirt, I crawled into his bed and climbed beneath the covers. His monkey, wide-eyed and rubber-faced, lay beside me as it had lain beside my son since infancy.

Retreating here had become a secret ritual for me, the only way I could relax enough to sleep. Lying in Scott Daniel's bed was like wrapping myself up in him. As I drifted in the haze between wakefulness and sleep, his favorite monkey in my arms, I could almost convince myself that he might burst through the door at any moment.

Memories of the day crowded my thoughts as I closed my eyes and drifted. The broken, agonized voices of the parents in the support group echoed in my consciousness while their sympathetic faces hovered before me, their eyes grazing mine. A few of those faces had held traces of skepticism when Steve explained how Scott had been our special gift from God, but not even Mary the agnostic social worker would ever be able to convince me otherwise. We had wanted so desperately to be parents; we had worked so hard to adopt Brittany. Once she came home, we settled back to concentrate on parenting, a job we loved.

Years later, with unbridled joy, disbelief, and a great deal of giddiness we announced Scott Daniel's pending arrival. The barren womb had become fruitful, and like Elizabeth, Hannah, and Rachel of the Bible, I wanted to sing and praise God in unbounded ecstasy.

Even in a shallow doze, I smiled at the memory. My doctor had warned me about late-life pregnancies; he had quoted statistics about complications, Down syndrome, and health risks to the mother. But

God proved faithful, and in the October of my forty-third year, I gave birth to a healthy son. Pastor John came to the hospital to pray with us, and I still remember how Steve, John, and I held hands over my hospital bed with the baby propped against my bent knees, taking in his first prayer.

God had been so generous—so how could he now withdraw his gift? We hadn't asked for a miracle baby, but we had fallen in love with him once he arrived. Why would God give us the unspoken desire of our hearts and then snatch it away?

Fully awake again, I rolled onto my back and opened my eyes. Streaming moonlight through the window made a rectangle on the floor, brightening the room enough for me to see the pictures on the ceiling. Scott Daniel had asked Steve to pin posters of his favorite basketball players above his bed, so in the gloom I could see the muscled profiles of Michael Jordan and Scotty Pippen, my son's personal favorite.

Unbidden, tears spilled from my eyes and trailed into my hair. Steve and Scott had often talked about getting tickets to go see Pippen play in Orlando, but life got in the way. Now that day would never come.

Turning onto my side, I felt the soft pressure of Scott Daniel's pillow against my cheek. How many nights had I peered through the door to see him sleeping here, his lips full and slightly parted, one arm wrapped around his monkey, one bare foot sticking out from under the covers. He loved wearing socks to bed but he kicked them off, so I was forever fishing them out of the sheets—

My thoughts came to an abrupt halt as the stairs creaked. I lay as if paralyzed while fear blew down the back of my neck. I would have heard a click if one of the bedroom doors had opened, so the person climbing the stairs was not Steve, not Brittany, and certainly not Scott Daniel.

Every muscle in my body tightened as I threw back the covers and placed my bare feet on the floor. Reaching for Scott Daniel's tee ball bat against the wall, I crept toward the hallway, where a dark shadow was moving toward Brittany's room.

My trembling fingers found the light switch. When the overhead lamp blazed, I found myself staring into the wide eyes of my daughter.

Fear faded to relief, then veered toward astonished anger. "What are you *doing*?"

Brittany blinked in the brightness.

My brain struggled to make sense of the situation. It was nearly one o'clock and a school night—and Britt had been in her room when I went to bed . . . hadn't she?

Mouth agape, I studied her. She wore a light jacket and shoes, and her purse hung from her shoulder. She hadn't been downstairs raiding the refrigerator.

I nailed her with an *I-mean-business* look. "Young lady, I asked you a question."

Lifting her chin, she met my gaze head-on. "I was with Charisse."

"At this hour? It's a school night, and your curfew is 10:30."

Disdain filled her eyes. "Nobody else has to be in that early."

"You do. So what were you doing just now?"

"Nothing."

"Nothing?" Anger, so successfully restrained earlier this evening, stretched its limbs inside my chest and pounded on my heart. Thrumming with rage, I marched to her room, threw open the door, and flipped the light switch. The bed was empty, though a decidedly lifelike lump lay beneath the quilt—a maneuver straight out of *Ferris Bueller's Day Off.*

Stalking toward her nightstand, I saw how she had managed to turn the lamp off—a timer, one of those square plastic gizmos you can buy at any grocery store, had controlled both the light and the radio with the aid of an extension cord.

For a moment I hovered between fury at her deception and wonder at her ingenuity. Fury quickly won out.

"This"—my finger trembled as I pointed to the timer in the outlet—"is pure deception, young lady. Why have you been lying to us?"

Brittany plopped on the bed, crossing her arms. "Well . . . I'm sorry. But my curfew is too early. Every other senior I know can stay out at least until midnight."

"You'll never convince me your friends' parents allow them to stay out until midnight on a school night. But that's beside the point—it's *1:00* A.M.!"

"Well . . ." She twirled a strand of flaming hair around her finger. "I guess we forgot to look at the clock."

I sputtered in stupefaction. "And where were you while you were forgetting to look at the clock?"

"Nowhere bad—just the Waffle House."

I stared at her in speechless incredulity. *The Waffle House?* Since when had my daughter acquired a love of pancakes and coffee?

I placed a hand on my hip. "You don't understand. Anything could happen to you late at night, anything at all. It only takes one drunken driver, one tired man on his way home from work—"

She rolled her eyes. "I'm not going to die, Mom."

I clenched my hand, resisting the urge to slap her impertinent face.

God would have to help me through this. He had given me this teenager, and in another minute or two I'd be more than happy to give her back.

I closed my eyes and clenched my jaw. What now, Lord? How much more do you expect me to handle?

Seventeen

THE SOUND OF VOICES WOKE STEVE FROM A RESTLESS sleep. He blinked at the green numerals of the digital clock, orienting himself to the time and place, then slid out of bed and threw on his robe. Brittany and Diana were going at each other about something, but what in the world could have set them off at 1:15 in the morning?

Diana's face was tight with fury when he entered the fray. Britty sat on her bed, her arms wrapped around herself, her chin jutting forward. Neither of his girls looked happy.

He brought his hand to his brow, shielding his eyes from the blinding light. "What's going on here?"

Diana whirled to face him. "I heard a noise and stepped out into the hall. I found our daughter climbing the stairs. While we thought she was asleep in bed, she's been out with Charisse. They think they're immortal."

"We weren't doing anything bad," Brittany mumbled.

"Wait." Steve held up his hand, fishing around for a misplaced thought, then found it. He gave his wife a triumphant smile. "She couldn't have been out. Her truck's been in the driveway all night."

Diana's brows lifted, graceful wings of scorn. "She had Charisse pick her up." She pointed to the nightstand. "Look behind that lamp—she purposely put her light on a timer to deceive us! And I want to know how long this has been going on!"

Steve looked at Brittany, who seemed to be weighing the consequences of the truth against those of a plausible lie.

Leaning against the doorframe, he folded his arms. "Where were you, Britty?"

She gave him a look of wide-eyed remorse. "The Waffle House. We go there because it's open twenty-four hours. But we don't do anything bad. We just drink Cokes and talk."

"Who was with you?"

Britt's cheeks went a deeper pink. "Um . . . Charisse."

"Anyone else?"

"No, Daddy."

Red flags flew at the word *Daddy*. She hadn't called him by that little-girl endearment since the last time he'd caught her engaged in intentional mischief.

He fixed a grim look to his face, one guaranteed to ensure compliance. "Your mother and I will not tolerate this kind of behavior. We don't want you out this late."

"But we weren't doing anything wrong!"

He lifted a hand to silence the outburst. "What you were doing doesn't matter. I worry about the drunks on the road, the oddballs who hang out in open-all-night places, the trouble you might encounter on the road after midnight. When your mother and I go to bed, we want to know you are safe and sound. We want you home."

He glanced at the timer in the outlet, disturbed by the evidence that his daughter had not only broken the rules, but had done so with premeditation. "You're going to be grounded for this—for a while, I think, probably as long as a month. We'll talk in a couple of weeks and see what lessons you've learned."

"Daddy!"

"That's it." He tightened the belt of his robe. "I'm not going to discuss this any further tonight."

Britty turned and buried her face in her pillow. She wasn't happy, but he could handle her anger.

Diana swept past him, leading the way out of the room. He followed, eager to hear her thoughts, but she had few to offer.

"Well done, Counselor," she murmured, each word a splinter of ice.

"You would have done something different?"

She didn't answer, but strode back into the darkness of their bedroom and got into bed, turning her back to him.

Steve slipped out of his robe, tossed it over the footboard, and pulled up the comforter.

Women. He had lived with two of them for over eighteen years, and he was no closer to understanding them than on the day he had married Diana. Scotty, on the other hand, had been as easy to read as large print.

Pain squeezed his heart in a sudden spasm. He missed his son. Never more than now.

Eighteen

"HELLO, SHARON, AND WELCOME TO THE PROGRAM."

"Dr. Diana?"

I forced a laugh. "Speaking."

"I can't believe it's really you."

I looked at Gary in patient amusement. "Last time I checked, Sharon, I was still me. What's on your mind?"

"Well . . ."

She paused, and that's never good. One of my brows shot up to my hairline while I silently asked Gary, *What gives with this one?*

I was about to disconnect the call when Sharon found her tongue: "Actually, Dr. Diana, I don't have a question for you. I called because I wanted to tell you something."

I checked the screen. "You told my producer you wanted to talk about a problem with your adult son."

"Actually, I wanted to talk to you about *your* son. I think it's terrible the way you've been carrying on as if nothing has happened when I know you have to be dying inside—"

I clicked the disconnect button. "Sorry, Sharon, but people who fib to Gary get cut off." I glanced at the monitor—Todd occupied the next space in the queue, and he was calling about a problem between his fiancée and his poodle.

"Good day to you, Todd; you're on the air. How can I help you?"

"Dr. Diana?"

"Who else?"

"Oh. Sorry."

Another case of broadcast blank-brain? "Todd, you have a problem with your fiancée?"

"I did, but—man, I heard what you did to that last caller. You were cold, Dr. Diana."

If he knew the details of the night I'd just endured, he wouldn't be so quick to pass judgment. "You think I ought to encourage people who lie in order to get on the air?"

"No, but—"

"Neither do I. Now state your problem or get off my show."

Beyond the window, Gary dropped his jaw.

"I, um—" The caller cleared his throat. "It's my fiancée."

"What about her?"

"My dog doesn't like her. My mother doesn't like her, either. She's a great little gal, but my mom keeps cutting her down—"

"Excuse me, but do you hear yourself, Todd? I'm having a little trouble understanding how you can recognize belittlement when you seem intent upon doing it yourself."

"Huh?"

"You just said you were engaged to a great little gal."

"Yeah. So?"

"So don't you see how condescending your attitude is? If your fiancée has grown up with people who criticize her, it's only natural she'd gravitate toward a man who treats her the same way. If you want your mother to stop belittling your girlfriend, I suggest you take a look at your own attitudes first."

Todd sputtered in confusion. "I don't belittle her—"

"Didn't you just call her a *little* gal?"

"Yeah, but I've always called her that."

"You don't think that's condescending?"

"Not when she's five-foot-one."

I stared at the screen, momentarily forgetting that dead air and radio don't mix. Behind the glass, I could see Chad laughing so hard he was in imminent danger of falling off his stool.

I pressed my hand to my forehead. "Your fiancée is short."

"Yeah. Comes up to my shoulder if she's wearing high heels."

"Well, then"—I shook my head, pretending not to notice Chad's histrionics—"I beg your pardon, Todd. I misread the situation."

Todd didn't miss a beat. "I think you misread that other caller, too. She was only trying to help you—"

"I don't need help with my personal life, Todd, and that's not what this show is about. So—tell your girl no one can make a doormat of her unless she lies down, and tell your mother to mind her manners and welcome this young woman to the family. As far as the dog goes—well, either come up with a way to keep them separated, or get yourself a new dog. Because the woman deserves first place in your heart."

I pressed the next button, then disconnected Todd. As a commercial for Neutrogena hand soap filled the speakers, I leaned back in my chair and exhaled a deep breath. "Good grief, when did our callers grow fangs?"

"You're okay," Gary reassured me. "You just have to remember they're trying to help. They listen to you every day, they've read about you in the newspaper, and they care about you."

"Thanks, but I don't want the show to turn into my own private pity party. Tell 'em when they call, okay? No talking about my problems. I'm here to talk about theirs."

"Help's on the way," Gary said. "Look at the list—Charity's on the line."

"Good. I could use a quotable quip this afternoon."

As soon as the intro faded into oblivion, I punched Charity through. "Charity? Welcome to the *Dr. Sheldon Show.*"

"Good morning, Dr. Diana." Her voice had that quivery, unsupported tone I always associated with older people. "This morning I ran across a particularly poignant quote I wanted to share with you."

I grinned at Gary. This woman was as predictable as the sunrise. "I'm all ears, Charity."

"It's from the Talmud, and it goes like this: 'The deeper the sorrow, the less tongue it hath.'"

My lungs contracted so I could barely draw breath to speak, but I forced out a reply: "True enough."

"I would imagine," her voice was soft with compassion, "that's why you don't want to talk about your son."

For a full five seconds I struggled to force words past the constriction of my throat. "And that, ladies and gentlemen"—I pushed the words into the mike—"is why I must ask you to refrain from broaching a difficult subject. Talk radio depends upon *talk,* and I can't talk about some things right now. Maybe not ever. So thank you, Charity, for expressing my reality so eloquently, and I'll thank you, listeners, not to mention my personal situation again."

I pressed the next button, then slumped in my chair as the *Dr. Sheldon Show* theme music led us into the top of the hour. According to the clock, we had sixty seconds before the newsbreak, so I pushed my chair back and stood. During the news I'd have time to walk down the hall and stretch my legs, maybe read a few of the e-mails that had come in during the last hour. I wouldn't be surprised if we had already received a handful either supporting or chastising me for reacting so strongly in this last segment.

The studio door opened. One of our interns, a red-haired youth named Craig Somebody-or-Other, stepped into the room, a sheaf of papers in his hand. He gave me a cautious smile. "Gary said you might like to see these."

"Don't worry, I won't bite." I took the letters and skimmed the first page. A rather bland greeting, thanks-for-changing-my-life, the usual stuff. I flipped through the others. "Anything good in here?"

Craig slipped his hands into his jeans pockets. "Nothing really controversial. Someone sent you a note about the latest healthcare bill before Congress—"

"Boring. People don't care about political issues unless there's a personal story attached."

"Well . . ." As Craig tilted his head, strands of hair that had come loose from his ponytail fell across his cheek. "There's a letter from a guy who says he wants to talk to you about something a little weird." His face flushed. "He, um, says he can clone your son."

Not sure I had heard correctly, I looked up from the page I'd been reading. "Say again?"

Craig took a half-step back. "He's with some group called Project One, and they're into human cloning."

"That's illegal in this country."

"The guy says he's from France."

I handed the stack of e-mail back to the intern. "He's a kook. Put these in my box, will you? I'll pick them up on my way out."

I pointed to the clock as I moved toward the door. "If you'll excuse me, I plan to make wise use of this break and take a walk down the hall."

At least he didn't follow me into the ladies' room.

Nineteen

ALONE IN HER BEDROOM, BRITTANY LEANED AGAINST the mountain of pillows on her bed and ran her fingers through her hair.

"So then what'd he say?" She kept her voice low. Though her mother hadn't specifically forbidden the use of the telephone, that was probably an oversight. The witch had certainly been mad enough to take away everything that made life endurable.

"He just grinned," Charisse answered. "Then he asked when you'd be free, 'cause he really wants to ask you out."

Brittany felt her cheeks grow hot. Being grounded was bad enough, but to have Zack Johnson *know* she was grounded was beyond terrible. "I am *so* bummed."

"Bummed because you're grounded, or bummed that he wants to ask you out?"

"Both." Brittany exhaled in a loud sigh. "Zack's timing stinks. Nothing in my life is going right now, and my parents are totally messed up. The witch is still furious, and my idiot dad keeps knocking on my door and coming in here to annoy me. He's been in twice since he got home."

"What does he want?"

"Nothing—he just comes in, messes with my hair or leans against the wall and tells me some stupid joke he heard from one of the kids in his office. Then he goes into his room and sits in his chair to cry. He thinks nobody knows what he's doing, but I hear him in there. He does that every day."

Charisse fell silent for a moment. "He's still sad about your brother?"

"They both are. I guess they just express it in different ways. Dad gets sad and Mom gets mad."

"What about you?"

"I'm okay. I mean, what can I do to change anything? They liked him better, anyway. He was their little angel. I'm their problem child."

A hollow clanging sound filled the phone, then Charisse snapped her gum. "Got a song for you. I wrote it this afternoon."

Brittany rolled her eyes, but she didn't dare complain. Charisse was a fairly decent singer, but her songs and guitar playing could use a little polish. Some of her lyrics made no sense at all, others had no real tune. But Charisse loved to compose, and Brittany felt she had to listen. After all, Charisse was the only person on earth who would sit and listen to her complaints.

"Girl with her dreams," Charisse sang, her voice cutting through the strum of the guitar. "Poor seventeen. Told what to think, how to dress, how to hide your deep distress . . ."

Brittany listened for three or four minutes, checked her watch, then picked up the remote and powered on the little television in her room. She hit the mute button as soon as images filled the screen—no sense in having the witch storm in here and declare the TV off-limits, too.

And Charisse wouldn't appreciate knowing she didn't have Brittany's full attention.

"That's where I'm stuck," Charisse said, abruptly stopping the song. "I can't think of a way to end it, and in performance you can't fade out the way they do on a CD."

"You'll think of something."

"I'd better. 'Cause this is going to be my signature song when we open the coffeehouse."

The coffeehouse was their brainchild, the Great Adventure they were going to embark upon as soon as they could manage to tear away from the Parents. They'd probably have to put in at least a couple of semesters at college to keep their folks off their backs, but then Brittany and Charisse were going to open The Spot, which would soon become the coolest hangout on the Gulf beaches. Charisse would sing every night while Brittany handled the business and made sure all the male hotties got good seats up front.

"Hey, I saw a For Sale sign on that biker bar just down the street from Luigi's," Charisse said. "It's closed now. We could go after school tomorrow and check it out."

"How are we going to check it out? We have no money."

"You don't have to pay just to look through a window, moron. We can drive over and look around. I know that place probably won't be available by the time we're ready to open The Spot, but the layout might give us some ideas."

Brittany wasn't sure how a biker bar would help them plan their coffeehouse, but anything was better than coming straight home. "Okay—wait, I forgot. I'm not supposed to go anywhere after school."

"Not even for ten minutes?"

"Not even. If the witch finds out, she'll add another month to my sentence."

"How will she find out?"

"She gets off work early, remember? She doesn't have to pick up the Scottster anymore—"

An unexpected lump rose in her throat, and she coughed to get rid of it. Trouble was, the more she coughed, the tighter her throat became so she had to cough again just to clear her airway.

Two minutes later, teary-eyed and wheezing, she thumped herself on the chest and managed a strangled question: "You still there?"

"Good grief, Britt. You okay?"

"Fine. Just breathed in the wrong way or something. What were we talking about?"

Charisse strummed the guitar a moment, then clicked her tongue. "Going to look at the biker bar. You said you can't go."

"Right. The witch is always here when I get home now, and if I'm late, she'll know it. She might be too busy to notice, but if she does, I'm busted."

"Bummer."

"Got that right."

They sat for a moment in companionable silence, then Charisse sighed. "Well . . . guess I better go at least *look* at my English book. I'll be grounded, too, if I don't pass Mrs. Parker's class."

"You'll pass."

"I wish."

"You will, you always do, you brain."

"Don't call me names."

"You brain."

"You moron."

"Get outta here."

"I would, if you'd let me get off the phone!"

They laughed, then hung up.

And as she lay back on her pillow, Brittany closed her eyes and knew that conversation would be the most fun she'd have all day.

Twenty

SLIDING TO THE EDGE OF MY CHAIR, I LEANED CLOSER to the dangling microphone. "Let me get this straight—you made an adoption plan for your baby eighteen years ago, and now you want to be involved in the boy's life?"

"Yes, that's right."

"Are you out of your *mind*?" I paused to let the words echo in the silence. "Bear with me, will you, while I spin a little analogy. Let's say life is a play, and the parents are the directors who train a child—he'll be the actor in this little drama. They place him on the stage, they clap madly when he takes his first step and says his first line. They are coaching from the wings, supporting our young thespian throughout every dramatic trial and tempest." I paused. "Janice, are you with me?"

"Still here."

"Good. Now—let's suppose our hardworking theater company is suddenly approached by another director, a woman who says she not only deserves a place in the wings, but on the stage as well. Our parent directors are trying to teach the child to be independent, they're allowing him to move away from them, but the new director wants him to move *closer* to her. How do you think that makes our hardworking parent team feel? And what about the child? With two sets of directors coaching him, how can he *help* but be confused?"

The caller, a woman from Alabama, sputtered in indignation. "But that's not fair—if it weren't for me, the boy wouldn't even be alive."

"Perhaps, but if not for those other people, he wouldn't be on the stage. If not for those people, you wouldn't have had the freedom to pursue whatever sort of life you've pursued for the last eighteen years. You may have made a selfless decision to make an adoption plan for your baby, and with everything in my heart, I applaud you for that. It takes a brave woman to realize that children deserve to grow up with a mother and a father who are absolutely nuts about the kid. For what you did eighteen years ago, I salute you, Janice. For what you want to do now, I say shame on you!"

Silence rolled over the phone line. I glanced at the control room window, where Gary and Chad were watching with wide eyes.

Maybe I had come on a little strong. Dr. Diana was supposed to be outspoken and occasionally outrageous, but a genteel lady from Alabama might not appreciate such brusqueness.

"Janice? You still there?"

"Yes." Her voice was lower now, subdued.

"Please." I gentled my tone. "Think again before you go knocking on that family's door. See if there's an adoption registry in your state. If by chance your son has registered and expressed an interest in a reunion, then and only then would you have my blessing to proceed. If he has not, please reconsider. Your son is at the age where he needs to make a life of his own. If he wants to meet you, he'll find a way to let you know. If he wants to move ahead with his life, let him. Eighteen years ago you made your choice. Now let the reunion be his choice."

Without wasting a moment, I clicked to the next caller, then grinned. "Good day to you, Charity, you're on the *Dr. Sheldon Show.*"

"Good morning, Dr. Sheldon! And how are you this lovely day?"

"We're all fine as frog hair, Charity. What's on your mind?"

"I ran across a profound thought the other day. I thought you would appreciate it."

I winked at Gary through the window, then propped my head on my hand. "All right, Charity. Can't wait to hear it."

"It's a quote by Samuel Johnson. He said, 'When grief is fresh, every attempt to divert it only irritates.'"

I drummed my nails on the desktop, knowing the sound would carry over the airwaves. "That's . . . interesting, Charity. What made you think of Sam Johnson today?"

"Why you, Dr. Diana. For weeks I've been listening to you try to divert people from your grief, and I know the effort has to be irritating your soul."

I answered in my breeziest voice. "Thank you for your concern, Charity, but my family and I are coping as well as anyone can expect."

I clicked on the next caller. "Stewart? Hi, this is Dr. Diana. Welcome to the show."

"I'm so glad I reached you. I've been trying to get through for days, but the lines are always busy."

I laughed. "What can I say? The problems of society just keep piling up outside my door. So what's your question?"

"No question, really. I just wanted to call and talk about the change I've noticed in you."

I glanced at the call screen. According to Gary's notes, Stewart from Chicago wanted to talk about his wife's meddlesome sister.

"I thought you had a sister-in-law problem, Stewart."

"I do, actually. But first I just want to say that lately I've been extremely disappointed in you."

"Oh?" I grimaced at Gary. "Sorry to disappoint you, Stu. But I gave up trying to please everyone a long time ago."

"It's just that I heard you were a Christian. And some of your recent responses haven't been very Christlike."

"Ohhhhh, I see." I pressed my fingertips to my temple, where another tension headache had begun to pound. "Tell me, Stu—do you read the Bible?"

"Sure."

"And in your Bible, did Jesus ever get upset?"

Stewart hesitated. "He was never mean or cruel. He couldn't have been, because he never sinned."

"I beg to differ, Stu, not about the Lord's sinlessness, but about the cruelty, because that quality is usually subjective. Do you recall the afternoon Jesus cleansed the temple?"

Three seconds of silence, followed by, "Uh-huh."

"I daresay some of those moneychangers thought Jesus was being a little heavy-handed, perhaps even cruel. And what about the Pharisees? Jesus did not mince words when he confronted them with their hypocrisy. But the Lord understood that sometimes one must be cruel in order to be kind."

"Um . . ."

"Get off your high horse, Stu, and don't toss my religion in my face. I could say a few things about people who read the Bible without understanding the larger context, but, unlike you, I'm going to practice a little self-control and keep my opinions to myself. For now, at least, I'm going to think of that Elvis song—know the one I mean?"

The ever-amazing Chad had successfully followed my train of thought. As I launched pious Stu into never-never land, Chad hit the next button and Elvis began crooning "Don't Be Cruel."

When we'd heard a good thirty seconds of the King, I gave Chad the cut signal and leaned into the mike. "Friends, let me tell you a story I heard the other day. Seems an old-time Quaker preacher had the original church in the wildwood, so to speak. His people came to Sunday meeting from all over the mountains, but, unfortunately, most of them had to pass by a big bear's cave on the way. The bear didn't take kindly to having his Sundays disturbed by so many churchgoing folk, so whenever he heard the sound of their singing on the path, he'd run out and bite a few, just for sport. Of course this upset the mountain folk, and pretty soon most of them stopped going to church."

Following my drift, Chad punched in a twanging banjo song for background music.

"Well, the preacher couldn't have that, no sir. So he went down the mountain to have a talk with the bear. He told him that God had meant for the animals and mankind to live in peace, and that the bear would be truly blessed if he could find it in his heart to turn the other cheek and not bite folks when they disturbed his rest. This sounded logical to the bear, who was a naturally God-fearing creature, so he promised to stop biting.

"Well, the church people began to come back to meeting and after a while they got brave enough to stick their heads in the bear's cave and speak to him. Some of the boys, though, became downright foolish. One afternoon they coaxed the bear out with promises of honey, then they pelted him with stones and clubbed him with branches. They beat that poor bear to a frazzle!

"The minister happened by the next day and heard the bear's moaning. As he knelt by the wounded creature's side, he heard about how those boys had not only lost their fear of the bear, but their respect as well. 'You told me I'd be blessed if I didn't bite,' the bear said. 'And I've kept my end of the bargain. But look what God has allowed!'

"The preacher shook his head. 'Friend bear,' he said, 'I told you not to bite. I didn't say you couldn't *growl*.'"

I clicked the next button, which played one of my exit riffs, then leaned in for a parting shot: "Think about it, friends. And forgive me when I growl."

I yanked the headphones from my ears, then leaned my elbows on the desk and massaged my temples. Half an hour to go before I could go home and forget about everyone else's problems . . .

The intercom at my elbow buzzed. "Dr. D? You've got a personal call on line six."

I glanced at the blinking row of telephone lights. Who could be calling on one of the private lines? Steve was at work and Brittany at school, but either one of them could be dealing with an emergency . . .

Rattled by an uncomfortable sense of déjà vu, I lifted the phone and clicked the blinking button at the far right. "Hello?"

"Dr. Diana Sheldon, please." The voice was cultured, masculine, and flavored by an upper-crust accent. European, probably. Maybe British?

"Speaking."

"My name is Andrew Norcross. I won't take up much of your time—"

"I'm in the middle of a show, Mr. Norcross, so if you're selling something—"

"I'm not selling anything, Dr. Sheldon. I wanted first of all to offer my sincere condolences on the death of your son."

I would have tossed him as easily as I bounced other callers who spoke of Scott, but the man's calm voice acted like a balm on my raw nerves.

"Thank you. But I haven't time—"

"Would you, Dr. Sheldon, like to hear about a miracle of modern medicine? Through our work in the field of reproductive technology, I believe odds are good we can reproduce and restore your son."

My hand froze on the phone. Was this some sort of sick joke? This man had to be a shyster, a con man, the worst kind of slime-ball ambulance chaser.

Fury flooded my voice. "Why, you—"

"I don't expect you to believe me or to make a decision now," he interrupted, his voice a soothing stream in my ear. "But you can discover the truth about our organization on the Web. I know you're grieving. And when your heart leads you to a place where you can move past the pain, visit us at www.projectone.org. You'll find the details of our program there."

The name snagged a memory in my subconscious. "You're with . . . that group involved in human cloning. And that's impossible."

"Why should it be? With samples of your son's tissue we can determine his complete genetic makeup and replicate it in the lab. The resulting boy won't *be* the son you lost, but he will be exactly *like* your son, genetically programmed in exactly the same way. Our motto is 'reproduction, not resurrection.' We can't bring your son back from the dead, but we can give you a baby with your son's exact genetic makeup. He would live in your son's environment, which has been changed only through the passage of time and circumstance." He hesitated a beat, then asked, "Why shouldn't you have another son identical to the one you so tragically lost?"

I could not speak. This was no bumbling unemployed worker with nothing better to do than listen to talk radio and moan about his personal problems—the man on the other end of this line was an articulate, thoughtful, and persuasive individual. Still, the idea of cloning was ludicrous—

He gave me no time to object again.

"Thank you for your time, Dr. Sheldon. I understand your reticence, even your doubt, but I believe you'll be pleasantly surprised when you read about our program. When you're ready, you can find my number on the Web page. Until then, I wish you well."

The line clicked, and suddenly the phone in my hand felt as heavy as a dead thing. I dropped it back into its cradle, my mind spinning with horror, bewilderment, and more than a niggling of curiosity.

I'm not quite sure how I got through the final half-hour of the program. The callers were unimaginative, their problems routine, my answers quick and to the point. Wedding protocol, a child's right to privacy, how to address the remarried father's new wife—I handled the questions easily, then pointed to Chad, who took us out with the bed while I made breezy small talk and promised an interesting discussion the next time we met.

The guys didn't even seem to notice my switch to autopilot. Thrilled with their technical prowess, they were high-fivin' each other when I looked through the window. "Not a single operator error," Chad crowed in my earphones as the bed faded into the noon news. "I love it when a show comes off without a hitch."

While Chad grinned and lined up the commercial breaks for the news, I took advantage of the quiet to turn to the laptop at my right hand. A high-speed modem connected it to the Internet, and within seconds I had arrived at a Web page featuring a picture of a perfect baby boy, umbilical cord still attached. "Clone Humans?" the caption read. "Why not?"

I scrolled down the page and began to read the text.

Our first goal at Project One is to develop a safe and reliable method for the cloning of human beings. Since the birth of Dolly, the first cloned mammal, several other experiments performed on mice, cows, and cats have demonstrated that cloning leads to healthy offspring. As of this writing, several human pregnancies involving clones have been established. Once the first cloned baby is born, we plan to offer our unique service to individuals throughout the world.

If you would like to be among the first to participate in our cloning program, please contact one of our project coordinators . . .

The Web site listed Andrew Norcross as the American coordinator, and added, "We anticipate the fees for our service will be approximately $300,000 U.S."

The article went on to describe how cloning would enable sterile, homosexual, or genetically impaired couples to have children. An affiliated program, ClonaPet, would offer the duplication of domestic animals, so "you will never have to say good-bye to a beloved pet again!"

A final blanket statement covered all the bases: "If you are interested in cloning for any reason, Project One has a program for you."

"Diana?" Gary's disembodied voice blared from the intercom. "We've got some ratings reports you might want to see."

"Coming." I clicked the Web page away, but not before making a mental note of the URL. Andrew Norcross, whoever he was, was probably just a slick salesman and these Project One people mere dreamers, but still . . .

I shoved the thought aside and stood. Zanies and nut cases were a given in the world of talk radio. If I were smart, I'd consign Andrew Norcross and his call to my mental trash bin and forget I'd ever heard of human cloning.

If I were smart . . .

My own admonition rang in my ears as I began the long drive home.

Like anyone else, I have flaws, and one of them is that I'm not as smart as I sometimes think I am. Growing up, my mother took great pains to avoid mentioning my intelligence—which was never exemplary, but occasionally noticeable enough to get me in trouble at home, especially when combined with my lack of humility. Seems I had a healthy ego without any sort of reinforcement—the self-esteem lessons they now teach in public schools would have turned me into a self-indulgent monster. I don't remember this, but to her dying day my mother swore that one afternoon in eighth grade, I calmly informed my parents they would soon need a dictionary just to converse with me.

(If I said that—and I'm still not sure I was that cheeky—I probably deserve the sassy daughter heaven sent me. In full humility I can say, however, that I have never deserved my son. Nothing I ever did could merit such a blessing.)

Though I had always thought of myself as reasonably bright, on the drive home from the station I was ready to cop to pure stupidity . . . because I could not get Andrew Norcross and his fantastic proposal out of my mind.

Clone Scott Daniel? At first glance the idea seemed ridiculous, even sacrilegious. Didn't the Bible teach that each individual possessed a single soul, and that soul went to heaven when the body ceased to function? I knew where my son was—Scott Daniel was in heaven with the Lord, waiting for us to join him.

Still . . .

In the past few months, medical science had pulled some pretty amazing rabbits out of its assorted hats. Technology hadn't been able to do anything to save Scott, though, and part of my brain still couldn't accept that a single glancing blow—a simple thump—could sever a child's spine and leave the emergency technicians with nothing to do but shrug their shoulders.

Was cloning a way to rectify that medical shortfall? Strange as it was, the idea made sense to me. I still could not accept that it had been God's will for Scott Daniel to die on March 24. I could believe Scott died because a driver was distracted, but I could not believe God had anything to do with the accident. Surely not everything that happened on earth was God's will. His perfect will could not include murder, rape, or terrorist attacks, could it? He did not want people to sin or behave foolishly. And hadn't Scott been acting a wee bit foolish when he darted into the driveway to chase that balloon?

I chewed on my lip, then shifted to the right lane where I could drive slower and think deeper.

If it had not been God's will for Scott Daniel to die . . . perhaps God was now giving me an opportunity to right a wrong.

Pressing my lips together, I lifted my thoughts toward heaven. *God, could it be? Five years ago you gave us an unexpected miracle; are you willing to grant us another one?*

Cloning was not so commonplace that we would be automatically assured of success. Despite Andrew Norcross's confident manner, I knew the process was still far from foolproof: doctors made mistakes, experiments went awry, embryo transfers failed. But if God put his creative hand on the process, perhaps I could have my baby restored.

I know it sounds crazy, Lord, but it's no crazier than me having a baby after so many years of infertility. It's no crazier than you telling Joshua to blow trumpets around Jericho or allowing Hezekiah to live another fifteen years after he begged for his life on what should have been his deathbed.

Reproduction, not resurrection, Norcross had warned. Still . . . wasn't reproduction the nexus of life? In my biology classes I had sat through countless films depicting the ageless struggle of sperm to enter the egg, salmon who leaped rapids to reach their spawning grounds, animals who sacrificed their lives in the drive to reproduce. Every living thing on the planet focused on reproduction; even Christ commanded us to go and bear fruit by sharing the gospel.

The thought brought a twisted smile to my face. God created Scott Daniel five years ago. Couldn't he help a few doctors re-create him?

The idea carried me all the way home.

Twenty-one

AFTER CLOSING THE CAR DOOR, STEVE TURNED THE key in the ignition, pointed the air conditioner's vent toward his face, and closed his eyes in the stream of cool air. Tears pressed against his eyelids, salty springs that had threatened to overflow several times during the day.

"God," he whispered, resting his hands on the steering wheel, "how am I supposed to do my job when every tenth or twelfth kid is a blond-haired, blue-eyed reminder of Scotty?"

Heaven didn't answer, but the simple act of asking the question eased some of the pressure upon his heart. All his life he'd heard that Christians were supposed to be overcomers; lately he'd felt fortunate to think of himself as an endurer.

Given his present circumstance, he couldn't think of a more stressful occupation than his own. He had gone into dentistry because the discipline appealed to him; he had specialized in the pediatric branch because he liked kids. But now his hands trembled when he held x-rays toward the light cabinet, and his voice often broke when he spoke to the youngsters in his chair.

Few of his young patients knew of the loss he'd suffered, and he worried that his emotional instability might frighten them. Kids were nervous enough around dentists—the sight of a weepy, red-eyed man behind a mask could only unnerve them further.

His staff knew everything, and they'd been surprisingly unembarrassed the first time he burst into tears without warning. Melanie had simply pulled him out of the exam room and walked him to his office with her steadying hand in the center of his back. Once inside, she'd handed him a box of tissues, then closed the door with a promise to handle things until he wanted to resume.

Now he breathed deeply, wiped his eyes with a handkerchief from his pocket, then put the car into gear. A few moments later he pulled into China Gate, his favorite Chinese restaurant, and went inside. At the counter, he ordered three dishes to go.

The young man behind the register raised an eyebrow.

"No Kung Pow tonight?"

Kung Pow had been Scotty's favorite. He loved the peanuts.

Steve shook his head. "Not tonight, thanks."

A few moments later he was heading home with the scents of fried rice and sweet-'n'-sour pork filling the interior of the old BMW. The sweet-'n'-sour was Brittany's favorite dish, and Steve had been thinking of her when he decided to pick up Chinese. She had scarcely spoken ten words to him since the night they had to ground her, so maybe this would help bring her out of her pout.

She'd always been a reserved, private child—more like Diana, really, because he'd always been willing to spill his deepest thoughts to almost anyone who cared enough to listen. Diana never shared her secrets unless the act of sharing was expedient and sensible, and the recipient of her thoughts could be trusted.

Brittany, on the other hand, never seemed to share her feelings with anyone—anyone over thirty, that is. She and Charisse Logan were as tight as ticks, but Steve couldn't remember the last time she had sat down and told him about her day. In all the length of his memory, he *knew* she'd never asked about his.

Maybe she was going through a phase. After all, weren't all adolescents self-centered?

He slowed for a red light, then stopped and tapped the steering wheel with his fingertips. He was no psychologist, but he was fairly certain eighteen-year-olds were supposed to be difficult. Kids at that age naturally pulled away, testing their independence while they tried to find their way in life. The parents, on the other hand, functioned like guardrails on a highway, getting bumped and battered as they struggled to keep the kid on the right road.

He had certainly given his parents fits at that age. At eighteen, he'd been running with a group of guys who stole beer from minimarkets for kicks, then spent the night drinking and playing pool in various family rec rooms. Only the grace of God had prevented him from being arrested or killed in an accident.

His blood chilled as his wandering thoughts tripped over a sensitive nerve. Accidents happened all the time, even to innocent kids like Scotty.

As the light turned green, Steve eased down on the accelerator and slipped back into thoughts of Brittany. She had been especially surly since Scotty's accident, and he suspected the roots of her discontent went far deeper than their recent discipline. Even before Diana caught Britty sneaking in late, the girl hadn't exactly been treating them with respect, much less love. Diana complained that Britt treated their home like a hotel, checking in only to use the phone, grab something to eat, and crash when her body ran out of energy. Sometimes Steve felt more like an answering service than a parent, and whenever he popped into his daughter's room to try to have some fun with her, he usually got a rude "Go away!" for his trouble.

Parenting a teenager was difficult . . . especially when compared to parenting a five-year-old. Scotty hadn't been perfect, but teaching him had been a simple pleasure compared to playing guardrail for a teenage girl determined to have her own way. Teenagers had access to such dangerous things—cars, drugs, guns, even sexual diseases. Every time the phone rang when Brittany was out late, Steve would snap to alertness while images of a thousand terrible tragedies flashed through his mind.

Bad things happened even to kids from good families. And if those kids *chose* to do stupid things . . . Steve shook his head. God must have legions of angels working overtime to save today's kids from their own risky behaviors.

The worst part of raising teenagers was knowing unleashed anger could drive them to do almost anything because kids tended to act first and reflect later. Practically every other week Steve opened the paper to read about another teen who had picked up a gun to do harm to others or committed suicide just to prove a point. He would never be able to forget the local boy who stole a plane and crashed it into a Tampa skyscraper. No one ever knew why.

He swallowed the lump that had risen in his throat and flipped on his turn signal. The most fiendish thing Scotty ever did in a tantrum was run into the dining room and yell "Greasy slimy gopher guts!" during one of Diana's dinner parties.

Steve bit his lip as another tide of tears threatened his eyes. "Please, Lord," he whispered, easing his car through the security gate at the entrance to his neighborhood. "Keep your hand on Brittany when I can't reach her. Don't let us lose our daughter, too."

Twenty-two

MY HEART LEAPED AS I HEARD THE CREAK OF THE rising garage door. Steve was on his way in.

I scooped up the Web pages I'd printed and thrust them into a folder, then walked to the entrance of the small study I used as a home office. Steve stood in the front hallway, a bag from China Gate in his arms.

"Hi, guy." I felt a little breathless, even giddy, but half hoped he wouldn't notice my eagerness until I was ready to talk.

I was in luck. He scarcely looked at me, but continued through the foyer toward the kitchen. "Hi. Britty home?"

"I'm not sure." I glanced at the computer screen to be sure I had clicked away Project One's Web page, then followed my husband. "She may have come in, but I was doing some work on the computer. I've been pretty much preoccupied the last few hours."

Steve grunted in a noncommittal reply, then set the bag on the kitchen island and began to unpack it. "I got that sweet-and-sour stuff she likes. I got you chicken and broccoli, if that's okay."

"That's great." I glanced back toward the stairs, then lifted my voice. "Brittany Jane!"

Steve winced. "She won't hear you even if she's up there. She's probably either on the phone or wearing her headphones."

I really didn't want to traipse up the stairs in search of my daughter; I wanted a few moments alone with my husband. "If she's hungry, she'll come down."

Perching on a barstool, I rested my chin in my palm and studied my husband. Grief had etched deep lines into his forehead, creases that hadn't been apparent only a few months ago. My face probably bore the same lines, but what if they could be erased with news of a miracle?

"I had an interesting call today," I began, easing into the subject that had staged a coup d'état of my thought processes.

"Someone on the show?"

"Someone who called during a break."

Steve opened a container, releasing the warm scent of soy sauce and rice into the kitchen. "So—who was it?"

I lowered my hand and adjusted the salt and pepper shakers someone had knocked out of position. "At first I thought he was a kook, but then I checked out his organization's Web page. The more I read about this group, the more interested I became. And now—okay, I'll admit it. I'm really curious."

Steve made a face as he pulled two pairs of wrapped chopsticks from the bottom of the bag. "We don't have a lot of cash to throw around right now, not with Britty going off to college in a few months. So if this guy was selling stock options or something—"

"Not stock options. He's into medical research." I paused as I heard the creak of the stairs. "But we can talk about it after dinner."

Steve nodded without comment. After twenty-two years of marriage and eighteen of parenting, our marital shorthand had advanced to the point that we could easily halt a conversation in midstream if one of the children popped into the room.

Brittany breezed into the kitchen, lifted her nose in what might pass for a nod of appreciation, then slid onto her favorite barstool.

Steve pushed a foil container toward her. "I got your favorite."

"Thanks." She pried off the plastic lid, then looked at the paper-wrapped utensils. "You expect me to eat with chopsticks?"

Steve grinned at her. "Give it a try. Might be fun."

Brittany rolled her eyes and slid off the stool. I watched in silence as she went to the drawer and grabbed a fork, then stalked to the cabinet for a glass.

I shifted my gaze back to my husband. "Good day at your office?"

He shrugged. "Fine."

"Mine, too. The usual kinds of callers, I guess. And Gary showed me a ratings report—we've picked up five new stations. We're finally making headway in the Northwest. Of course, some of these new stations don't have the morning slot free, so now I have to remember not to say 'good morning' on shows that will be rebroadcast in the middle of the afternoon."

"That's great, Di."

Taking his foil container, Steve perched on another barstool. Once he had moved away from the counter, I stood to glean whatever was left in the bag—a container of chicken and broccoli, an egg roll, another pair of chopsticks, and a handful of fortune cookies.

Turning, I pulled a plate from the cabinet and scooped some rice from the open container, then spooned a healthy portion of the chicken and broccoli over it. At the pantry, Brittany popped the top on a can of Coke and slurped at the rim.

"Brittany!" I made a face. "I hope you don't do that in public."

She poured a stream of caramel-colored liquid into her glass. "None of my friends would care."

"Well, *I* care. And anything you do unconsciously becomes a habit soon enough."

She rolled her eyes in reply. Not wanting to wage war over something so trivial, I backed off, then opened the fridge long enough to pull out a jar of dill pickles. Long ago I'd learned that a dill pickle after a meal killed my craving for something sweet. I figured pickles had kept me from gaining thirty pounds over the years.

I wrapped my palm over the jar, then twisted. Nothing.

"Here, Steve." I slid the jar over the counter. "I need some brawn."

He gave me a quick grin, then untwisted the lid with one quick motion. I speared a pickle with a fork, then set it on a dessert plate to sit until after my meal. Dill pickles, on my sensitive teeth at least, are best served at room temperature.

Taking my plate, I took the barstool next to Steve at the counter, willing my eyes not to glance at the empty table to our left.

The square pub table had been perfect for the corner of our kitchen—informal and antique, in happier days it brought all four of us together over meals when our schedules allowed us to eat together. In the days following the funeral, however, we grazed through the kitchen like roaming horses, nibbling from the dozens of casseroles that had materialized in our refrigerator.

Now we were eating as a family again, but none of us had made a move toward the antique table. I don't think any of us had the heart to sit across from Scott Daniel's empty seat.

Steve positioned his chopsticks between the fingers of his right hand, then glanced at our daughter. "How was your day, sweetness?"

She shrugged and leaned back in her chair—a maneuver I'd forbidden a hundred times. Not only was she weakening the joints of my chairs, but if those back two legs slipped on this tile, she would almost certainly fracture her skull. The last thing I needed was another visit to the hospital.

I was about to rebuke her again when her face split into a sudden smile. "Mrs. Parker threw up in English class."

I grimaced. "Must we hear about this now? We're eating."

Steve furrowed a brow in concern. "Your teacher? Is she all right?"

"Yeah, we think she ate something that disagreed with her."

Steve's chopsticks froze in midair. "That could be serious. If there's food poisoning in the school cafeteria—"

"There's not. Mrs. Parker is too cheap to eat at school; she always brings her lunch. But at least we got a substitute and got to goof off the rest of the hour."

Brittany's smile was wide and real, the first sign of genuine pleasure

I'd seen on her face in weeks. And what had brought it on? Goofing off and the sickness of a teacher.

I drew a deep breath and regarded my broccoli chicken. I could launch into another lecture, but Brittany had heard my entire repertoire. Besides, she was smiling, and we were eating dinner like a family.

I shouldn't spoil it.

We sat in silence for a few moments, Steve managing fairly well with his chopsticks, me fumbling to keep up with him, and Brittany unabashedly eating her dinner with a fork.

"It's not fair," I finally said, trying to inject a note of humor into the heavy silence. "I think you're so good with those things because you work with thin little instruments all day."

Giving me a wicked grin, Steve waggled his chopsticks at me. "Practice makes perfect, Diana darling."

"I don't have the patience for it." Dropping my chopsticks to the counter, I picked up a fork and winked at Britt. "Maybe our daughter has the right idea."

For my efforts at camaraderie, I got another roll of the eyes. She gobbled a last bite of pork, then slipped from her chair and grabbed her glass. "I've got homework."

"No Coke upstairs, young lady," I called before she could make a break for it. "Your carpet already looks like a minefield."

She huffed again, then set the glass on the counter. I knew she'd be back for it once I vacated the kitchen.

But for now I was glad to see her go. I waited a moment, then allowed my thoughts to swing back to the subject I'd been about to broach when Britt came downstairs.

No time like the present, they say, and the hour certainly seemed appropriate. Steve was as relaxed as I'd seen him in days.

Steeling myself to my course, I plunged ahead. "Remember the call I mentioned earlier? The guy who called on my break?"

Steve regarded me quizzically for a moment, then nodded. "Yes—the one with the Web page?"

"That's right. He works for a company called Project One. Medical technology."

Steve took a big bite of chicken, then lifted a brow and swallowed. "So you said."

"They are researchers involved with cloning . . . people."

My husband's face twisted into the human equivalent of a question mark. "Don't tell me you're taking this guy seriously."

"It's not as bizarre as it sounds, Steve. According to what I read on their Web page, we should not think of clones as drones or science fiction monsters. A clone is merely the identical twin of someone else, separated through time."

His brows rose as he leaned back in his chair and twisted to look at me. "Okay—so why did this guy call you? Is he trying to get you to do a segment on cloning?"

My heart thumped against my rib cage. Might as well tell the truth, the whole truth, and nothing but the truth.

"Not exactly—he didn't mention the show at all. He called because he'd read about Scott Daniel."

The line of Steve's mouth clamped tight for a moment, then his throat bobbed as he swallowed. He lowered his chopsticks, braced his hands against the table, and met my gaze head-on. "I'm not sure where you're going with this, Di, but I don't think I like it."

I waved his concerns away. "Don't make snap decisions. The idea turned me off, too, until I did some reading. Cloning isn't what you think."

"I don't know what I think. It's too new, too far out, and, if memory serves, it's illegal in this country."

"Legality is not an issue—they can perform the procedure in a country where cloning *is* legal." I let the silence stretch a moment, then reached out to gently touch his arm. "The people at Project One have a saying, Steve—cloning is reproduction, not resurrection. I know we can't have Scott Daniel back, but we can have a boy just like him. We can give that boy another chance at life."

"Have you lost your *mind*?" Steve gave me a look that said his brain was working hard at a new set of problems. "I don't know why you would ever think"—his voice broke—"we could replace Scotty."

"I'm not trying to replace him! I'm just trying to make things right!" I shifted to face him. "Give me a few minutes, Steve, will you just *listen*? Let me explain everything, then you can make an informed judgment."

He crossed his arms, his face locking in neutral. "I'm listening."

I hesitated, wishing for a moment that I'd brought my notes from the study. "Okay. Well, first it's important to realize that a clone is not an exact replica of the original person. We won't have another Scott Daniel, but we'll have a boy genetically identical to him. He will have all of Scott's inbred abilities and the same tendencies that are built into a kid, but he won't be the same. And we won't expect him to be."

A muscle worked at Steve's jaw, but he didn't interrupt.

I forced a laugh. "It would actually be a great experiment in nature versus nurture—noticing the differences, I mean. But what they would do is take a cell from Scott's tissue samples—and the medical examiner has all the genetic material we'd need—and insert the DNA from one of Scott's cells into a female egg—one of mine or somebody else's, it doesn't matter. The egg will have been emptied so it's nothing but living cytoplasm. When Scott Daniel's DNA is inserted, the egg will begin to divide. When it reaches the embryo stage, it will be implanted into a woman . . . and that woman could be me."

A little overcome by the sheer wonder of the process, I paused to draw a deep breath. "Just think, Steve—I could have the baby. Our miracle boy would be born all over again, but this time we'd know exactly what to expect. The baby would look just like Scott Daniel and he'd be hard-wired like Scott Daniel, but he'd be different, too. And we'd have another chance to parent him."

Steve frowned in a way that made me wonder if he was trying to remember Scotty's birth or trying to forget every word he'd just heard.

His next words settled that question: "I think the very idea is repugnant. That sort of manipulation is against nature. It's not right."

I knew I had married a man who thought with his heart instead of his brain, but never had that tendency annoyed me more. Couldn't he grasp the logic of my argument?

"Everything we do these days is against nature! Do you think it's *natural* to have plastic surgery, or take pills, or get false teeth? We've learned how to use technology to our advantage, so why not use this?"

His brows drew together. *"God* creates people, not man. He makes each of us unique—"

"We are unique individuals, yes, but at this moment the planet is populated by over one hundred fifty million people whose genetic codes are *not* uniquely individual. Identical twins, for instance, and triplets. Do you find twins unnatural? Of course not. Do you find triplets repugnant? I don't think so. In fact, I seem to recall you describing the Brown triplets in your practice as *adorable."*

Steve spread his hands. "I don't know, Di. Don't you see why this guy called you? He wants to use you. You're a celebrity, and since Scott's accident you're even more in the public eye. If he gets you to sign on to his cause, you'll be setting a dangerous precedent. Human life has been cheapened enough with stem cell research and embryos being created to be used as living collections of spare parts. Do you want to endorse the way they are tinkering with stem cells and modifying human DNA? What if they make mistakes we cannot rectify?"

"Project One is concerned with cloning, Steve, not genetic engineering. They are two completely different things. Genetic engineering involves the modification of human DNA; cloning is simply the copying of it."

"But those people aren't going to stop at one threshold. If you give them permission to proceed with this kind of research, human genetic engineering is the next step."

I forced my lips to part in a calm, curved smile. "Read your medical journals more thoroughly, hon. Gene therapy has been going on for years. And it's changing lives for the better."

"But what about the cheapening of human life? Cloning will not always be successful, so what about the babies who die when something goes wrong?"

"People die all the time, Steve." My voice filled with a harshness I could not suppress. "You and I know that better than anyone. Yes, the cloned child might die through miscarriage or even stillbirth, but every pregnant woman faces that risk. And do you know how many patients sign up for experimental cancer treatments every year? Thousands. Should they be restricted from trying new protocols just because something might go wrong and they might die?"

His eyes rested on me, alive with speculation. "You're comparing apples to oranges. It's not the same."

"I disagree. And death is part of life. Over forty thousand people die in auto accidents every year in the United States, and yet nobody has ever suggested we do away with automobiles. Yes, some cloned embryos might die . . . but maybe they weren't really embryos, only collections of cells. Who can say?" I paused to push a stray hank of hair behind my ear. "I think that's a risk I'd be willing to take."

Steve looked at me in bewildered horror, but didn't speak.

"I'm not asking for a decision right now." I lowered my voice. "I just want you to think about it. I'm not completely sure if this is right for us, but I think I'd like to talk to this man from Project One and investigate some of the details."

A range of emotions played across my husband's face—uncertainty, fear, and a trace of anger—then he reached out and gently took my hand. "I know you miss Scotty, Di. But we can't bring him back."

I lifted my chin. "You don't have to tell me what I already know. I just want to do a little research. To see if maybe—"

"It isn't right, Diana. I'm not as good with argument as you are, but I know when something is wrong. And this has wrong written all over it. But if you want to have another baby—"

"It took us twenty years to conceive the first one. The odds of me getting pregnant again are about a million to one." I pulled my hand from his, knowing I wouldn't win the argument tonight. But the seed had been planted, and Steve would be considering the idea for the next few days. And while I knew his doubts were strong, his love for Scott Daniel was stronger.

While he pondered, I was going to launch a full-scale investigation . . . and contact Andrew Norcross.

I gave Steve a quick smile, then carried my dishes to the sink.

Two hours later I sat before my computer in the study, fretting at the keyboard as I typed in yet another search phrase. I didn't really want to know all the scientific details involved in the cloning procedure, but it would help if I could assure Steve that the process was safe and effective. I thought I had a good understanding of the medical procedure, but in my research I stumbled across some interesting considerations.

I had forgotten that an American company, Advanced Cell Technology, first announced the successful cloning of a human embryo in October 2001. Horrified by the implications, the U.S. House of Representatives promptly voted to ban human cloning. The Bush administration went on record in favor of the ban.

Public reaction dumbfounded the researchers at ACT. The CEO of that company, Dr. Michael West, told the press he never intended to clone a human being, but had instead taken the first steps toward therapeutic cloning. "We took a human egg cell and removed its DNA," he told a reporter from CNN. "So now we have the beginnings of life with no blueprint. And we put a human cell from a different person into that egg cell. The egg cell then does somewhat . . . wonderful things. It takes the patient's cell back in time, so that it's embryonic again. And it's sort of, you know, back to the trunk of the tree of cellular life. So that we could then make anything identical to the patient."

West went on to say that his work centered on treating illness, not creating human lives. "We're talking about human *cellular* life, not a human life," he told the reporter. "A human life, we know scientifically, begins upwards, even into two weeks of human development, where this little ball of cells decides, 'I'm going to become one person or I am going to be two persons.' It hasn't yet decided. No cells of the body of any kind exist in this little ball of cells, and that's as far as we believe it's appropriate to go in applying cloning to medicine."

I clicked the print key so I could show Steve a copy of the article. I knew he'd be concerned about the possible destruction of human life, but if those cells were only the *potential* for human life . . . therein arose another problem. Could we differentiate between life and *probable* life? In God's eyes, when did a person become a person? A lump of skin was cellular life, but it certainly wasn't a person. An embryo, on the other hand, *was* a person, even if tiny and dependent. If the scientists pursuing therapeutic cloning could train a little ball of stem cells to grow into a kidney, they were creating human organs, but not human life.

Could science determine when personhood begins?

My head ached from all the technical terms I'd digested in the last hour. Technically, a fertilized egg, or *zygote,* contained the forty-six chromosomes that inhabited every human cell, but as it grew it moved through other stages, becoming a morula, blastocyst, embryo, and fetus. I read that many dedicated pro-lifers—a term I'd always used to describe myself—claimed that any being with forty-six chromosomes was a person, but I had to admit that definition seemed too simplistic and even inaccurate. After all, people with Down syndrome had forty-seven chromosomes; were they not people? And apes had forty-eight, so you could not say that a being with "at least forty-six" qualified as human.

The *morula,* I learned, was the proper name for the shapeless mass of sixteen cells existing four days after fertilization. The term *blastocyst* described the cells' development from the morula stage to the *bilaminar,* or two-layered stage, which began during the cells' second week. At fourteen days, the *primitive streak* appeared—a visible marking that would eventually develop into the spinal column. Until the appearance of the primitive streak, the morula, blastocyst, or embryo could divide to become twins or even triplets.

So how could we say a blastocyst was a person?

I shook my head, weary of my internal debate. None of this really mattered to me; I wanted to *have* a baby, not destroy one.

"Many religious people," I read on a seminary-affiliated Web page, "oppose cloning on the grounds that it is impossible to know if the soul can be cloned. Since the soul is invisible and immeasurable, who but God can say whether or not it exists inside a clone?"

I clicked my tongue against my teeth. My personal theory, unprovable but logical, held that the soul emanated from the invisible and immeasurable breath of life God exhaled into man in the Garden. That spark of life—which man had yet to replicate from nonliving matter—passed from parents to child. I couldn't say with perfect certainty at which stage of cell development the soul formed, but neither could any theologian.

Two weeks earlier I'd spent ten minutes with a caller who insisted that life began at conception. Recognizing the beginning of an abortion discussion—which usually provoked great passion, but turned at least half my audience off faster than slime on a dinner plate—I sought to direct the old debate down a different trail.

"You're wrong, my friend," I'd told him. "Life doesn't begin at conception. It began in the Garden of Eden, when God breathed life into Adam. Life was passed from Adam to Eve when God formed a woman from man's living rib, and it's been passed from parents to children ever since."

"Yeah, but scientists can make babies in a test tube now."

"Can they? They can't do squat without a living egg. The spark of life, or whatever you want to call it, has to exist first. Think about it— your hand is alive as long as it's attached to your body—cut it off, and those cells die within minutes. Likewise, a sperm and egg are alive, so when they join to form the beginning of an embryo, life is not created, it's merely transformed."

"Well . . . okay. But I don't believe in a literal Garden of Eden. That's just a myth."

"So are you, caller. Ciao."

I had disconnected him and moved on, but now my own words whirled in my brain as I read a paper on religious arguments against cloning. A flush of pleasure flooded my cheeks when I discovered an actual term for what I had expressed to the caller: *traducianism,* the belief that a child inherits a soul as well as a body from its parents.

Somehow I'd missed that one in my college Bible classes.

The idea made sense, even in a cloning situation. A baby created from Scott Daniel's DNA would still be the genetic offspring of my chromosomes and Steve's. The DNA, a nonliving blueprint, would be placed into a living egg to direct the cell's division and growth. The embryo would be sheltered and nourished by my own body. If there was a chance, however small, that the soul was somehow transmitted through the living egg, then I'd stipulate that we harvest one from my ovaries. The doctors would undoubtedly protest on account of my age, but I would insist.

And life would beget life. The resulting child would possess a soul every bit as vibrant and alive as Adam had been in the Garden of Eden.

I rested my chin in my hand, feeling a smile stretch against my palm. Steve would accept this argument. Once he felt the baby's first kick, he'd know God had blessed us with a new life and a new soul. Still—

My smile shriveled. Steve had other concerns, more practical arguments that couldn't be dismissed by polysyllabic words and foggy theology.

Was it right for us to pursue a risky procedure? I remembered reading about the first successfully cloned kitten back in the spring of 2002—scientists tried one hundred eighty-eight times and created eighty-two embryos before achieving one successful pregnancy. Andrew Norcross had assured me that the technology had improved, but what if it had not?

What if I got four months into the pregnancy and discovered the developing fetus was abnormal? As a Christian, I considered all life a sacred trust because it sprang from the hand of God. If the cloned baby developed some sort of severe problem, would I have the heart to carry it to term and deal with the consequences? Some people might be quick to point out that the clone had sprung from *my* hand, not God's, therefore I would be bringing one more suffering child into a world filled with suffering children . . .

Could we afford to care for a severely disabled child? We had a daughter preparing for college; our retirement years loomed on the horizon. We were no longer young. I was forty-eight, Steve fifty, and the care of a severely deformed or dependent child would drain our energy and financial resources. We were financially stable, but three hundred thousand dollars for medical fees to Project One, none of which would be covered by insurance, would take a healthy bite out of our retirement savings. I would still have my career and Steve could always count on a profit when he eventually sold his practice, but the nest egg we had spent years building would be gone—

"You're still down here?"

I flinched as Steve's voice broke into my thoughts. He stood in the doorway, his arms crossed as he frowned at my computer screen.

Instinctively, I swiveled my chair to block his view. "I was doing some research."

The corners of his mouth were tight, but determination shone in his eyes. "I've been thinking about it, Di, and cloning is just a little too 'brave new world' for me. I don't think we should do it."

I looked away. In the interest of domestic peace, I didn't want to contradict him at this late hour, but I didn't see how he could have given the idea enough thought. After all, I'd spent the entire night doing research while he'd been sitting in his favorite chair. How could he make up his mind so quickly?

"Don't make a hasty decision." I propped my head on my hand. "I'm going to call this man from Project One and I'll ask him about all the issues troubling us. I'm not completely sold on the idea, either. It's a lot to think about."

My words seemed to reassure him, for the line of his shoulders relaxed. He nodded toward the stairs. "Coming up?"

"In a little while. I just need to clean up a few things down here."

He nodded. "Okay."

He turned to leave; I swiveled back to my computer. But before reaching for the lamp a few moments later, I copied Andrew Norcross's number from the Web site onto a sticky note, then slapped it onto a page in my calendar.

Twenty-three

ANDREW NORCROSS AND I PLAYED PHONE TAG FOR three days. After the conclusion of my Tuesday show, I finally managed to reach him. He apologized for my difficulty in pinning him down, but explained that due to the controversial nature of Project One's work, he maintained an office at an undisclosed location in New York. "This is my cell phone number, but I'm not always available to answer it."

I laughed at the thought of this cultured man holding clandestine meetings in darkened alleys. "How on earth do you conduct business?"

"We have a post office box where you can send whatever documents we need, but for meetings, I'll come to you rather than have you come here."

Sitting in the studio, I turned away from the windows and faced the blank wall. "Sounds secretive—and, to be honest, such secrecy hardly inspires confidence, Mr. Norcross."

He chuckled. "There is no need for concern, Dr. Sheldon. When you are ready to make a commitment, we'll fly you to France, and you may inspect any of our facilities. My superiors are very open about our operation, but necessity forces them to be a bit publicity-shy, particularly in the States."

"I would like to meet with you," I told him. "My husband and I have some concerns and questions about the entire process."

"I would love to come down. Do you have room in your schedule on Friday?"

I blinked. "You'd come so soon?"

"Certainly. We know how important it is to act while interest is keen, and experience has taught us the value of face-to-face meetings. Let me know when you have time available, and I'll arrange to meet you."

I checked my calendar, suggested a lunchtime meeting, and Andrew readily agreed. I gave him our home address for his files, then suggested that we meet at an Applebee's restaurant near the station. I also offered to pick him up at the airport, but he insisted he could find his way with no trouble.

"I'll look forward to meeting you," I said, "but I have to be honest—my husband has expressed serious reservations about the entire idea, so this trip may be a waste of your time."

"I would be surprised if you both didn't have reservations. In fact, I consider thoughtful hesitation a good sign—you're asking hard questions, and we want our clients to know everything before beginning a procedure. Don't worry, Dr. Sheldon, I'm sure we'll be able to dispel any worries you might have."

I ran my hand through my hair, steeling myself to ask the question uppermost in my mind. "Before you go, there's one thing I really must know."

"Yes?"

"Why did you call me?"

The bluntness of my inquiry didn't seem to rattle him. He laughed, then answered with a smile in his voice. "Your celebrity was a major factor, of course. We would not have heard of you if not for the press coverage of your son's death. But if we can turn your tragedy into something good, if we can demonstrate how cloning has the power to mend broken hearts and a broken home, we'll be taking giant strides forward. In a few years, perhaps, you may be part of the reason we won't have to be so secretive about our office locations."

"But what if my husband and I don't want to go public with the story? We have always tried to shield our children's privacy."

"And we will respect your wishes once the baby is born. The news of your pregnancy and the child's birth will make headlines, but after the delivery you will be free to live your normal life. I would imagine we would want to hold a press conference in the hospital where you give birth, but we would never send reporters to your doorstep."

I frowned, remembering the media's intrusion on the day of Scott's funeral. "Sometimes they come without prompting."

"If they do, you will deal with them as you always have. Frankly, we enjoy working with celebrities because they are accustomed to dealing with the press. You would not have a press-free life even without your interest in cloning, and you have already established boundaries between your professional and personal lives."

I glanced toward the window, where a pair of interns were casting covetous glances toward Chad's soundboard. Norcross was right; I had lived in a goldfish bowl for years. Surely this would be nothing new.

"You're right, Mr. Norcross. After what we went through at the funeral, I think we can handle a birth announcement."

"I look forward to meeting you, Dr. Sheldon."

I thanked him, then hung up. And as I lowered the phone, I realized Steve had been right about one thing—Andrew Norcross had been up front about Project One's blatant plan to use my celebrity to advance their cause.

But would it really matter? They would use my name, but with God's help, I would bring a beautiful new life into the world. Surely the end result would be worth whatever price I had to pay.

Twenty-four

STEVE POINTED TOWARD HIS REGULAR BOOTH AND nodded at the hostess as he passed. "Good afternoon, Shirley. Mind if I seat myself?"

"No problem, Doc." She grinned as he walked by. "Want your iced tea now?"

"Bring it on."

After sliding into the booth, Steve plucked the laminated menu from its holder, even though predictability was one of the nice things about eating in the same restaurant every afternoon. The waitresses at this Denny's knew what he liked: unsweetened iced tea, a small garden salad with French dressing on the side, and either a club sandwich, French dip, or veggie burger, depending on his mood.

Today he didn't know what sort of lunch his mood dictated. Last Thursday he'd been emotionally hung over from the parents' support group meeting; his stomach had been too queasy for anything more than a plain club sandwich. Last night he had made a point of skipping the meeting—not that Diana noticed—but the quiet night at home had done little to improve his outlook. The thick cloud of grief that had surrounded him since Scotty's death had not abated, but a new current stirred the air—Diana's notion of cloning. She had set up a Friday lunch meeting with that fellow from Project One, and Steve had promised he'd be hospitable and open-minded.

He still didn't feel right about pursuing the cloning idea, but Diana had a knack for making the far-fetched sound perfectly plausible. Daunting on the radio, she was nearly irresistible in person. When she took it upon herself to present a case, people were usually nodding in agreement before she had moved from point one to point two. Last year she'd gone before the Hunter's Green community association to promote the idea of salary increases for the two guards who staffed the security station. Before she'd finished, the association had voted to grant Christmas bonuses, too. If Diana had spoken five more minutes, Steve wouldn't have been surprised to discover that the association had voted to raise monthly maintenance fees to establish a Hunter's Green Security Guards' Retirement Fund.

He had just decided that the glossy picture of a French-dip sandwich amounted to culinary pornography when a deep voice broke into his concentration. "Afternoon, Dr. Sheldon. They let you out of that office for lunch?"

He looked up. Wilson McGruder, one of nearly a dozen pastors on the staff of his church, stood with one hand tucked into his belt, the other pressing against the edge of the table as if for support. The elderly McGruder ministered to the "senior saints," a large and active group of older adults who, when they weren't in church, spent most of their time traveling from one tourist attraction to another.

Steve was surprised McGruder even knew his name.

"Pastor." He extended his hand. "Sorry for not standing, but this booth has me pinned."

"No problem, young man." McGruder shook his hand with a firm grip, then inclined his head toward the empty bench. "Do you mind if I join you a moment?"

Steve smiled. "Not at all. Join me for lunch if you like."

"Ah, no, I don't want to be a bother." The older man slipped into the booth, then folded his hands on the table. With the sure instincts of a homing pigeon, Shirley came toward them, order pad in hand.

"Just an iced tea for me," McGruder said, "and whatever the doctor's having can go on my tab."

Steve protested, but the pastor waved his objection away. When Shirley had taken Steve's order and retreated to the kitchen, McGruder leaned forward.

"I'm glad the Lord set you in my path today, Dr. Sheldon. I've been meaning to tell you I was very sorry to hear about your son."

With an effort, Steve pushed words past the boulder in his throat. "Thank you, Pastor."

The minister's dark eyes, startling beneath a shock of white hair, drifted toward the window. "I go to a lot of funerals in my work, and there's something beautiful in the death of an elder who knows the Lord. The death of a child is no less beautiful, for I know the little ones go straight into the arms of Jesus, but it's harder for those of us who are left behind with our questions."

Steve could do nothing but nod.

Shirley returned a moment later, two iced teas in hand. Correctly divining the prevailing mood, she set the glasses on the table and left without a word.

"Is there anything we can do for you, son?" McGruder's eyes glinted with kindness. "We're here to serve you."

"Everyone has been very kind." Steve pulled a pink packet from the sugar rack, ripped it open, and dumped the stuff into his tea. "We had enough food at the house to feed a battalion."

"Ah, but the weeks following a funeral are the hardest. After the food and the guests disappear, that's when loneliness smacks you upside the head."

Steve closed his eyes until he could rein in his emotions. This man wasn't just spouting words; obviously, he had lived through the emotions he was describing. Of course, a man of his age had undoubtedly experienced many things.

"Pastor"—Steve opened his eyes—"what do you know about human cloning?"

The man's heavy brow furrowed. "Cloning?"

"Yes. My wife has been doing some research on it, but I'd appreciate hearing a minister's opinion."

McGruder snorted with the half-choked mirth of a man who wasn't sure he should be laughing. "Son, what I know about cloning could fill the head of a pin three times. I'm afraid I don't keep up with those kinds of things."

Steve shrugged to hide his disappointment. "That's okay."

The pastor scratched his head. "There was one thing, though—let me recall. I think—no, that was something else—yes, that was cloning. I was preparing a lesson on cults for the saints' Monday morning Bible study, and I ran across a new group. Seems to me they were into cloning, though I never understood why."

Steve frowned. "A cult?"

"Yes. Wait a minute—there, I remember. They're called the Raelians, and they're nuttier than fruitcakes, in my opinion. Founded back in '97 by a man named Rael. He claims that the name of God in the Old Testament, Elohim, isn't a reference to Jehovah at all." He squinted at Steve. "Because Elohim is plural, don't you see. Apparently the idea of the Trinity hasn't occurred to them."

Steve didn't see, but he nodded.

"Anyway, these Raelians say that since Elohim is plural, God must have been a race of superior beings—aliens—who began life on earth through a sort of cloning process. They think Jesus was resurrected through cloning, too. According to them, he really did die on the cross, but the aliens levitated his body and sent a clone back to earth."

Steve sat back, stunned. "That's crazy."

"Not to them." McGruder shrugged. "There's a cult born every month, seems like, and they get nuttier and nuttier. But the Bible says people will believe a lie in the last days. Since folks have been believing lies for years, I take that verse to mean people of the last days are going to believe the most illogical things you could ever imagine."

Steve glanced out the window. "These Raelians—are they American?"

"Praise God, no. We have more than our share of cultists, but these guys are European. I forget which country they hail from."

Steve shifted his gaze back to the pastor's face. "Could it be France?"

McGruder looked thoughtful, then nodded. "I think that's it. I'd have to check my notes to be sure, but I'm sure it was someplace in the European Union. They started a company, you see, to do human cloning because it's illegal here. I didn't pay much attention to that part of what I was reading, though. Didn't seem relevant to the senior saints. And I couldn't imagine anybody buying into that heresy."

If only you knew.

Steve drew a deep breath. "Pastor, apart from the cult business, how do you feel about cloning?"

The man sighed as he ran his hand over the crepe at his throat. "I really don't know enough about it to comment, Steve. Wish I did."

"What if I told you it was almost like artificial insemination or in vitro fertilization. Those procedures are performed all the time these days. In a church as large as ours, I'd be willing to bet some of our own members owe their children to IVF or AI."

A smile gathered up the wrinkles at McGruder's lined mouth. "You know, sometimes I miss the good old days. Having babies was a lot less complicated then. Most children could tell who their parents were without having to consult a medical record."

"I know." Steve sipped his tea, then lowered the sweating glass to the table. "So you don't have any strong feelings about the cloning procedure itself?"

McGruder shook his head. "I don't know what to say, son. I can only tell you I'd be highly suspicious of anyone affiliated with people who find it more sensible to trust aliens than God. I find it much simpler to believe in a loving God who created me, chose to bless the earth through Israel, and will take custody of my immortal soul at death than to spend my time and money trying to clone myself over and over just so I'll last until the aliens come back."

"Me, too." Steve leaned back as Shirley approached with his lunch. After thanking her, he looked at the plate and lifted the top of the bun.

McGruder leaned forward and sniffed the veggie patty suspiciously. "That thing really fit to eat?"

"It's healthy."

"But is it good?"

Steve grinned and reached for the catsup. "Anything's good if you put enough catsup on it."

"I'll leave you to your lunch, then." Grinning, the pastor slid his hand over the check Shirley had left on the table. "Sorry I couldn't be of more help, son. But if I come up with something useful, I'll let you know—if that would be all right."

"That"—Steve extended his hand toward the older man—"would be much appreciated."

Twenty-five

I WAS NOT HAPPY TO HEAR THAT STEVE WANTED ME to cancel my appointment with Andrew Norcross because old Pastor McGruder believed in aliens.

"The appointment's for tomorrow afternoon," I pointed out, settling into the easy chair by our bedroom window. "He may already be at a Tampa hotel. I can't cancel now; it'd be bad manners."

"I don't think manners matter much in this situation." Steve sat on the edge of the bed and pulled off his shoes. He'd been called to the emergency room after dinner—one of his young patients had been in an auto accident and needed several permanent teeth replaced—and we hadn't had a chance to talk. Now he was tired, obviously irritable, and in no mood for compromise.

"I can't believe you're still pursuing this." He threw me a sideways glance, his face flushed in the light from the overhead lamp. "I thought you were about to give up on the idea."

"Well, I haven't. I'm not going to give up until I've given Andrew a chance to answer my questions. For Scott Daniel's sake, I'm going to persevere."

"This afternoon I did a little research of my own—did you know Project One is affiliated with the Raelians?"

I frowned. I'd seen the name on one of the Web sites I'd visited, but I'd been so interested in the process I really hadn't paid much attention to the fine print at the bottom of the page. "And who are they?"

"The cult Pastor McGruder told me about. Apparently they believe aliens created all human life, and through cloning we're supposed to stay alive long enough to see them come again. I don't understand it all, and neither does Pastor McGruder. I'm not sure the Raelians understand what they're supposed to believe, but they're really into the idea of cloning."

I snorted. "I doubt Andrew is affiliated with little green men from outer space."

"But he might be affiliated with the Raelians."

"So what if he is? I don't necessarily agree with my Muslim dry cleaner, but I still need to get my clothes cleaned."

"Your dry cleaner isn't involved in your family life . . . and he won't be using your name to promote his business."

Steve had me there. Andrew had freely admitted that the people at Project One intended to use my name to promote their work. If their work included preaching the doctrine of aliens . . . I blew out my cheeks. That would mean trouble.

I picked up the novel I'd been trying to read ever since Scott Daniel's accident. "We'll just have to ask Andrew about it tomorrow. If he is a Raelian or whatever, we'll tell him to keep the medical aspects of our case separate from the religious aspects of whatever it is they believe."

"Some things are too closely linked to be separated."

"Anything can be separated, Steve. Even an atom."

My husband didn't answer, but the piercing look in his eyes stirred something in my soul—whether it was guilt, anger, or grief, I didn't care to analyze.

I dropped my unopened book onto the floor, then shifted to face my husband. "Honey, forget about the aliens. I want you to come to this meeting tomorrow with an open mind. I told Andrew we'd meet him at the Applebee's near the station—"

"I'm not going to the meeting."

"But you promised!"

"I promised I'd be hospitable. I didn't promise to go." Steve spoke in a firm and final voice, and I knew he would not change his mind. My rock of Gibraltar could be as stubborn as stone, too.

Girding myself with resolve, I lifted my chin. "I'll go alone, then. But I am going. It's too late to back out."

In that moment I knew we had come to a crossroads—never in the twenty-two years of our marriage had I opposed him so completely. Usually we talked through problems when we disagreed, and nine times out of ten Steve saw the wisdom in my arguments. But by the set of his chin and the look in his eye, I knew he wouldn't be changing his mind, at least not within the next twenty-four hours.

I glanced at the clock—11:15. I should be going to bed, but the thought of crawling beneath the sheets with such a stubborn man made my stomach clench. Besides, years ago we had promised never to go to bed angry with one another. That promise hovered above us now, inviting me to apologize and attempt to bridge the gap that yawned between us . . .

I knew what I *should* do. I should apologize, I should soothe his ruffled feelings, I should put off all talk of cloning for another day . . . but I couldn't do any of those things. Not anymore.

So I wouldn't go to bed.

As my heart pumped outrage and indignation through my veins, I stood and picked up my book. "You're tired, and I want to read, so I'm going down to the study. Don't wait up."

"I won't."

I left him, my heart pounding as I jogged down the stairs. Why couldn't he see how important this meeting was? Cloning might be the only way to make our family complete again. We had lost Scott Daniel, but we could fill that empty space.

We had to. I have tasted desperate desire only a few times in my life—first, when I met Steve and knew I would never be happy without him at my side; second, when it became apparent we were not likely to have biological children and I yearned for a child of my own; and third, when I learned that I was pregnant with Scott and begged God to give me a healthy baby.

On each of those three occasions I had prayed like Hannah, weeping and groaning with emotions too deep for words. And each time God had answered, so I was confident he would answer my prayers again.

As I turned the corner and entered my study, Charity's quip of the day washed through me, shivering my skin like the touch of a wandering spirit. This morning she had called in the first hour to share the words of some nameless mystic: "Life contains two tragedies," she told me, her voice wavering over the airwaves. "One is not to get your heart's desire . . . the other is to get it."

The only tragedy here, I resolutely told myself, would be for Steve to ignore my pleas and my research. We would have another son, and God would smooth our path and keep this baby from harm.

I had never wanted anything so badly in my entire life.

Twenty-six

IN THE UPSTAIRS BATHROOM, BRITTANY STEPPED closer to the locked door and pressed her ear to the surface. Her parents must have assumed she was asleep in her room, for they had made no effort to lower their voices.

Her parents never argued—at least, not like the people she saw on television. Her father was so easygoing he wouldn't even honk at drivers who weren't paying attention at traffic lights, and Ms. Counselor always said yelling accomplished nothing.

Her parents conducted their arguments in supercharged voices, and the discussion Brittany had just heard was intense enough to cut through the space between their bedroom and the hallway. She had been caught by the mention of Scott Daniel—a name rarely spoken these days—then the conversation veered off to cults and space aliens. She had no idea what her parents were arguing about, but one thing was clear: her mother desperately wanted to talk to someone named Andrew, and her father just as desperately wanted to avoid talking to this person.

Who was this Andrew guy? And why did he have the power to make her usually reasonable parents bark at each other?

She turned out the light, then cautiously opened the bathroom door and peered into the hallway. A light still burned through the half-open door of her parents' room, but she had heard her mother go downstairs. Mom was probably in her study, which meant she was either working late or too ticked to stay in the same room with Dad.

Slipping like a shadow through the darkened hall, Brittany entered her own room and closed the door. After diving for the comfort of her bed, she huddled beneath the comforter and curled into a ball.

Around her, the house waited like a living thing, silent and anxious. Last week her parents had been yelling at her. Tonight they were fighting with each other. Next week—who knew?

What had happened to them? Their family wasn't perfect, but it had never been as messed up as some of her friends'. Both her parents were as straight as sticks and as predictable as June weather. Sometimes she wished one of them had a secret life, something really juicy, but they had no skeletons in the closet, no tattoos in private places, no gay siblings or cousins who rode with the Hell's Angels. Her parents were the most conventional, boring people on the planet . . . which was why she couldn't understand why they were arguing about aliens.

What did aliens have to do with the Scottster?

She lay perfectly still, the only sound the rhythm of her pulse in her ear. Why did things have to change? If Scotty were still alive and sleeping in the room next door, Mom would have come by to tuck him in. On her way through the hallway, she'd have thrust her head into Britt's room, made a face at the mess, then pointed an accusing finger at the pair of half-empty Coke cans on the window sill.

A few minutes later Dad would have come through the hallway, stomping over the floor like a giant as he did his ridiculous "Fee Fie Foe Fum" routine, bellowing about smelling the blood of "his Scotty son." In time, he would have come to Britt's door, too, but he would have rapped lightly with his knuckles and offered some stupid knock-knock joke he'd picked up from one of his patients.

The sweetness of the image drew tears from some deep place far behind her eyes. She dashed the wetness away, then pressed her face into her pillow.

Why was she feeling so weepy? Her childhood was long gone, and she didn't want it back.

Scott was gone, too . . . and, at the moment, her parents were way beyond her reach.

But life had to go on, didn't it?

Twenty-seven

WORN OUT BY MY ARGUMENT WITH STEVE, WHEN I did go to bed I fell asleep almost immediately. For a while I tossed and turned in a fretful doze, then my hold on reality relaxed and at last fell free. Through the magic of sleep and the subconscious, my brain transported me to a dream landscape almost as vivid and real as the world around me.

I found myself again sliding out of Gary's car in a numb sense of panic. This time, however, he had not dropped me at the morgue, but at the children's hospital.

I stood on the concrete sidewalk wearing the same plaid skirt I'd worn the day Scott died. I carried the same purse on my arm, and if I had checked the screen of my cell phone, I knew I'd see Steve's number displayed there. He had called me to meet him . . .

"Diana!" Steve's voice, electric with tension, cut through the shushing sounds of passing cars. Still wearing his lab coat, he stood near the hospital entrance. "This way."

I hurried to join him. "Where's Scott Daniel?"

"Somewhere in here." He paused before moving through the automatic glass doors, and as I looked into his eyes I saw no trace of grief or sorrow, only the fear of a parent who had received news of an accident. "Come on, let's get to him."

He didn't have to ask twice. I followed my husband, easily keeping pace with his long-legged stride. We passed the receptionist's desk, where a pair of elderly men with trembling hands were pulling Medicaid cards from their wallets; we hurried by a long line of pregnant women in wheelchairs, all of them staring into space with expressionless faces.

My heart was pounding in a joyous rhythm by the time we reached the elevator. I caught Steve's eye. "I knew it was all a mistake. He's alive."

Concern and confusion warred in Steve's eyes. "Of course he is. They would tell us if he weren't."

"I know." I smiled, then looked away, barely able to repress the fount of hysterical laughter bubbling up within me. Steve didn't know what I knew, how absolutely awful this day could have been . . .

My heart lifted when the elevator chimed. I stepped forward, eager to charge ahead, but when the doors opened a mob of faceless men, women, and children flooded into the hall. Shoved and turned by the crowd, I cried out in frustration, then finally reached the elevator. I had lost Steve, but I jabbed the nearest button and sighed in relief when the double doors finally slid together.

The elevator deposited me on a floor unlike any hospital ward I'd ever seen. The walls gleamed like alabaster, and milky fog streamed around the ankles of the nurses monitoring the hallways. Part of my brain registered this as odd; the larger part of my brain drove me forward. An orderly in white stood behind the desk, and when I asked for Scott Daniel Sheldon, he pointed to a room directly behind me.

A sudden chill climbed the ladder of my spine as I approached the door. I knew I was dreaming, but I didn't want to wake. If I could be with Scotty, I could adjust to the faceless people and mist-carpeted hallways. Better to have Scott living in a dream than dead in the real world.

I pushed on the swinging door, then stared at the multitude in the room. Steve and Brittany sat by the bed, while Pastor John, Gary, and several of our friends from church lined the walls. Bouquets of flowers stood on tables and shelves, spreading their sweet fragrance throughout the room.

I hurried to my son's side. He looked small and pitiful in that big bed, but his skin was rosy, his lips full and pink. The small scratch still marred his cheek, but his hand, when I held it, was warm. Leaning over the bed railing, I turned his hand and pressed my fingers to his wrist—a pulse, strong and regular, flowed through those blue veins.

"He's alive." I whispered the words over the whoosh and click of the machines in the room.

Steve dropped his hand upon my shoulder. "Yes, sweetheart, he is. But we're waiting to hear what the doctor will say."

Ignoring my husband, I trailed the back of my hand along my son's sweet face. "Scott Daniel, wake up, honey." I spoke in the lilting rhyme with which I used to wake him as a baby. "The sun's come up and so should we, snugglebugs though we may be."

No answer. I began again, a little louder this time. "Wake up, sweetie. The sun's come up and so should we, snugglebugs though we may be—"

The phone rang, interrupting, and I turned to glare at it. But there was nothing on the bedside table but a plastic pitcher and a paper cup.

Reality jolted me back to wakefulness. The phone on my night-stand was ringing . . . at 1:20 A.M.

Shock yielded quickly to fury. I fumbled for the phone, then snapped, "Hello?"

The phone clicked as the caller hung up. Fuming, I dropped it back into its cradle, then lay back down and raked my hand through my hair. The caller had to be one of Brittany's friends, someone who could tell by my voice that this was not a good hour to call.

Good thing he or she hung up. If I knew who had interrupted my time with Scott Daniel, I'd probably go for his or her adolescent throat next time we met.

I turned onto my side and closed my eyes, my mind grasping for the dream, reaching for it with terrible longing. But the thin sleep I had enjoyed proved to be all my body would accept.

A cruel joke, courtesy of my subconscious mind.

After an hour I got up and went downstairs to read and weep . . . alone.

Twenty-eight

OVER THE THUMP OF THE MUSIC THAT CARRIED US into the noon news, Gary's voice buzzed in my ear. "Good show, Dr. D."

I looked up at him through the window, gave him a thumbs-up, and slipped the headphones from my head.

I didn't have time to hang around and chat. In exactly fifteen minutes, I was to meet Andrew Norcross at the restaurant down the street.

I grabbed my purse, hurried through the hall, then stuck my head through the doorway of the sound studio. "Anything urgent, guys?" I glanced at the correspondence folder. "Anything that can't wait until tomorrow?"

Gary glanced around his desk, then shrugged. "Don't see anything. But the paychecks haven't arrived yet."

"Don't care about the paycheck; I'm outta here. Call me later if anything comes up, but I'm going to be incommunicado for a couple of hours."

To emphasize my statement, I pulled my cell phone from my purse, dramatically pressed the power button, then winked. I left them to wonder if I had a secret life, then smiled my way through the usual cluster of interns gathered in the hallway. Today they were holding court outside the country music studio, and as I peeked in the window, I realized why—Marcia Lane, a beautiful and buxom rising star from Nashville, was sitting at the mike for a live interview while her latest hit, "'How Can I Miss You if You Won't Go Away?" warbled through the speakers over the door.

The sun was warm on my face as I moved through the parking lot and unlocked my car. Summer would be upon us before we knew it, then my walks through the parking lot would become mad dashes to hurry from one air-conditioned sanctuary to another.

Scott Daniel had always enjoyed summertime. I had taken him to a water babies class as an infant, and after that he could never seem to get enough of the pool. I had to be careful, though. The chlorine would turn his beautiful hair a strange shade of green if we didn't slather on the conditioner after every swim.

I found myself smiling. Was a love of the water a result of nature or nurture? Would the new baby like the water as much as Scotty did?

Applebee's was buzzing by the time I arrived. I stood in the entry-way with my arms folded and tried not to be conspicuous as I scanned arriving customers. I knew Andrew was traveling alone, so I could safely ignore groups of women and couples. I found myself examin-ing young-to-middle-aged men with the concentration of a surgeon.

When a taxi pulled up at the curb, I knew I'd found him. A tall, thin fellow with a leather briefcase stepped out and rubbed the back of his neck with one hand while studying the front of the building. He wore a dark, tailored suit unlike anything modeled by the locals.

With a confidence born of certainty, I moved toward the door and motioned him in. "Andrew Norcross?"

His narrow face split into a smile. "Dr. Sheldon?"

"Welcome to Tampa. I've got the hostess holding a booth for us."

I immediately felt at ease with my guest. Having been a student of psychology and a professional counselor, I can usually form an accu-rate impression of people within a few moments of meeting them. Andrew was handsome in a European model sort of way—gaunt cheeks, wavy hair, dark eyes. His hands were clean, his nails mani-cured, and the corners of his eyes crinkled into nets when he smiled—and he smiled a lot.

I felt a frisson of guilty pleasure because Steve hadn't come.

After exchanging introductions and pleasantries, we studied the menus and placed our orders. Nerves had tightened my stomach into a ball, but I didn't want Andrew to feel uncomfortable eating alone. I ordered a mandarin orange salad.

Once the young waitress had taken our menus, I folded my arms on the table and looked across at my guest.

"Good flight?"

"Uneventful, thank goodness. I'm hoping for another quiet flight this afternoon."

Working around the heavy table, he pulled his briefcase onto the bench and proceeded to extract a folder and a glossy brochure. My mouth almost watered at the sight of the papers—I hungered more for information than food. "I really appreciate your coming all this way, Mr. Norcross."

"Please call me Andrew."

"All right. I'm afraid I must begin by apologizing for my husband."

He lifted a brow. "Has he been detained?"

I smiled, trying to put a pleasant face on the situation. "I'm sorry, but my husband is a dentist, you know, and sometimes things . . . come up. He won't be joining us today."

A look of concern crossed Andrew's face, then he shrugged and smiled. "The organization prefers that I meet with both prospective clients, but since we also work with single parents, I'm sure we'll be fine. I know you'll relate all the information." He leaned forward and handed me a brochure featuring a beautiful blond boy on the cover. My heart twisted. The boy could have been Scott Daniel's brother.

Andrew wasted no time coming to the purpose of our meeting. "As you know, Dr. Sheldon, we are a not-for-profit organization, but we do have operating costs—quite extensive expenses, as I'm sure you can appreciate. The controversial aspect of our work has forced us to be slightly clandestine about the operation of our labs, but I can assure you everything is regulated. The French government monitors our medical and research facilities, and an independent panel of accountants audits our books each year."

I nodded, eager to move into the more difficult aspects of the discussion. "I understand all that, Andrew, and I have no problems with your organization. My husband, however, heard some troubling news—something about Project One's affiliation with a group called the Raelians."

Andrew's smile deepened. "I'm not surprised you are concerned."

"Are you tied to them?"

"Project One's founder is affiliated with the Raelians, yes. And many Raelians have registered with our company for one project or another—cloning has religious significance for them, you understand."

"Actually, I don't understand at all."

"It's not relevant to your situation. The important thing for you to know is that Project One is an independent entity with no official ties to the Raelian Movement. We accept no monies from them, nor do we distribute any funds to them."

I leaned back against the seat, wondering if a separation of funds was enough to counter Steve's objection. The Raelians' bizarre beliefs had so turned him against the concept of cloning—

"Correct me if I'm wrong," Andrew pressed into my thoughts, "but don't several American religious groups dabble in commercial enterprises? The other day I was watching a religious show on television, and they offered a credit card to supporters. Apparently every time someone uses the card, a small percentage of the transaction amount goes to support the Holy Water Spring Retirement Community for Sensible Saints."

His comment brought a smile to my face. "I'm not sure you've got the name quite right, but yes, you're correct. Religious groups use all sorts of means to raise money."

"Does your husband find that offensive?"

I shifted my gaze toward the window as I considered the question. Steve had strong opinions about religion and money. While he wasn't opposed to students selling candy to support the Christian school, he didn't think it right for the church youth group to do the same thing. I could scarcely see the difference, but according to Steve, the Lord's church should be supported by tithes from the Lord's people. The Lord's school, I supposed, would have to survive on tuition and candy bar sales.

Sighing, I turned back to Andrew. "That question has too many variables for me to answer."

A smile found its way through his mask of uncertainty. "Perhaps he will be content to know the Raelians do not use Project One for fundraising or proselytizing. We are a business operation, pure and simple."

"Yet one tied to a religious group."

"Don't other organizations sponsor programs as a service to their members? Look around—in this country alone you can find Catholic hospitals, Christian retreat centers, Baptist universities. The other day I saw an ad for a Christian mortgage company. Those people offer a service because they believe it will benefit people of like mind. But they do not forbid others from enjoying the same service, nor do they always proselytize."

"Point taken, but we are accustomed to those groups and affiliations. I'm afraid my husband finds the Raelians a little strange. Incomprehensible, actually."

Andrew quirked a brow. "Try explaining the doctrine of transubstantiation to someone who's never heard of Jesus Christ."

I laughed. "Where are you from?"

"Britain. But I lived all over Europe as a child; my parents fell victim to a case of wanderlust, I'm afraid. I've only been in the States two years."

"Long enough to get a good feel for our society, though."

He grimaced in good humor. "It took several months to readjust my perceptions of America. From watching American exports on

European television, I formulated a notion that all Americans were like the people on *Jerry Springer* and *Baywatch*."

He glanced at the brochure on the table. "I suppose we should get back to our discussion. Is there anything you'd like to know before I launch into the standard spiel?"

"I think you can skip the spiel and cut to the heart of the matter. I've already done a bit of research, so I think I know all I want to know about the actual cloning process."

"So you've covered the basics."

"I'm familiar with the process—in nontechnical language, at least. But I'd like to know more about certain ethical issues." I tented my hands. "My husband has strong reservations, and I imagine my radio audience will, too—if we decide to go through with this."

Andrew nodded. "The most important thing to remember is that a clone is not a carbon copy. It would be more accurate to describe a clone as a time-delayed identical twin of the original. The clone and the donor would have different fingerprints. Remember Cece, the first cloned cat? He and his donor were different colors. Because a clone will grow up in different circumstances than the donor, environment will play different roles in shaping certain characteristics. A clone will not inherit the donor's memories, personality, or likes and dislikes. A strong likelihood that he or she will develop in the same way exists, but so does a chance the clone will not."

As the waitress approached, I leaned back into the booth and smiled. The new child would encounter different things than Scott Daniel, but he'd probably look the same and have a similar personality. And, when a few years had passed, I'd have another opportunity to capture Scott Daniel's goofy gap-toothed grin on film.

Andrew, who had ordered tea, set his cup off to the side and seemed more eager to talk than fuss with his drink.

Fine with me.

When the waitress had walked away, I pushed my soft drink to the side, too. "One thing does concern me, Andrew—no matter how safe the procedure becomes, I fear many Americans will be resistant to the idea of cloning. We are a nation of freethinkers, and people believe clones will be like zombies, mindless Frankensteins who will wander through life as a mere shadow of the donor. My husband and I would face this prejudice—as would my son."

"Nothing could be farther from the truth. Clones are real people, and in the United States all people have rights and responsibilities. I've heard the same arguments in Europe. People think we are creating clones to create a race of slaves, but that's ridiculous. Once a cloned child is born, he or she will be protected by the same laws protecting other individuals. Clones are fully human, and they must share in human civil liberties."

"Once the child is *born*." I underlined the latter word. "Therein lies another potential problem. Fetuses do not always have rights under American law, and my husband and I both strongly disagree with the devaluation of preborn human life. We would not want you to create a dozen embryos and use only one. We would not be comfortable with the implantation of, say, four embryos, and the selective abortion of the weaker fetuses—"

"Then you do not have to deal with those things—we will not implement those strategies in your situation." Dismissing my concerns with a shrug, Andrew unwrapped the flatware in his napkin, then withdrew the spoon. "After studying the matter for some time, I feel the only objection to cloning that holds any merit at all is the claim that the technology is not yet foolproof. But we have come amazingly far in the last few months, and I can almost guarantee you will not be confronted with a problem in the embryo stage." He plucked a lemon wedge from a plate on the table, squeezed the juice into his tea, then dropped the rind back onto the plate. "Again, let me remind you—cloning is not genetic engineering. We are not modifying human DNA, we are simply planting it to grow in new soil."

I parked my chin in my palm. "My husband, if I may be frank, is more than a little dubious about the entire idea. He spoke with a pastor at our church, an older fellow who knows nothing about modern technology, and Steve got a little rattled. I've a feeling our pastor simply dismissed the idea as playing God."

Andrew shook his head in weary resignation. "We hear from religious protesters every week. In contrast to abortion, which results in the *destruction* of human life, we are about the *creation* of life. Moreover, we hear that 'playing God' argument every time medicine takes a major step forward. At one time the arguments against birth-control pills and heart transplants consisted of the same two words. When people see what good can come out of advanced technology, the protests usually die away."

I accepted a glass of water from the waitress, then set it on a napkin. "All right, Andrew, I'm now thinking more like a radio host than a mother. When—if—word of this gets out, I know I'm going to be hounded on my show and in the press. People will be calling me everything from Mary Shelley to Hitler. What am I to say when they accuse me of personally ushering in the end of the world?"

"Don't let the critics shake your confidence. Tell them cloning is perfectly ethical, legal, and well on its way to being accepted worldwide." Andrew opened the brochure and flipped several pages. "Cloned children are perfectly protected under existing American law, but regulations concerning the actual cloning process still need to be instituted around the world. On these pages you'll find operational guidelines that were proposed by our people, approved by the International Association of Physicians, and subsequently adopted by the European Union. They do not yet exist in this country, of course, because cloning is still illegal here."

I leaned forward to peer at the page.

"First," Andrew said, "human clones should have the same legal rights and responsibilities as any other human being. Second, no living person should be cloned without his or her consent. An individual should be entitled to automatic copyright for his or her own genetic code. Just as you cannot take my published words and use them for your own benefit, one person should not be able to benefit from the DNA of another without consent."

I stared at the page, my mind opening to a new realm of possibilities. "I hadn't thought of that."

"It's important. Imagine what might happen if someone got ahold of Michael Jordan's hairbrush. They could take the DNA from a single strand of his hair and impregnate scores of women with Michael Jordan clones. Those children may grow up to hate basketball, but they'd all have Michael Jordan's body, his genetic code, and whatever elements are hard-wired into his personality. That sort of identity-theft should be illegal."

I closed my eyes, imagining an entire room of Osama bin Laden or Hitler clones. That idea alone could generate hours of discussion on my show.

"Third"—he glanced down at the page—"human clones should only be gestated and delivered voluntarily by adult women. Though the Japanese are currently working on an artificial womb and some researchers have theorized that clones might successfully gestate in the wombs of cattle, we know human embryos are profoundly imprinted during the prenatal period. Infants who miss out on the sounds of human conversation, touch, and even music during gestation would be severely deprived at birth."

I could only stare at him. The implications of what he was describing were enormous. The people at Project One might be kooky in their theology, but someone had demonstrated a great deal of wisdom by preparing these regulations.

"Finally"—Andrew tapped the last paragraph on the page—"the cloning of convicted murderers and other violent criminals should be banned. Since evidence suggests that a propensity for violence can be inherited, the use of criminals' DNA for cloning should be prohibited under any circumstances. The world does not need another Stalin, Lenin, or Hitler."

I smiled as the opposite thought occurred to me. "But what about the world's truly wonderful people? We could create another Anne Frank . . . another da Vinci and Ben Franklin."

His mouth curved in a smile. "Can you imagine the inventions da Vinci and Franklin might come up with if they were allowed to work together? With today's technology at their fingertips, there's no limit to what they could achieve."

"Amazing." My thoughts drifted toward the future, where my own beloved son might attend medical conventions with clones of Thomas Edison and George Washington . . .

"Many people have talked about the possibility of correcting the mistakes of the past," Andrew said. "Now we have a chance to do just that."

His comment snapped me out of my reverie. "Correcting a mistake?"

"Like the Holocaust. Those who complain that cloning will somehow cheat the world of genetic diversity fail to realize how we could actually restore the genes of millions of people who died under Hitler's regime. Consider the hundreds of thousands of doctors, scientists, and scholars murdered in Stalin's purge—wouldn't it be wonderful if we could restore those people?"

"You're not worried about overpopulating the planet?"

He laughed. "I doubt we'll engage in the mass production of human beings until food supplies are likewise being mass-produced. With the help of genetic engineers, other groups are cloning food products—super-productive fruits and vegetables, disease-resistant livestock, and the like." He lifted his glass, but paused before bringing it to his lips. "I've learned never to say never, Dr. Sheldon. While we wouldn't be able to restore every Holocaust victim, enough locks of hair and bits of bones remain for us to make tremendous headway in righting the wrongs committed by a previous generation."

While the idea of restoration intrigued me, I was far more fascinated by the possibility of righting a *recent* wrong—Scott Daniel's death. So far Andrew had talked philosophy; I needed practical details.

I cleared my throat. "Andrew, if I were in your position, I would want to be sure any prospective parents were mentally healthy before proceeding."

He nodded. "Naturally, family stability is a major concern. In that sense, we're a bit like an adoption agency. We want to be sure our babies are going to live with stable parents."

I held up my index finger. "My family, on the other hand, is recovering from a death in the family. I'm not sure *stable* is a word that describes us at the moment."

He reached out and lightly touched the back of my hand. "I think I know what you're going to say, Dr. Sheldon, and I understand. We know you will need time to grieve, but the process of cloning takes time, too. We'll have to get tissue samples from you, then we'll have to do the actual DNA implantation. If you're to be the egg donor, you'll have to take hormones in order to produce several eggs at the proper time, then you'll have to travel to Europe for the implantation. You'll go through the nine months of pregnancy, then you will welcome and raise your child."

His smile held a tinge of sadness. "I'd say that was the easy part, but I think you're experienced enough to know that grief and motherhood often go hand in hand, right?"

I looked away as tears stung my eyes. The man was perceptive. From the first moment we hold our little ones, mothers know the grief of letting go is inevitable.

"We may be a little more flexible than most American adoption agencies," Andrew went on, rambling, I thought, to cover for my sudden weepiness. "For instance, we would have no problem approving a single woman who wished to become a mother through cloning, or a homosexual couple. We don't hold our clients to an outmoded definition of family, but we do expect prospective parents to be of sound mind and body."

Steve would have seen red upon hearing Andrew talk about new definitions of family, but what did Project One's unconventional views have to do with us? Besides, Steve didn't spend his days listening to callers try to explain their convoluted interpersonal relationships. I did, and I knew the stereotypical family had become a thing of the past. As of the year 2000, the "two parents with their own children" designation applied to only 24 percent of American households. The situation of the American family wasn't ideal, but few civilizations throughout history had been as stable.

I dashed tears from my eyes, then watched silently as the waitress advanced and set two salad bowls before us. I picked up my fork and speared a bite of chicken, giving Andrew implicit permission to eat while we talked. "You mentioned tissue samples—where am I to get those?"

Andrew picked up his knife and fork. "I'm assuming an autopsy was performed after your son's death? The medical examiner should have tissue samples on file. They may even still be fresh—unfrozen, that is. If there were no other choice we could use something as simple as a strand of hair, but an assortment of cells would be far better."

"Will the ME give them to me?"

His dark brows drew downward. "Not usually. Often you'll have to engage a lawyer to see results. Sometimes an intimidating letter in the right tone will persuade an ME to hand over tissue samples. But you might have to get a court order to see results."

I bit my lower lip. "And then?"

"You have a medical examination. If you're not yet menopausal—"

"I'm not."

"—then you take hormones designed to encourage hyperovulation. When the time is right, you will fly to France, where in our lab the doctor will remove several eggs from your ovary. They will be emptied of all genetic material, then one will be injected with your son's DNA. The others will be placed in storage."

"If my eggs . . . aren't suitable?"

"Then we will use another woman's. The origin of the eggs is not really important, because none of the egg donor's DNA is passed onto the clone. Once the egg is denucleated, nothing remains inside but cytoplasm."

And perhaps the spark of life . . . the seeds of a soul.

Automatically, my hand dropped to my lap and touched the soft place where I had carried Scott for so many months.

"I would really like to use my egg, Andrew. I don't want a donor."

He hesitated over his salad, one brow lifting, then he shrugged. "I don't foresee a problem."

"Once the egg divides, what then?"

He held up a warning finger, stalling me until he had swallowed his last bite. "Once the embryo has reached the six-cell stage, it will be implanted inside your womb. You will remain under our doctor's care for a few days so we can monitor your hormones to be sure your body doesn't reject the pregnancy. When all is as it should be, you will fly home and return to your normal activities. Go to your regular obstetrician, have whatever tests he or she recommends. Within forty weeks, you will give birth to a normal child who will be the genetic offspring of you and your husband . . . and the identical twin to the boy you lost."

I had read the material, I had pondered and weighed it until I could have provided many of the details myself, but hearing Andrew explain the procedure in a matter-of-fact voice reassured me, for his was the voice of authority. I, on the other hand, was a new convert desperately seeking a smidgen of faith.

"And you say several women are now pregnant with clones?"

He stared at me, his eyes sparkling, then gave me a tentative smile. "I shouldn't say anything." He lowered his voice to a conspiratorial whisper. "But the first two clones were born two weeks ago. A set of twins, delivered in London. Mother and boys are absolutely healthy. To be safe, however, they're going to keep the news quiet until the boys are three months old."

I felt a tide of gooseflesh ripple up each arm and crash at the back of my neck. "You're not kidding?"

His grin widened as he shook his head. "My supervisors would have a fit if they knew I told you. But I thought you should know.

You won't be the first in the world, if that pressure worries you. You might not even be the first American woman. You'd definitely be *among* the first, though. A pioneer in the field of fertility technology."

I sat back, letting my gaze rove over the diners beyond our booth. Cloning was no longer a dream, nor was it mere scientific prattle. It had happened, it would happen again, and it could happen for me . . . if I were willing.

"Who?" I turned back to Andrew. "Who did the London woman clone?"

One corner of his mouth quirked upward. "I'm not at liberty to divulge that information. I can tell you, however, it was someone remarkable."

I pressed my hand to my forehead as images swirled in my brain like bits of glass in a kaleidoscope. Who had been cloned in London? Winston Churchill? Prince Charles? No—they wouldn't clone a living person without his permission. But what if they'd *had* his permission?

I smiled as an absurd idea lifted its head. Given the long life spans of women in the royal family, rumor held that Queen Elizabeth might reign for another twenty or thirty years, leaving Charles with little time to do the job for which he'd been born. What if *another* Prince of Wales had been created? A pair of identical princes—another heir and a spare. The younger versions of Charles would have every hereditary right to rule and every opportunity to reign if he died soon after the queen reached the end of her natural life span. William and Harry might object, of course, but so far those young men had not shown any burning desire to assume the throne . . .

I shook my head, clearing away the fantastic ideas. Five years in talk radio had expanded my thought processes far beyond the rational realm.

"Okay." I took a deep breath. "So cloning is possible. It's probable. Now tell me about the expense."

Andrew lowered his fork, then slowly clasped his hands. "The process is quite costly. But I've been in touch with my superiors back in France. Because of the favor you'd be doing us—because, as we discussed, we fully intend to use your name and position to advance cloning in the United States—we are prepared to offer you a 50 percent reduction in fees. We will cover everything—the implantation, research, hormone treatments, even hospitalization, should you require it—for one hundred fifty thousand dollars."

I caught my breath. Since I'd been expecting to hear a figure twice that amount, I felt like I'd won the lottery.

"One hundred fifty thousand? That's all?"

"Absolutely. And payment can be spread out over the time of your treatment, but we'll need a deposit. The typical amount is 10 percent."

Fifteen thousand dollars . . . about what I'd intended to pay for Brittany's college tuition next year. But fifteen thousand, even one hundred fifty thousand, was a paltry amount when compared to the value of my son's life.

My thoughts shifted to more practical matters. "What about the publicity? When, exactly, would it begin?"

"From our side, not until after the pregnancy is established. You, of course, are free to tell anyone you like of your plans—we would only ask that you not reveal our office locations on national radio." He grinned. "We have attracted enough controversy; we would naturally be reluctant to invite more."

"Thank you, Andrew." I picked up my fork and punched at a piece of chicken hiding among the lettuce folds. Slipping through the restraints of my self-control, a smile spread over my face. "I'll go home and discuss these things with my husband. I'm quite sure we'll be sending you a check next week."

Dollar signs and baby booties danced in my imagination as I drove back to the station. Coming up with one hundred fifty thousand dollars wouldn't be easy, but we could manage it. Throughout our married life, we had taken financial chances—stepping out in faith to buy our first house and the dental office, taking our first scary steps into the stock market—but God had always provided what we needed. I was convinced he would provide this time, as well.

Well, Lord, you've opened a door . . . now provide the means we'll need to go through it.

Sitting at a red light, I took a mental inventory of our financial affairs. The bill-paying checking account was always in a state of flux. The savings account was only slightly more substantial, for even though we made regular deposits, unexpected expenses regularly drained it. That left our retirement accounts, the equity in the house, and the money-market fund we had opened as a savings account for Brittany's college tuition.

I didn't want to sell the house—I wanted our new son to grow up in the same room that had sheltered Scott Daniel. But we'd been living in the house ten years, so a home equity loan or a second mortgage wouldn't be out of the question.

And both Steve and I were well employed. My husband made a good living from his practice and I was one of the highest-paid radio personalities in Florida, if not in the nation. I hadn't checked Dr. Laura's paycheck stub lately, but at contract negotiation time my agent had assured me I was on my way to playing in her league.

Once I told Steve how easily we could restore our son, his reservations would ebb away. The expense might give him pause, but he'd soon agree it would be money well spent. After all, he had never been tight-fisted; we both believed money was something God gave us so we could minister to the needs of others. What better cause for our investments could we find? Perhaps our example would encourage a doctor in Italy or France to clone St. Francis of Assisi or even St. Paul.

I laughed softly as a sudden thought occurred to me—a clone of Paul raised in a messianic Jewish household! In a century with satellite television and the World Wide Web, what a preacher that firebrand would make! Modern medicine might even find a way to heal the troublesome illness he had referred to as his "thorn in the flesh."

I pulled into the parking lot, shut off the engine, then leaned against the door as an indefinable feeling of *rightness* swept over me. Jesus spoke of the "pearl of great price," the thing a man would sell his soul to gain. I knew the analogy pertained to salvation, but couldn't the pearl also stand for other precious things?

For me, the pearl of great price would be the restoration of my precious son. For him, I would empty my bank account, mortgage the house, sell my own blood.

One hundred fifty thousand dollars was nothing.

Twenty-nine

WITH SOME DIFFICULTY, I MANAGED TO TEMPER MY excitement while I returned to the air studio, taped a series of promos, then ran to the grocery store to pick up a short list of family necessities. As the grandfather clock in the foyer chimed six o'clock, I swept into the kitchen on a tide of rising euphoria. Steve and Brittany were eating sub sandwiches at the bar while my dinner, still wrapped in waxed paper, waited on the counter.

I heaved the grocery bags onto the stove, then cast my family a faintly reproving look. "What? No waiting for the mother?" The note of cheer in my voice contradicted my rebuke, and at the sound of it both Steve and Britt looked up, clearly suspicious.

Not willing to broach the subject of cloning with Brittany in the room, I grabbed my sandwich and sat next to Steve, forcing myself to relax. I would explain the cloning project to him first, get his approval, then tactfully approach Brittany. Thoughts of a new brother or a pregnant mother would not thrill her, but by the time the baby came she'd be away at college. She could begin her new life while we started over again with our new son.

I took a bite of the low-fat club sandwich. Amazing what they could do with meats and peppers and a little lettuce. "Delicious." I smiled at my husband. "Thanks for getting dinner."

"What are you so cheery about?" Steve gave me a dubious glance. "Pick up a couple of new stations today?"

I shrugged and swallowed. "Maybe. Things are going well with the show."

Brittany must have sensed something in the air, for she gulped the remainder of her sandwich, took a perfunctory swallow of her Coke, then left the table, beverage in hand. I watched her carry the forbidden glass up the stairs and decided to let the infraction slide. I needed to speak to Steve, and I didn't want to wait.

"I had lunch with Andrew Norcross today." I kept my tone light and bright. "He was very interesting and well-prepared. I think you would like him."

Steve kept eating, but his eyes said, *Oh, really?*

I pressed on. "Because we'll be helping Project One by allowing them to go public with our story, they're willing to give us a break on the fees. They'll take care of everything—all treatments, services, and follow-up, for one hundred fifty thousand."

Steve found his voice. "Dollars?"

"That's right."

"American dollars?"

"Of course, American dollars! And I was careful to mention all your concerns. Yes, you were right, the founder of Project One is a Raelian, but the cloning group in no way disseminates his religious beliefs. And Andrew assured me they will respect our pro-life convictions. They will withdraw several eggs from my ovary, but they will use only one at a time for the DNA transfers. If the first embryo doesn't implant, for instance, they'll process another, but they will not create several embryos and then freeze them. I told him we couldn't allow that."

He lifted one brow, suggesting in marital shorthand that I had taken leave of my senses. "And you *trust* him?"

"Of course I trust him. They are ethical people; a board of directors oversees every step of the process. Furthermore, they have considered details I wouldn't have thought about in years. Here." I spread the brochure on the counter. "I read most of this after lunch and now I'm even more impressed with their organization."

Annoyance struggled with disbelief on his face as he stared at me. "You're still serious about this?"

"More than ever."

"And nothing I said means anything to you."

"Of course it means something, Steve—but Andrew had an answer for each of our concerns. He explained everything to me, and if you read this brochure, you'll see that cloning is safe, practical, and quite possibly the answer to several medical problems." My voice broke with huskiness. "It *is* possible, Steve. The first cloned twins were born last month in London, with no complications. We could be the first Americans—"

"Is that what's driving you?" His eyes sniped at me. "Are you doing this for the *publicity*?"

I took a wincing breath. "Is that what you think? I'm not pursuing this for publicity, I'm doing this for us. I want to restore our family."

He looked away, his eyes brimming with threatening tears. I shifted my gaze back to my sandwich.

I'd sprung a lot on him tonight and I shouldn't push. He needed a few minutes to collect his thoughts, to lick his wounded feelings, to find the humility to admit he'd been wrong to object to my plan.

Steve glanced at the pages of the brochure, then cleared his throat and met my gaze. "Where do you think we're going to come up with one hundred fifty thousand dollars that aren't in our budget?"

I swiveled to face him. "I've been thinking about it all day. We have fifty thousand in Brittany's college fund, so I could take the deposit—fifteen thousand—from that. And we have at least two hundred thousand invested in the house, so we could get a second mortgage or a home equity loan."

"It wouldn't be fair to dip into Britty's college fund for this. I also don't think it's right to risk our house for a procedure that may not work. We're already making huge mortgage payments. How are we supposed to afford a second?"

He met my gaze without flinching, and for an instant I felt like a spoiled ingénue telling her father that she really, *really* needed a new dress for the debutante season.

The feeling didn't last. I wasn't a spoiled girl; I was a mature woman with a successful career. "We can afford it, Steve. We'll just cut back for a while. And Britt won't need all that money this year. If for some reason we're not able to completely reimburse her account, we could always take out an educational loan."

"So you want us to pay for a student loan, a second mortgage, the original house payment, and two car payments? The only thing free and clear around here will be Britt's truck."

I snorted. Brittany's old red pickup—the vehicle of her dreams and her sixteenth birthday present—hardly deserved to be called a truck, but at least it was paid for. The insurance premium, however, made me see double every six months.

Leaning forward, I propped my elbow on the counter and pinched the bridge of my nose. Closing my eyes, I murmured, "Don't give me grief about money, Steve. You don't pay the bills, so you don't have the headaches. I think I know what we can handle."

"If it's causing you so much stress, maybe I should take the check-book."

"It's not stressful." Lifting my head, I met his gaze. "I know we'll be fine, we always are. Hasn't God always provided what we needed?"

"I'm glad you finally got around to thinking about God."

The remark stung. Did he think I hadn't prayed about this decision?

Leaning back in his chair, Steve fixed me in a stern-eyed gaze. "Diana, you could bring home an entire encyclopedia of information saying cloning is okay, and I'm afraid I wouldn't change my mind. I've been praying about this, and I have a clear sense that cloning is not for us." Dampness shone in his eyes as he rubbed his hand over his jaw. "Maybe it is okay for some people, I don't know. But I don't think it's God's will for us. It won't bring Scotty back and it won't ease our pain."

His voice fell to a whisper. "Our son is with God, Diana, he's not waiting in some test tube or petri dish. I don't think cloning will honor the Lord."

For the first time in my life, I could not find words to fit my emotions. My usually reserved husband had exerted his authority without apology . . . but I didn't like his decision. He was wrong, I *knew* he was wrong, but I didn't know how to convince him he was making the biggest mistake of his life.

"Steve." I reached out and brushed his hand with my fingertips. "I know what you're feeling. You're still grieving for Scott Daniel—so am I. You think you need more time. Well, you'll have the time you need because the cloning process won't happen overnight. It'll take months, probably more than a year. And while we're waiting you'll move past the pain and soon you'll be ready to move forward and embrace the idea of a new child. But you can't give me an emphatic denial now. We'll need to put some things in motion as soon as possible, and these things can't wait. Besides"—I forced a laugh—"we're not getting any younger. So if we're going to be parents again—"

"You talk as if we're not parents at all." Raw hurt gleamed in his eyes. "Diana, we still have two children—Scotty in heaven, and Brittany right here."

Beneath the table, I clenched my fist, desperate for him to understand. "I haven't forgotten anything, and I've been praying, too. And I really believe this is God's will for us—"

"God's will?" His voice cracked. "How can you know cloning is God's will?"

"Easy. We know God sent Scott Daniel to us, right? And we know God wants us to raise our children in the nurture and admonition of the Lord. But we didn't get to raise Scott Daniel; the accident took that opportunity from us. Cloning will turn back the clock, and out of all the people in this country, God sent *us* the opportunity to restore our son—"

"Have you lost your mind? No one can turn back the clock."

"Now we can."

"No! God wills that we live this life as it comes, that we remember our time on earth is only temporary—"

"It's not that temporary!" I was shouting now, but I didn't care if Britt overheard. "You can't tell me it was God's will for a five-year-old miracle to be snatched from our hands before we even had a chance to walk him to first grade! The loving God who gave Scott to me wouldn't take him like that! You can never, ever convince me otherwise!"

"You think you know God's mind?" Steve laughed, the sound hoarse and bitter in my cozy kitchen. "You spend all day on the radio talking to people as if you *are* God, and you only point them to him when you can't think of anything else to say. You're what people call a 'worldly Christian,' someone who gives godly advice only when your own self-reliance, common sense, and intuition have failed."

Helpless to halt my rising anger, I scraped my hand through my hair. "What are you talking about? I do more good for people on the radio than you do in that stuffy dentist's office!"

He flushed, his features contorting with shock and anger. "I do what God called me to do." His words were sharp, as pointed as an ice pick. "And I thought you were doing what you felt called to do. But if you think you're being called to pursue this cloning thing, you're not hearing God. I don't know who you're hearing, but it's not God."

"Who are you to say what I'm hearing?" I gripped the edge of the counter, my temper rising beyond my limits of control. "Where is it written that God speaks to only the man?"

"A husband is supposed to be the spiritual leader in his home."

"Then stop wallowing in your grief and start leading! You're not doing anything, Steve—you sit in your easy chair every night and cry for half an hour, as if that would help anything. At least I'm trying to do something constructive."

"You call cloning constructive? You will destroy our privacy and expose all of us, even Brittany, to the glare of international publicity. With this cockeyed scheme you will attract more wackos and vigilantes than that stupid show of yours could draw in a hundred years—"

"While you're doing nothing! *Do* something, Steve. Help me put this family back together!"

My words hung in the silence, vibrating in the space between us. For a moment Steve gaped at me, his eyes blazing with amber fire, then he slowly placed his hands on the table, palms down.

We had both said more than we should have. We had both ventured beyond the boundaries of safe discussion into the territory of personal insult. And we both knew it.

But neither of us felt like apologizing.

"I am grieving for my only son." Steve stared at the tips of his fingers as if he'd never seen them before. "I loved him. And Scotty deserves to be missed."

"I loved him, too. And I know he deserves another chance at life." The words slipped out before I could stop them, and while I knew they weren't technically accurate, they expressed the yearning of my heart.

Steve looked at me, accusation mingling with anger in his eyes.

Slowly I stood and placed my trembling hand on my husband's shoulder. "Steve, please try to understand. I haven't forgotten God in all this. I believe he sent Scott Daniel to us as a miracle, and I believe he had nothing whatsoever to do with that terrible accident. God didn't kill our son. And now he's given us a chance to—"

"God may not have killed our son"—Steve lifted his head—"but he certainly allowed the accident. And with all my heart I believe he took Scotty's soul to heaven."

I lifted my hand, unable to remain in physical contact with a man who would offer such a simplistic defense. "Then tell me *why*." I sank back to my stool, facing my husband. "Why did God take our son when it would have been no big deal to have Scott avoid that car? Or suffer a broken arm instead of a broken neck?"

Steve shook his head. "I don't know."

"But I want answers!"

"Sometimes we can't find the answers this side of heaven."

Frustrated beyond words, I slid off the seat and backed away. "I want answers, I *need* them! If God isn't going to provide any, I'm going to find them on my own!"

When an audible gasp broke the heavy silence, I looked up to see Brittany standing in the kitchen doorway, her hand wrapped around the doorframe as if for support. White-faced and teary-eyed, she stared at us a moment, then pivoted on the ball of her foot and strode toward the stairs.

"Now look what you've done." Rebuke saturated Steve's voice. "As if she didn't have enough on her mind."

"Britt? What terrible things are on her mind? School and zits are not the most pressing problems in the world, you know."

"You, *Counselor*"—he spat the word—"should know how traumatic it is for children to hear their parents arguing. As far as I know, this is the first time she's found us like this."

I drew a long, quivering breath, mastering the fury boiling within me. "Most kids deal with more than this every day. Brittany has been sheltered her entire life; maybe it's time she caught a glimpse of the real world. Kids need to know their parents sometimes argue."

"But she's hurting! She lost a brother."

"We lost a *son*. And we'll lose another one if you don't support me in this."

Steve's eyes went hot with resentment, and I knew I'd lost the battle. Despite my assurances, proofs, and pleas, he would not help me bring another child into this family.

I looked at him, biting my lip until it throbbed like my pulse, then slowly shook my head. I'd explained the situation as best I could, but my words were powerless against Steve's stubborn will. If God was going to restore our son, he was going to have to either change Steve or show me some way around him.

Abandoning my husband in the silence of the kitchen, I turned and retreated to my study.

Thirty

"YOU OKAY, BRITT? YOU SOUND FUNNY."

Brittany sniffed, then dabbed at the end of her nose with a tissue. "I'm fine. Just having an allergy attack."

"Oh." Charisse fell silent. "So . . . you want to do something tonight, or are you still grounded?"

Brittany hiccuped, a lingering result of her sobbing. "I'm still grounded."

Charisse sighed. "Bummer. But hey—I heard that. Are you drunk?"

"I wish." Brittany threw the wadded tissue in her palm to the floor. "I'd give anything to get wasted and forget about this place."

"So—wanna sneak out later?"

Biting her lip, Brittany considered the idea, then decided against it. With her parents squalling and squabbling, either one of them might be roaming the house in the wee hours of the morning. She'd get caught for sure.

"Can't. I'm not feeling good, either."

"Too bad." Charisse strummed the guitar. "Well . . . since there's nothing else to do, you wanna hear my new song?"

"Sure." Brittany lowered her head to the pillow, then positioned the phone on her ear. "Play away. I'm listening."

As Charisse strummed and sang a new song that made no sense at all, Brittany closed her eyes against the hot geyser that pushed at the backs of her eyelids. She brought her fist to her mouth in an effort to stop any sound that might rise from her throat, because if Charisse heard her crying, she'd ask what was wrong.

And Brittany couldn't say.

All she knew was that nothing in her life was right. Everything in her world—her house, her schoolwork, her car, her makeup, her clothes, her shoes, her weight, her hair, even the dozens of nail polish bottles lined up on her dresser—absolutely nothing about any of it was good. Zack Johnson had been avoiding her in the halls, and who wouldn't? Nobody wanted to be around anyone who oozed *loser* from every pore.

She'd been a loser from the beginning. Her birth mother hadn't wanted her, so she'd dumped Brittany at Social Services. Mom and Dad had been good for taking her in when nobody else wanted her, but then Scotty came along, and their hearts filled with love for their *own* kid . . .

While Charisse sang, Brittany bit her fist and struggled against the tears she refused to let fall.

The shadows beneath the palms and hibiscus were already deep and dark when Steve stepped out onto the front porch. Thrusting his hands in his pockets, he walked down the steps toward the sidewalk, taking comfort in the soft scuffing sounds of his shoes on the concrete. Such an ordinary sound on an ordinary night, coming from an ordinary American home.

Except nothing in his house was ordinary anymore.

A tear trickled down his cheek. He swiped it away, angry at his own weakness. How could one loss disrupt a family so? He knew some marriages splintered over the deaths of children, but he had always assumed his marriage could survive anything. After all, he and Diana were Christians, reasonable people, and financially stable. They had a lovely daughter who was successfully growing into young womanhood, and they'd had a darling son who charmed a smile out of everyone he met. They maintained successful careers, as many friends as time would allow, and a comfortable home in a tidy, gated neighborhood.

How could their lives fall apart in a single instant?

He strolled down the sidewalk, passing his neighbor's house where a TV blared through a cracked downstairs window and music drifted from their thirteen-year-old girl's upstairs bedroom. The Hudsons were nice people—Janice was a dedicated schoolteacher, and Robert a pharmacist down at the local Albertson's. With their three teenage girls, they attended Mass once a week and seemed to weather every storm life sent their way. But as far as Steve knew, life hadn't sent them many storms. Their daughters were good students, athletic, and pretty. Probably the most serious problem the Hudsons had to face all year was the damage they'd discovered at the corner of their front porch.

Subterranean termites, Bob had confided to Steve, his eyes somber. Trouble with a capital *T.*

Steve quickened his pace, moving into the circle of light provided by the streetlight in front of the next house. He didn't know the Emersons, but according to the grapevine the quiet, elderly couple wanted nothing more than to enjoy their retirement years and occasionally entertain their grandchildren. A single light burned in an uncurtained window downstairs, and through the panes Steve could see a sedate living room with traditional furniture and groupings of smiling family portraits on the walls.

He averted his eyes, not wanting to invade his neighbors' privacy. They hadn't invaded his, even immediately after the accident. This modern neighborhood was tidy and circumspect; each resident minded his own affairs and pretended not to notice when the sounds of raw, real life seeped past the boundaries of the carefully clipped lawns. Once a year, on the first Saturday in July, they met in the street for a neighborhood block party—skateboarding kids at one end, moms in the middle, dads with barbecue grills and beers at the business end. They talked, they laughed, they engaged in polite games of one-upmanship.

You got a raise? How nice. I made partner.

You bought a Lexus? Nice car. I went with the BMW.

Steve grimaced as he considered this year's convocation. This summer he could top them all: *You had a baby? Good for you. We're carrying America's first clone.*

Staring down at the sidewalk, he snorted softly. His neighbors had no idea what had been happening in his house. Through the last few difficult weeks, he and Diana had continued to smile and go to work, toiling in the traces of their daily lives as if nothing had happened . . . when in fact their world had turned upside down.

From an open window he heard the sudden sounds of barking. From within the shadows of anonymity, a man yelled, "Sadie! Shut up!"

Steve increased his pace, not wanting to upset the animal further. In another month, maybe two, none of these windows would be open, for Florida's muggy heat would lie upon them like a blanket even at this first hour of dark.

How could Diana presume to know what God had in mind for their family? He was supposed to be the head of the house, and thus far he'd had nothing but unsettling feelings when she mentioned cloning and the idea of another baby. In his youth it was hip to call these feelings *bad vibes,* and the expression still fit. A creeping unease slithered at the base of his gut whenever he thought about the Raelians, and the entire Project One setup felt a little too sci-fi for his comfort. Diana might well be right about the promises they'd made to her, but how would she know if those scientists decided to tinker with the DNA they transferred? And how could she guarantee they wouldn't create a half-dozen embryos and freeze several for future experimentation? Their labs were located in France because the United States wouldn't allow this sort of organization to operate within its borders. Though Steve didn't always trust the government, he had to respect the men and women who had studied the situation and declared cloning a bad thing. If they'd seen enough danger to prohibit the practice, their conviction was good enough for him.

Still . . .

He loved his wife, and struggled to understand her point of view. She had lost the only baby she had carried within her womb, and he grieved with her for that loss. But she needed to understand his feelings, too. He had lost the boy into which he had deposited all his father-son dreams. Diana and Brittany shared that unique mother-daughter thing where one day they were best friends and the next they were hissing at each other, but he and Scott had experienced a father-son bond the girls would never understand. Though Scotty was still young, already the two of them had ventured deep into male bonding. He had taught Scott how to bait a hook. They had begun to play ball together, and Scotty had even begun to ask questions about the day when he would become a daddy . . .

The memory brought a twisted smile to Steve's face.

"Will I ever have a little boy?" Scotty had asked one day as they fished on the bank of Walsingham Lake.

"Sure you will, son."

"But where will he sleep?"

"I'm sure he'll have his own room, just like you do."

Scott's little face squinched into a knot. "But where will Brittany and Mommy sleep?"

Steve had patiently tried to explain that they would not always live together because one day Scotty would leave home to go live somewhere else—

As he had . . . sooner than anyone expected.

Another squadron of tears ran down Steve's face, silent, steady sentinels of the grief that still overflowed his heart. He had learned not to resist them. They sprang up whenever summoned by memory or thought, they flowed until the reservoir had emptied. In time, perhaps, the bitter springs would not flow as freely, but Steve doubted they would ever disappear completely.

Amazing, that a mature Christian could feel such pain. He had been taught by godly parents, he knew the Scripture, he knew Scotty was with Jesus. With all his heart he believed the Lord would comfort, heal, and carry every daily burden. With all that knowledge he had hoped to alleviate the agony of death, but the pain would not be denied. When Paul wrote, "O death, where is thy sting?" he must have been writing with an eternal perspective in mind. Here, on earth, death still stung like an adder.

Scotty had been a tender tree planted in the fertile ground of Steve's affection, and death had ripped the young tree out by its roots. Despite his certain faith, Steve would never think of heaven without feeling the ache of the empty hole in his heart.

Sighing, he wiped his cheeks with his shirt cuffs and pressed into the darkness, circling the block. Diana knew the Scriptures, too. As a professional counselor, she knew about grief and its effects on those who mourn. But that knowledge had not helped her after the accident. She insisted on handling the situation like a clinician, pressing toward cloning while denying the clawing pain ripping her soul apart.

"Doctor," he murmured, slipping his hands into his pockets as he looked up at the star-spangled night, "heal thyself."

What had happened to his wife? In the beginning she had mourned as he had, but while he continued to weep, she had girded herself in determination. The only tears she had shed lately were tears of frustration brought on by another of their arguments.

She no longer slept in Scotty's room, no longer clung to the boy's stuffed monkey. For a few days Steve had actually felt jealous of her quick recovery, but now he wondered if she was healing at all.

Then again, what did he know? He knew how to treat teeth, not hearts.

Diana had always been quicker to respond than he. In basic temperament, they were opposites—Diana was an introvert, but when she turned on the charm she could be bright, persuasive, and delightfully domineering. In household matters he usually deferred to her because she always researched their options and made sound recommendations.

This time, however, grief had wrecked her reasoning and skewed her thoughts. She might have law and logic in her corner, but he had an unswerving conviction that cloning was wrong. Scotty could not be replaced, and God had brought them to this dark place for a purpose. Whether or not they discovered that purpose . . . well, it didn't matter. Some answers could only be found behind heaven's door.

So . . . his family had come to a rough place, and his job was to steer them safely through it. But to please Diana, he would either have to capitulate and approve her plan to bear a clone or suffer the consequences of denying her. Those consequences would not be pleasant. He had never seen such determination in her eyes.

He hesitated beneath the sheltering arms of a huge live oak on the corner, a thick old tree that had barely escaped a neighborhood association vote to cut it down. Yes, it did obscure the streetlight, and yes, it did shed several pounds of leaves in the spring. But the regal tree had probably outlasted more hurricanes, tropical storms, and winter freezes than any soul in the neighborhood.

If only he had half the strength of that tree.

He lifted his eyes to the spangled sky serving as a backdrop to the gently swaying branches. "Do I give in to her, Lord? Or do I hold my ground?"

He heard no answer in the darkness, no divine message through the whispering branches. But an inexplicable peace settled about his heart, and, clinging to it, he turned and began to walk back home.

Thirty-one

ON MONDAY MORNING, I DRESSED AND HEADED OUT early for the office, grateful beyond words for a job that offered distraction and distance from my recalcitrant husband. At eight minutes past nine, the intro to my show began. Perched on my swiveling chair, I adjusted the headphones to a more comfortable position, then checked my notes for the monologue. I usually began each hour with a brief intro about family life or life in general—something to warm up the audience and give callers time to get to the phone. As my producer, Gary, willingly played Ed McMahon to my Johnny Carson.

As the intro died out, I leaned into the mike. "Good day to you, guy friends and gal pals across the fruited plain! Dr. Diana Sheldon here, bringing you words of wisdom from the home front, the house front, and the business front, wherever you happen to be."

I tapped my pencil on the desk. "I was thinking about something on the drive to the studio today—sort of mentally planning my day, you know, and thinking about what I'd have to do when I left work this afternoon. Then my mind flipped back to the days when my children were small. I don't know about you, but when my kids were babies I prided myself on motherly conscientiousness. No ready-made baby food for my offspring, no sir! Instead I bought fresh vegetables, cooked them, puréed them in the food processor, then I froze those smashed foods in ice cube trays."

Behind the window, Gary grinned and leaned into his mike. "What's an ice cube tray?"

I groaned. "Heaven help us, I keep forgetting my producer is on the young side of thirty. An ice cube tray, my naive ignoramus, is one of those plastic things with dividers. You fill them with water and place them in the freezer, and in an hour or two you have frozen ice cubes."

"Some of them were metal," Chad added helpfully. "My parents had metal ones in their icebox."

"Spoken like a true antique aficionado." I placed one hand on the mike to whisper into it. "Help me, friends. I am surrounded by American youths. The studio next door is filled with youngsters, and you should see the hallway . . . but I digress."

Grinning, I leaned back and resumed my normal banter. "As I was saying, I was so proud of feeding my children home-prepared foods with no additives, no preservatives, nothing but foods as natural as God made them." I thumped the desk for emphasis.

Gary recognized his cue. "And then?"

"Then my kids grew up. And they began to eat fast-food French fries, hamburgers, and fried chicken fingers. My son thought pizza was one of the major food groups. When my daughter decides it's time to get married, she'll probably choose Styrofoam as her china pattern.

"But the worst of it is what this relaxed attitude about food has done to me. Saturday I was in the kitchen, thinking I would do something dramatic like actually boil a couple of eggs for egg salad. I thought it was about time I made an honest-to-goodness home-cooked meal for my family, so I decided to whip up some egg salad. I was pretty sure I could find some bread smashed up behind something in the freezer."

Chad pressed the sound effect button. In unison, a chorus of awed voices whispered, "Wow."

I laughed. "You *should* be impressed. Anyway, I found a couple of eggs in the fridge, dug out and dusted off a saucepan from the cabinet, and put the eggs on to boil." I paused dramatically. "Then I approached the most daunting step of the adventure."

From the control room Gary quipped, "Was one of the eggs, um, occupied?"

I groaned. "Ugh. Nothing so gross. No, I opened the fridge and launched a search-and-rescue mission among the many bottles stuffed inside those plastic compartments built into the door. Finally, success! I discovered a jar of mayonnaise with about half an inch of mayo at the bottom."

"So?" Gary asked. "What was the problem?"

"Well, this is April, right? So I thought I should check the expiration date, because everyone knows mayo can go bad and breed salmonella. So I turned the jar sideways and upside down until I found the date in tiny little letters: July 13."

"So you were good to go, right?"

"Not hardly. The date was July 13, 1998!"

I pointed at Chad, who punched the next button and sent a funky riff out over the airwaves while a prerecorded announcer reminded listeners of our toll-free number: 1-888-555-HELP.

I didn't even have to resume my patter before the phone lines lit up. Relieved, I glanced up at the computer screen, then punched the line for the first caller. "Hello, and welcome to the *Dr. Sheldon Show!*"

"Dr. Diana?"

"Good day, Charity."

"How'd you know it was me?"

I laughed. "I see all, my friend. I'm assuming you have a snippet of wisdom to share with us today?"

"Oh, yes. Friday I heard that one woman moaning about her husband's weight."

"And you can shed some light on the subject?"

"Yes, indeed. Are you ready?"

"Lay it on me."

Charity cleared her throat, and, on cue, Chad pressed a button launching the sound effect of a drum roll.

"Overweight," Charity said, "doesn't happen overnight. It snacks up on you."

Ch-ching went the sound machine.

I groaned. "Very punny, Charity."

"I know. Wasn't it cute?"

"Uh-huh. Got anything else for us?"

"Not today. But maybe I'll call again tomorrow."

"I'll look forward to it." I clicked to the next caller, a man named Bill from New York. "Good morning, you're on the *Dr. Sheldon Show.*"

"Dr. Sheldon! Let me first say that I love your program and agree with you 98 percent of the time."

Uh-oh. That remaining 2 percent was going to give me trouble. I worked a smile into my voice. "Thank you, Bill. Did you have a question?"

"Why, yes—at least, I think it's a question, maybe I just want to pick a bone with you."

Automatically, my hand went toward the phone. If Bill from New York felt compelled to talk about Scott Daniel—

"The other day I heard you say you were a Christian."

My hand relaxed. "Yes, I am."

"Well, don't you find your beliefs to be discriminatory? To my knowledge, Christianity is the only organized religion that says only its adherents are going to make it to the next life. Most other religions see God as the person at the hub of a wheel, and just as there are many spokes in a wheel, there are many ways to reach God."

I glanced at Gary, then exhaled noisily. "Boy, Bill, you like to start off the week with a bang, don't you?"

He chuckled. "Well, that's why they pay you the big bucks, Dr. Diana."

"Yeah, right." I laughed along with him. "First, let me take exception to your claim that Christianity is the only religion that limits entrance to heaven. I think you'll find that most cults are quite specific in their beliefs that *they* are the chosen ones. They keep people in their group through fear and intimidation."

"Well, I wasn't sure about that. But you've got to admit, Christianity is pretty specific. I grew up in a hellfire and brimstone kind of church, and I've heard all those speeches about 'narrow is the path and few there be that find it.'"

"I'm glad you were listening. Yes, the path is narrow, but heaven is not some sparsely populated country club. It's going to be filled with people. Sociologists tell us that as many as 70 percent of all humans ever born never live to celebrate their eighth birthday"—I felt the old knot rise in my chest, but kept going—"and Scripture indicates that children go to heaven when they die. If you add to that figure the millions of babies murdered by abortion every year, and then add those who profess Christ—let's say that's 10 percent of the forty billion or so people who have ever lived on earth—the grand population of heaven is going to be more than thirty billion. That's nearly three-fourths of all human beings ever created."

"Yeah, but—"

"No buts about it, Bill. Doesn't it make sense? I mean, why would God, who knows the future, create the human race if he planned to send the vast majority of us to hell? I don't believe he would."

"Yeah, but you're set in your ways. And you can't say that other religions are worthless. Anyone who teaches peace and love and tolerance is doing good for humankind—"

"Forget your hub-and-the-wheel analogy, Bill, and let me tell you a more appropriate story. There was once a king who had three sons. He also had one ring of pure gold. Concerned about rivalry among his sons after his death, he had two rings fashioned from false gold and upon his deathbed he ordered his wise men to give the three rings to his sons. Calling his sons near, he told them the truth: one ring was real, two were false, but the person with the pure ring would always be kind, good, and blessed of God. So, Bill, what do you think happened next?"

"For the love of heaven, how am I supposed to know? You're spinning some silly story while I'm trying to—"

"Of course, Bill, thanks for playing. All three sons strove to be kind and good because each of them wanted the people to believe he had been blessed with the real ring."

"See? See?" Bill was practically beside himself, shrieking into the phone. "I'm *right*. All religions have value if they teach people to live peacefully with one another."

"Anyone who practices good will be regarded as good by those who can't see the secrets of the human heart," I answered. "But all the good in the world won't change the truth—only one son had the real ring. The other two were living a lie. Think about it."

I pressed the next button, sending us into commercial, then leaned back and stretched. Though it was only Monday, the morning felt more like Friday.

A glance in the mirror this morning revealed that fatigue had settled in pockets under my eyes. Steve and I had endured the weekend in an awkward state of truce, pretending politeness and burying our noses in newspapers or books whenever circumstances forced us to sit in the same room. Pleading a headache, I slipped out of church after the early worship service, leaving Steve to teach his Sunday school class alone.

I spent most of Sunday afternoon in my bed, surrounded by copies of the *St. Petersburg Times*, the *New York Times*, and the *Tampa Tribune*. Talk radio demanded a working knowledge of current events, and Steve left me alone to read most of the day, coming in at 11:00 P.M. to change, shower, and crawl under the covers on his side of the bed.

At least Brittany seemed immune. She'd asked for and received permission to spend most of the weekend at Charisse's house.

Chad's voice buzzed in my headphones. "How's the level in there?"

"Good, Chad. Everything's great."

"Got a couple of local calls on the line," Gary said, making small talk while my prerecorded voice extolled the virtues of all-natural bee pollen supplements. "Their topics will play in Peoria, though."

"That's fine."

I rocked in my chair, waiting for the commercial to run out, then idly tapped my fingers on the desk during the ten-second lead-in. I was anxious to finish the show and get out of the studio, for this afternoon I planned to visit the bank. I needed to mail a cashier's check for fifteen thousand dollars to Project One in New York.

As the intro died away, I clicked on the phone and greeted my next caller. "Cynthia? Welcome to the show."

"Dr. Diana?"

"That's me."

"I'm having a terrible problem with my husband. I know you believe in marriage at all costs—"

I cut her off before she could put more words in my mouth. "Wait a minute, dear. Marriage at all costs? I don't think I've ever said that. Doesn't even sound like my lingo."

"Well . . . I mean, you believe in marriage."

"Yes, I do. But first tell me about the problem with your husband."

"Well—we just aren't getting along these days. We fight all the time, and I've been asking myself whether it's better for my kids to live in a quiet house with one parent or a stressful house with two."

"Let me ask you this—did you come from a divorced family?"

The caller hesitated. "Yeah."

"And do you have a career?"

"I'm a nurse."

"Okay. How many children, and how old?"

"Two boys—they're five and three."

I let out a low whistle. "So tell me why you'd be willing to contribute to the divorce rate in order to stop squabbling with your spouse?"

"Well . . . isn't it true that children are happier when their parents are happy? And divorce happens half the time, I hear. I don't think my kids would be hurt if we split up."

"That 50 percent divorce rate statistic is a lie, Cynthia. Think about it. They tell us in any given year two million marriages and one million divorces are recorded, so people assume half the people who get married also get divorced. But that's not comparing the *total* number of existing marriages to the *total* number of divorces. When you look at it in the proper perspective, the divorce rate is about 13 percent."

"So? It still seems like everyone I know has been divorced at least once."

"You need to widen your circle of friends, dear. And have you considered what divorce is doing to our nation's kids? We are sowing troubles we'll reap in later years and future generations. Psychologists tell us three out of five children of divorce feel rejected by at least one parent. Five years after their parents' divorce, more than one-third of divorced children perform markedly worse in school than before the divorce. And half still suffer from the slings and arrows of parents who fight as much *after* the split as before! So don't tell me you want to divorce your husband for the sake of your children. I don't buy it."

When I heard nothing but silence from the other end of the phone, I wondered if I had misread the situation.

"I would never"—I lowered my voice—"tell a woman to remain in a marriage if she is being abused or threatened, or if her children are in danger. If that is your situation, my advice would be to take your kids and get out. But if you and your husband just can't get along, for the love of Pete, solve your petty problems and learn how to cooperate! Marriage is a partnership. Every day one of you is going to have to surrender to the other, and in successful marriages, partners take turns being flexible."

"I guess," Cynthia said, "but it seems like I'm always the one giving in."

"Then you tell your husband it's time for a change. If he loves you—if he's committed to your marriage—he'll listen. Love isn't lording your will over someone, it's learning how to bend when the winds blow. Choose your battles carefully, Cynthia; don't force your hand on unimportant issues. But when something really matters, stand your ground and state your reasons for feeling as you do. And perhaps your confidence can sway your husband to see things from your viewpoint."

I paused, giving her a chance to respond, but apparently Cynthia had nothing to add.

"So, listeners—get with the program so many of our grandparents followed. Think of marriage as a lifelong journey, not a short-term fling. For the sake of our children, let's show a little character and make things work."

I pointed to Chad, who let the next commercial roll, then propped my chin on my hand and studied the list of callers in the queue. A woman named Doris wanted to talk about her husband's annoying postretirement habits, a homeschooled child had a question about her mother's discipline, a man named Stephen was having a problem with his wife. Americans had nothing but problems, and over the course of my career, I'd heard about everything. Each day in the studio was different, but few days held any surprises.

Thinking it might be interesting to hear the male side of a marital disagreement after Cynthia's call, I waited until the commercial played out, then leaned into the mike.

"Hello, Stephen, welcome to the *Dr. Sheldon Show*."

"Good day, Dr. Diana."

I froze as my husband's voice reverberated through the studio.

For an agonizing moment my mind went blank. Score one for Steve—he'd managed to surprise me. I stared at the computer screen, not daring to look at Gary lest he see the panic on my face, then forced out my usual reply. "Go ahead."

"I'm calling about something that's happened in my family. Nearly a month ago, we lost our young son in a tragic accident."

"I'm sorry." The words felt stiff and heavy on my tongue.

"Thank you. My wife and I grieved together for a while, but now she seems intent on chasing a ghost. She will not let our son go."

Closing my eyes, I wavered between reason and emotion. The professional, rational side of me knew the proper response, but my emotional side recognized the trap my husband had set. He wanted me to say something like "She needs to move on" or "No one can live in the past," but those instructions didn't apply in our situation. We didn't *have* to move on; we had another choice—but I knew he wouldn't mention the word *clone* on national radio.

"I'm very sorry for your loss," I said, shifting into semiautomatic mode, "but your wife will handle things in her own way. Give her time—she might surprise you."

Before Steve could say anything else, I hit the next button. Chad's head jerked up as one of our prerecorded comedy bits began to play, and Gary shot a puzzled look through the glass.

"Listen," I whispered into the phone, knowing we were off the air. "I don't know what you think you're doing—"

Steve interrupted in a calm voice. "I'm trying to help you see reason. Maybe if you look at yourself from another perspective—"

"Get off the phone and don't ever call here again."

I punched the disconnect button, then dropped the receiver into the cradle. While my prerecorded voice laughed and whooped it up on the airwaves, I held my head in both hands and tried to gain control of my seething emotions.

Gary and Chad probably thought I was sick and needed a break—and they wouldn't be far off the mark. The encounter with my husband had left me feeling queasy.

The guys didn't know the truth. And I wasn't about to tell them.

I was still boiling from Steve's little telephone stunt when he came home at six o'clock. I sat in the study, my nerves stretched tighter than a bowstring, and waited for him to pause in the doorway and say something.

I wasn't prepared for the sound of a second male voice.

"Come on in, Pastor," Steve said, his tone unusually bright for this hour of the day. "Have a seat in the living room, and I'll get us something to drink. Diet Coke okay with you?"

"That's fine, Steve, thanks."

I cringed as I recognized the voice of John Thompson, our pastor. For a moment I searched my memory, wondering if I'd forgotten about a dinner appointment, but found nothing. Which meant Steve had invited the pastor to our home for some sort of ambush.

That realization fanned the anger that had been boiling beneath my skin. Spontaneous human combustion suddenly seemed possible.

I heard them move from the foyer into the hallway, then their voices echoed in the kitchen amid the chink of ice cubes and glasses. Steve would probably settle the pastor into a comfortable chair, place a soft drink in his hand, then come to fetch me.

I glanced toward the door. My purse lay on the table, so I could grab my keys and run out the door, later claiming I had to make an emergency run to the grocery . . .

"Diana." Steve leaned against the doorframe and peered in at me. "Do you have a few minutes? I've invited Pastor John—"

"I heard." The laserlike glare I shot at him could have sliced through steel. "What is this, a sneak attack?"

Steve took a half step back, his face a mask of pleasant blandness. "It's nothing of the kind. I wanted to talk to John, so I invited him to the house. You're welcome to join us, but only if you want to. I understand if you have work to do."

I narrowed my eyes. Steve was not usually the conniving sort, but this charade wouldn't have fooled even an innocent like Scott Daniel.

"I have a lot of work." I gestured toward the printed wire reports scattered over my desk. "But if I get caught up with my reading, maybe I'll come in."

"That'd be nice." Without another word Steve left me, and a moment later I heard him rummaging around in the kitchen, probably searching for some snack that would hold the men until dinner.

I stared at the computer screen, then gave my reflection a lopsided smile. My husband was not a subtle man; obviously he'd called in reinforcements. Apparently he thought the Reverend John Thompson could attack my stance on cloning, but I doubted our minister was up to the challenge. Trouble was, neither of them would realize the futility of their position if I retreated from the battlefield.

With quiet assurance I stepped out of the study and joined the men in the kitchen. Steve had done his best to provide refreshments for his guest, setting a plate of battered Oreos in the center of the kitchen island.

Pretty pitiful battle rations for a mercenary.

"Give me a minute, guys." Breezing past Steve, I opened the cupboards and found fresh chips and a jar of salsa, then arranged my offering on our best snack tray. After setting it on the counter and making certain each man had a full glass of soda, I took a seat at the bar across from the pastor.

I gave him my brightest smile. "John, I know you didn't stop by just to chat about Steve's Sunday school class. So why don't you tell me why you're here?"

Fire the first shot, if you dare.

The pastor looked at me, a betraying flush brightening his face. "Well, yes, Diana, Steve asked me to stop by to talk to you about this matter of cloning. He thought I might be able to shed some light on the subject."

I cocked a brow in his direction. "Have you light to shed?"

A cheap shot, maybe, but if he was unprepared, he deserved it.

"Well"—he glanced around; I had the feeling he was looking for notes—"I believe it's intrinsically wrong, and that's the most important thing. People who say these little cloned embryos are not human are mistaken. If allowed to grow, those cells will develop into a human baby just like those cloned sheep cells grew into a lamb—"

"But the cells are not always allowed to grow, John. Some of them are halted before the egg divides past the six-cell stage. It's not an embryo yet, no organs, nothing but elementary stem cells."

"It's human, isn't it?"

"Yes, if you mean that it has forty-six chromosomes like every other human cell. But the cells of your thumb have forty-six chromosomes, too, and while they're human, they're not a person."

He frowned. "We shouldn't be playing God with this kind of thing."

"An old argument, John, and not effective. Are we playing God when we shock someone's heart back to life? When we do a heart transplant? God does hold the power of life and death, but sometimes he allows men to wield that power, too. Would you outlaw defibrillators because they can literally bring people back from the dead?"

John glanced at Steve, then spread his hands. "I can't argue science with you, Diana. You know more than I do about the technology. So let me ask you—why do you feel you have to clone your son? You know the process won't bring Scotty back."

I stiffened, a little surprised by the feint and counterattack from another direction. "I know cloning won't bring Scott Daniel back, but it will right a wrong. I honestly believe God never meant for our son to die that day. So maybe he is allowing us to explore the miracle of cloning so we can have another chance with a genetic twin."

Lines of concentration deepened under John's eyes. "God is sovereign, Diana. He doesn't make mistakes. Scott Daniel died, so you have to accept that God took him home."

Swallowing hard, I lifted my chin. "God didn't take Scott Daniel from us. He wouldn't do that."

"God ordains everything that happens in the lives of his children." John spoke in a soft and careful voice. "If you are a Christian, everything that happens to you is filtered through his perfect will."

I shook my head. "He may not have stopped Scott's death, but I'll never believe he actually *permitted* it. Why would he? It makes no sense."

Drawing a deep breath, John pressed his hands to his knees. "Your daughter Brittany drives a red pickup, right?"

Steve nodded. "That's her."

John smiled and looked at me. "Okay. Suppose, Diana, Brittany came to you and asked permission to take Scotty to the candy store. She knows she can't take him without your approval. You grant that permission, so even though she's driving, the trip is happening according to your will. If you hadn't agreed, Brittany would not have the authority to take your son. The ultimate decision was yours."

I nailed him with my sharpest glare. "Are you saying Satan took my son with God's permission?"

The pastor's eyes clouded with hazy sadness as he lifted his hands. "I don't know, I don't know if we *can* know these things. But this I do know—Scripture tells us that the Lord does not abandon anyone forever. Though he brings grief, he also shows compassion according to the greatness of his unfailing love. For he does not enjoy hurting people or causing them sorrow."

"He hurts people?" I had steeled my heart in defense, but those words slipped away from me like the mewling of a kitten caught in a crossfire. Hastily, I reinforced my defenses. "I serve a God of *love*. He doesn't do evil things."

"God is not the author of evil, but neither is he its victim. He takes the evil that happens to us, even the evil we bring on ourselves, and uses it for his highest good."

I lifted a finger. "That's why I think good can come from cloning. If Scott Daniel had not died, we would never have considered it. God will bring good out of it, but I can't believe he did this to us on purpose."

The pastor closed his eyes and opened his mouth—a clear signal that my volley had utterly missed the mark.

"If you believe God merely allowed this tragedy to happen," he said, speaking as slowly as he would to a child, "then you must also believe he was either unable or unwilling to intervene. If he was unable, then he is not greater than evil, and therefore not an all-powerful God. If he was unwilling, then he behaved far more callously than any father I can imagine."

Lost in confusion, I stared at him. He was painting pictures of a God I didn't recognize, and I'd been a Christian most of my life.

"If, as you say, God took my son"—the words tasted sour in my mouth—"then *why* did he do it?"

The pastor smiled, but with a distracted, inward look, as though he had transferred his attention to a field of vision beyond my reach.

"I don't know why," he said simply, "but God does. And if you seek him, he may give you the wisdom you need to understand."

Aghast at the answer, I looked at Steve. My husband was staring at the floor, twin tracks of tears on his face.

"I do believe one thing," Pastor John said, standing. "When tragedies like this happen in our lives, God is far more interested in our reactions than our actions. So I would caution you to be careful, Diana and Steve. Don't run out and do things you might regret. Turn your thoughts inward and see if God might be trying to do something in your spiritual life. Spiritual things, after all, are eternal things. Nothing else really matters, does it?"

Stunned by an assault I hadn't counted on, I sat at the counter in silence as the pastor bent to pick up a cracked Oreo, nodded a farewell, then accompanied my husband out into the night.

That night I visited the hospital again. The dream came back with startling clarity, rushing into my consciousness the moment I began to drift in sleep.

I stepped out of Gary's car, felt the familiar scratch of my plaid skirt, saw Steve standing near the door.

"Diana," he called, looking as if he'd been waiting for me. "This way."

Overcome by an eerie sense of déjà vu, I didn't speak, but followed him through the doors, past the reception desk, and down the hall where the pregnant women in wheelchairs were still staring into space. I drew a deep breath as we paused at the elevator and took a moment to look around—the corridor to my right ended in a brick wall; to my left I saw the bustling waiting area and dozens of people who waited restlessly to see a physician.

The elevator chimed. This time I braced myself for the onslaught, stepping aside as the faceless, animated mannequins poured out of the elevator and scattered into the waiting room. Steve vanished again, but I didn't hesitate. I stepped into the elevator, pressed the only button, and soon found myself on the alabaster floor with the white-garbed nurses.

I didn't pause to ask for Scott Daniel's room, but turned immediately for the place I'd last seen him. Though I knew what to expect, a thrill shivered through my senses as I crossed the threshold and saw my son lying in the hospital bed. Steve and Brittany were there, still keeping a vigil, while Gary leaned against the back wall. Pastor John had left the room, as had the friends who'd been present on our previous visit, but they didn't matter.

Only Scott Daniel. I moved immediately to the bed and leaned over the metal railing, pressing my lips to his warm forehead.

He lived. My son still lived.

"He's alive." This time I spoke the words in a firm voice, to be heard above the mechanical clicks of the machinery around the bed.

As before, Steve dropped his hand upon my shoulder. "Yes, sweetheart, he is. But we're waiting to hear what the doctor will say."

I ran the back of my hand along Scott's round face. "Wake up, honey." Again I whispered our good morning refrain. "The sun's come up and so should we, snugglebugs though we may be."

He did not wake, but I thought I saw a slight flutter behind his eyelids.

I leaned closer to whisper directly in his ear. "Wake up, Scott Daniel. The sun's come up and so should we, snugglebugs though we may be."

No answer, but was that a flush on his cheek?

"I think his color's improving." I tossed the words over my shoulder to anyone who would listen, then paused. Brittany and Gary had left the room, leaving me alone with Steve.

Steve's voice, firm and final, fell upon my ear. "We have to wait for the doctor."

"Scotty?" I leaned far forward, gently drawing my son into my arms. Perhaps that was the problem. At home I used to crawl into bed with him, holding him close as I recited our little rhyme. "The sun's come up and so should we, snugglebugs though we may be—"

"Diana?" The resonant voice behind me was familiar, but I couldn't place it. A quick downward glance revealed dark shoes and pants topped by a white lab coat. The doctor, surely.

I returned my gaze to my son. "Don't you think he looks better, Doctor? I thought I saw a little movement a moment ago."

"He's gone, Diana." He spoke the words without malice, but they fell with the weight of stones in still water, spreading endless ripples of pain and betrayal.

"Noooooooooo." Biting back a sob, I traced a thread of gold in Scott Daniel's hair. "He's alive."

"His body is being kept alive through the science of machines, but his soul departed long ago. He is safe and happy, but he is not here."

Unable to speak, I shook my head. How could this idiot doctor say such things, when I held a living, breathing boy in my arms? Scott Daniel was here with me, the scar on his cheek was *healing*, for Pete's sake, and I would not let him slip away.

"Diana." The doctor's voice was closer this time, and gentler, almost as if he stood behind me whispering in my ear. "You have to let him go."

"I can't."

"You must. You can't live in this place."

"I can." The words felt like daggers ripping up my throat. "I will. I will stay here for as long as it takes my son to wake up; I'll sleep for the next two weeks if I have to—"

A hand squeezed my shoulder and I turned, ready to rail against the doctor who refused to see the life still burning in my son. But the room melted into blackness, and when I focused my eyes, I found myself lying in bed. A shadow-shrouded Steve leaned over me.

"You okay?" His voice sounded uneasy. "You were whimpering in your sleep."

Wearily, I lifted my head. By the dim glow of the bathroom night-light I saw the outline of our bed, the nightstand, the fringe on the window blind. Drab, dark reality.

"Sorry." I dropped my head back to the pillow. "Dreaming, I guess."

He grunted and turned away from me; a few moments later I heard him softly snoring.

When I was sure he slept, I buried my face in my pillow and released the hot tears of loss and fury that had begun to rise the moment he woke me.

Thirty-two

STEVE'S PASTORAL AMBUSH WAS NOT ENOUGH TO upset my campaign. Though that skirmish had momentarily bewildered me, one truth remained: the Bible had nothing to say about cloning. Since I still believed the Project One opportunity could be part of God's plan for us, I pressed on.

I had hand-delivered the letter with my fifteen-thousand-dollar cashier's check to the post office on April 21. Within a week I received a "to-do" list from Andrew at the New York Office of Project One.

First on the list: obtain Scott Daniel's tissue samples. On my most formal stationery I immediately fired off a letter to the Pinellas County medical examiner; a week later I shot off a second note.

Finally, on May 13, I received a response. Dr. Joseph Spago, the ME I had met on the day of Scott Daniel's death, replied with a form letter regretfully stating that he could not release the tissue samples for my use. To do so would violate policy.

Ten minutes after opening the envelope, I was on the phone. After navigating a bewildering voice-mail maze, I punched in Dr. Spago's extension, answered several annoying prerecorded queries, then finally found myself talking to the man I sought.

I reminded the doctor that we had met in March.

"Dr. Sheldon." Immediately his tone became solicitous. "Of course I remember meeting you. What can I do for you?"

"I'm holding a letter from you, Doctor, refusing to release a selection of my son's tissue samples."

From the way he awkwardly cleared his throat, I realized he hadn't recognized my name when he signed the letter.

"I'm sorry, Dr. Sheldon, but it's against our policy to release specimens. We have to keep specimens from all unnatural death cases in the event some sort of litigation arises. This is particularly important in accident cases like your son's."

"But you have several samples from my son's body. I'm only asking for one."

A second of silence followed, then, "May I ask why you want this?"

Rolling my eyes, I turned my chair to face the window. "I don't think that information is pertinent to my request. I am a parent, I want a tissue sample from my son's body—preferably one that has not been frozen."

"I'm truly sorry, Dr. Sheldon, but the answer has to be no. I would love to oblige you as a professional courtesy, but I answer to higher authorities."

I sighed. "All right, then. What would it take for me to obtain one of those samples?"

He exhaled into the phone. "I'm not positive, but since we are responsible to the courts, I suspect nothing less than a court order will suffice."

"Thank you, Doctor."

I disconnected the call, scribbled a few notes on a legal pad, then reached for the phone book. Steve and I had not met with our lawyer since revising our wills shortly after Scott Daniel's birth. This call would be a surprise.

Parker Oliphant, our family lawyer, seemed genuinely pleased to hear from me. "Diana Sheldon! Don't tell me someone has decided to sue you for radio malpractice."

"Nothing so tedious, I'm afraid." I leaned back in the chair and stared at the ceiling, mentally marshaling my facts. "I'm in the midst of an unusual situation and I could use your help. I'm thinking a strongly worded letter might do the trick."

I heard the creak of his chair. "What's the story?"

"It concerns my son, Scott Daniel." Against my will, a lump rose in my throat and threatened to strangle my words. "You may have heard about the accident a few weeks ago."

"I did and I'm very sorry. I sent a card; did you get it?"

"Yes, and thank you very much." In truth, I had no idea if I saw Parker's card—the kitchen table had been littered with stacks of cards and letters I hadn't had the courage or the heart to open. Steve's receptionist, Gerta Poppovitch, had acknowledged them for us.

"Parker, what I'm about to explain is controversial, so I'd appreciate it if you kept this quiet. I'm not sure of all the legal terms or procedures, but I need you to write a letter to convince a judge to release tissue samples held by the Pinellas County medical examiner's office."

The chair squeaked again. "There's no need to do that, Diana. If you're planning to sue the driver who struck Scott, the ME will automatically provide the data we need—"

"I'm not suing, Parker. The accident was . . . an accident."

A deep silence echoed over the phone, broken only by the scratching of a branch against my windowpane.

"I'm sorry, Diana, if I'm sounding a little dense—but why did you want this tissue sample?"

"It's for medical research, Parker—for the baby I plan to have next year. I don't want to go into details, but I desperately need one of those tissue samples. I'm asking you to do whatever you must to get it for me."

Silence rolled over the line, then he said, "You're talking about cloning."

"Yes."

Parker did not respond for a long moment, but I could hear the ghostly chatter of a keyboard as he made notes about the conversation. "Well," he finally said, "as the parent, you have more right than anyone to your own child's tissue. After all, after the autopsy the ME's office signed the body over to you, didn't they?"

"Yes. They said they needed to keep samples in case of possible litigation, but that's a moot point in our situation. Besides, I'm not asking for every tissue they have, just a representative sample."

The keyboard chattered again. "Steve's on board with this?"

I drew a deep breath, torn between truth and a careful dodging of the question. "Well . . . not exactly. Will it matter if he disagrees with me?"

"Only if he openly resists you."

"So if Steve says nothing, the judge will grant my request?"

"The odds are pretty good."

"But if Steve wants to fight me?"

"Then you're in trouble. The judge might even dismiss your request as frivolous."

I hesitated, counting the costs. I was about to suggest something that went against everything I'd believed for years and every precept I'd ever proclaimed on the air. Families were the basis of America, and nothing mattered more to a happy family than a happy marriage, but could I be happy if Steve refused to allow me to restore our son?

If he did not change his mind—and from everything I'd seen, I didn't think he would—could I be happy remaining in this marriage? *With* Steve, I'd continue to be an example of a faithful wife, but inwardly, I'd be dying. *Without* Steve, I could be a happy single mother, devoted to my son.

I'd been married for twenty-two years . . . but I'd only been allowed five years as Scott's mother. I'd been cheated, but by having another son I could bring balance to my life.

Gathering my courage, I asked the question that would change everything: "What if I petition the court as a single woman?"

I heard Parker's quick intake of breath. "But you're not single."

"I could be."

He laughed, but I heard no humor in the sound. "I don't know what you're thinking, Diana, but I think you'd better work things out with Steve before you petition the court. A judge is not likely to think highly of your mental stability if you can't decide whether or not you want to be married."

I thanked him for his time, promised to call later, and hung up.

Dinner that night was strained, but for once I wasn't the primary cause of the disruption. Steve had come home at five and gone straight to the kitchen, where he deposited takeout boxes from Durango's. Eager to see a smiling face, he'd tiptoed up the stairs to greet his daughter, then caught Brittany smoking in her bedroom.

Ten minutes later we all sat at the kitchen counter, silent and tense. Steve kept shooting pained glances in Britt's direction while she fastened her gaze to her plate and stabbed at a slice of roast beef until the meat had more holes in it than a sieve.

When I could bear the tension no longer, I looked at her. "Are you done?"

Her jaw tensed. "Yes."

"Then you may be excused."

Bolting like a deer before the hounds, she pushed back from the table and stomped toward the stairs, but not before grabbing a box of cheese crackers from the pantry.

I noted the food and sighed, wearily making a mental note to vacuum her carpet tomorrow. No one could mess up a bedroom faster than my daughter.

Once she had gone, I pulled the ME's letter from my pocket and slid it across the counter.

"What's this?" Steve asked, his expression blank.

"Read it."

He pulled his glasses from his shirt pocket and read with a stony expression. As he folded the page again, however, a look of triumph flashed in his eyes.

"So the medical examiner won't cooperate. Surely that's a sign."

"What are you talking about?"

"A sign from God. If he had wanted us to pursue cloning, he would have smoothed the road before us."

Crossing my arms, I stared at him. "Maybe you're wrong. Maybe he's making our way difficult to stretch and test our faith. After all, he certainly didn't make things easy for Paul or the disciples."

"They were working to advance the kingdom of God. You're trying to advance a personal cause."

"For the love of Pete, will you make sense? Why can't you agree with me?"

"Because you're wrong. You're in denial, Counselor, and you can't see how you're lying to yourself."

Something rose within me, a bitter and acrid emotion I had never felt toward any living person . . . yet it was directed toward my *husband*. How could this be happening to us? I was a Christian, I loved Steve, and until now I had always wanted to be a submissive wife. Hadn't I gone with him to that stupid support group when everything in me railed against it? Yet this time he had gone too far. He was forcing me to live a life I was never meant to live.

"I'm going to ask you one last time." Rancor sharpened my voice. "Will you support me when I ask for a court order to get those tissue samples? Will you help me parent our new son?"

He dropped his fork, touched his lips with his napkin, then lowered it and met my gaze head-on. In a voice as steady as my own, he answered. "I will not."

A trembling rose from deep within me, but I would not weep. "Then I'll move forward without you. And you know what that means."

The set of his jaw did not change, but his brow wrinkled and something moved in his eyes. "I suppose I do."

"I want a divorce."

I thought my statement would shock him. Perhaps it did. But in that moment he did not flinch, nor did he protest. We both sat as immovable as rocks, two partners caught in a standoff because neither would capitulate.

"You have no grounds for divorce," he finally said.

"How about mental cruelty? You have denied me the one thing I desire most in life—my child."

He looked at me and blinked hard. "I have never been cruel. I have been firm."

"That's what most abusers tell their wives."

His brows shot up. "Oh, come on, Diana. You can't say I have abused you."

"I prefer to cite 'irreconcilable differences,' if anyone asks. But your refusal to support me feels like cruelty."

"I can't help your perceptions! Besides, I meant you have no *biblical* grounds to divorce me."

"Abuse isn't a biblical reason for divorce, either, but I would never tell an abused woman to stay with her husband." I straightened in my chair, readjusting my shattered dignity. "Besides, I think the Bible makes that point about adultery being the only allowable reason because people were putting their spouses away so they could marry someone else. I'm not planning to remarry. I want to have my baby. I'd love to reunite our family, but if you can't join us . . ."

I shrugged and lowered my gaze, hoping he'd understand. I hadn't fallen out of love with him—after twenty-two years of marriage we weren't exactly passionate in our relationship, but our marriage was comfortable and I had always considered Steve my best friend. I knew I shouldn't toss that aside, but neither should he ignore my desperate desire to restore our son.

I cast him a sidelong glance. "I'd love to be married to you forever, Steve, but I'm going to have this baby. If you change your mind, and if you don't hate me after all this, well, maybe there's hope for our future together. But if you can't support me, I want a divorce."

I watched a host of varying emotions twist his expression as he looked out the window. First, emotion softened his eyes, then a random thought tightened the corners of his mouth. "You know what this makes you," he said, his eyes averted. "The biggest hypocrite to ever hold court on radio."

"I am *not* a hypocrite." I threw the words like stones. "I have always been true to my beliefs in public and in private."

"I've heard you tell callers how divorce hurts children. You say parents should bend, practice give-and-take—"

"I've been bending for twenty-two years. And as far as our children are concerned, Scott Daniel is dead, Brittany is finished with childhood, and the new baby won't even draw breath if we stay married."

His squint tightened. "You talk as if we already have a third child. We don't. We shouldn't. Not like this."

"I should, I can, and I will, whether or not I have your help. If you won't join me, I'll have him without you. If I have to leave you to do it, I'll leave."

Picking up his fork, Steve stared down at his plate. "Suit yourself." The words were a hoarse whisper. "But you won't take our daughter. I won't lose two children."

That statement felt like a slug hitting the center of my chest. "You can't be serious. Daughters belong with their *mothers.*"

"Daughters belong in a stable and loving environment." Calmly he picked up his knife and proceeded to slice his roast beef. "At this moment, I'm the one who can best provide what Britty needs. I'm sure any judge would agree after my lawyer describes your plan to put this family on the front page of every newspaper in the nation."

Shock whipped my breath away. The room seemed to spin, the bright yellows and reds of my kitchen mixing in a mad whirl. Instinctively, I reached out to grasp the edge of the counter, then closed my eyes and held my head to stop the nauseating sensation of vertigo.

I don't know how long I sat there—four minutes, maybe five—

but when I lifted my head again, Steve had risen and walked away. Three plates remained on the counter, all of them filled with food no one had eaten or enjoyed.

I stood and carried my dishes to the sink, then used a fork to scrape my untouched beef into the disposal. The act reminded me of the surfeit of food we'd known after Scott's accident. No one wanted to eat when death came calling.

Even when death struck a marriage.

Thirty-three

AT ONE POINT IN MY CHILDHOOD—I'M NOT SURE, but I think I was six or seven—I decided to run away. I even picked out the place I would run to, a pretty little home by the lake. My parents and I often drove past that house on our way to church, so I had mentally mapped out the route I'd take to reach it. Any people who lived in such a nice house, I reasoned, had to be nice, too.

I had no real reason to leave home, but kids on TV and in books ran away all the time. My parents were loving and firm, not monsters. Still, I planned my escape.

One afternoon I went so far as to pull all the things I'd need from my bureau drawer. Item by item I pulled out shirts and shorts, socks and underwear, and I remember being shocked when I turned to discover that I had emptied my entire dresser. I either had inflated ideas about my needs or a pitiful lack of clothing.

One night after my mother tucked me in, I thought about how much I would miss her when I ran away. Despite my best efforts to hide it, a tear slipped down my cheek and caught my mother's attention.

She knelt by my bed. "Diana, honey, what's wrong?"

I shook my head. "Nothing."

"Are you sure?"

I was sure of one thing—I couldn't tell her about my plan to run away. So I lied and told her I was fine, I wasn't upset, everything was a-okay. Which it was.

I think all my life I've been planning to run away. I've just been waiting for a reason.

I didn't want to divorce Steve. I didn't believe divorce honors God. I knew it would damage my testimony before an unbelieving world. And, as I was constantly telling my radio audience, I believe in marriage and partnership and staying together for the sake of the children. I hated what a separation or divorce might do to Brittany, even at her age.

Still . . . Steve and I had reached an impasse, a place where I could not bend and he would not yield.

Wednesday morning found me searching the classified ads in the station's break room. Apartments were plentiful in Tampa, and several were located within a ten-minute drive of the station. I'd need a two-bedroom, of course, because Brittany would have to come with me . . .

If Steve would let her. I dropped the paper, abruptly aware that I was moving too quickly. Steve could be stubborn when he wanted to be, and last night he'd indicated he'd fight me for custody of our daughter.

I'd need a good lawyer.

I glanced at my watch. With only ten minutes till air, I didn't have time to start a search through the yellow pages. But I'd work on it in the afternoon, because with each day of waiting my eggs and Scott Daniel's tissue samples grew older.

I could not afford to waste time.

Thirty-four

STEVE STEPPED THROUGH THE PRIVATE EXIT OF HIS office and stood for a moment in the parking lot, wincing in the glaring sun. Lately life itself seemed intent upon causing him pain.

"You okay, Dr. Sheldon?"

Prying one eye open, he saw Melanie Brown standing beside him, her eyes sheltered by a pair of wire-rimmed sunglasses. Her shoulder-length blonde hair ruffled slightly in the breeze while her lips curved in a soft smile.

"I'm fine." He brought two fingers to the brim of an imaginary cap, then pointed to the sun overhead. "Just a little blinded, that's all."

"You should get some Ray-Bans." She moved toward her car, a lima-bean-colored VW bug she'd named Lily. Pausing by the door, she eyed him with concern. "You want me to pick you up a pair of sunglasses while I'm out for lunch? I'd be happy to do it since . . . well, I know things are rough for you right now. You probably don't feel like going to the mall."

He resisted the urge to snort in derision. A crowded public shopping center was the last place on earth he wanted to visit on his lunch hour, but she didn't need to know the reason for his melancholy.

"Thanks, Melanie, but I'll be fine. You drive carefully, now."

She flashed him a smile and got in the car, then waved before pulling out and driving away. He watched her leave, realizing that she was going to have lunch amid a happy bustle of people while he ate a sandwich by his son's grave.

Grief tiptoed close to press a cold palm to his shoulder. Angrily he shrugged off the chill, then slipped his hand into his pocket, searching for his keys.

What had happened to his carefully ordered world? In the last few weeks his wife, formerly a fount of wisdom and stability, had morphed into a woman he scarcely knew, let alone understood. He had tried talking, waiting, and empathizing, but though two months had passed since Scotty's accident, she showed no signs of returning to her old self. Somehow she had turned a corner he thought she'd never reach, and last night she had been dead serious when she asked for a divorce.

He found his keys, unlocked the car, and slid into the seat, leaving the door open so the heat could escape. Slipping the key into the ignition, he started the engine, then positioned the vent to blow cool air onto his face.

A divorce. When he was a kid, his mother had nearly worn out Tammy Wynette's recording of that tune. As Tammy warbled on about her pending D-I-V-O-R-C-E, he had sounded out the word and wondered what in the world could be so bad people had to spell it in a song.

Now he knew. Divorce was awful enough when it happened to other people; when it happened to you, it was like a death. Worse than death, actually. Scotty's accident had been a shock, but death had come swiftly and almost painlessly for Scott. Divorce tore the limbs from a family torso and left the raw nerve endings exposed.

If this divorce went through, Brittany would be ripped in two. At a time when she desperately needed both parents and wanted neither, what would she do?

He'd been praying ever since Diana first mentioned the horrible word. He'd asked God to change her heart, but somehow he knew God didn't force his will on his creations. Free will was both a tremendous gift and a tremendous burden . . . especially to those whose loved ones used their freedom to make destructive choices.

He closed the car door, then sat for a moment with his hands braced against the steering wheel. He didn't know what to do next. An inner voice urged him to take action, but as he saw it, he had only three choices: capitulate to Diana and proceed with the cloning; resist her efforts in the cloning and the divorce; or allow her to proceed in her plans with no resistance whatsoever.

The first option was untenable for several reasons. First, he did not want to be associated with the Raelians, no matter how loose their affiliation with Project One. Second, producing a replacement twin for Scotty seemed disrespectful to his son's memory. Though Steve felt certain he could love another child should Diana want to again consider adoption, he did not think it fair to expect another baby to fill Scotty's shoes. Third, the idea of cloning disturbed something in Steve's spirit, and throughout his life he'd come to rely upon the peace of God as a sure indicator that he'd chosen the right thing.

If he resisted Diana and contested the divorce, the media would be drawn to their family like fleas to a hound. Diana's career would suffer, Brittany would be tormented, and his practice, built on years of trust, might collapse. No parent would want to take their child to a dentist whose name appeared regularly in the tabloids.

He shuddered to think how reporters might turn innocent moments of their family history into lurid escapades for the gossip trade. Snoops from the *Tattler* or the *National Gossip* would take one look at their children—one adopted, then, thirteen years later, a miracle birth—and portray Scotty's arrival as some sort of alien encounter or, even more believable, the result of an adulterous fling. Brittany, whose exotic flaming-haired loveliness stood out in any crowd, would be fodder for photographers and reporters who might say or do anything to pry a provocative quote from her lips.

But those things would be only background for the real story once Diana's plans to bear a clone became public knowledge. Even divorced, they'd forever be known as the "Warring Clone Couple." The resulting child, if he survived, would inherit a legacy of speculation, rumor, and gossip . . .

Steve couldn't allow that. He loved his family too much.

Which left only one option—to allow Diana to make her choices freely, to step back and make it easy for her. Didn't the Bible say something about letting an unbelieving husband or wife go free? God wanted his children to live in peace.

Trouble was, Diana wasn't an unbelieving spouse. She was as strong a Christian as he was, but in the last few weeks grief had strapped blinders over her eyes. He could think of about ten spiritual principles her recent decisions had violated, including that verse about wives submitting themselves to their husbands . . .

Diana was a twenty-first-century woman. She didn't submit to many people. On the night he'd brought Pastor John to the house to try to speak sense to Diana, she'd faced him with the steely resolve of a gunslinger with nothing to lose.

He chuckled bitterly as the words of an old-time preacher came back to him on a tide of memory. "My wife and I have been married fifty years without a single argument," the preacher had said, thumping the pulpit for emphasis. "In the beginning, we made an agreement—she'd let me decide the major issues, and she'd take care of all the minor matters. And in fifty years of marriage, we've never had a major issue come up."

Steve exhaled a deep breath. His marriage had been much like the preacher's until God tossed a decidedly major issue into his lap. Trouble was, his wife was not willing to let him lead.

Sighing, he put the car into reverse, then turned to look behind him. The parking lot was clear, which was more than he could say for his future.

Brittany crossed the threshold, then winced as the security system beeped softly. She'd learned how to get around her mother's little tattletale setup at night by going out a window, but just once she'd like to come home from school without the house announcing her presence.

The soft glow of a lamp came from her mother's study, accompanied by the plastic clatter of the keyboard. Maybe her mom was concentrating and wouldn't notice as she slipped through the foyer.

Lowering her head, she moved past the doorway to the study, then felt her heart sink when the computer clatter ceased.

"Britt?"

She paused in mid-stride. "Yeah?"

"Good day?"

Brittany took a step back, enough to bring her within view of her mother at the computer desk.

"Okay day."

Her mother nodded, then turned back to face the computer monitor. That was it, then.

She hesitated. "Dad home?"

"Not yet." Her mother's voice was flat, abstracted.

"He picking up dinner?"

Her mother shook her head. "Don't know. Haven't spoken to him."

All right. Brittany rolled her eyes and moved away from the door, digesting her mother's diffident reply. Her parents usually kept close tabs on each other, especially at dinnertime. They had an arrangement—Dad picked dinner up on Mondays, Wednesdays, and Fridays, Mom cooked on Tuesdays, Thursdays, and Saturdays, reserving Sundays for leftovers. But even when Mom didn't cook, Dad usually called ahead to ask her what she wanted for dinner . . .

Brittany paused with her hand on the banister. Something was rotten in Denmark, as Mrs. Parker would say, something foul. Something not even Diana Do-Right and the World's Most Perfect Kiddie Dentist could handle.

She snorted softly as she climbed the stairs. Life as the child of two nearly perfect adults (or so everyone thought) had been hard enough before the Scottster died, now things were really spinning out of control. Diana Do-Right was looking a little frayed around the edges, and Dumbo Dad hadn't been himself in days.

Going into her room, Brittany swung her backpack onto the bed, then closed the door and turned the lock. She moved to her CD player, slid in her favorite disc, then slipped on her headphones and turned up the volume.

Closing her eyes, she let the drums and rants of the lead singer take her mind off home. Better to think about life on the streets of New York and in the L.A. hood than to dwell on the miseries of life at 3957 Hunter's Lane in Pinellas County, Florida.

Funny, though . . . until her parents started fighting, she would have sworn her mother was getting better. Dad was still moping around the house; she often found him sitting in his easy chair with damp cheeks. But in the last few weeks, Mom had almost seemed like her old self. She spent a lot of time at her computer, she walked with the old spring in her step, she had resumed her complaining about clutter in the house. Last Saturday afternoon Britt had heard sounds coming from the Scottster's room. She had peeked in to find her mother sealing all of Scott's stuffed animals in plastic bags and storing them in the closet. The rubber-faced monkey had disappeared from the bed, the plastic robots had been swept from the shelves, Scott's raincoat had vanished from the hook by the closet door. Everything, Brittany guessed, from looking at the neat piles in the closet, had gone into storage.

She wasn't sure what that meant, but she'd seen enough Lifetime television movies to know that people who did such things had usually accepted a tragic event and were ready to move on with their lives. Apparently Mom was ready and Dad wasn't, so maybe that accounted for the trouble between them.

Stretching out on the bed, she rested one hand on the book she was supposed to read for homework and clutched her pillow with the other. The friction between her parents was something new . . . and a little unnerving. She'd seen them get a little snappish with each other when they were tired, in a rush, or if one of them had just come home from a really bad day at work. But when one was down, the other managed to be up, and by talking things out they somehow managed to level out.

She rolled onto her back and stared at the ceiling. Maybe that was the problem with her folks now—Dad was down, Mom was up, and the talking wasn't working.

From the depths of her book bag, her cell phone rang. Brittany sat up and dived for it, then checked the caller ID. She felt a little flutter in her stomach. She knew this caller.

Snatching off her headphones, she pressed the talk button. "Hello?"

"Britt? It's Zack."

Holding the phone against her ear, Brittany settled back onto her pillow and grinned. "Whatcha doing?"

"Nothing. What's up with you?"

"Nada. Just lying here."

"Cool. Hey, I was thinking—you wanna go over to Tampa tonight? There's a new band playing in Ybor City. They're supposed to be really good."

Brittany bit her lip. Technically, she was well past her month of being grounded, though neither Mom nor Dad had officially come out and said she was off the hook. But even if she was free to go out, these concerts went late—the no-name bands usually started playing at nine or ten, and the featured groups didn't take the stage until eleven or twelve. But she hadn't gone anywhere all week and she was bored.

"I'd love to go—but I can't leave here until ten. Can you pick me up then?"

"Yeah. For you, I'll wait."

She glanced in the mirror, glad he couldn't see the blush that had risen to her cheeks.

"And Zack?"

"Yeah?"

"Don't come to the front of the house. Just pull to the end of the street and park in the cul-de-sac. I'll walk down and meet you there."

"Whatever you say."

As she clicked the call away, Brittany considered her plan. She'd come up to bed early, turn out the light, let her parents think she'd gone to sleep. Their house lay a good sixty yards from the end of the street, so she could go out the window, shimmy down the oak tree, and walk down the sidewalk in darkness. Once the concert was over, she'd reverse the process to beat the security system.

Sighing, she closed her eyes and pulled the headset back over her ears. Her parents wouldn't even know she was gone.

Thirty-five

THE REMAINING DAYS OF MAY STRETCHED THEM-
selves thin while Steve worked to preserve his home and family. After
Diana's startling request he had gone to his pastor, who listened sym-
pathetically and with genuine tears in his eyes. When Steve finished
explaining their situation, Pastor John promised to pray for the family, then gently reminded Steve that if the divorce went through, he
would have to give up his Sunday school class and resign his position
on the elder board. Church policy was based upon literal Scripture: a
man could lead in the church only if he were blameless and "the husband of but one wife." No divorced persons need apply.

Steve had left the pastor's office with a new emotion stirring in his
breast: shame. Not only had he failed to keep his wife and daughter
safe from an attack on their family, he had also proved himself an
unfit example for other believers. When he went home to sleep in the
guest room that night, he lay down in misery so acute it manifested
itself in real stomach pains.

After two weeks of pointless arguing with Diana and persistent
pleading with God, Steve climbed the stairs to talk to his daughter.
Diana thought they should talk to Brittany together, but something
in Steve wouldn't—couldn't—give Diana that satisfaction. Display a

united front now? How could they, with the fabric of their family torn in two? Refusing to participate in that charade, Steve waited until Diana left the house to speak at a Tuesday night meeting of professional women, then he climbed the stairs.

They had come to an arrangement. Brittany would graduate from high school on Friday, May 30, and Diana wanted to file for divorce as soon as possible after the milestone event. "To hurry the medical examiner," she'd said, crossing her arms. "My lawyer sent a letter, but it had no effect. The only way to get the tissue samples is by a court order, so we'll have to file a petition."

Without being told, Steve knew she wanted to petition the court as a single woman. No judge would grant her petition if her husband protested, and some might not even grant it if the *ex*-husband protested. But after pondering and praying about the matter through many sleepless nights, Steve had come to a decision: he would not fight her. Not in the divorce, not in the court petition, not in the cloning. If he resisted, Diana would blame him for any subsequent troubles or failures. If he stepped back, she would have no one to blame but herself.

At the head of the stairs he turned and looked at Brittany's closed door. Diana would be furious that he had spoken to Britty without her. But her actions had caused this standoff, and their daughter deserved to know the truth from someone who wanted to hold the family together.

He knocked on Britty's door, received no answer, then tried the knob. Locked, as usual.

He knocked harder. "Brittany!"

Pressing his ear to the knob, he heard rustlings from within. Finally his daughter opened the door and stared at him in puffy-eyed bewilderment.

"What time is it?" she asked, her voice heavy with sleep.

"It's 7:30." He stared into her messy room. The golden glow from a lamp on the table revealed schoolbooks scattered on the floor next to an assortment of magazines. The comforter on her bed was rumpled, and the noise she called music buzzed from the headphones on her pillow.

He looked at her in concern. "You feeling okay? You don't usually go to bed at seven o'clock."

She closed her eyes. "I'm tired, Dad. I need a nap."

"You can sleep in a few minutes, then. I want to talk to you."

Huffing in resignation, she moved to the bed and sat on the edge of the mattress, hugging her pillow to her chest while she lowered her head. Steve pushed a pile of jeans from the chair at her desk, then sat down, his gaze roving over rows of nail polish and cans of hair goop.

Had she ever used this desk to *study*?

She lifted her head. "Am I in trouble?"

"No, nothing like that." He swiped at an imaginary piece of dust, then smoothed the desktop with a fingertip. "Brittany, your mother and I have been talking about some pretty serious matters for the last couple of weeks."

Her eyes narrowed.

He drew a deep breath. This was not going to be easy.

"This is hard to explain, honey, but your mom and I have come to a place in our marriage where we cannot go forward together. Neither of us has been unfaithful to the other, you don't need to speculate about anything like that. But because we can't stay married, I'm going to leave the house this weekend, after graduation. Your mother says she's going to file for divorce. If she does, I'm not going to contest it."

Both her eyes were wide now, her mouth a small *O*.

"I know this will be hard for you," he continued, lowering his gaze to her stained and strewn carpet. "So as much as I'd like to have you with me, I'm going to let you stay here this summer so you'll be in a familiar place as you get ready for college. But if you want to stay with me at any time, all you have to do is let me know. I love you, Britty, and I want to be near you. The thought of leaving—I can't—I'm sorry."

Sorrow ripped at his voice, leaving him with tatters of useless phrases, and when he looked up again, his daughter's eyes had gone glassy with wetness.

"I'm so sorry, honey." He stared at her, his heart breaking under the weight of a million regrets. "I wish it didn't have to be this way."

"You're getting a *divorce*?"

"It's what your mother wants."

"My parents will be divorced." She spoke in a tentative, flat voice, as if taking the words for a test drive.

He pressed his lips together as an unexpected surge of anger caught him by surprise. If someone had told him he'd ever hear those words from the lips of his child, he never would have believed it. Even during the most difficult times, *divorce* had never been in his vocabulary, but he hadn't counted on Diana finding the audacity to speak the word.

Brittany clutched the pillow and stared at the crumpled comforter on her bed. "Most of my friends have divorced parents." She released a hollow laugh. "I'll finally fit in."

"Britty—"

"Is it—" She looked up, a question on her face. "Is it because of what happened to Scott?"

He sighed, wishing he could explain, but it wouldn't be fair to burden her with the full story now. If Diana persisted in her plan, Brittany would understand soon enough.

"Scotty's death put a strain on our relationship, but we could have made it through."

Her eyes filled with anguish. "Is it because of me? Because of something I did?"

Compassion flooded his heart. "No, honey. You should never think that." He rose and crossed to the bed, then pulled her into an embrace. "You didn't have anything to do with this. Trust me on this one. In time you'll understand, but for now . . . well, just trust me. In a few weeks I may not be married to your mother, but I'll always be your father and I'll love you forever. Never forget that."

He released her and stepped back. She stared at him with a slightly bewildered expression, as if a question lurked in her mind, but not the courage to ask it.

"You had nothing to do with this," he repeated, in case the unspoken query had been spurred by guilt. "This is something between your mother and me."

He turned then, leaving her in the numbness of discovery, but he knew the tears would begin to flow soon enough. He was well-acquainted with grief, and he knew she would pass this night in soul-searing tears. As much as he wanted to spare her, he couldn't.

As for him, a new emotion took up residence in his heart. For making him hurt his daughter and for bringing agony upon them all, rage toward Diana boiled at the core of his soul.

Brittany sat in stunned silence as the door closed. For a moment her mind went blank—she could not seem to formulate words, even clear thoughts—then a sharp surge of sadness pricked the heavy balloon of guilt she had been carrying for months. Remorse poured out in a flood, streaming down her cheeks.

She had often hoped her parents would split up. When she was feeling defiant, she used to fantasize about divorce bringing an end to that "united front" her mother always babbled about. Sometimes she secretly envied friends who spent weekends with their dads in apartments on the beach or summers with their moms someplace a world away.

Still, wishing was one thing and reality something else altogether. She could scarcely imagine her parents separated. How could Diana Do-Right do something as crazy as this? Was this one of those nutty midlife crises they were always poking fun at on TV? Or was her mother having an affair? Her father had said she wasn't, but maybe he was lying. Maybe her mother was lying to them both.

Her eyes lifted to the mirror above her cluttered dresser. She saw herself there—young girl, big eyes, pale skin, flaming-red hair. Abandoned at birth and now abandoned again.

Her face twisted, her eyes clamped tight to trap the sudden deluge of tears, but there were too many. Bending from the waist, she buried her face in her pillow and gave vent to the agony of confusion and hurt.

How could her parents do this, and right when she needed them to be there for her? Graduation, which should have been the best night of her life, would be a sham. She would stand between them in photographs, everyone would smile at the camera, but the whole thing would be a lie. Everything in her life was a lie, and everybody a liar.

She hated them—her mom and dad both.

Her dad drove her crazy with his teasing and nosing into her business, but she couldn't imagine him not being around when she needed twenty bucks or her truck was making weird noises. And as annoying as his continual questions were, she couldn't imagine walking out the front door without hearing him ask where she was going and when she'd be coming back.

And as much as she resented her mother for bringing them all to the brink of divorce, she couldn't imagine living without her, either. While it might be fun to visit Dad in an apartment somewhere, living without Mom would be like living in a house without electricity. On good days, in the old days, she seemed to keep the house warm. Without a doubt, she kept the house running. She was the one who reminded Dad of school events, who made the dentist appointments, who paid the bills, who did little things like keeping fresh flowers on the kitchen table and in the foyer . . .

"Oh, man." Brittany sat up and reached for a tissue, then blew her nose. She couldn't think when her head was stopped up, and her head felt like a ball of water, wet and slippery and gross. Last night, out with Zack, she had felt pretty and flirtatious and mature.

Good thing he couldn't see her now.

After blowing her nose again, she rolled onto her side, punched her pillow, and wiped her cheeks with her shirtsleeve. Maybe the divorce wouldn't matter. After all, she was eighteen, legally an adult, and she'd be off to college in less than three months. She wouldn't even be living here, so the problems of home shouldn't really matter. Dad would help pay her college bills and Mom would handle all the paperwork just as she handled everything else. When Christmas came around, she'd spend a few days with Mom and a few days with Dad . . . but where would she spend Christmas Eve?

She balled her hands into fists, fighting back the hot tears swelling behind her eyes. Why was this so terrible? She'd probably be like 97 percent of the other kids in her freshman class, just another girl whose parents had two different addresses.

Cold, common sense rose up to shine the hard light of truth on her words. No—it would not be life as usual if her parents split up. The word *divorce* tasted terrible on her tongue, and she still couldn't accept the possibility. And though her dad had said the breakup had nothing to do with her, an inner voice whispered that she'd been flirting with disaster for over a year. Every time she slipped out the window, every curfew she broke, every lie she told added to the stress in her parents' lives. Though they didn't know the half of what she'd done—and maybe never would—she was not blameless. She had been rebelling against her family for months, and the stress had finally cracked the foundation.

Maybe this was God's way of paying her back. He knew what she'd done. He saw everything and kept records, didn't he? In Sunday school she'd learned to think of him as a shining and holy old man who sat in a big white chair surrounded by angels and hundreds of black books on stands. Every time you did something to break one of the rules he put a black mark next to your name, a mark that could be erased only when you repented and confessed and prayed in Jesus' name.

But even when you did those things to make it right, you still had to suffer the consequences. And this time she'd committed one sin too many, piled on the straw that broke the proverbial camel's back.

Her family was broken, and she could do nothing to fix it.

Thirty-six

ON MAY 30, STEVE AND I JOINED THE HUNDREDS OF other parents jamming the War Hawk stadium to witness the high school graduation. We sat together in chilly silence, our shoulders not touching even once, and applauded like zanies as Brittany crossed the stage to accept her diploma and have her tassel moved from one side to the other.

As I watched, I couldn't help but think that the timing of our divorce, while not perfect, was probably the best it could have been. Our daughter was preparing to leave home for college; she was already cutting ties to high school friends. Loosening the apron strings that bound her to us was a logical next step. The divorce could not touch any fond memories she retained of her childhood, and I was reasonably sure Steve and I would remain civil in the years ahead. I had even dared to dream of reconciliation after the baby's birth—if Steve could find it in his heart to forgive me for this struggle, I knew his love for Scott Daniel would lead him to love the new baby. Love for our family would bring him back.

After the graduation ceremony we drove back to the house, then Brittany ran upstairs to change into jeans and a sweater. We waited until she came down; we hugged her and kissed her and sent her out to celebrate with her friends. Then Steve calmly told me good-bye and went to his car, which he had discreetly loaded with suitcases before the graduation ceremony. As I watched from the doorway, he slid into the BMW and drove away to his new apartment, his new furniture, and his new life.

As we had agreed, I went into the study and turned on the computer. In March 2002, Florida had become one the first states in the country to offer uncontested on-line divorces. For two hundred forty-nine dollars, conveniently payable by credit card, applicants could spend thirty minutes answering a series of questions and have their divorce petition filed in court. Petitioners would have to appear at the final divorce hearing, but the on-line application appealed to me. It was fast, private, and inexpensive.

Because Steve had decided not to contest the divorce, I made no demands on him. With lucrative careers, we agreed neither of us needed money for alimony or child support since Brittany's college fund would cover her expenses until she was ready to step out on her own. We agreed that I would keep the house until Brittany left for college, then we'd put it on the market and I'd move to a smaller place. When it sold, we'd evenly split the proceeds.

My dreams of keeping the house so the baby would grow up in Scott Daniel's room had fled with Steve's refusal to support the idea. Without Steve's income, I was now counting on selling the house to reimburse the money I'd borrowed from Brittany's college fund and to finance the cloning. If all went well, the house should sell just as I needed the balance of Project One's fee. I'd still be short about thirty-five thousand, but if I cut down on expenses and asked my agent to book me for a few profitable speaking engagements, I'd eventually be able to cover the balance.

Time passed. Moving in the relaxed haze of a steamy Florida summer, I went to work, spouted advice, then came home to sit by the pool with Terwilliger. Whenever a pang of loneliness struck, or I found myself listening for Steve's key in the door, I would remind myself that I had done a desperate thing for a valid reason. Within a year, God willing, I would have my son again. Then, if God willed, perhaps Steve would come home.

I kept a watchful eye on the calendar, counting off the days, and stored my emotions on a shelf. Next year, when I was snuggling with my son, I would call Steve, apologize, and beg him to consider rekindling our marriage. Until then . . . I'd steel myself to the sight of his empty chair, his unrumpled pillow, and the spotlessly clean second sink in our master bath.

On June 30, four weeks after filing our divorce petition, Steve and I stood in a judge's chambers, assured him we were parting amicably, and walked out of the Pinellas County courthouse as unmarried individuals. We crossed the courtyard and stepped onto the asphalt parking lot together without speaking, then walked side by side to our cars. We reached his BMW first.

I hesitated. With my wealth of experience in counseling I should have known what to say, but nothing had prepared me for this good-bye.

Steve stood still, staring at his keys as he spread them over his palm. Only the tightening of the muscles in his throat betrayed his emotion. "Will you answer one question for me?"

Squinting at him through the hot glare of the June sun, I felt perspiration trickle down my spine as a suffocating sensation tightened my throat. "What question is that?"

He looked at me with something very fragile in his eyes. "Do you still love me at all?"

I could not bear the touch of his gaze, and the look of hurt behind the question. I crossed my arms and looked away to safer territory. "I'll always love you, Steve. But now it's time for me to love our son."

I held my breath, hoping the enormity of what we had just done would bring him to his senses, but he only lowered his keys and unlocked the door. "Good-bye, Diana."

That was it, then. No second thoughts, no last-minute promises. Only a weight of sadness on his lined face, and a brief good-bye.

"Bye." Feeling guilty and selfish, somehow I forced the word over the despair in my throat, then lowered my head and hurried through the parking lot.

The next morning I sat at the studio microphone rubbing the naked joint of my ring finger as I listened to yet another "I-can't-get-along-with-my-mother-in-law" call. This man, at least, had experienced a unique situation. The last time he had forgotten to call and say he'd be coming home late from work, his mother-in-law had rushed to comfort her distraught daughter (who was certain her hapless husband was having an affair), then locked the hardworking man out of his own home. "It's all because my wife's first husband was a no-account jerk," Jim told me. "They seem to think I'm the same way, but I'm not."

I pushed a heavy sigh over the airwaves. "Jim, are you up for a story?"

"Uh—sure, Dr. Diana."

"Okay. Picture an old-timer sitting on his front porch in his rocker, watching new folks drive into town. A family comes by, and they stop to ask for directions. 'We're thinking about moving to the country,' the husband says, 'and we're wondering what this town is like.'

"The old-timer narrows his eyes a minute, then says, 'Well, tell me about your old neighborhood.'

"The wife rolls her eyes and says, 'Oh, things are terrible where we're living now. The neighborhood is going downhill, the people are a bunch of snobs, and the schools are just awful.'

"The old-timer shakes his head. 'Hate to tell you folks this, but things are pretty much the same here. If I were you, I'd just keep going.'

"So they did. A few minutes later another family pulls up for directions, and the husband comes out to ask about the town up ahead. The old-timer gives them the once-over and says, 'Suppose you tell me about the place you're living now?'

"The wife steps out and says, 'Oh, it's a perfectly lovely town; we hate to move. The schools are wonderful, the location is lovely, and the people are as nice as can be. We wouldn't move at all, except—'

"'That's okay,' the old timer interrupts. 'I don't need to hear anymore. You just mosey on into town, and I think you'll like what you see. You're going to feel right at home.'"

I hesitated a moment. "Jim, you still with me?"

"Yeah, Dr. Diana."

"Do you understand? What did my story say to you?"

"Umm . . . that I should move out of town?"

I glanced at Gary, who was rocking with laughter behind the window. "Not quite, Jim. The point of that story is that the town didn't change; the attitudes of the people made all the difference. People with a negative outlook tend to carry that perspective into everything they do. Not always, of course, but I'm amazed at how certain people manage to find the negative in everything. I have a feeling your mother-in-law may be one of those people."

Jim managed a choking laugh. "So I'm stuck with her?"

"Yes—and no. What your mother-in-law did was wrong. You have a right to enter your own home whenever you choose. But instead of fixating on your mother-in-law's overreaction, why don't you concentrate on pleasing your wife? Call her when you're going to be late. Bring her flowers, tell her there's no woman in the world that can match her smile. Make her feel loved and special, and she'll stop doubting you. Treat her with the same consideration you'd like to receive, and I guarantee your mother-in-law will run out of reasons to lock you out of the house. Her attitude will change, but it might take time."

Jim stuttered for a moment, then grew quiet. "I guess that'd work. But the woman's still a witch."

"She's a crazy-maker," I said, laughing. "Know what crazy-makers are? They're people who drive us nuts, but they also make us stronger. Learn to live with a crazy-maker, and you'll learn to tolerate the other trials in your life."

I looked up when I heard a tapping on the studio window. Gary was standing at his desk with a printout in his hand. He pointed to the paper, then drew his index finger across his throat in an abrupt gesture.

Glancing at the clock, I saw that we had five minutes until the newsbreak, but Chad could fill the time with commercials and one of our prerecorded bits if some emergency had come up.

"We'll be back with more of your calls after the news," I said, keeping my tone light. When Chad hit the first commercial, I slipped off the headphones. I was about to stand and go into the control room, but Gary burst through the studio doorway, the mysterious paper in his hand.

Leaning back in my chair, I gaped at him. "Have we declared war on somebody?"

He smiled a grim little grin as he handed me the ragged page. "The news of your divorce just hit the wire. I think you'd better read this, then we have to decide how we're going to handle the matter."

Keeping one hand over my fluttering stomach, I skimmed the wire report. Beneath a headline of "Pro-Family Radio Psychologist Knocks Blocks from Beneath Crumbling Marriage," I read that my divorce had become part of the public record. An astute journalist had obviously seen the court report this morning and called Steve at his office. "When asked the reason for the divorce," the reporter wrote, "Dr. Steve Sheldon would only say, 'Ask my wife.'"

I groaned. "Wouldn't you know they'd go after Steve?"

"He's easier to reach than you." Gary took the paper from me. "So, how do you want to handle this?"

I took a deep breath. "How broad is the coverage?"

"I think it's a safe bet that it's national by now. This came out on the wire half an hour ago, which means CNN will probably put it in their noon news loop. By tomorrow it'll be old news and you'll be playing defense."

I nodded, understanding his point. "So if I address it today—"

"Your audience will see you as being straightforward and honest. It's hard to paint something as a scandal if no one's trying to hide it."

Running my hand through my hair, I weighed my options and settled on a decision. For the last four weeks I'd been considering different ways of announcing my divorce. I knew the news would become public; I just hadn't expected it to hit in the middle of my show.

I picked up a pencil and reached for my notepad. "After the news break, I'll address it in the monologue. Find me some moving background music—something soothing without too many violins. Maybe the soundtrack of *Pearl Harbor*."

Gary nodded and went out while I twirled the pencil between my fingers and stared at the blank page. How could I tell thousands of devoted listeners that one of the stoutest defenders of marriage in the modern world had felt it necessary to divorce a loving husband? It would have been easy to say Steve was abusive or controlling, but I could not sully his reputation to save my own skin. Besides, we'd be seeing blood in the water on this one no matter what I said.

I'd have to account for the divorce . . . and soon I'd have to explain the cloning. My lawyer had already filed my petition for the court order to obtain the tissue samples; we were only waiting for a judge to review the case and give us a ruling. If all went well, I could be pregnant within a matter of months.

So I owed my audience two revelations, and reaction to the second might well overshadow disappointment for the first. It'd be a coup for the network if I broke the cloning story on my show. Project One wanted to share my story with the world, well, why not share it with my audience first?

My gaze drifted toward the windows where Gary and Chad worked. Unfortunately, I hadn't told my staff about my plans for the baby. It hardly seemed fair to drop that bombshell on them without warning because a subject this huge would change the nature of the show for weeks to come. Cloning would become the hot topic of the *year,* and Gary would find himself fielding callers who used words like *traducianism* and *denucleated*. Some of our conservative listeners would find my plans so shocking they'd leave in droves, while we'd undoubtedly attract new listeners from the fringes where UFO and conspiracy buffs dwelled . . .

If I dropped both bombs today, I'd be facing major damage containment and an eventual audience readjustment. But why not press ahead? Our nation's recent history was replete with examples of people who'd been caught in far worse things than divorce and survived by moving ahead with their lives.

During the news break I jotted down a few thoughts, then sat silently as the intro music played. As the last refrain of the "Dr. Diana theme" faded away, I lifted my notepad and saw that my fingers were trembling.

"Welcome back, friends, to the *Dr. Sheldon Show.* This monologue will be a little different, but I need to take a few moments to share my heart with you. For five years now, I've been listening to your problems and offering honest, truthful answers, and now I'd like you to hear about a problem I've experienced. The media has painted me as some sort of sanctimonious holier-than-thou counselor, and that's not an accurate picture. I believe God ordained specific principles to create a healthy, functioning human society. I also believe certain bedrock philosophies, when followed, result in strong homes and happy families.

"Which is why it breaks my heart to sit with you and reveal that yesterday my twenty-two-year marriage ended in divorce. My ex-husband is a good man, a fine man, but we can no longer remain married. You've often heard me speak of the importance of maintaining a united front when raising children—well, my husband and I have turned in two different directions. I do not wish to reveal private details in a public forum, but you should know that we are both committed to loving our children to the best of our ability and we are fully aware of the stress divorce can bring. But unhappiness in the home can bring stress, too—as can a marriage in which two people can no longer agree on the basic requirements for a life together."

I paused, searching for words beyond those on my notepad. "I know some of you will have strong feelings about this—some may even think I have betrayed you by seeking a divorce when I have always stressed the importance of marriage. All I can do is remind you that I have never said you must remain married no matter what. Neither my husband nor I have been unfaithful in this marriage; no third parties were involved. We are aching, publicly and privately, so don't feel you must throw stones to make sure we're feeling an adequate amount of pain."

I glanced up at Gary, who had no idea of what was coming next. "Now I want to tell you something else—something I have never revealed in public. Modern science has given me a unique opportunity to experience a miracle."

Lowering the phone in his hand, Gary looked at me with a troubled and questioning expression.

"As most of you know"—I paused to clear a frog from my throat— "I lost my beloved five-year-old son a few months ago. Scott Daniel was the joy of my life. Now, through the miracle of technology, medical researchers have given me a chance to bear my son's identical twin. He won't be the same child, but a genetic duplicate. I will carry him in a normal pregnancy, I will love and cherish him just as I loved and cherished Scott Daniel before the accident claimed his life. And once again I will experience the inexpressible joy of motherhood."

I shivered, overcome again with the wonder of the future, then pointed at Chad, who rolled the soft version of the riff that signaled a return to the telephone queue. "Before I take your calls"—I dropped my voice to a whisper—"be forewarned. Today I will not discuss my divorce or my future plans. Tomorrow, perhaps. I know this news will ignite controversy, and I'm prepared to deal with the repercussions. But I must ask you to respect the privacy of my daughter and ex-husband. They are not public figures, and they have a right to privacy."

I glanced up at the screen, and saw that Cheryl from Waco wanted to ask if I had the recipe for the Cabbage Soup Diet. Ordinarily I'd have consigned her call to the bottom of the heap, but today such triviality seemed a blessing.

Thirty-seven

STEVE GLANCED TOWARD GERTA POPPOVITCH, WHO had just slammed the phone down in an unusual display of temper. "Sorry, Dr. Steve," she said, catching his eye. "But those reporters are about to drive me buggy."

"Ignore them." He picked up a patient chart on the counter, then flipped it open and tried to make his brain focus on his handwritten notes. His ability to concentrate seemed to have vanished along with his marriage, and he found himself taking twice as long with patients as usual. Melanie, bless her heart, covered for him whenever she could, but by four o'clock he usually had a waiting room filled with impatient parents who pointedly glanced at their watches and grumbled about homework to finish and dinners to prepare.

He was falling apart. Losing Scotty had been hard enough; losing his marriage in the face of intense publicity was a nightmare beyond anything he had ever encountered.

Yesterday Diana had gone public with the news of their divorce and her plans to clone their son, and last night a phalanx of reporters had been waiting outside Steve's building, cameras at the ready. He charged through them and their stinging questions, and in between each panting breath he heard himself muttering "No comment, no comment" as though he had developed an acute case of Tourette's syndrome.

Hurrying into the apartment, he leaned against the door, a new kind of fear quaking his body from toe to hair. His phone was ringing; the answering machine blinked with thirty-seven messages from representatives of the media and one call from Diana, who had phoned from the station to tell him she had broken the news.

How considerate.

The situation hadn't improved with the dawn of a new day. Another corps of reporters had been waiting outside his apartment when he left for work, and through the tiny window in his office he could see another group waiting on the sidewalk outside his office building. Gerta said at least half a dozen parents had canceled their children's appointments, and the children he did see were more nervous than usual, spooked, no doubt, by the reporters and the harried look in their dentist's eye.

Through all the confusion, Melanie had been a godsend. She double-checked his charts before giving them to Gerta to file; she flagged suspicious teeth on several x-rays before he entered the exam room. And when he paused in the break room and debated running the media gauntlet to fetch a cheeseburger for lunch, she had offered to go pick something up and run it right back. He gratefully accepted her offer, and within minutes she had gone out and returned with two taco salads.

"Don't worry, Steve," she said as they ate together in the tiny break room. "This won't last forever. They'll probably keep after Diana, but as long as you refuse to have anything to do with her, you'll fade out of the picture." She lightly laid her hand on his wrist. "And if and when you need to talk to someone, know this—I'll be there for you. Anytime."

He did not answer, but winced slightly, as if her touch had nipped his flesh. A month ago the eager look in her eye would have set off his inner alarms and sent him into a hasty retreat, but he was no longer a married man.

He was single. And, according to his church, no longer an example of virtue.

Not knowing what else to do, he took a bite of his salad and gave her an appreciative smile.

Thirty-eight

FOUR DAYS AFTER BREAKING THE BIG NEWS TO MY radio audience, I sat alone in my kitchen, absorbing the sounds and silences of a nearly empty house. Terwilliger slept under the table and atop my foot, his legs twitching as he whimpered in sleep, probably chasing a cat in his dreams.

Poor little guy. Until the accident he had belonged to Scott Daniel. In the past four months he had drifted from person to person, trying to find another constant companion. "Looks like you're stuck with me," I murmured, glancing down at his chunky little body. "Everyone else is leaving."

I sipped my coffee and counted the chimes from the grandfather clock in the foyer. One. Two. Three. Three o'clock, and no husband coming home later either for dinner or with dinner. I didn't expect to see Brittany until at least midnight, if then. Since graduation, she had taken to spending most of her time with her friends, and I wanted to give her the freedom a high school graduate deserved. Steve was worried because she didn't want to be with either of her parents, but I assured him her avoidance of us almost certainly had less to do with the divorce than with the fact that she'd be leaving for college in less than two months. She wanted to be with her friends, period.

Over the last few days, the oddest sense of disconnectedness had crept over me. I was the same person I had always been, with the same coworkers, friends, and job, yet there were moments when I felt like that man in the *Outer Limits* episode who wakes up to find that he's somehow managed to sleep through the world's nuclear destruction. Whether walking through the house or driving in the car, I kept wondering who would care if I decided to stop off at the grocery instead of going home. If I obeyed a wild notion and drove to Fort Lauderdale one afternoon, would anyone notice that I hadn't been home at dinnertime? If I collapsed in the bathroom, how many hours would I lie on the tile floor before someone realized I needed help?

The term *single* fit me about as well as a size 3-X jacket; the word felt uncomfortably loose and revealing.

"You'll get used to it," I told myself, lifting my mug. "You can get used to almost anything."

I took another sip of my coffee, an afternoon pick-me-up I sorely needed. This morning's show had been a near-disaster. Three-quarters of the callers seemed more intent on blasting my decisions than listening to reason, and when I spoke logically or recited facts, they resorted to yelling, as if an argument could be won by sheer volume.

The other callers, the 25 percent who supported me in the divorce, the cloning, or both, were more enthralled than interesting. I was so brave, so courageous, such a model for others, yada, yada, yada. While it was nice to hear from people who didn't think I'd evolved into the wicked witch of the west, those callers tended to put me—and my other listeners—to sleep.

The most comforting words had come from Charity, who had not failed to call with her quote of the day. "A ship in the harbor is safe," she had said, "but that is not what ships are for. Maybe you should launch out into the unknown, Dr. Diana."

Taking her words to heart, I now sat with my trusty legal pad and struggled to come up with ideas for a slightly adjusted format—something to take my focus away from traditional conservative family issues but not deny the foundational principles I still espoused.

I scratched on the notepad, then held it up to consider what I'd written: *Technology with a Twist.*

I grimaced. That tag sounded more like some kind of cocktail than a radio program. One of my colleagues at the station used "the fusion of entertainment and enlightenment" as his promo line, so maybe I could go with something like "modern thought meets universal truth."

Then again, why not describe the show as the WWF of modern ideas? The World Wrestling Federation wouldn't mind . . . but their lawyers might.

Sighing, I dropped the notepad, then rested my elbow on the table and propped my chin in my hand.

I hated to admit it, but Steve's absence had been a shock to my system. He'd taken an apartment in Clearwater Beach, only a fifteen-minute drive away, but the thought of him living in another zip code unnerved me. I'd known I could not walk away from twenty-two years of marriage without feeling some major side effects, but the little things were affecting me most.

Like no snoring to break the deep silence of the night.

No one to take out the garbage without being asked.

No one to keep me company when I waited up for Brittany to come home.

I nearly jumped out of my skin when the phone shattered the stillness. "For the love of Pete," I grumbled, pulling my foot free of Terwilliger's warm little body. "Get a grip, Diana."

The phone had rung almost constantly during the last week, but old news was not news, so I hadn't fielded any press calls today. As I predicted, the news of my plan to bear a clone overshadowed the announcement of my divorce. I stalled most of the reporters with a comment about how it was premature to discuss the future, and every night I thanked God for the security guard outside my gated community. Though the press hounded Steve and me persistently for a couple of days, no one had bothered Brittany. I doubted if anyone had been able to find her.

I scanned the caller ID, not willing for my solitude to be interrupted by a telephone solicitor or a reporter, then hastily picked up the receiver. Someone was calling from the station.

"Diana?"

Gary's breathless voice alarmed me. "Is something wrong?"

"Did you hear?"

"Did I hear what?" Automatically, my gaze shifted toward the television in the family room. If there'd been some sort of disaster, Gary would want me to know as soon as possible so we could discuss how to handle it on tomorrow's program.

"The network dumped us. The word came down a few minutes ago—this morning was the last show we'll do from WFLZ."

Unable to speak, I stood as if fastened to the floor.

"Diana? You there?"

I gulped, forcing down the sudden lurch of my stomach. For a moment the color ran out of my kitchen and the hum of the phone faded into oblivion.

"That's—that's impossible," I managed to stammer. "They wouldn't dare dump us. We make them too much money. Even with the controversy—"

"They dared and they did. I spoke to Conrad Wexler myself, who said they hired you to speak for family values and parenthood, not science freaks and cultists."

"*Cultists?* Who's he been talking to?"

"What's this about, Diana?" A note of panic vibrated in Gary's voice. "You didn't say anything to me about cults. And you didn't warn me that we were stepping into a weird area. One minute I'm thinking you're brave for coming clean about your divorce, and the next minute you're telling the world you're taking us into the honest-to-goodness Twilight Zone."

I pressed a hand to my face. "Hush, Gary. I need to think."

"Why didn't you do that sooner?"

"I did. But I didn't foresee this." I turned and leaned against the kitchen counter, my thoughts racing. Score one for Conrad Wexler—he had managed to surprise me. Landed a knockout blow when I wasn't looking. But though my stomach felt empty and my lungs breathless, I wouldn't be down for the full ten-count. No way.

"Let's see—did you call the station's lawyer to ask for clarification? Maybe there's a clause or something to prevent this. They can't dump us for no reason."

"They have a reason. You can't change the format of your show without approval."

"We didn't change the format."

"Not officially, but you changed the content, and they say that's the same thing. And Conrad Wexler didn't sound exactly reluctant to let us go. I think he was personally offended by what he's heard about your plans."

"Wexler? I thought he was a progressive liberal."

"He's a conservative Catholic. Before last week he was one of your biggest fans."

"But he employs all those raunchy talk-show hosts—"

"He's a businessman; he goes with what makes money, as long as it doesn't cross a certain line. I didn't know where his line is, but obviously you've crossed it. So we're out. Out of the station, out of the network. We get six weeks of severance pay, and that's it."

I pressed my hand to my forehead and rubbed the tender spot at my temple. My eyelashes began to twitch, a sure sign of stress. I used to drop everything and call Steve when things like this happened . . . now I could only call on God. But he was enough.

Father, help. Please. You brought me to this place, so please see me through.

Drawing in a deep breath, I forced myself to calm down. "Don't worry, Gary, and don't pack your suitcase. I'll have my agent get on top of this."

"You do that. But he'd better be prepared for both barrels. Wexler didn't mince any words with me."

I hung up, then moved to the kitchen sink and bent to brace my arms against the counter. Gary had to be exaggerating, but he wouldn't joke about us being fired from the network. Being dropped by one station was troubling enough, but if we lost the network, we didn't lose one station, we lost more than sixty that wouldn't turn around and pick us back up—not if they wanted to stay in good graces with the higher-ups, that is. Worst of all, we lost our facility, our access to equipment, our support system.

I was no longer a successful radio star; I was an unemployed has-been.

I had to call my agent. But in a minute, when I wasn't feeling so nauseous.

I turned on the water, ran my fingers through the cool stream, then rubbed the pulse points at my throat. What would I do without my job? I'd been depending on that income to make a living; I'd been counting on the network for health insurance and maternity leave benefits.

Unbidden, Steve's name floated to the front of my brain, but I shoved it aside. He was a good man, the sort who would help if I asked, but I couldn't ask him for anything now.

Not even for the baby's sake. From the moment I had realized Steve could not approve of the cloning, I knew I would not ask him to support the baby in any way. If he would not acknowledge our son, I didn't want him to have any claim to the boy. The baby would be mine alone, an amalgamation of my body and Scott Daniel's DNA.

But without a job, how could I support myself and come up with the money I needed for the procedure? If I dipped into Brittany's account, I'd bankrupt her future . . . and her trust.

I lowered my head, feeling like one of those weepy people who called my show to complain about suffering the consequences of their own foolish actions.

Overcome by despair, I leaned over the sink and wept.

Thirty-nine

RECALLING CHARITY'S QUIP ABOUT SHIPS LEAVING the safety of the harbor, I licked my wounds, called my agent (who was as distressed as I about the bad news, and no help at all), then set about reordering my future. I spent the July 4 holiday at my desk, outlining a plan that would take me out of radio and into the adventure of my life.

Because the Prime Radio Network was the biggest in the business, I knew my career in radio was over. No other network could match my salary or Prime's market base, so unless I wanted to do a Sunday morning show for some little independent station in Kalamazoo, I would have to surrender the idea of a radio talk show.

But TV loomed as a distinct possibility. At my age I wasn't exactly Miss America material, but neither would I send viewers screeching in horror. I could come up with a format and tape a couple of shows at the local public broadcasting studio. I'd have to rent the facility and pay the crew, but I would consider it an investment in my future. While the tape made its rounds at the networks, I would concentrate on getting Brittany off to college, selling the house, and winning permission to use Scott Daniel's tissue samples.

My lawyer had petitioned the court the day after the issue of our divorce decree, and he warned me that the process of judicial review could take four or five weeks, maybe longer. I saw the delay as God's perfect timing. By the time I had legal access to Scott Daniel's tissue samples, everything else should have fallen into place. Britt would be on her way to school, the house would be listed with a real-estate agent, and I could leave the area, maybe head out to New York, Los Angeles, or one of the other major markets.

Brittany wouldn't care where I went. She would have said farewell to her high school friends and she'd be excited about meeting new people at college. Steve would probably be thrilled not to have me living across town, and maybe he'd find it easier to start a new life if I weren't in the picture.

Then again . . . perhaps he'd come out to visit after the baby was born. And maybe, if love and nostalgia softened his heart, Steve would see that my idea was actually a blessing and he'd change his mind about accepting our son. If he did, I'd willingly come back to Tampa. We could remarry and start over in a cozy condo on the beach, one with a guest room where Brittany could stay when she came home on breaks from school. I could get a local studio to host my TV show. If Oprah could make Chicago her signature town, I could do the same for Tampa.

My celebrity as the mother of the first American clone would help my career if I used it carefully. Instead of focusing so much on traditional values, my TV show could explore the world of contemporary medicine and shifting ethical boundaries. I'd still maintain my pro-life positions, condemning fetal experimentation and partial-birth abortion, but I wouldn't be such a hard-liner that I couldn't be open and receptive to new ideas. Good things could come out of modern medicine and reproductive technology. I would stress that years ago people were repulsed by the thought of test-tube babies, but now such procedures were common. Perhaps my first show could be about heart transplants, which had once seemed a perversion of the natural order.

As the mother of the first American clone, I'd be the perfect person to embody all that was good about medical technology. Together my son and I would help bring a fearful nation into a new century of possibilities.

The Project One folks would be thrilled if I moved to TV, and my son would be a living advertisement for their work. Perhaps they'd even sign a contract promising to sponsor my show—a promise that would be appreciated by the networks. My agent would *love* to sell a program with a tested format, a well-known host, and a wealthy sponsor ready and waiting.

As the day wore on, I felt my flagging self-confidence begin to rise. At dinnertime I interrupted Gary at his family picnic to tell him we were moving the show to television. He sounded a bit distracted as I explained my plans, but he thanked me for calling and wished me a happy Fourth of July.

Eleven P.M. found me doodling dollar signs and possible salary figures on my notepad when the phone rang. I glanced at the caller ID. The number was Charisse's, so Britt was probably calling to tell me she'd be stopping by to pick up twenty bucks for the late movie . . .

Sighing, I reached for the receiver.

"Yeah?"

"Hey." Charisse giggled, and at the sound of her laughter I knew trouble was afoot. Brittany was supposed to be with Charisse, but the girl's casual greeting told me otherwise.

"So"—the smack of her gum cracked over the line—"did your mom see the hickey on your neck?"

Like a witness to an unexpected accident, I sat absolutely still. During the ensuing silence, Charisse stopped cracking her gum.

I would have given anything to see the look on her face.

"No." I switched into Motivated Mother Mode. "I didn't see anything on my daughter's neck. Should I look again, Charisse?"

Dead silence filled the other end of the line, then I heard a click. Charisse obviously had few defense mechanisms, but at least she hadn't tried to lie.

I lowered the phone back into the stand, then dropped my head onto my hand and groaned. I didn't even know Brittany had a boyfriend—or did she? Maybe the girls had gone to a party where they played those adolescent kissing games. That didn't sound like something Britt would do, but who knew what kids these days were up to? Or maybe Charisse was kidding, and the mark on Britt's neck was only a bruise. Or maybe there was no mark on my daughter's neck at all.

Yet one thing was clear—Charisse thought she had been speaking to Brittany. Despite the lack of a biological link between us, Britt had picked up my vocal inflections. She was always telling me it drove her crazy when people said she sounded like Dr. Diana.

I reached for the phone to call Steve, then dropped my hand as an acute sense of loss sideswiped my heart. Old habits were hard to break. I was the custodial parent; I would have to deal with this. Rationally.

My daughter apparently had a love bite on her neck, and Charisse knew all about it while I knew nothing. And—a new realization dawned—my daughter, who was supposed to be spending the night with her best friend, was in fact AWOL and I had no idea where she could be.

I felt an instinctive stab of fear, then took a deep breath and pushed the pain away. This was the twenty-first century, and Brittany had been carrying a cell phone since her fifteenth birthday. Apart from those toddler leashes parents needed in airports and amusement parks, the cell phone was the best parental tool ever invented.

I reached for the phone again, punched in Britt's number, and waited.

The phone rang.

And rang.

And rang.

Still holding the phone to my ear, I stood and pushed the lace curtain away from the window. Her red pickup was nowhere in sight.

I closed my eyes, trying to recall the events of the day. Britt had slept late, not coming downstairs until nearly lunchtime. I'd been working hard on my proposal when she went out the door, and I had barely managed to flap my fingers in an absent-minded wave when she said good-bye.

Biting my lip, I disconnected the call, then flipped through my address book for Steve's new number. Maybe she had gone to the beach to see her father. If they had been watching a movie or doing something, she might have decided to stay at his place instead of going on to Charisse's house . . .

Someone picked up after the third ring. I nearly melted in relief when a female greeted me, then I tensed.

This was *not* my daughter's voice.

"May I speak to Steve, please? It's his—it's Diana."

"Just a minute."

Was it my imagination, or did that voice cool when she realized who I was?

I cleared my throat when Steve came on the line. "Sorry to interrupt—"

"You're not interrupting. It's just a little Fourth of July party for the office staff."

"At 11:00 P.M.?" I squinched my eyes together, unable to believe that a serpent of jealousy wriggled in my breast. What business was it of mine?

"Melanie's son is watching a video." Steve spoke in a soft, almost weary voice. "She wouldn't let him borrow it, so he's staying till the end."

"Oh." I felt a flush burn my cheeks. How could I sit here and act like some sort of green-eyed monster when our daughter was missing? "Listen, Steve—is Britt with you?"

"I haven't seen her." The softness fled his voice, replaced by sharp concern. "Where is she supposed to be?"

"She's supposed to be at Charisse's house, but Charisse just called here to inquire about a hickey on Britt's neck."

"What?"

"You heard me." I glanced at the clock. Nearly 11:15, and still no sign of my daughter. Her curfew was midnight on weekends, so she wasn't officially overdue yet, but it wasn't like her to go out without telling us where she was going . . . or was it? She'd been spending the night with Charisse for years, and we had never had any cause to doubt her word.

"Steve, I'm worried."

"Don't panic. Did you call her?"

"Of course. She didn't answer her phone."

"Maybe the battery's dead."

"Not likely. She keeps it charged—heaven forbid that she miss a call from one of her friends."

"Is it possible she went to some other girl's house?"

"Anything's possible—but who else?" I raked my hand through my hair, frantically trying to come up with other names. Brittany had been a member of a large peer group in middle school, but as she grew older, the girls drifted apart. She and Charisse had been best friends for the last three years.

I couldn't come up with a single name. "I don't know. I can't think of anyone."

"Good grief, Diana, she and Charisse have to hang out with somebody. You know kids of that age, they travel in packs."

"I know, but I don't know any of her other friends. They don't go to our church, and I don't think they even go to her school."

My thoughts whirled away, then zoomed back to focus on one sharp and disturbing realization. As a teenager, I was always bringing my friends home because Mom and Dad kept a supply of frozen pizzas in the freezer and cases of soda in the pantry. Britt had *never* wanted to bring her friends to our house, and deep inside, I knew why. She didn't want everyone to know she lived with Dr. Diana the radio shrink and Dr. Steve, the kiddie dentist with the big treasure chest.

I brought my hand to my forehead. "Think, Steve. What do we do?"

"What time did you tell her to be home?"

I swallowed hard, trying not to reveal my growing irritation with his questions. "I didn't tell her anything; she's supposed to be at Charisse's."

"Does Charisse know where she is?"

"Obviously not, since she called here expecting to find Britt."

That fact alarmed me more than anything. Even Charisse didn't know where Brittany was, and I was sure those two knew almost everything about each other. So if Britt had a secret she hadn't shared with her best friend—

"Steve, I'm scared."

"Wait till midnight, then call the police. She has to be somewhere."

"But where?"

Disturbing images blurred in my brain—Brittany strapped in her seat belt while the pickup sank in a culvert, lying battered and unconscious in a hospital bed, or drugged and being raped at some out-of-control Fourth of July party-—

"Lord, help us," I whispered. "Bring our baby home."

Forty

HEARING THE RISING PANIC IN DIANA'S VOICE, STEVE took a deep breath to calm the racing of his own heart. "Why don't you call her?"

"She didn't answer the first time!"

Steve gripped the phone, resisting the alarm that had sent a surge of adrenaline through his bloodstream. Diana needed calm counsel, not words to fuel her fear. "Try again. Maybe she was in the bathroom or something."

"All right. I'll call her. And so help me, when I reach her I'm going to let her have it for scaring us like this—"

The phone clicked. Steve pressed the talk button and punched in his daughter's number, determined to reach Britty before Diana did. His wife—*ex*-wife—was angry, and she didn't always think straight when in the grip of fury.

Fortunately, he had Britty's cell phone programmed into memory, and he heard it begin to ring a moment later. "Come on, Lord, let her pick up," he whispered, breathing a prayer into the phone. "Just let her be okay."

From the backseat of Zack Johnson's car, Brittany heard the phone ringing inside her purse.

Again.

"Ignore it," Zack whispered, his breath coming in short gasps.

"I ignored it last time. What if something's wrong?" Grateful for an opportunity to pull away, she sat up and reached for her purse, digging the phone out after only four rings.

"Hello?"

"Britty, where are you?"

Her father's voice slammed into her conscience with the force of a speeding locomotive. A shiver ran up her spine, a shudder that had nothing to do with the rush of cool air on her bare skin.

"Daddy?"

"You're supposed to be at Charisse's—but obviously, you're not. So would you mind telling me where you are? Your mother's frantic."

Brittany glanced behind her, where Zack leaned against the seat, one hand reaching out possessively to stroke her arm. Instinctively, she pulled away.

"I'm with a friend."

"Well, you'd better get home. Your mother's not happy that you lied about where you were going."

Brittany pressed her lips together as a wellspring of shame rose within her. She wanted to confess, to cry out that she was sorry for something far worse than her father would ever imagine her doing, but she couldn't say those things in front of Zack. And she still needed him to take her back to the beach where they had left her pickup.

"I'm going," she whispered. "I'll be home soon."

She rested her forehead on the back of the front seat. Why did everyone make such a big deal about sex? There had been no wonder here tonight, no oneness, no passion. Only discomfort, awkwardness, sweat . . .

And fear.

"I'm going home, Dad," she repeated, half hoping he'd hear her unspoken need. "I'm sorry."

"Okay." His voice was calmer now, the worry replaced by relief. "I'll call you tomorrow, okay? Even though you're not living with me, I still care about what's happening to you."

She wanted to cry, to hang her head and weep until she shuddered with hiccuping sobs, but she couldn't do that here.

"Okay, Dad."

She hung up the phone, then lowered her head and cast Zack a sidelong look. "I'm busted. You need to take me back."

He gave her a smile, and she could see he hadn't noticed the change in the quality of her attention. "Aw, baby, the night is young. Let the old coots wait awhile."

"You don't know my parents—and you especially don't know my mom. If I'm not home in half an hour, she'll call the cops. And she won't just go to bed—she'll sit up waiting for me. The longer she waits, the madder she'll get."

Zack heaved a heavy sigh, then pulled his T-shirt from the back of the front seat. "Okay, babe, good enough."

She stared at him. "Zack, do you love me?"

He laughed. "'Course, Britt."

Spurred by an innate modesty, she turned to look out the window as she fumbled with the buttons of her blouse. He loved her. So maybe the pain was worth it.

Her phone rang again, and without looking Brittany knew who was calling. She debated whether or not to answer, then decided she'd better.

"Hi, Mom," she said, just after hitting the talk key. "I'm on my way home."

"Where are you?" Her mother's voice was an angry buzz.

"In Madeira Beach."

"Where in Madeira Beach?"

"Um . . . in the park. I'm with a friend, Mom, and we're on our way home."

"Have you lost your mind, girl? You're supposed to be at Charisse's—"

"I'll be home in a few minutes."

She clicked the phone off and dropped it into her bag, wishing she could cut herself off from the last few months of her life as easily.

Forty-one

AFTER HANGING UP THE PHONE, I COULDN'T RELAX; I couldn't even sit still. The public park in Madeira Beach was a good half-hour away, and if Brittany was with someone, she might have to drop the friend off someplace . . .

Restless, I went up to my daughter's room, turned on the light, and looked at the usual assortment of teenage girl clutter. Nothing in the scattered clothes or magazines explained why my daughter had become a liar.

What had happened to my Britt? When had she changed, and how had I missed the signs?

I looked over the top of her dresser, then opened her underwear drawer and lifted out stacks of panties, bras, and socks. Nothing to explain how the good Christian girl I had raised could tell me bold-faced lies.

Had she *planned* to stay out all night? She regularly spent the night with Charisse; sometimes Friday and Saturday nights on a weekend. How many times had she actually been out running around the county, sleeping who knows where . . . and with whom?

My heart shook off the disloyal thought. Brittany wasn't a bad girl; she had never given us anything more than ordinary teenage trouble, and I had always considered myself an expert in differentiating between normal growing pains and outright rebellion. Our adult friends thought of Britt as sweet, polite, and relatively dependable. Sure, she rolled her eyes a lot and avoided us like the plague, but I attributed those things to adolescence, not character flaws. Besides, she had accepted Christ at an early age and she went to church with us every Sunday morning.

So how could she be the kind of girl who would lie and sneak around behind our backs?

I opened another drawer; nothing but shorts.

Another; bathing suits and tops.

I moved to the nightstand, where a stack of slick magazines toppled onto the floor as I opened the door. I scanned them for signs of incriminating evidence, but they were just magazines—not the sort I would have chosen, but how could I stop her from spending her allowance on junk when I wasn't around?

Sinking to the floor, I made a face at one particular cover—the magazine was called *Skank,* and one headline read, "Does he love your bod or your brain? Five ways to tell." The headline beneath it proclaimed, "Sticky fingers? Ten ways not to get caught."

Caught—what, *shoplifting*?

I pitched the magazine into the trash, then bent to look under the bed. Amid the childhood detritus of trolls and beheaded Barbies, I found a collection of CD cases. After pulling them out, I skimmed the names of the groups and realized I'd never heard of any of them. But I was not a fan of punk rock or whatever the kids were listening to these days, and Britt often went to concerts for local bands who burned CDs as easily as we used to make cassette tapes.

On a whim, I flipped open one of the plastic covers and read the words of a song. I don't know how they sounded set to music, but the lyrics were bad poetry and contained profanity that would have made my mother faint and attitudes that made my heart shrivel. Rebellion, despair, talk of suicide and hopelessness . . .

I dropped the CD cover as anguish seared my soul. Did my daughter *enjoy* listening to this junk? If she did, she had been feeding her heart and mind with soulless drivel while I sat before a microphone and admonished the parents of America to be vigilant about what went into their children's ears.

"Garbage in, garbage out," I whispered, gazing at the trash my daughter had chosen for entertainment. I knew each younger generation tried to be a little more outrageous than the previous one, and my generation had been pretty wild. I'd come of age in the seventies, when pot was cool and rebellion expected. But I had been a Christian, and my religious convictions had kept me from making really serious mistakes.

"What happened to my daughter, God?" The words came out as a wail. "Why haven't the things that worked for me worked for my daughter? Why haven't the things we've drummed into her since childhood kept her on the right path? Is she ignoring everything her father and I ever told her about truth and goodness and purity, or did we fail her somehow? Did we teach her about truth often enough and loud enough, or did we only assume she would pick up what she needed to know from Sunday school?"

I sank to the edge of the bed as my heart bulged with a question I didn't have the courage to speak aloud: *Were we to blame for this?*

The anxieties that had been lapping at my brain crested and crashed in a terrifying, painful roar—what had happened to my daughter's soul? I would have sworn her commitment to Christ was genuine. As a young girl she regularly read her Bible, she went on missions trips with the youth group, she seemed to honestly enjoy her relationship with God. But if she were a sincere believer, how could she live like this? Why wasn't the Spirit of God knocking her flat with conviction?

I lowered my head as tears welled in my eyes. Perhaps wishful thinking had skewed my perception of Brittany. Maybe it was all a lie—her salvation experience, her participation at church, her testimony. Peer pressure was a powerful force even in the early teen years; maybe she had only said and done the things she thought we expected her to say and do. Now that she had achieved a degree of independence, maybe she was showing her true colors away from our home and our supervision. Psychologists had a saying: the person your child is away from home is the person they'll become at maturity. I'd always taken comfort in that truism because no matter how often Britt rolled her eyes at us at home, in public she had always been well-mannered and polite.

What if I'd never seen the real Brittany?

Feeling as though some large, lumpy object pressed against my breastbone, I swallowed hard and braced myself to face the truth. I was losing my daughter. I *would* lose her, unless somehow I could identify the problem and correct it.

That's when I saw the leather corner of a blue book jutting out from beneath the mattress. I pulled it out and ran my hand over the leather cover.

A diary. An expensive one that did not lock, but closed by means of a leather strip that looped around the spine and fastened at the edge.

Should I read it? Ordinarily I would not pry into Britt's thoughts, but this was no ordinary night. I was fighting for my daughter's life, for her *soul,* and at the moment I was woefully unprepared for battle.

With trembling fingers, I untied the leather strap. Propping my back against the side of the bed, I flipped open the pages and began to read. The back of the book was blank, but at one point Britt had been faithful to write every night.

Thursday, September 5:

I swear, Mom never comes in my room anymore except to gripe about how messy it is! She's been a real witch lately, and I think she's all freaked out about the Scottster at kindergarten—as if that were the end of the world. Now it's like the only time she thinks of me is just to yell about something—my room, or the fact that I came in ten minutes late. Ten minutes! Like the fate of the universe hangs on ten minutes.

I wish she'd just go to bed and leave me alone—I mean, none of my other friends have a warden for a mother, just me. And Dad's just as bad. He's so dumb sometimes. Everybody loves him, but not everybody has to live with him.

Sometimes I'm so angry I just want to leave. Sometimes I think about getting married and not inviting them to the wedding—that'd serve them right. Sometimes I think about my mother being in a car wreck and in the hospital, and find myself wishing it would happen. At least she'd be out of my hair a few days. I think I could watch her drive into a lake and just sit there, not even getting up to call 911.

My Dumbo Dad could be in the car with her, I don't care. I'm sick and tired of living here. I'm sick of their rules and everybody telling me what I'm supposed to be. Everybody thinks I'm some kind of angel girl because of who my parents are, and that's not fair. It's like I've never had a chance to be who I am—whoever that is. I'm told what to think and what to wear and what kind of music to listen to. People think I'm one way, but they don't know the real me at all. I guess only Charisse does, but she's always in such a fog. She doesn't have a clue about anything really important.

Most of the time I hate them. I hate Scott. I hate everybody at church and at school. I hate my entire messed-up life.

Britt hated *Scott*? Trying to comprehend what I was reading, I checked the date again, then realized she'd written this well before the accident. I'd been telling myself this was mere backlash to the emotional trauma of losing Scott, a reaction to grief and loss, but Brittany had been feeling this anger for nearly a year.

I sat perfectly still and felt my heart break. It was a sharp, searing pain, probably much like the warning pang of a heart attack—the sort that makes old men clutch their chests and fall to the ground in agony.

How could she? Sadness pooled in my wounded heart, a gray despondency unlike anything I'd ever felt before. How could my beloved daughter have felt such rage toward us? We had never done anything but try our best to love and protect her.

I flipped to the back of the diary, then ruffled the pages until I found a more recent entry.

Saturday, June 14

Z has been asking me to sleep with him. I haven't yet—probably because I'm a little afraid of the whole idea, but I might change my mind. I've been so crazy lately, and Z seems to be the only person in my world who actually has his act together. He got a summer job at the record shop in the mall, and C and I like hanging out there. Sometimes Z and I slip into the stock room and make out for a while. It feels a little scary and weird, but maybe that's what love is.

I used to think I would never have sex before marriage because my parents would kill me if they found out, but I don't think that's so major anymore. I mean, what's the big deal? It's not like they're going to find out, with Dumbo Dad living in Clearwater and the witch with her nose stuck to the computer screen. The best thing about graduating is that they don't bug me as much as they used to about coming in on time . . . or maybe the witch just doesn't care anymore.

I do know this—all that stuff about marriage being holy and pure and for life is a crock. I always thought my parents loved each other, but you should hear them now. I don't know what's going on in their heads, but I know it's not good. It sure isn't holy and pure.

All I know is that Z says he loves me and I believe him. And if he asks, you know, the question again, I'll probably say yes.

Why not?

I froze as the front door slammed. My head felt numb and my heart still throbbed from the knowledge I'd just gleaned, but the sound of the door roused me to action. I stood, about to shove the diary back under the bed, then stopped.

No. There should be no more secrets between us.

Wrapping my courage around the strands of my raveled, bleeding heart, I tucked the diary under my arm and went to greet the daughter I no longer knew.

Forty-two

THE SHADOW MOVING ACROSS THE FOYER'S TILED FLOOR was too large for Brittany, and for a moment my breath caught in my throat. Then the unidentified visitor moved into the circle of lamp light.

Steve.

I had never been so relieved to see another adult in my life. "Steve," I called, clinging to the banister as I crept down the stairs. With its heavy secrets, the diary beneath my arm felt like a fifty-pound weight.

I paused at the bottom of the steps, not certain how to begin. If ever a situation called for a united front, this one did.

Stepping closer, he looked up at me. "Forgive me for letting myself in. Old habits, you know." His shoulders rose in a faint, helpless shrug. "I decided to come help you. Not that you need help, but . . . I thought I should be here."

The wave of indignation I'd felt earlier came flooding back. "What about your party?"

"Everybody went home when I told them I had a family emergency."

I closed my eyes to trap a sudden rush of tears. *Thank you, God, that I still have an ally in Steve.*

"I'm glad you're here." I stepped off the stairs and showed him the diary. His questioning gaze traveled from the book to my eyes, so I hurried to explain. "I found this in her room. I don't usually snoop, you know, but I had to see if I could find something to explain why she would lie to us." I took a deep, unsteady breath. "I discovered I don't know our daughter at all."

He slipped his hands into his pockets, then inclined his head toward the living room. "Want to sit and talk?"

"I'd like that. She's not home yet, but I expect her any time now."

We moved into the living room, where Steve sat on the couch while I sank into the wing chair. I turned on the lamp, then opened to the page I'd been reading when he pulled up.

"She hates us," I said simply. "She thinks of me as a witch, and you're Dumbo Dad—and those, I think, are her more affectionate terms for us. But what frightens me is the anger she expresses here. I can't believe any child raised in a loving home can feel this way. I certainly never hated my parents like this."

"You're not Brittany." He spoke softly, though his eyes glowed with the same pain I felt. "I don't think we can judge her through the lens of our experience."

I propped my elbow on the arm of the chair and pushed at the hair on my forehead. "I don't know what to do. We should send her to a counselor, I suppose."

His sharp laughter caught me off guard. "Do you honestly think Brittany would agree to see a counselor? For heaven's sake, Diana, she's lived with a counselor for eighteen years! Counseling is the last thing she wants!"

"But she needs it! I've only read a few pages of this, and I'm scared to death. The girl who wrote this is filled with hate, and anger, and fear. She's also thinking about sleeping with some guy. I'm frightened for her."

He brought his hand to his stubbled jaw, then gave me a brief, distracted glance and tried to smile. "What would you tell a caller who called your show with this problem?"

I blinked at him. "What would I—I can't answer that. It's different when it's your own child."

"It shouldn't be. You're the professional counselor, the family expert. You've been telling people what to do for years."

Whether or not he intended it, the words stung. I sat back, a frown puckering my mouth as I realized how right he was. I was a phony. My show was a sham. The so-called advice I'd been dispensing over the airwaves held about as much value as empty air.

Disappointment struck like a blow to my stomach. I lowered my eyes, looked at my empty palms, then shook my head. "I don't know. If she doesn't repent and turn around, I might say the parents have to kick her out. After all, if they allow her to continue to lie to them, aren't they enabling her to continue doing wrong?"

I hauled my gaze from my helpless hands and returned my attention to the man on the sofa. "It's not like this is the first time Brittany has lied. Remember the timer and the lamp? Only the Lord knows how many nights she fooled us with that setup. Now I'm wondering how many nights she's been out running around when we thought she was with Charisse. Sometimes tough love is the only option. Sometimes you have to be tough if you want to preserve your own sanity . . ."

I let my words trail off, not willing to verbalize all the pictures that had crystallized in my mind over the past half-hour. Though I had never imagined my daughter in such scenarios before, I now pictured her sporting hookerwear and sipping from a bottle of Scotch in a den of drug dealers. What if she had contracted a venereal disease? What if she had had an abortion? Would I even know about it?

Looking at the man who had once been my best friend, I longed for the protectiveness of his arms, then shoved the longing away. "If you were the professional counselor, what would you advise?"

He brought up his hand to cover his mouth, closed his eyes for a moment, then let his arm fall to his side. "I don't have a clue, but I know who does. What other parents do and say doesn't matter in this situation. What my folks did with me or what yours did with you doesn't count for anything. We've just come through a terrible ordeal, and this situation is unique."

"Other families have gone through terrible ordeals—"

"Their experiences don't have anything to do with us. There's only one person I trust to prescribe behavior for us now, and that's who I'm going to ask for advice."

I gave him a look of sheer disbelief. Steve had never read a psychology book in his life, as far as I knew, unless he'd taken to reading them in the five weeks since he'd moved out.

"And that expert would be?"

"The heavenly Father."

Silence stretched between us. I lowered my gaze as a fresh wave of guilt washed through my soul, followed by a tide of indignation. I thought about God all the time. I had been praying for Brittany in the last hour. What else was I supposed to do?

I smiled to cover my annoyance. "And how are we supposed to arrange an appointment with God?"

"Think about it—how does he react when we are filled with anger and hate? And we do resent him sometimes, even though we're his children." Steve trembled slightly, as if a chilly wind had blown over him. "I resented him plenty after the accident. I couldn't understand why he'd take Scotty . . . and once I asked why he'd take our son, who adored us, and leave us with a teenager who didn't give a flip about our family. But even in the face of my ugliest honesty, he didn't turn away. Even when I angrily pounded the arms of that easy chair, he never left my side. His Spirit kept telling me to trust him . . . one day at a time."

A trace of unguarded tenderness shone in Steve's eyes as he met my gaze. "She may choose to walk away from us. But no matter how angry you are for Britty's betrayal, no matter how hurt you are by what you've read, you can't give up on her, Diana."

"Part of me wants to." I thought of the vitriol running like a flaming thread through her diary. "Honestly, right now I'm ready to get her out of the house. She's been running around for God knows how long, lying to us, hating us—how can she hate us when we're the ones who work to put clothes on her back and a roof over her head? We've done nothing but support her and love her; we've tried to teach her the right things. We've brought her up in the best home we knew how to make, yet look how she has chosen to repay us!"

Steve rested his cheek in his hand. "I know, honey. I'm feeling the same things. But we can't make a mistake now, because our reaction to this could affect the rest of her life. We have to think and pray and proceed carefully."

"The parent of the prodigal," I murmured, my thoughts wandering.

"What's that?"

"Something our 'quip of the day' lady said a few weeks ago. She said that at some time, every parent is the parent of the wandering prodigal, with nothing to do but keep the house open to hope."

"She's right." The warmth of Steve's smile echoed in his voice. "She's exactly right, Diana. We have to hope and pray that Brittany comes around."

I listened, I heard, but I wasn't sure I was ready to take his advice. God might be long-suffering and forgiving . . . but I wasn't God.

Forty-three

IN A SUDDEN FLASH OF REVELATION, BRITTANY REAL-
ized that nothing felt as awful—or as wonderful—as walking into
the foyer and seeing her mom and dad in the living room beyond.

Awful, because she'd been caught in a lie . . . and the lie was the
least of what she'd done tonight.

Wonderful because her parents were together.

Terrible because neither of them looked inclined toward sympathy. Somehow the infamous united front had pulled together over
the divide of divorce.

Better face the music.

Drawing a deep breath, she took a step forward. "I'm sorry."

Ignoring the apology, Mom straightened in her chair. "Where
were you?"

"And who were you with?" Dad's brows lowered in a frown.

Crossing one arm over her chest, Brittany knew it'd be best to
tell the truth . . . or as much of the truth as they could handle.

"I was with Zack Johnson." She glanced from her mom to her
dad. "You don't know him."

Her mother fixed her in a hot glare. "You told me you were spending the night with Charisse."

"I didn't."

"Is this the first time you've lied to us?"

Looking at the floor, Brittany weighed her options. If she confessed to a few things, maybe the other things would remain hidden. "No. I've been out a couple of times with Zack."

When she looked up again, her father wore a look of astounded horror. "What do you *do* all night?"

"Nothing, Dad." She shrugged. "We go to Dunkin Donuts or Steak 'n Shake . . . or sometimes we just go to the beach and talk. A couple of times he's taken me back to Charisse's house."

Mom's hand went to her throat. "Charisse's mother lets you come in at all hours of the morning?"

"Charisse's mother goes to bed." Brittany dared to meet her mother's burning gaze. "I just tap on Charisse's window, and she gets up to let me in."

"Brittany—" Her father leaned forward, resting his elbows on his knees. "I don't understand why you felt it necessary to lie to us. If you want to date this boy, why didn't you bring him home to meet us? We're not opposed to you dating. We're not monsters."

Lowering her gaze, Brittany shrugged.

"Your father asked a good question." Her mother's voice came out hoarse, as if forced through a sore throat. "Despite what you think, we are not your jailers. I am not the wicked witch, and your father is a far cry from a Dumbo Dad."

A shiver struck Brittany's spine. Shifting her gaze, she saw a blue book on the coffee table. *The* blue book.

Her mother had read her diary. No wonder she was hacked.

She dared to risk indignation. "You *snooped*?"

"You gave me reason to," her mother answered in a level voice.

"I've always respected your privacy, but you lied to me. And when you break trust, Britt, you lose privileges. Even the privilege of privacy."

Brittany crossed one arm over her chest. "Can I go upstairs now?"

"I'm not sure we're done here." Mom looked at Dad. "Anything you want to say to your daughter while we're together?"

Dad nodded. "You bet there is."

Forty-four

I SANK BACK IN MY CHAIR, ALL TOO RELIEVED THAT Steve had come and was now talking to our daughter. He had been right about one thing: I was too hurt, too angry, and too wounded to handle the situation rationally. I couldn't forget what Brittany had written about me driving into a lake and how she wouldn't call 911 if I were drowning.

What had I done to evoke that kind of hostility? I had done nothing but love the kid, sacrifice for her, and pray for her. I hadn't been a perfect parent, but I'd done the best I could . . . hadn't I?

When Steve and I first married, I had wanted a baby more than anything. After nearly three years of riding the infertility roller coaster, we decided to adopt—and signing the agency agreement had been a huge leap of faith. Steve was just beginning his practice, still paying off school bills, and I was struggling to finish my master's degree. Money was tight in those days, but somehow we obtained a second mortgage on our small home and forked over a check to the adoption agency. We passed another anxious eighteen months before the agency placed Brittany Jane with us.

As sure as I lived, I knew God wanted us to be parents. Steve loved children, and motherhood was the desire of my heart. How could a loving God fail to grant the position he had designed us to fill?

He didn't. At six weeks of age Brittany came home, a tiny, beautiful pink bundle of smiles. We adored her, and I finally felt truly fulfilled. I took her everywhere, even to school when I studied in the library. When I walked up to get my diploma, I carried Britt in a Snugli on my chest.

I had been made for motherhood, or so I thought. When Brittany went to school, I took pains to be available whenever needed. I served as a room mother, I baked dozens of cookies for her class and served as a minivan chauffeur on field trips. I attended every science fair, speech meet, concert, and fund-raising event. Steve, who by that time had built a thriving practice, reserved Saturdays and Sundays for family outings and church.

I thought life couldn't get any better. And when Britt entered middle school and wanted to be let out of the car at the corner so her friends wouldn't see her with me, I reminded myself that this behavior was typical for the age. Pulling away was natural and normal; she had to learn to stand on her own within her peer group. She was becoming an exotically beautiful young lady, and my heart sang every time I looked at her.

Then Scott Daniel came. My thoughts turned again to diapers and sleepers, but this time the miracle had happened within my own body. I breast-fed him—a wonder!—and sometimes I think we bonded in a way Brittany and I never had. Because my radio career began while I was pregnant with Scott, I worked extra hard to do all the things I had done for Britt. I didn't have time for much else, but by then Brittany had dropped out of her extracurricular activities, and seemed intent on pretending she didn't even have parents—

I felt the truth all at once, like an electric jolt through my spine.

I had nearly lost my daughter.

"We love you, Britty," Steve was saying, "and you will always have a home with us. But if you lie to us, if you demonstrate that you cannot be trusted, you will face the consequences. If you cannot function as a part of this household with a compliant spirit and a willing heart, you are free to leave. We will help you pack your things, and we will set you free."

His voice softened as his eyes filled. "We don't want you to leave. We want to support you in college; we want to stand by you through life. But if you cannot live with us, Brittany Jane, you can live without us. The choice is yours to make."

Britt's chin wobbled as she looked up. "I'm sorry." Her gaze fell on the diary, and I knew she had to be thinking of all she had written—things I hadn't even read.

"Take some time," Steve said, "and think about your decision, because this isn't something you can dismiss with a simple apology. I'm sorry we haven't caught this pattern of disobedient behavior sooner, and I apologize for not being as vigilant as I should have been. Now you need to decide whether you want to be part of this family or step out on your own."

Her face twisted. "How can you say that? This isn't a *family* anymore."

Oh, no. I would not allow her to shift the blame for her misdeeds to our shoulders. And if she wanted to match pain for pain, the events of this night had left me armed and bristling for battle.

"You said you wouldn't even call for help if I drove into the lake—" Anguish choked off my voice. I stared at her. "You wouldn't care if I *died*?"

Her eyes filled with tears, but I couldn't tell if they sprang from shame, fear, or guilt. I waited, but she did not apologize, nor did she deny a word she'd written.

And in that moment I experienced what psychologists describe as the fine line between love and hate. My passionate yearning for my daughter, wounded by her words, flamed into an equally passionate revulsion.

"Finish up with her," I told Steve, weeping as I rose from my chair. "I can't stay here."

Leaving them together in the living room, I crossed the foyer in swift steps and let myself out into the darkness.

forty-five

S TEVE LOOKED AT HIS WEEPING DAUGHTER AND KNEW
she'd not soon forget this night. This was not a simple matter of being
caught in a lie. Tonight they had pulled back the curtain and seen
their daughter as she really was.

Charisse's phone call had been a blessing in disguise. If she hadn't
called, and if Diana hadn't found the diary, they might still believe
their daughter was no more than a moderately troublesome teenager.

"We love you very much, Britty." He stood in order to look
directly into her eyes. "But you've hurt us deeply—not only by your
actions, but by your words."

Her chin trembled when he gestured toward the diary. He thought
she wanted to deny the things she'd written, but couldn't.

He slipped his hands into his pockets. "I know it hasn't been easy
being our kid. That's why we're offering you a way out. But home is
the place where you'll always be welcome, and we're the parents who
will always love you."

Weeping in earnest now, she sank to the love seat in front of him.
"I could live with you." She paused to swipe at her cheeks. "Mom's
mad at me, so if I lived with you—"

"Your mom's anger will pass, but it's going to take her a while to get over the hurt. I'm hurt, too. You can't treat us with hate and disdain and expect us not to feel anything in response."

"I'm sorry, okay?" She shifted, clearly unwilling to meet his gaze. "Can I go upstairs now?"

He nodded. "If you have nothing to add, I suppose we're done here."

Rising, she whirled away and took the stairs two at a time.

Exhaling slowly, Steve sank back to the sofa and watched her go. He would have liked to see something more from her, some sign of genuine brokenness as opposed to regret that she'd gotten caught. But for better or worse, this situation was finished. She would decide how they'd play the next act.

He lowered his head to his hand. Never in a hundred years would he have believed he'd reach the point where he'd have to ask his beloved daughter to leave home, but he couldn't stand by and do nothing while she lived in rebellion.

Abashed at his choice of words, he shook his head. It felt ridiculous telling a kid to leave home when there was no more unified home to leave. Most kids would do what she had suggested—if they had a falling out with Mom, they'd move in with Dad until things got tough there, then they'd hightail it back to Mom's house. Back and forth, like some kind of human ping-pong ball, forced out only when both parents had endured all the trials they could handle . . . or they just couldn't care anymore.

Thank God, he still cared. And, though she had been cut to the quick, Diana still cared. The bond between her and Britty had been forged years ago, and it would grow strong again when Britty began to raise a family of her own. Maybe then she would learn how to see her parents as individuals, not as authority figures. Looking through the scope of hindsight, perhaps she'd appreciate the family she had enjoyed in her youth.

He closed his eyes as another bolt of remorse struck him. *Had* enjoyed? Why did he always find himself thinking in past tenses?

He stood, then crossed the foyer and went out the front door. Pausing on the front porch, he listened. A midnight silence enveloped the neighborhood, with no televisions, no music, no clattering skateboards to disturb it. Overhead, a wind whispered through the sheltering oak near the sidewalk, rustling like the silken swish of the black dress Diana used to wear on special evenings out.

The memory tugged at him, drew him onward. A light burned from the neighbor's front porch, and somewhere in the distance a dog barked. Steve stepped into the sultry darkness and began to walk, adding the quiet jingle of the change in his pocket to the night sounds.

He'd passed three houses when he saw Diana standing beneath the live oak. In the slanting silvery rays of moonlight she stood on the sidewalk, her shoulders bent, her head bowed, her hands pressed to her face . . . receiving, no doubt, her tears.

He quickened his pace to join her, and she looked up at the sounds of his steps on the sidewalk. When he opened his arms, she stepped into them willingly.

Without speaking he held her, all his loneliness and confusion fusing together in one surge of terrible yearning.

Forty-six

FEELING AS THOUGH DEVILISH HANDS WERE SLOWLY twisting the joy from my heart, I leaned against Steve's chest and cried out my anger, sorrow, and frustration.

"Why is God doing this to me? I'm not Job! But he's taken everything, beginning with Scott Daniel. He took my son, my job, my career, and now he's taking my daughter—"

Steve's hand, which had been stroking my shoulder, suddenly froze. "Your career?"

Pulling back, I palmed tears from my cheeks. "The network fired me when I announced my plans to proceed with the cloning. I'll be okay; my agent thinks I can get a TV show, but it couldn't have happened at a worse time."

He reached into his pocket, then offered me a handkerchief. "I'm sorry."

Grateful for his thoughtfulness, I took it and blew my nose. "Thanks. Really." Squinting, I looked up at him. "Is Britt okay?"

"She went up to bed. I imagine she'll cry herself to sleep, but this night has given her a lot to think about."

I pressed a hand to my temple, where I could already feel my veins warming up to a major migraine. "Me, too. I can't believe I never saw any signs of her feelings."

"We did see signs, Di. We misinterpreted them." Pausing, he looked at me, and I wondered at the speculation in his eyes. "What'd you say a minute ago about God doing this to you? I thought you had decided God had nothing to do with it."

I shook my head. "Maybe Pastor John had a point. All I know is that I really do feel like Job. It's like God decided to take everything I loved just to see if I'd curse him and die."

I paused to blow my nose, then dabbed at it with the handkerchief. My stomach writhed and knotted under Steve's compassionate gaze. I didn't know how to explain all the feelings storming my heart—I've always found it easier to verbalize thoughts than emotions—but I knew this man would listen without judging me too harshly.

"I tell you one thing—I'm ready to give up on advice-giving. I'm a fraud."

"Now, Diana—"

"It's true! I try to tell other people how to raise their children, and look at me! I can't raise a daughter, and I couldn't protect my son. I'm an utter failure, and—" Fresh tears choked my throat. "I can't even stay married!"

"Hush, now." His hands fell on my shoulders, then he lowered his head until his brow rested upon mine. "Diana, you're being too hard on yourself. I lost a son, too. My daughter's in trouble, too."

"But your entire life isn't falling apart. You still have your practice."

"That's crazy, Diana. I lost you, and *you* were my life. The practice is just busywork."

Amazed that he could still hold me with tenderness, I looked at him through a haze of tears.

"And you're forgetting something about Job. Job was a righteous believer, but he wasn't perfect. He was clinging to something even during all his trials, something God wiped away in the end."

Frowning, I pulled away. I thought I knew everything about Job, but I had no idea what Steve meant. "Job had nothing but his nagging wife, and who'd want to cling to her?"

Steve laughed. "I wasn't talking about his wife; I was referring to his pride. Even in his suffering, Job was proud of himself . . . until God showed him how small he was."

My husband—no, my friend—gave me a smile that gleamed in the moonlight. "What are you clinging to, Diana?"

Crickets chirped an accompaniment as I considered the question. What *did* I have left? I'd been stripped as thoroughly as an abandoned car. All I had now were dreams of the future and a desperate desire to hold my child again—

My thoughts came to an abrupt halt. The most important thing in my life since Scott Daniel's accident was the cloning. That hope kept me going, yet it had splintered my marriage and fractured my family.

I swallowed hard. Surely God wouldn't ask me to give up an opportunity he had provided.

Steve pressed through my silence. "Diana?"

"I know what you want me to say." I crossed my arms. "You want me to change my mind about the cloning. But I can't. It's my pearl of great price, the thing I am willing to give everything for."

Steve shook his head. "You've misunderstood the analogy."

Again, I had encountered stubborn stone. "I understand it fine! I know it's about salvation, but sometimes a verse can apply to more than one situation. And I really believe God sent the cloning opportunity our way. I think you're wrong to disagree with me. I think our divorce is wrong. I think Brittany's made wrong choices in her behavior. But most of all I think it'd be wrong to give up on my baby."

He looked at me then, and in his eyes I saw pity mingled with regret. "I should be getting back." He slid his hands into his pockets. "I've a full day tomorrow."

"Me, too," I answered, though I had absolutely nothing on my calendar. I'd probably sleep late and spend the afternoon sending out résumés.

"Before I go, though, I want to say this—you are doing your dead-level best to avoid facing reality, Diana. Scotty is gone, and there's nothing you can do about it. You can't bring him back. You can't replicate him. God brought him into our lives, yes, but God also took him away. And I have to believe he had a reason."

I resisted the childish impulse to throw my hands over my ears. "I don't want to hear this."

"Of course you don't. It's too painful. But in the last few months I've learned that grief is like standing in twilight. You can run west toward the setting sun, hoping to avoid the darkness, but the fastest way to see sunshine again is to walk east through the night. It's not easy, because grief is a lot darker than dusk. But it's the surest and least exhausting way to live in the sun again."

I stared at him, surprise mingling with indignation. Who was *he* to give me counsel? I had two degrees in psychology and one in biblical studies. He was a *dentist.*

Steve's face twisted in a small grimace, and I had the uncomfortable sense that he'd read my thoughts. "One thing I know," he said, featherlike lines crinkling around his eyes. "God is in the dark, too. I feel his presence every minute."

A wave of guilt slapped at my soul. How long had it been since I felt God's presence?

I raised my hand as if to ward away the question, then shook my head and turned toward home. We walked back together, then Steve got into his car while I walked into the dark house without him.

Forty-seven

STEVE WAITED UNTIL HE HEARD THE SLAM OF THE front door and the click of the deadbolt, then he started the car and pulled out into the street. With every yard he traveled, the emptiness in his soul seemed to expand.

He was driving away from the two women he loved most in the world, and both were in terrible pain. Both of them needed him.

Neither of them wanted him.

His fingers tightened around the steering wheel. Once he'd told his Sunday school class that he hadn't really understood the depths of God's love until he became a parent; tonight he was glimpsing the depths of God's forgiving mercy.

He loved them; he saw the error of their ways and the denial in their hearts. Brittany had been showered with love and affection from the moment they grafted her into their family, and nothing would ever make him stop loving her.

So why did she resist him? Why hadn't she broken down in remorse and fallen into his arms? Her feeble "I'm sorry" meant, "I'm sorry you caught me," nothing more. Defiance had still gleamed in her eyes when she raced up the stairs, and soon she would be away at school where they'd have no way to supervise her.

All they could do was pray.

He pulled up to a red light. A teenage couple sat in the car next to him, the girl draped over the boy, the boy energetically chewing something as he bounced in time to the throbbing rhythm of whatever was pounding through his speakers.

Looking away, Steve shook his head. Why were people so stubborn?

Diana was the worst. She could be as stubborn as a stuck door when she made up her mind to believe something. No amount of pushing or prying could shake her free of her convictions.

Yet he understood what drove her toward cloning. Her ability to love deeply was one of the things that had first attracted him to her. She brought passion to her projects, she threw herself headlong into whatever causes she felt led to undertake, and he'd always stood with her, supporting her.

This time, though, he couldn't follow her.

The light changed. He waited until the teenager in the next lane had roared ahead, then he eased down on the accelerator and turned the car toward Clearwater Beach.

He pressed his hand to his chest, where his heart literally ached.

Father . . . why does love have to hurt so much?

Forty-eight

I SLEPT THAT NIGHT IN A SHALLOW DOZE IN WHICH dreams mingled with inchoate fragments of memory. I sought my dream of Scott Daniel, but it was Brittany's face, pale and sorrowful, playing on the backs of my eyelids, followed by Steve's sad smile as he said good-bye on the front porch.

Waking was a relief. At seven o'clock I flung off the heavy comforter and padded down the hall, then quietly peeked into Brittany's bedroom. Something in me feared she had slipped away for good in the night, but her form lay beneath the covers, her red hair streamed across the pillow.

Closing the door, I breathed a prayer of thankfulness and climbed back into my big bed. After drawing the heavy comforter over my shoulders, I nestled into the warm space I had occupied all too short a time. But wakefulness had deposited remnants of reality upon my pillow, needling thoughts that weren't about to let me retreat into unconsciousness.

Unasked, my ex-husband had come when I needed him.

My daughter had been lying to us for months.

Steve still loved me.

My virtuous daughter wasn't virtuous.

Steve would come back if I could give up the most important thing in my life.

Brittany hated me with a passion.

If I didn't want Steve, some other woman would be happy to move into the space I had vacated. Steve was a good man, handsome, faithful, and a good provider. Furthermore, he was the marrying type. It wouldn't be long before some single woman caught him on her radar and flew in to intercept.

I had nearly lost my daughter—and I might lose her still.

Steve would not come back unless I gave up the cloned baby . . .

But I couldn't lose the baby, too. At the moment, the baby was the most certain thing in my future.

I lay with my eyes closed for fifteen minutes, then gave up the struggle to sleep. I climbed out of bed, showered, and went downstairs for my morning caffeine. Twenty minutes later I was sitting in my study with the yellow pages open.

I called the first three realtors listed, made appointments for them to see the house, and promised myself I'd sign an agreement with the first one to show up with an adequate marketing plan. Within seven weeks Brittany would be leaving for college, and even if the house sold tomorrow, it'd take at least six weeks for us to de-clutter, pack, and handle the paperwork required for closing.

I spent the rest of my Saturday interviewing real-estate agents. One dear lady hugged me three times when hearing of my sad situation (divorce, empty nest, job relocation); the second woman made regretful *tsk*ing noises as we toured the house.

I hired the third agent out of sheer weariness. He shook my hand, produced a listing agreement, and told me the sign guy would plant the "For Sale" sign first thing Monday morning.

Brittany and I avoided each other for the rest of the day. She did not go to Charisse's house, but stayed in her room. Something in me hoped she was tossing out trashy magazines and obscene CDs, but when I walked past her door, nothing in her room had changed.

After dinner I moved through the house with a notepad in one hand and a pencil behind my ear, making a list of all the cosmetic things I'd have to do to sell the house. The paint on my shower ceiling was peeling; the paintings in the stairwell would have to come down so I could patch the nail holes and repaint the wall. The carpets would have to be cleaned; the sod patched, fresh flowers planted in the pots beside the front door. Maybe geraniums, since they were bright and easy to grow . . .

Since I'd put all Scott Daniel's things in storage for the new baby, his room was pristine. Brittany's room—well, I'd just promise prospective buyers that I'd install new carpet and paint the walls in September. No sense in cleaning a room that would be a wreck again by nightfall.

On Sunday Britt and I went to church. We sat together in the service, not looking at each other and not speaking. The sermon was on God's sovereignty, and I found myself praying that Brittany would listen.

Our pastor talked about the media in today's society, and I found myself thinking of the terrible magazines I'd seen in Britt's bedroom. Then he read God's message to the prophet Isaiah: "I am the one who exposes the false prophets as liars by causing events to happen that are contrary to their predictions. I cause wise people to give bad advice, thus proving them to be fools."

I could only hope Britt would realize she'd been reading bad advice.

She spent all Sunday afternoon in her bedroom, venturing out only long enough to eat and dart into the bathroom. I tried talking to her about trivial things like the weather when she came into the kitchen, but my attempts at conversation fell flat.

Sunday night I went into her bedroom and stood in the doorway. Britt sat upon her bed, one leg crossed, the other dangling over the edge of the mattress.

"I love you, Britt"—tears weakened my voice—"I'm sorry for the times I wasn't there for you."

A shadow of annoyance crossed her face. "What are you apologizing to *me* for? I'm the one who messed up."

"We all mess up, honey. But just as the Lord forgives us, we need to forgive each other. I need you to forgive me, and I'll forgive you."

She lowered her gaze to the magazine on her bed, though the twitch of a muscle in her jaw told me she was upset. I waited for a response, but she said nothing.

"Britt? Do you forgive me?"

"Yes." The reply was sharp.

"I forgive you, too." I spoke in as gentle a tone as I could manage. "And tomorrow will be a new day, a new week. We can each start over with a clean slate."

She didn't answer, but I walked forward and drew her stiff body into my arms, holding her long enough to whisper again, "I love you, honey."

I wouldn't have been surprised if she were rolling her eyes while I hugged her.

She didn't dissolve, she didn't confess, she only remained silent. I left her sitting there, knowing I had done the best I could at the moment. What was it Charity had said? At some time every parent is the parent of the wandering prodigal . . . and prodigals had to *want* to come home.

I rose early on Monday morning. After a cup of coffee, a quick shower, and enough newspaper reading to convince me I wasn't the most miserable woman in the world, I went to my desk with a blank legal pad. I had never submitted a formal proposal—my radio career had begun almost accidentally after I accepted a six-week gig as a temporary host. Our ratings soared, my position became permanent, and my career blossomed when we were picked up by the network.

I wrote the word *staff*, then scrawled, *Gary Ripley, producer.* That much was easy; I couldn't imagine doing a show without Gary. We'd been together so long he could practically read my mind, and I was certain he would welcome a move to television. Radio had its perks, but the potential demographics of television made it look like small potatoes. Our earning potential would rise dramatically, too, and Gary certainly wouldn't mind making more money.

I grinned, thinking of him working on-camera like producer Michael Gelman, who had a huge on-screen presence on *Live with Regis and Kelly*. Gary was a handsome guy, young enough to draw the eighteen-to-thirty-four demographic, and the camera would eat him up. So would my audience.

I tapped the pencil against my cheek as I considered other possible staff members. Chad would probably get a kick out of being employed by a television network, but he worked for other radio shows, too, so I wasn't sure he would want to leave WFLZ.

Maybe I was putting the cart before the horse. We had to sell the concept of the show first; we could worry about staff later. And my agent would know what sorts of personnel perks were negotiable.

I had just fleshed out an introductory statement—*Dr. Diana Sheldon, renowned radio host and experienced counselor, offers moral and ethical perspectives on the latest medical technologies, with an emphasis on reproductive technologies*—when the phone rang, scattering my thoughts.

I picked it up. "Hello?"

The caller was Cynthia Somebody-or-Other, calling from the personnel office of WHGK in Fort Lauderdale. Her voice was warm and friendly.

My thoughts focused immediately. "WHGK? Are you a talk-radio format?"

"That's us." My heart did a double-beat. Could they have heard about my availability? I wasn't looking for a job at an independent station, but if this was the door God opened . . . Working in Florida might be a good option for Brittany's sake, since she would be going to Florida State.

I took care to match Cynthia's friendly tone. "What can I do for you?"

"I'm calling about Gary Ripley. He has applied for a position and listed you as a reference. Do you mind if I ask you a few questions about Mr. Ripley?"

My mouth went dry. "Um, sure." I took pains to sound cheerful as I assured her that Gary was a good worker, innovative, reliable, and visionary.

"He was my right hand," I said, uncomfortably aware that I was speaking of him in the past tense. "I don't know what I'll do without him."

Cynthia Whoever seemed oblivious to the note of desperation in my voice as she thanked me and hung up. Dropping the handset back to the phone, I clapped my hand to my cheek and considered the paper on the desk before me.

Gary, who'd been my shadow for the last five years, had decided not to hitch his wagon to a falling star. Obviously he hadn't believed my assurances that we'd find a spot in television, and he had wasted no time applying at another station—probably half a dozen. Gary never did a thing halfway, and with his credentials he'd be hired within the month. Which left me alone, with no producer to help me shape the program, no friend to help me pitch the idea.

At least I still had my agent. As long as I paid him, he wouldn't jump ship.

I ate a tasteless lunch of tomato soup and stale crackers, then went back to my study and tried to focus on my task. Six weeks of severance pay wouldn't last long, and I needed to pay my lawyer and set money aside for Project One's fee.

Time to type up the official proposal. I slid into my desk chair and rolled across the tile floor, then picked up the legal pad and propped it against the printer. I had no sooner clicked on the icon for my word processing program than the phone rang again.

I stared at it, wondering if this was yet another call from a personnel office. Gary would be thorough, and as much as I wanted to tell anyone who called to go jump in a lake, I couldn't do that to a friend.

Sighing, I picked up the phone. "Hello?"

"Dr. Diana Sheldon?"

Gritting my teeth, I glanced at the caller ID. No station call letters this time, just a private number with a Fort Lauderdale area code. Probably someone from WHGK wanting to know where to send Gary's first paycheck.

"Speaking."

"You don't know me, but I've been dying to talk to you."

Inwardly, I groaned. *This* was the reason I had an unlisted number. At work I took calls from the public all day; I did not want to do telephone counseling at home. Besides, hadn't this person heard I was out of the business?

"I'm sorry," I said, "but I really can't take counseling calls now. And how did you get this number?"

"Please, Dr. Diana—" The woman's voice wavered. "A friend gave me your number; she saw it somewhere in her office. I called because I have to know about cloning. I desperately want to do it, and no one here seems to understand why this is something I have to do."

I didn't hang up. Despite the intrusion, I leaned forward on the desk.

"Tell me your story."

"I have a son—his name is Tyler; he's three months old. He was perfectly healthy at birth, but he developed pneumonia when he swallowed some amniotic fluid. The doctors gave him a drug—too much, actually—and it severely damaged his lungs. We've filed a lawsuit and we'll soon have the money to do the cloning procedure. I've read about your situation in the paper, and my husband and I know our best answer is cloning."

"Really." I felt myself begin to relax. If Steve were here, I'd put him on the extension to hear this woman's perspective. Maybe then he'd begin to understand that it was perfectly rational to want to produce a twin who could continue when one child's life had been prematurely ended.

"Do you have access to Tyler's tissue samples?"

"Yes. He was genetically perfect at birth, but with his damaged lungs the doctors say he may not live past the age of three or four. So I want to have another baby—"

"Wait." A sudden chill touched my spine. "Your son is still living?"

"Of course. Our doctors all agree a lung transplant is Tyler's best chance at a normal life. And since he is still young and small for his age, there's a good chance the clone's lungs will grow quickly to catch up."

I felt a sudden coldness in my stomach, as though I had swallowed a fist-sized chunk of ice. "I'm sorry. I didn't catch your name."

"Glenda. Glenda Jones."

"Well, Glenda, let me see if I'm understanding the full picture— you want to conceive a child in order to use his body for spare parts? You want to give this new baby's lungs to your present son?"

"That's the idea." Her voice held a note of surprise. "I thought you understood."

"But . . . that's illegal." My mind flashed back to Andrew's reasoned defenses of the cloning procedure. "Cloned children are perfectly protected under existing American law. You're talking about infanticide."

"I'm talking about a late-term abortion." Glenda spoke in an eerily calm voice. "My doctors haven't exactly endorsed the plan, but I've done enough research to know it's perfectly feasible. I'll go overseas to have the clone implanted. Then when I'm full term, I'll have a late-term procedure and the doctors will use the fetal lungs for a transplant. You'll probably deliver first, so you'll get all the publicity while my husband and I quietly do what we must to save our son."

Stunned beyond words, I sat still as the full import of her words hit me. She was talking about a D&X, or partial-birth abortion, in which a surgeon delivers a late-term baby feetfirst. We had debated the issue on my show often enough that I could recite the horrific details verbatim. The surgeon used his fingers to deliver the baby's lower extremity, then the torso, the shoulders, and the neck. The skull, however, would become lodged at the opening to the uterus, for the mother's cervix would not have dilated enough for it to pass through. The baby would be turned upside down, his spine facing the ceiling. While his little arms and legs kicked, the surgeon would slide the fingers of his left hand along the baby's back and hook the shoulders with his index and ring fingers. Next the doctor would take a pair of blunt, curved Metzenbaum scissors in his right hand. He would carefully advance the tip, curved edge down, along the spine and under his middle finger until he felt it contact the base of the skull. He would then force the scissors into the baby's head. Once the blade had entered, he would spread the scissors to enlarge the opening, then remove the blade and insert a suction tube to draw out the infant's brain . . .

A tremor wriggled up the back of my neck. If this woman needed a healthy set of infant lungs, she would wait until the last possible moment to have the abortion, for the lungs developed only in the last stages of pregnancy.

With the phone in my hand, I trembled until I thought my teeth would chatter. I had assured Steve such monstrosities would not happen in this country. Yet they could, and desperate people like Glenda would be certain they *would*.

A quiet voice reminded me that desperate mothers could do unimaginable things.

"Glenda"—my voice sounded strangled to my own ears—"I can't endorse what you're planning."

"I didn't call for your endorsement." Her voice had gone chilly. "I called for a phone number. I'd like you to place me in touch with the group who does the cloning. I understand their main office is in France?"

I closed my eyes. "I can't give you that information."

Silence hummed over the phone line for a moment. "I can't believe you'd refuse me. What do you want? Glory? We aren't trying to steal your thunder."

"I don't want . . . thunder."

"Then why are you refusing to help? Of all people, I thought you'd understand."

"I do understand." I closed my eyes as a window in my mind began to open. "More than you know."

"Well?" She waited, and when I did not respond, she huffed in my ear. "I can get it somewhere else, you know. I'll find that number. I'd do *anything* to save my son."

"I know."

She drew an audible breath and pressed on. "I was real sorry to hear about what happened to your little boy. That's why I thought you'd understand—when your child is sick and dying, you'll do anything to save him."

Troubled by images of a lifeless infant in a doctor's hand, I opened my eyes. My gaze fell upon a photograph of Steve, Britt, Scott Daniel, and me on our last trip to Disney World. Things had been so happy then, so normal. What would I give to return to that time?

"Not anything," I said, then hung up the phone.

For three days Glenda's conversation haunted me. Every time the phone rang I worried that she had called back, each chime of the computer made me flinch in the fear that she or some other desperate woman had found my e-mail address.

When I went to bed and closed my eyes, I did not dream of Scott Daniel. Instead, the vision of a prone infant in a surgeon's gloved hand fluttered across my eyelids. I dreamed of dead babies, I heard their cries in the wail of the lovelorn cat next door.

Waking in the throes of a nightmare, I would roll over and doze again, only to see images of clustered cells dividing to line up beside a primitive streak. These roly-poly circles, each colored by a brilliant string of forty-six chromosomes, marched across the movie screen in my mind and jiggled to the funky musical riff from the *Dr. Sheldon Show*. Disney's *Fantasia* animators would have been hard-pressed to compete with my imaginative subconscious.

I woke every morning more tired than I'd been when I went to bed.

I tried to concentrate on my daily routine, but other thoughts intruded. Most persistent was my personal theory that the egg and sperm must somehow contain a divine spark of life. If I was right—and I still believed I was—then those invisible seeds of a soul had to be present in a morula and a blastocyst, too. The flame of divine life flickered in every cell, no matter how small or undeveloped. And since we legally protected the eggs of bald eagles—which could be fertile or infertile, but were certainly only *potential* eagles—should we not also protect potential babies?

Science seemed to indicate that human life began approximately two weeks after conception. But some questions could not be settled by science . . . some matters depended upon higher disciplines and spiritual wisdom.

When cleaning off my desk one afternoon, I saw a notepad covered in my own scrawlings. At the top of one page I had written, *How can we say a blastocyst is a person?*

Now I wondered how we could know a blastocyst was not two people, or even three. More to the point, how could I have imagined that these matters had nothing to do with me?

I wanted to discuss these thoughts with someone, but Brittany was rarely at home and I doubted she'd be interested. Steve might have listened if I called, but I'd given up the right to telephone him at any hour with random musings.

So I carried my thoughts to bed, where they churned and stewed in my weary psyche, then spilled out into my dreams.

The moment I opened the car door, I knew I had returned to the hospital in my recurrent dream. The steady whoosh of cars on the highway provided an accompaniment to the pounding of my heart, and Steve's greeting sent a thrill down every nerve of my body.

Despite the events of the last few days, Scott Daniel had not left me. In this hospital, at least, he still lived and breathed.

"This way," Steve called, and I ran after him, nearly passing him in my eagerness to reach Scott's room. I gave the old men at the receptionist's desk only a passing glance; the pregnant women in wheelchairs could have been mere wallpaper. Reaching the elevator before Steve, I slapped the call button with my palm, then leaned against the wall in order to avoid the flood of faceless folks who would pour out in only a moment.

The dream did not disappoint. The elevator chimed, the animated mannequins rushed forward, and I whirled into the elevator without so much as a backward glance. As I pressed the single button, I realized that this was what psychologist Frederik van Eeden had called a "lucid dream"—a dream in which the sleeper knows she is dreaming.

I knew it, all right, and I didn't care. Reality had become so difficult in the last few weeks that I couldn't wait to see Scott, to be his mother again.

When the elevator doors opened, I ran through the sea of mist to his room, then pushed the door open. Unlike the other times, Steve had not arrived before me. No one kept a vigil with my boy, but he was not completely alone. A dark-haired doctor in a white lab coat stood in the curtained shadows, his clipboard shining through the gloom.

Ignoring the physician, I hurried to Scott's bedside, then pressed my palm to his cheek. Thankfully, it was still warm.

"He's alive." I breathed the words as a prayer of gratitude.

"Of course he is," the doctor answered in a low voice that was at once powerful and gentle. "But he's not here, Diana."

"He will be when he wakes up." I trailed a fingertip down the length of Scott Daniel's nose. "Wake up, sweetie. The sun's come up and so should we, snugglebugs though we may be."

I waited, listening to the click and hiss of the respirator, but Scott did not respond.

"Diana." The doctor spoke again, his voice commanding my attention. "You have to let him go."

"No." Refusing even to look in his direction, I kept my gaze fastened to my son's sweet face. "He's only asleep. He'll come back to me; I'm trying so hard to bring him back—"

"Diana." The man's voice wasn't much above a whisper, but the effect was as great as if he'd shouted in my ear.

I cast an irritated look over my shoulder. "Don't you have someplace else to be?"

From the corner of my eye, I saw a smile light his face. "My place is with you and Scott. I've been with you both all along."

I shuddered and fought down the momentary unease that twisted my stomach. "You're a figment of my imagination—a fantasy physician, probably inserted by the part of my brain that insists on facing reality."

"Scott Daniel is happy in my Father's house . . . and you need to have faith in my promise."

Have faith in *what* promise? That was the trouble with dream doctors, they didn't have to make any sense.

Dropping my hands to the railing at the edge of the bed, I whirled to confront the meddlesome physician . . . and what I saw turned my knees to water.

The doctor's lab coat fairly shone with such brilliance my eyes began to sting. His hair gleamed like spun silk under the hospital lights while his eyes glowed with power, authority, and compassion.

When he spoke my name again, I understood how he had summoned the dead from Hades and calmed the stormy seas. Slowly, I released my grip on the bed railing and dropped to my knees, the floor tiles cold under my hands as my heart knocked in fear and dread.

Something—perhaps the instinctive drive for self-preservation—woke me. I lay flat on my back, my sweating palms pressed to the bedsheets, my eyes fixed on the spinning ceiling fan overhead. My heart felt as heavy as a stone within my chest, weighing me down so I could not move.

After a long while, I found my voice. "It was a dream. A lucid dream. That's all."

But I lay without turning until the rising sun fringed the window blinds and a mockingbird heralded my return to a new day.

forty-nine

ON FRIDAY I MANAGED TO SHOVE TROUBLING thoughts about dreams and medical ethics aside long enough to input the final changes on my proposal for a televised *Dr. Sheldon Show*. My agent had been talking up the program since Monday, but I knew he'd need something polished in hand to seal the deal.

At 11:00 A.M. I was doing my best to nibble off the remaining vestiges of my right thumbnail when the phone rang. I glanced at the caller ID—the name was unavailable, but I recognized a New York area code.

I snatched up the phone. "Hello?"

"Diana Sheldon, please."

"Speaking."

"Dr. Sheldon, this is Les Phillips, director of programming at the WB Network. I talked to your agent this morning, and we're very excited about the possibility of hosting your new television show. We'd like to bring you to New York to discuss the possibilities. Would you be open next week?"

A rush of pleasure warmed my face as my hand flew to my desk calendar. "Any particular day?"

"How about Tuesday? I know that's short notice, but we have a morning slot we're trying to fill. Your agent has given me a brief synopsis of what you'd like to do, but we're anxious to talk to you personally. We'd like to get things started before you go to Europe to have the procedure done."

My fingers froze on the calendar pages. "You want the program to address cloning?"

"We want to follow your pregnancy from the first moment. We'll begin with a prime-time special covering your court battle for the tissue samples, and we'll be sure to mention the sacrifices you've made in order to follow this dream to its conclusion. We'd like to get some shots of your son and have you talk about him on camera."

"Oh." I couldn't come up with anything more profound; my brain was reeling.

Phillips laughed. "We are absolutely gonzo about this idea. Not since Katie Couric had her colonoscopy on live television has anyone done anything like this—and your ratings will leave Katie in the dust. The country's first cloned child—it's killer! And we'll be with you every step of the way." His voice lowered to a conspiratorial tone. "Your agent mentioned the matter of your expenses, of course, and I'm pleased to report that our network would be more than willing to cover all costs related to the procedure."

"You'll pay all the expenses? The fees, the travel—"

"Everything. After all, we'll be putting your life on public display. Your agent says you're okay with this."

I bit my lip. "To a point. Once the baby is born, I'd want to be left alone."

"No problem. It's the conception and delivery we're most interested in. If at a later date you want to show his picture on the air so viewers can see how he's growing up, that'd be great. By that time your show will have branched out into other areas, and I'm sure other reproductive technologies will be in the spotlight. We'll expect you to keep our viewers on the cutting edge of the reproductive revolution."

"I see." I would be the first, so the network wanted to capitalize on my opportunity. They'd pay for the privilege, though, which meant my financial worries would end.

I struggled to think of a question that would make me sound intelligent instead of dumbfounded. "Would the show be filmed in New York?"

"That's negotiable. It's possible we could film in Tampa, since that's your home base. We'll rent a studio, and you could have input in the hiring of capable staff. Sure, I think we could consider a satellite show. We're certainly willing to negotiate."

I leaned back in my chair. This offer would mean coast-to-coast coverage of my pregnancy, as well as national and international publicity . . . and both Steve and Brittany would despise that kind of attention. But Britt would be away at college, so she wouldn't be faced with it every day, and if Steve was determined to remain an ex-husband, he would be out of the picture.

That thought brought another in its wake, along with a chill that struck deep in the pit of my stomach. Steve might be out of the picture, but I'd be influencing hundreds of women like Glenda Jones, women who urgently wanted a child, and couples who were willing to work within existing laws to chase their desperate desires.

People like me.

Cold, clear reality swept over me in a terrible wave, one so powerful I struggled to breathe. For weeks—months—I had been focused on my desire to restore my son, but if I went on national television, the same women who went to their hairdressers to demand Jennifer Aniston haircuts could go to Project One to demand cloning for any number of reasons . . . and in this country those developing babies would not be protected until birth. What if pressure from those people caused American politicians to rethink their positions on cloning? Science would declare open season on morulas, blastocysts, and human embryos, all of which contained the seeds of eternal souls.

Project One wanted publicity; they would get it from me in spades if I went through with this.

"I can't." I heard myself say the words before I consciously gathered the courage to bend them to my will.

I heard the rustling of papers over the line. "You can't come next week?"

"No—" I closed my eyes, a sick feeling deep inside me. *Dear God, what was I thinking?* "I can't come at all. I can't do the show."

"If the lack of privacy concerns you, I promise we'll handle the matter in good taste." Phillips's tone suggested he was trying hard to speak clearly to a novice. "Your agent says you know how to handle the press—"

"It's not the publicity."

"The money, then. We're completely agreeable to a fair salary in addition to the fees we'll be paying. And nearly everything is open to negotiation."

I realized I was crying only when I tasted the salt of my tears running into the corners of my mouth. "You don't understand, Mr. Phillips. I can't take your job . . . because I can't go through with the cloning."

My refusal fell on the stony ground of his silence, but I lifted the family photo on my desk and held it against my heart. "I'm not sure I can explain my reasons in a way you'll understand, but my decision is irrevocable. It has taken me a long time to see things clearly—*Too long, Lord. I'm so sorry*—But I know one thing—what you're suggesting would cost too much."

"But we're paying for everything!"

"I'm talking about the currency of human life."

I thanked him for his time, then hung up. Moving on legs that felt like wooden stumps, I climbed the stairs and went into Scott Daniel's room, then sat on the edge of his bed as comprehension began to seep through my despair.

What had I done?

A few days ago I had been wondering why the Spirit of God hadn't knocked my daughter flat with conviction while I should have wondered the same thing about myself. Every parent at some time is the parent of the wandering prodigal, but in this situation *I* was the prodigal and God the parent . . . how long had he been waiting for me to understand? He had tried to speak to me through people, through his Word, even through my dreams, and I'd turned a deaf ear to every plea.

A snatch of Scripture from last Sunday's sermon drifted back to me on a current of memory: *I am the God who kills and gives life; I am the one who wounds and heals.*

I thought of how Britt had chafed against the rules I had instituted to protect her. She would say I was trying to wound her, when in fact I wanted only to love her.

God had led me to the valley of the shadow of death, and I had refused to walk through it. I had kicked and screamed and railed against his will, then I calmly plotted a course around the valley, thinking I could join my family on the other side unscathed.

What a fool I'd been. I had hurt all the people I loved most. By taking matters into my own hands, I had systematically destroyed my life.

I thought God was intent upon wounding me.

He wanted only to draw me closer.

I had been running from that severe love since Scott Daniel's accident, chasing the fading sunlight rather than stepping into the darkness and holding tight to my loved ones.

"God, forgive me. I've been so blind." Dredging the admission from a place beyond logic and reason, I closed my eyes. "Forgive me for being selfish, proud, and stubborn. Open my eyes now to the things that matter, to the things you'd have me do."

By the time I had finished unburdening my guilty heart, the shadows had shifted from the Tampa Bay Bucs wallpaper to the red-uniformed tin soldiers. I stood on trembling legs and crossed to the closet where I had stored Scott Daniel's toys.

Reaching up, I took the plastic-shrouded monkey from the top shelf, then pulled away the wrapping. Sinking onto the bed, I gathered the yellow-and-black monkey in a tight embrace and inhaled the scents of foam rubber, my beloved son, and love.

Bending over it, I bowed my head as the tears began in earnest.

Fifty

STEVE PULLED UP TO THE HOUSE AND PARKED ON THE curb, then got out and slipped his keys into his pocket. Diana had said she was going to hire someone to cut the grass, but obviously she hadn't gotten around to it. His once-beautiful lawn, which grew like a jungle in the rainy months of summer, was looking a little wild. The red-and-white For Sale sign in the center of the lawn sat in a tuft of grass six inches high.

He pressed his lips together as he walked to the door. No sense in ragging on Diana about the lawn, she'd obviously had a lot to do in trying to sell the house and find a new job. In addition to that, she still had to deal with Brittany.

Brittany was doing better, Diana had said in her call, but she wanted him to come over to discuss something important. No, she couldn't discuss it on the phone and no, it really couldn't wait.

So here he was on a lovely Saturday morning, a man who should have been playing golf or trying to forget about his problems instead of running homeward every time his wife—*ex*-wife—called for help.

He rang the bell, and a moment later Britty opened the door. She looked thin around the eyes and cheeks, but she smiled when she saw him. "Hi, Dad!"

"Hi, kiddo." He gave her a hug, then peered past her into the foyer. "Is your mom around?"

"She's in the study, probably gabbing on-line. You can go on in if you want."

"No—I'll wait in the living room. She'll come out when she's ready."

He moved toward the formal living area they had used more in the last month than in the ten years they'd lived in this house. But he wasn't about to go into her study as if he belonged there. Diana had set the rules; she had relegated him to the position of *Outsider*. And Outsiders didn't go into private areas unless they were invited.

Britty had followed him, and now she leaned against the wall, her eyes alight. "Want something to eat? Some cookies, maybe? I made some last night."

He sank onto the sofa. "You didn't go out?"

"No." Her face fell. "That wouldn't have been such a hot idea. But Mom dug out her old recipe for snickerdoodles and we made a batch. They're pretty good, if you want one."

"Sounds good to me."

He placed his hands on his knees, about to rise, but she whirled away. "I'll get them," she called over her shoulder, moving down the hall.

He leaned back as an odd sense of disappointment slapped at him. So . . . even Britty wanted to treat him like a guest.

A moment later a shadow fell across the carpet. Diana stood in the doorway, and at the sight of her frayed smile he had to fight an overwhelming desire to enfold her in his arms. "Thanks for coming, Steve."

"No problem." He tried to grin as if he hadn't a care in the world. "What's up? You having trouble with your car?"

"No."

"Britty need an application signed? You need a tax form?"

She drew a deep, audible breath. "I need some brawn."

He laughed. "Diana, you can't call me over here every time you need someone to open a pickle jar—"

"It's not a pickle jar. It's something bigger."

Her eyes were gleaming with some emotion he couldn't define. Fear, perhaps? Insecurity?

"I need you," she began again, "to help me pull up the sign out front. Because we're not moving. Because I'm not going anywhere, not even to France."

He stared at her, searching her face, probing for the meaning behind her words. "You mean—"

"I'm not going through with the cloning, Steve. I called off my lawyer. I can't afford it."

So money had prevailed where he could not.

Looking down to hide his disappointment, he rubbed a smear on the arm of the sofa. "I'm sure the house will sell, Diana. And you'll find a job."

"It's not the money, it's everything else." She caught his gaze and held it. "I can't afford to lose you or Brittany."

Warmth spread through his bloodstream as his reserve began to thaw. "What are you saying?"

She lifted one shoulder in a shrug he had once found charming . . . and still did.

"I'm saying you were right. I was afraid to go through the darkness of grief. But earlier this week I began to understand that my actions were not only destroying my family, but others, too—people I have never even met." Her gaze lowered. "The cloning opportunity is not of God. I thought it was, but it couldn't be. I should have listened to you."

As a feeling of glorious happiness sprang up in his heart, Steve took her hand, drawing her to his side. "I'll be with you in the dark, Diana. I've been feeling my way through it for the last several months . . . and I think I've found the way out."

Her chin trembled. Her lips parted as if she would speak, then she closed her eyes and nodded.

Steve drew his wife into his arms and held her as she wept.

He stroked Diana's cheek, felt her tears on his fingertips, then buried his face in her shoulder and went quietly and thoroughly to pieces.

"I'll be with you, darling," he whispered when he could speak again. He ran his fingers through the strands of her hair. "Every step of the way."

Fifty-one

SIX MONTHS LATER

Humming along with Alan Jackson, I pressed the live mike button as the strains of his latest hit drifted away.

"Hold on tight, darlin'," I murmured in my most velvety voice as the music faded. "Lovely tune, isn't it? Now we have Thomas on the line, calling from Largo. Thomas, you there? What's on your mind tonight?"

"Lynda, is that you?"

"I'm right here, Tom." I smiled, warmed by the reminder of how quickly the listeners of country music's WCTY had warmed to "Lynda Love," the golden-voiced gal who spun tunes and talked to callers during the lonely hours of nine to midnight every weekday night. The program director had correctly figured that an out-of-work psychologist with a gift for gab might be just the person to charm the lonely and lovelorn.

As for me, I couldn't have been happier. Steve listened every night, often calling in to keep me company on the air, and once or twice Brittany had called from Tallahassee, where a friend of hers sometimes picked us up on the Web broadcast.

Steve and I had remarried in mid-August. He restored my wedding ring to my finger only a few days before we drove Brittany to Tallahassee and deposited her in a freshman dorm. She seemed to be doing well in school, and surprised us now and then with calls "just to talk." It was, I told Steve, as if she was finally beginning to see us as something other than parents.

"But we'll always be her parents," he'd protested.

"That's true. But this past year she saw us as authority figures, not people. One day I'd like to be her friend."

After writing Andrew Norcross to say I would not be pursuing cloning, I received a short note in reply. My deposit, he informed me, was nonrefundable, as it had already been spent on research.

Regretfully, I chalked up the cost to the price one pays for experience.

I paid a lot during those tumultuous four months—personally and with the emotions of the people I love. But God was merciful to me, and, like Job, he restored my losses. My husband was back in my home and my heart; my daughter, though still independent and reserved, seemed more open to us now that she was away from our direct supervision.

And my sweet Scott Daniel, my son, waited for me in heaven. I look forward to joining him there one day.

I enjoyed my new job even more than the *Dr. Sheldon Show*. The pressure was gone, and as "Lynda Love" I was able to be sweet and sentimental as opposed to sharp and synthetic. Instead of doling out principles and witticisms, I listened, I commiserated, sometimes I even wept. I became a different person, a lot softer and more sympathetic.

Sometimes I was a little dumbfounded when I realized that even a professional counselor could be blindsided by grief, but the human mind is amazing. It can nurture delusions; it can rationalize the vilest of crimes. Those who operated the ovens at Auschwitz learned to think of their Jewish prisoners as dirt, not people. And so they sent thousands to their graves.

I shuddered to think how close I came to falling victim to a similar sort of tunnel vision. Only the prayers of my husband and the grace of God kept me from going down a path that could have resulted in disaster not only for me, but for thousands of deluded people who could not see the dangers inherent in the work of Project One.

I learned that God is sovereign over the tragedies and triumphs of life. He is never caught by surprise, never perplexed by the things that happen. And he is so loving and powerful that he orchestrates even the tragedies of our lives so that good results from them.

Rebirth. Restoration. Renewal.

I realized all these things and more after submitting myself to the sovereignty of God. By accepting Scott Daniel's death instead of trying to circumvent it, I finally found peace.

I still had dark days . . . and sometimes the sight of that rubber-faced monkey spurred fresh tears. But Steve was right. God walked with me in the darkness, too.

On line one, Thomas from Largo was saying his teenage son was being rebellious.

"You're not alone, Tom. How old is your son?"

"Seventeen."

"That's a tough age."

"I just don't know what to do with him. He doesn't listen, he rolls his eyes at everything I have to say, and when he loses his temper—man, look out. We nearly had a fistfight the other night. My wife and I are counting the months until we can send him off to join the armed services."

I laughed softly. "I hear what you're saying, Tom, and I'm also the parent of a teenager. I sent my child off to college a few months ago, and I have to admit I had mixed feelings. Part of me was glad to see her go—for some of the reasons you've expressed and because I think life itself can teach her things she won't accept from me right now. But another part of me was sad to see her leave. I'll miss her and I worry.

From this point forward, she'll start to make her own choices, and that scares me silly. What we see as loving concern, our kids see as over-protection."

"So . . . how do you get through it?"

I smiled at the question. I was a slow learner, but the Lord had reminded me that I loved Brittany more than life, and not because she was my only remaining child. I loved her because of who she was, and because her arrival in our family had been no less miraculous than Scott Daniel's.

I hoped she would forgive me one day for forgetting that.

"How do I get through it? I pray, Tom. Deeply, fervently, and with tears, I lift my daughter up to the Lord and trust him to take care of her. When she asks for my advice, I'll give it, but until then I'll pray."

"Well, we pray, too," Tom drawled, "but sometimes it seems like our prayers aren't goin' much higher than the ceiling."

"Oh, they're going all the way up." I laughed softly. "You know much about oysters, Tom?"

"I know I don't like to eat 'em."

"Me, either. But you should also know that oysters are one of God's most wonderful creations. When a grain of sand enters their shell, they don't even try to eject the irritation. Instead they embrace it, pull it close, and surround it with their very essence. In time, their ability to wrap beauty around trouble results in a pearl."

I clicked the next button, which sent a stream of soft music over the airwaves. "That's what you need to do with your son, Tom. When he irritates you, embrace him, pull him close, and tell him you love him more than anything. In time, my friend, you'll have a pearl."

As the Dixie Chicks began to sing "Doctor, Please Bypass This Heart," I settled back in my chair, picked up the phone, and joined Tom in praying that the love of God would touch his son.

Discussion Questions / Study Guide

1. Some of Diana's actions may seem far-fetched to you, but grief often drives individuals to behavioral extremes. Have you ever suffered extreme grief? How did it affect you?

2. Diana enters deep denial after Scotty's death, confusing her desires with God's leading. How was God directing her during this time? Why did she miss hearing his voice? Has there been a time you felt you were hearing God's voice only to find out later that you'd been listening instead to your own desires? How did God help you through this time? How can we ensure we're really hearing God's voice?

3. What was ironic about Diana's philosophy of wifely submission in a Christian marriage? How does submission relate to our relationship with Christ?

4. At certain points of the story, you may have wondered if Diana's commitment to Christ was genuine. But isn't it possible for

believers to step out of fellowship with God and stray from his intended path for us? What must we do to restore that fellowship?

5. How did you feel about Diana's early views on cloning? Her later views? Do you think science will ever be able to pinpoint the moment a soul is created? Why or why not?

6. What sort of mother is Diana? What could she have done differently in Brittany's situation? Have you ever had reason to doubt your ability to parent your child in difficult situations? Where do you find help in those times?

7. This story illustrates how one wrong decision can systematically destroy everything in our lives. As Diana says, "Hurt people, hurt people." If we do not find healing, or if we do not repent and turn back, we drift farther and farther from the place we should be. Has someone you know experienced a similar situation?

   Perhaps there's someone in your own life who has hurt you deeply—is it possible that person was acting out of his or her own pain? What, if anything, can you do to encourage reconciliation?

8. Since the beginning of recorded history, man has pondered the meaning of suffering. God is not the author of evil, but neither is he its victim. As novelist Randy Alcorn says, "God is not only more powerful than any evildoer, he can take the worst evil and use it for the highest good . . . We can't figure out how that works. (Why should we expect our finite minds to understand the workings of the infinite God? Isaiah 55:8–9.) Fortunately, our inability to understand how it works never diminishes the sovereignty of God."
   What does this story teach you about the power of God?

Author's Note

NO WRITER TRULY WRITES ALONE, AND I OWE MANY thanks to many people.

First, I must thank the guys at the *Glenn Beck* radio program at WFLA in Tampa for letting me pop in one morning to observe. Thanks also to friend, minister, and novelist Al Gansky for providing up-to-date information on cloning and teaching me the meaning of *traducianism*.

Thanks to Susan Richardson, Marilyn Meberg, and my secret pal for reading through rough drafts and providing expert comments. Marilyn's delightful book *The Zippered Heart* provided the basis for the bear-and-the-preacher story. Robin Jones Gunn contributed the parents-as-guardrails metaphor.

The statistics about the population of heaven come from Dr. Harold Willmington's wonderful book, *The King Is Coming* (Tyndale House), and he cites the following verses to assure us that young children go to heaven upon death: 2 Samuel 12:23; Matthew 18:1–6, 10; 19:14; Luke 18:15–17.

Thank you to the community of writers known as ChiLibris for providing fellowship and the answers to all sorts of odd questions.

And now, the disclaimers:

This book is a little unusual because the most far-out situations are based in truth and the most ordinary are completely fictional.

Yes, the Raelians do exist; yes, apparently they do believe aliens created human life; and yes, they are intent upon human cloning. I am afraid we may see the successful cloning of a human infant in the next few years. The information about ACT is true. You can find Dr. Michael West's interview with CNN at http://www.cnn.com/2001/TECH/science/11/25/cloning.west.cnna.

Yes, much to my chagrin, the state of Florida does allow on-line divorces.

And while my family does contain two teenagers and a husband, all of them would want you to know they have not been depicted in this book.

Also Available from WOMEN OF FAITH *fiction*

The Note
by Angela Hunt
When PanWorld flight 848 crashes into Tampa Bay killing all 261 people on board, journalist Peyton MacGruder is assigned to the story. Her discovery of a remnant of the tragedy—a simple note: "T - I love you. All is forgiven. Dad."—changes her world forever. A powerful story of love and forgiveness.

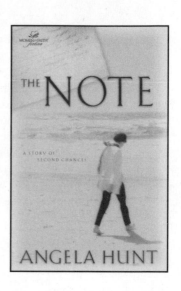

Stranded In Paradise
by Lori Copeland
Tess Nelson feels she can juggle all the areas of her life and make a success out of any situation. That is, until the rug is pulled out from under her and she loses her boyfriend, a job promotion, and is sent on a trip to "get herself together." When a tropical storm hits her would-be island paradise, Tess meets a fellow traveler who possesses the peace, inner-strength, and courage her soul aches for. Filled with humor and an unforgettable cast of characters, this is a story of letting go.

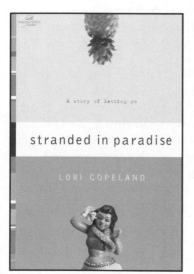

W PUBLISHING GROUP™
www.wpublishinggroup.com
A Division of Thomas Nelson, Inc.

A Time to Dance
by Karen Kingsbury

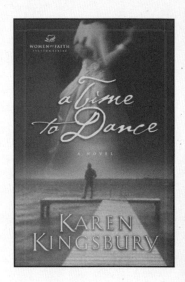

The decision has been made. After 23 years of marriage, John and Abby are getting a divorce. But before they can tell their family, their daughter announces that she is getting married so they postpone their own announcement until after the wedding. But as the big day approaches, they wonder if the decision they've made is irreversible or if they can find once again what they've been missing for so many years. The time for love, the time...to dance.

A Time to Embrace
by Karen Kingsbury

Like newlyweds, the reunited John and Abby Reynolds laugh, love, and dream of a long future together. But in an instant, a car accident changes the Reynolds and their entire community. The driver of the car fully responsible for the accident is Jake Daniels, the high school football star who knows John Reynolds as Coach, mentor, and friend. In the wake of this near death accident, can tragedy be overcome by the possibility of a transforming miracle?

W PUBLISHING GROUP™

www.wpublishinggroup.com

A Division of Thomas Nelson, Inc.

Sandpebbles
by Patricia Hickman

Recently-widowed March Longfellow efficiently commandeers the lives of her son, and the staff members of the small-town newspaper she owns, all the while grappling with grief and issues unresolved before her husband's fatal boating accident. When a new pastor comes to town and his family's lives become intertwined with her own, March finds her life thrust into a new direction—one she cannot control. As March begins to release the things of the past, God rekindles her faith and offers her renewed hope for love.

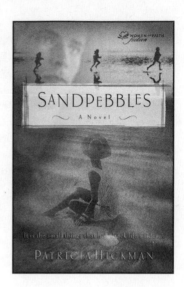

Covenant Child
by Terri Blackstock

When Amanda's husband dies unexpectedly and her two step-daughters are given over to their grandparents, Amanda desperately tries to keep ties with them through support money and letters—unbeknownst to them. Now she struggles to understand the wounds and scars of two girls she longs to know—trying to overcome their cynicism and doubt—and prove her love is genuine and her gifts come with no strings attached.

W PUBLISHING GROUP™
www.wpublishinggroup.com
A Division of Thomas Nelson, Inc.

The Immortal
by Angela Hunt
A man claiming to be 2000 years old says he is on a holy mission to prevent a global cataclysm. To uncover the truth, Claudia must re-examine her beliefs as she delves into ancient legends of the Wandering Jew, biblical warnings about the Antichrist, and eyewitness accounts of the Crucifixion, the Inquisition, and the Holocaust.

The Justice
by Angela Hunt
If the U.S. didn't expect a woman President in this century, they really didn't expect a woman President with blood on her hands. After the assassination of her running mate, Darryn Austin finds herself Queen of the free world. She appoints Paul, an old college flame, a cabinet member in order to ensure him a seat on the Supreme Court and secure a reliable ally. But after circumstances in his life trigger a radical personal conversion, Paul becomes a threat to the President a threat she is willing to eliminate. As Paul grapples with guilt and the possibility of God's existence, readers will question truth, faith and the condition of the heart.

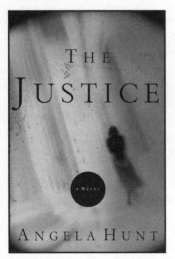

W PUBLISHING GROUP™
www.wpublishinggroup.com
A Division of Thomas Nelson, Inc.

Other books in the Heavenly Daze Series

The Island of Heavenly Daze
by Lori Copeland & Angela Hunt

To a casual visitor, the island of Heavenly Daze
is just like a dozen others off the coast of Maine.
It is decorated with graceful Victorian mansions,
carpeted with gray cobblestones and bright wild
flowers, and populated by sturdy, hard-working
folks—most of whom are unaware that the
island of Heavenly Daze is not just like the other
islands of coastal Maine. The small town that
crowns its peak consists of seven buildings, each
inhabited, according to divine decree, by an
angel who has been commanded to guard and
help anyone who crosses the threshold.

Grace in Autumn
by Lori Copeland & Angela Hunt

It's November, and as the island residents prepare
for the coming months of cold and snow, they are
surprised by God's unexpected lessons of humility,
trust, and hope. Authors Lori Copeland and
Angela Hunt revisit the Island of Heavenly Daze
in the second book of the highly acclaimed series
about a small town where angelic intervention is
commonplace and the Thanksgiving feast a
community affair.

W PUBLISHING GROUP™
www.wpublishinggroup.com
A Division of Thomas Nelson, Inc.

A Warmth in Winter
by Lori Copeland & Angela Hunt

Readers have already fallen in love with the quirky personalities that inhabit Heavenly Daze. In *A Warmth in Winter*, the unforgettable characters and humorous circumstances offer poignant lessons of God's love and faithfulness. The story centers around Vernie Bidderman, owner of Mooseleuk Mercantile and Salt Gribbon, the lighthouse operator, who despite the vast differences in their struggles are being taught about the ultimate failure and frustration of self-reliance.

A Perfect Love
by Lori Copeland & Angela Hunt

Despite the blustery winter chill, love is in the air in Heavenly Daze. Buddy Franklin is searching for someone to change his lonely life, Dana and Mike Klackenbush are trying to reestablish the friendship that led them to marriage three years before, Barbara and Russell Higgs are contemplating babies, and Cleta Lansdown is determined to keep Barbara, her married daughter, close to home. As always, the folks of Heavenly Daze triumph, learn, laugh, and love—and readers will do much of the same!

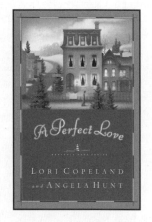

Hearts at Home
by Lori Copeland & Angela Hunt

Edith is trying to lose weight in every way imaginable to get into a certain dress by the time Salt and Birdie's April wedding rolls around. Olympia dies suddenly, leaving her daughter Annie the beloved old house, which she can't afford to keep and maintain on her professor's salary. Plus, Caleb tells her he's being "transferred" at the end of the month! Annie has to learn how to find God's will . . . and open herself up to a new love that's been under her nose the entire time.

W Publishing Group™

www.wpublishinggroup.com

A Division of Thomas Nelson, Inc.